A Bunch of Strays

A Novel of the Outback

by

Marie Mahood

Central Queensland
UNIVERSITY
PRESS

© Marie Mahood

First Published 1996 by
CQU Press
PO Box 1615
ROCKHAMPTON QLD 4700
Tel: 07 4922 8144
Fax: 07 4922 8151
Reprinted in 1996
Reprinted in 1998
Reprinted in 1999

National Library of Australia
Cataloguing in Publication entry

Mahood, Marie

A Bunch of Strays: a novel of the outback.

ISBN 1 875998 10 1.

1. Title

A823.3

Typeset by CQU Press
in Garamond Narrow 11pt and Lucinda Calligra Regular

Printed and bound by
Watson Ferguson & Co.
Brisbane, QLD.

Cover Painting is The Breakaway by Jan Hendrik Scheltema (1861-1938)
Illustrations by Liz Mahood.

*Dedicated to
the Battlers, past and present,
of the Australian Outback.*

All characters, station runs and
small towns in this story are fictitious,
and any resemblance to any person,
place or incident is purely co-incidental.

Acknowledgements

Special thanks to John Morris for permitting us to reproduce the painting *The Breakaway* by Jan Hendrik Scheltema on the cover of this book. This painting is part of John's private collection.

Special thanks to Liz Mahood for her illustrations throughout the book.

ARTS QUEENSLAND

Sponsored by the Queensland Office of Arts and Cultural Development

This project has been assisted by the Commonwealth Government through the Australia Council, its arts funding and advisory body.

CONTENTS

PART I *Skeeter Ryan*

Chapter 1
Skeeter finds a mate — 3

Chapter 2
A flood, a bushfire, and a magic Christmas — 11

Chapter 3
An unexpected ally — 19

Chapter 4
Two pounds a week and all found — 29

Chapter 5
Introduction to The Wet — 35

Chapter 6
Cattle-buyers and horse traders — 43

Chapter 7
Cook on the grog — 53

Chapter 8
Visit to Halley's Cut — 67

Chapter 9
Christmas down south — 77

Chapter 10
*The War ends and
the outback plans a celebration* — 83

Chapter 11
Race-meeting at the Crossing — 91

Chapter 12
Weddings, planned and impromptu — 97

PART II *Serendipity*

Chapter 13
The Grand Tour — 107

Chapter 14
A virgin block beckons — 115

Chapter 15
Post-war Darwin. Mick stakes his claim — 123

Chapter 16
A muster proposed and rejected — 131

Chapter 17
Homestead camp established. A trip to town — 139

Chapter 18
Parrot Hill attends a muster. The padre visits — 147

Chapter 19
Cyclone and bush surgery — 157

Chapter 20
New boss at Parrot Hill — 165

Chapter 21
Cattle-duffers in the back country — 173

Chapter 22
Welcome visitors from the West — 179

Chapter 23
Fight at Felix Creek. Fire at the Homestead — 189

Chapter 24
Christy's future at risk — 199

Chapter 25
Alan gets his break — 207

Chapter 26
The law steps in — 215

Chapter 27
Trial at Eversham — 223

Chapter 28
New Evidence: Injun Joe meets his match — 231

Chapter 29
A man's got a right to protect his home and family — 239

Part 1
Skeeter Ryan

Chapter 1

Skeeter finds a mate

Skeeter slid adroitly into the gap between two of the rounded boulders which overlooked the rabbit warren, and watched with rising panic as the farmer strode purposely towards her retreat. The old sod must know she was there; he wouldn't be strolling round his paddocks at this hour of the morning for nothing. Old Mean Johnson never did anything for nothing. He was on to her for sure.

She did not relinquish her grip on the still-twitching rabbit until the moment when she saw him pick up her tracks in the dew-wet grass, pause, and then stare in the direction of the warren. She tried to stuff the rabbit further into the crevice, out of sight, hoping against hope that he would miss the sugar-bag, with the three still-warm bodies inside, lying just out of sight beyond the largest boulder, along with the five traps she had already taken up.

But Mean Johnson came relentlessly on, and the moment for flight was past. There was nothing to do but brave it out. As she stepped out into the open the child was suddenly conscious of the whole scene as if she were seeing it as an onlooker, and not as one of the central figures. She was aware of the fine quality of the early morning light and the long pencil-thin shadow of the gum sapling at the outer fringe of the warren. Every blade of grass seemed to separate itself from its fellows, and stand like a green sentinel about to witness an execution. The rabbit, which she now saw herself holding, was a limp amalgam of thousands and thousands of grey and white hairs with two staring eyes like wet and gleaming gems. Then a magpie shrieked suddenly from the sapling, and she was back in the picture, and the man was upon her.

"You boys been told often enough what I'd do if I caught any of you on my farm!" He stood six feet away from her, legs solidly apart, and his arms folded across the broad expanse of grey woollen chest. His inspection began at the dirty bare feet, took in the too-large shorts and shapeless pullover, and then rested on the small face and the shock of unkempt red hair chopped off raggedly just below the ears, too long by far for a boy.

"Well, bugger me, it's a girl!" He whistled slowly between his teeth, and surveyed his victim with a new curiosity. "Whose kid are you, Ginger, come up here to pinch me rabbits and stamp all over me crop?"

Skeeter stood up straighter and shoved the rabbits toward him defensively. "I'm Marion Ryan and here's yer mouldy old rabbit. I was doing you a favour, Mr Johnson, taking rabbits instead of 'em eating your crop, and I don't stamp on it, either. I always walk on the edge, like you c'n see from my tracks."

The man ignored the proffered corpse, and walked around the boulder outcrop and stooped to pick up Skeeter's sugar-bag and traps.

"Four, eh?" he said, "What d'you get for them?"

"Threepence a pair," mumbled the child, wondering frantically how she could reclaim her traps and make her escape.

But Mean Johnson wasn't in any hurry to let her go. She stood by miserably as he picked up a stick and began prodding at the burrow entrances. With a snap her last trap went off, and he tugged it out of the earth and dropped it with the others at her feet. "There's plenty other places for rabbits," he said, "why'd you come here, when I got notices to prosecute on every paddock?"

"The boys set all the other real good places, Mr Johnson, close enough to walk to, and they belt me, or they pinch my traps or rabbits. Sometimes I don't get one. On your place, mostly I get five or six every day, because the boys are too windy of you to come here."

"And you aren't, Ginger?"

Skeeter hung her head and made no reply.

"Ninepence a day, eh? That's a lot of money, five bob a week about."

"No, not always." She was almost, but not quite, snivelling now. "I only sell two pair to the rabbitman; we eat any over ourselves. Mum makes pies."

"And you give the quids to Mum, do you, to help out because you've got no Dad?"

His voice wasn't gravelly anymore, just curious, and suddenly Skeeter found herself, astonishingly, telling old Mean Johnson what she had never breathed to a soul before, not even Mum, to whom she lied daily about her catch. "No, Sir, I only give her half. The other half I've been saving, for two years now, since I was eight. I'm saving to buy my land. You got land. I'm gunna have some too, one day."

Ralph Johnson gaped momentarily, and then grinned into the earnest freckled little face staring up at him.

"So you want to buy a farm, Ginger, do you? Well, bugger me!"

"Hell no," Skeeter burst out, "not a farm. I'm gunna buy a cattle station, a cattle station way up north."

Some sixth sense told the man he must not laugh. Then with a stunning clarity he realised that, standing before him, right here in this paddock, was the only other human he'd ever met who could have understood the lonely dreams of the boy he'd been thirty years before, and had, until this moment, almost forgotten.

He picked up bag and traps and thrust them towards her.

"In that case, Ginger, you'd better run, or you'll miss the rabbitman, and be late for school into the bargain."

She didn't thank him, but snatched the bag and traps and ran.

He watched as the small figure reached his boundary fence, climbed through, and set off at a fast clip down the track that led to the outskirts of the township and there converged onto the only gravelled road which the settlement boasted. Then he turned back towards the farmhouse where his breakfast awaited him.

"She ain't got the complexion for it, not up north," he murmured to himself as he strode along. "But maybe that won't stop her, at that!"

He stopped as another thought struck him. Sixpence a day from the rabbitman, but what about the skins? A couple of dozen skins a week would have to be worth something. He wondered where she sold those, or if she sold them. Some kids didn't, he knew, judging from the messes of entrails, heads and skins he'd occasionally found left for the crows, and it was a fair job to prepare half a dozen skins on top of going round the traps and bargaining with the rabbitman, and getting to school on time. He glanced towards the sun, not seven o'clock yet. Yes, he decided, she'd have time to do it, not today, maybe, because he'd held her up, but most days she would.

By the time Ralph Johnson was back in the farmhouse kitchen warming his hands at the big kitchen range, and pouring his first cup of tea for the day from the big enamel pot on the hob, Skeeter had squatted down beside the scribbly gum just off the track, swiftly gutted her catch with a pocket-knife, and made slits in one of the hind legs so she could force the other leg through. Then she hooked each rabbit by its hindlegs over the stump of a branch to get enough purchase to pull the skin down in one movement, so that the body hung pink and glistening from the branch, with its coat dangling inside out below it, still attached pathetically to the head. Skeeter pulled each one from the branch hurriedly and hacked the skins and heads free from the bodies with practiced slashes of her pocket knife.

The rabbit van was parked in a grove of trees close by the beginning of the gravelled road, and three or four boys were still bargaining with its owner, who was not averse to classifying a small doe as a kitten worth only a penny if he thought he could get away with it. He never tried it on Skeeter. He paid her in a sixpenny piece rather than the two threepences she demanded, and insisted that he had no more change, and because of the lateness she could not stay to argue. There was no point telling her Mum she'd had no luck this morning because the tell-tale flecks of fresh blood on her pullover would give her away, so she resigned herself to handing over the full amount, comforting herself that she would undoubtedly find a way to make it up in the near future.

In the kitchen of the weatherboard cottage Maggie Ryan was spooning porridge into the plate of her five-year-old son when Skeeter entered and went straight to the dresser, on which stood the small earthenware jar which housed the family's current wealth. She lifted the lid and dropped the sixpence inside.

Maggie glanced up and smiled at her daughter. Not yet thirty, she had all the classic beauty of her Irish ancestors from whom she had inherited her black wavy hair and dancing blue eyes; mother and daughter were as alike as chalk and cheese, for Skeeter seemed to have inherited all the physical genes of her unknown father, and none of the Ryans', who, whatever else they may have been, were all outstandingly beautiful. It was this characteristic that had been Maggie's downfall, for when she had gone to Perth to work as a housemaid at seventeen, she had attracted more than one upper-class young man, and one of them had duped her into believing that he was promising to marry her. When he confessed he was already married, and gave her a large sum of money and the address of an old woman who was a practising abortionist, Maggie had taken the money and returned to the cottage, and her widowed father, to await her confinement.

Her second confinement was quite another matter. Davey was the result of what she called a little bit of fun, and a long time without it, and there was nothing more the town gossips could say because they had already said the lot, day-in and day-out, ever since she had stepped off the train with a bun in the oven five years earlier. As far as the township was concerned they might have been virgin births, because Maggie's lips were sealed. Davey was a Ryan through and through, and if his father was local, no-one could hazard a guess, and Maggie wasn't telling.

George Ryan, carpenter and odd-job man, sometimes wondered at his daughter, because he knew that she could have married more than once in the first years after her return home, and provided her baby daughter with a stepfather and the security of an honest surname, but he only brought up the subject once.

"With all due respects, Pa," she spat at him, "men are only good for one thing, and I've got that, and I don't intend to be a slave to one for the rest of my life!"

He reasoned that if it suited her the way it was, it more than suited him, and there he let the matter rest. And when Skeeter came home bawling from her first day at school, he intercepted her at the woodheap, rolled over a stump, took her on his knee, and taught her the little rhyme, "Sticks and stones will break my bones, but names will never hurt me!" And Skeeter believed him immediately, allowed him to mop up the evidence of tears, and then ran inside to tell Mum of the exciting new world of school.

At nearly ten, Skeeter knew herself to be the luckiest kid in town, and revelled in the freedom that the taint of her illegitimacy bestowed upon her. She was never going to be accepted as a 'little lady', or be invited to the birthday parties of the other little girls and boys, so she lost no time in bemoaning the fact. She could do all the things the 'little ladies' could not. She was the only girl in town who could go rabbiting and earn herself some money. She could wear shorts instead of silly dresses which inevitably got caught on barbed-wire fences when she climbed through them. She owned a pocket-knife, which was her most treasured possession. And instead of playing after school in other little girls' yards, she roamed in the bush, climbed trees, and learned to swim in the creek. Few taunted her at school, for she was always top of her class, and could run faster than anyone else in the school, and, not being a lady, she could use her fists if she needed to. Even the big boys, with bigger fists and longer reaches, preferred not to tangle with a small girl who lost no opportunity of reminding them that she was smarter than they were, and was quite capable of waiting her chance to ambush them with a hail of stones, and then sneer as she outran them.

Skeeter had not been altogether truthful in her claim to Mean Johnson that the boys belted her. Skeeter was a loner, and she liked it that way, and if the other kids were scared to trespass on Johnson's farm, or brave Johnson's bull, then Johnson's farm was the place for her.

The inevitable gossip which she overheard made Skeeter think about her situation rather than just accepting it, and the more she thought about it the more astounded she became at the reasoning of her family's critics. Obviously, the only crimes they seemed to have committed was to have a family without a father as boss, and to survive what the grown-ups referred to as The Depression without asking the Government man for Susso, whatever that was.

In her eyes Grandpa was far better than any of the fathers of her schoolmates. She listened unabashedly to any adult conversations she could overhear, and she kept her eyes open, did Skeeter. She knew there were fathers in town who boozed at the pub, and then went home and bashed their wives and kids, and she sometimes saw the evidence of the beltings on her schoolmates. She knew there were fathers who didn't get drunk, but belted their kids anyway, and others who couldn't find enough work to feed their families properly, so that the poor kids begged for the orange peels and lunch scraps of those who did have a school lunch.

Skeeter envied none of them their fathers, and came to the conclusion that Providence had smiled upon her in providing her with a Grandpa instead. For Grandpa was rarely without work, and her family never went hungry, and Grandpa had such a store of yarns and bush lore that Skeeter would have undoubtedly forgiven him the occasional dry day if he had been a tardy provider.

Skeeter loved Grandpa equally as much as she loved Mum. Mum was a different kettle of fish to Grandpa, but Skeeter always knew where she stood with Mum; she gave a straight answer to a straight question, and never complicated a decision with pointless restrictions based on what people might think. If Mum made a rule Skeeter respected it as based on good honest reasoning, and did not often break it. When she did, and was belted for it, she knew the punishment was deserved, and did not resent it.

Skeeter lied to her mother daily about her rabbit catch, not because she believed Maggie would demand the whole of the payment, but because she knew that her practical mother would respond with scorn to her dream, and the dream was too precious to risk being diminished by the criticism of one of the people she loved best.

Perhaps she also lied by omission, for she never told Maggie of any of the taunts or gossip she heard. It didn't matter much to her, and nothing could be done about it, so there seemed no point in repeating it. On the rare occasions when a taunt involved her in a fist fight, and she returned home with a bruise or torn clothing, she lied to her mother about the cause, and accepted the punishment for unruly behaviour without comment. Skeeter was aware of the core of bitterness which directed her mother's attitudes, and instinctively knew that she would only add to it if she whined about the silly taunts. She was happy enough at school, for the taunters were in the minority, and she joined in the games at playtime, and was accepted as a leader and organiser by most of the other girls, though she never had any special friend. She knew that it was their mothers, and not they, who omitted her name from the birthday party and Sunday picnic lists, but as she privately thought such parties must be 'cissy' from the discussions she heard, she was pleased rather than hurt that she was not included.

It was the practice of the fourth standard teacher to allocate the classroom desks according to the results of his Friday tests, and more often than not Skeeter occupied the place of honour in one of the double desks in the front row. She was seated there one morning when the lesson was interrupted by the headmaster with a new pupil in tow. He murmured something to Mr Gardner, and handed over his charge, who stood with surly expression and downcast eyes while the other children inspected her with interest and muted whispers. She was half-caste Aboriginal, skinny, barefooted, but neatly dressed, and she clutched a brown-paper parcel which obviously contained her lunch.

"What's your name, child?" queried Mr Gardner, at the same time casting a harsh eye towards the whisperers in the body of the class.

"Elsa," quavered the little girl, "Elsa Kickett."

There was a titter in the front row. Skeeter inspected the newcomer with just as much interest as her fellows. They had never had a coloured child in the school before.

"Well, Elsa, you must put your lunch in the cloakroom," (the child clutched it more firmly to her) "when you arrive tomorrow. The monitor will put your name on the shelf to show where you keep your things. But for now, you can sit in the spare seat at the back beside -er- Annie."

There were three spare seats in the classroom, but one of them was beside a boy, and boys and girls did not usually sit together. Of the two girls Annie was the meeker, a slightly retarded child at the bottom of the playground pecking order. But Annie, though she may not have known her sums or her spelling, had no doubts whatsoever of her social status. She leapt to her feet with a cry of outrage, and for the first and only time defied her teacher.

"I'm not gunna sit next to a nigger, and you can't make me. I'll tell me father on you," and her voice trailed off in a snivelling wail.

Other little voices joined in. Mr Gardner was no longer in charge.

Skeeter glanced at the innocent cause of the uproar and noticed that the eyes were no longer downcast, but narrowed in an almost murderous glance of hatred, and the puny shoulders were drawn back. Elsa was a fighter, Skeeter liked that. She jumped to her feet, picked up her pad and pencil, and strode to the back row. "Here," she ordered the snivelling child brusquely, "Take your pad and get out. Go and sit in my seat. I'll have yours, and Elsa can sit beside me." She tugged the hesitant Annie off her seat by the back of her dress, and pushed her out into the aisle. Mr Gardner was suddenly beside them, holding Elsa by the elbow.

"Thank you Marion, that is a kind gesture. Annie, go to the front. Now, the rest of you, not a word, or you'll get the stick, one and all. On with your sums, and, Marion, will you go to the cupboard and get a pad and pencil for Elsa, and then show her how we do long multiplication sums." Mr Gardner was back in control.

When Skeeter came back with the pad and pencil Elsa was still sitting stiff and erect in the seat, staring mutely ahead. Skeeter slid into the seat beside her, and leaned over to whisper, "Just as well you've got me next to you. That Annie's got nits in her hair, and you'd catch 'em for sure."

Elsa's face turned towards her, and the lips split into a broad white grin, and the brown eyes sparkled. "I've got a friend," thought Skeeter, as the black curly head and the red-gold head bent together over the intricacies of multiplication.

The friendship of Skeeter and Elsa endured one long glorious winter, through the bright spring and into the wheat harvest school holidays summer. Elsa lived with her half-caste parents and two older brothers in a camp on the bank of the river, while her itinerant horse-breaker father worked on the surrounding farms. Ted Kickett owned two horses, which he grazed on the common or along the river bank, mild old fellows which had pulled the two carts and the family's belongings over most of the outback roads of Western Australia.

Maggie raised no opposition when Skeeter begged permission to spend Saturday afternoons with Elsa, though the Kicketts' camp was three miles away on the other side of the river. The Ryan love of horseflesh, any horseflesh, had bubbled over in Skeeter, and Elsa taught her to ride bareback, and had opened to her another source of revenue.

"You can get threepence a pound for dead wool," Elsa confided. "Dad says the butcher will buy it if we collect enough. Dad sees the dead sheep sometimes on the farm when he's going to work, and he says we can have the horses on Saturdays to go and pull the wool." So Skeeter took a sugar-bag, and watched the crows and followed the stink as Elsa told her to do, and plucked extra strands of wool caught on old fences, and listened to Elsa's matter-of-fact stories of sheep stations in the north-west, and bananas and other strange fruit which grew along the Gascoyne River where the Kicketts' real home was.

"Half the kids at the Carnarvon school are yella-fellas like me," she told Skeeter. "And some of the white kids are our cousins. It's miles better than this old Mudjinup school, and I reckon we'll be going back up there when Dad finishes down here."

Skeeter hoped devoutly that Mr Kickett's work in the district would never end, accepted that sooner or later it must, and lived for the day. Her tenth birthday came, and Maggie invited Elsa to tea and to stay overnight, and after tea they sat on the lawn in the moonlight, and Elsa told Grandpa the blackfellow names for the stars, and Grandpa told both of them the white man's names, and how you could find your way at night by following the star paths. Then Maggie made cocoa for them all, and brought out the birthday cake and set it up on a kerosene case and lit ten little coloured candles in the moonlight. Skeeter blew out all the candles in one go, and made her wish, a variation of her standard wish. She wished she could see the stars up north, where Elsa insisted they were both bigger and brighter. Then she cut her cake and handed out big slices for everyone, and counted herself the luckiest girl in the whole of Australia.

On Christmas Eve the Kicketts began to pack their belongings, and about ten on Christmas morning the two loaded carts trundled up to the Ryan's cottage, with Elsa's oldest brother and mother driving, and Mr Kickett riding a young chestnut gelding he had taken in lieu of payment for his last job. The horses were unharnessed and turned into the Ryan paddock, and the two families celebrated Christmas together, with two bottles of beer for the men, and four bottles of lemonade for the women and children, kept cool in the shade of the back step under wet sugarbags. In the late afternoon the horses were reharnessed, and everyone shook hands all round, and Grandpa said, "You're a white man, Ted," to Mr Kickett, which Skeeter thought was a funny thing because he wasn't, he was a half-caste, and then the family climbed into the carts, and Mr Kickett mounted the colt, and off they went down the road, none of them looking back, not even Elsa.

Chapter 2

A flood, a bushfire, and a magic Christmas

During the year which followed the Kicketts' departure a number of things happened, some good, some bad.

The year began well, when Maggie raised her annual two bob each way to ten bob each way on an outsider at the New Year Picnic Races, and the city book-maker who came to the bush to make a killing was forced to pay out, when an entirely unknown, unlikely-looking dark-horse, romped past the post to take the Mudjinup Cup. Jilgee's owner/rider and Maggie were the only two backers at 100 to one, and Maggie, who announced to all and sundry that the Ryans could always tell a good horse when they saw one, confided that night to Grandpa that Ted Kickett had told her about the horse on Christmas Day. It belonged to the farmer who had paid him with the chestnut colt, and Ted did know a good horse when he saw one.

Maggie bought a wireless with part of her winnings, and proposed to put aside the rest for music lessons for Skeeter. Skeeter, who could already raise a handy tune on Grandpa's harmonica, whined that she didn't want to learn the piano, because the lessons and practice would take up the valuable time after school which she needed to set her rabbit traps, but Maggie seemed adamant.

The wireless, one of the few in town, in pride of place in the parlour, opened up a new world to the Ryans. They had never bought a newspaper, cheap though they were, because Grandpa could not read or write, only sign his name, and Maggie said she had enough to do on the home front without bothering what was happening elsewhere. But now there was the radio news every evening, to which Maggie and Grandpa immediately became addicted, and Skeeter's favourite serial, 'Dad and Dave'.

March came in hot as midsummer, and no signs yet of any autumn rains, and a man called Hitler occupied the Rhineland, which made Grandpa pull a long face and tell Maggie that it sounded like 1914 all over again, and sooner or later we would have to fight the mongrels. Grandpa had been a Light-Horseman in the War, but he didn't talk about it much, except on Anzac Day, when he always got drunk after the parade, and chewed peppermint lollies when he came home for tea, so that Maggie and Skeeter couldn't smell the beer on his breath. Then he would say he was glad little Skeeter was a girl, no matter how much she wished she wasn't, and Maggie would say "Eat your tea, Pa, and don't bother the child."

But that year Grandpa did not get to the Anzac Parade because he was in the cottage hospital with a broken ankle. He had slipped off a roof he was mending two days before Anzac Day, and he asked Skeeter if she would march for him and wear his medals, but Maggie told him war was for stupid men and to leave Skeeter out of it.

The right time for planting the farmers' wheat came and went, and still no rain, and when Grandpa came home with his crutches, there were less and less people wanting him for jobs. Maggie suddenly stopped talking about finding a piano teacher for Skeeter, and took on a job herself, doing the ironing every Tuesday for the bank manager's wife. Sometimes Skeeter felt a little guilty as she halved her rabbit money secretly each morning, and dropped a threepence or a sixpence into the old Lactogen tin in the wooden trunk in the room she now shared with Davey. If things get really bad I'll give it to them, she decided, appalled at what her sacrifice would mean. She could hardly remember when she hadn't been saving for her land, and to lose her stake and have to begin all over again was something she could not bear to think about. But even though Maggie now sold the butter she made twice a week, and the family ate dripping instead on their bread, they never went hungry, and Skeeter began to hope that she would not be called upon to make the sacrifice.

There was still enough food in the Ryan house to give the occasional meal to the tramps who called in apologetically asking if there was any wood to chop, but there were more and more tramps on the roads, and Maggie told Skeeter that she must never talk to any of them unless she was in her own yard. Skeeter believed that Maggie thought the tramps might be so hungry that they would steal her traps or her rabbits from her, and she promised vigorously that she would give the tramps a wide berth.

There was more and more talk of the drought on the wireless news, and when the first of the farming families began to drift into town and set up their camps along the river where the Kicketts had once lived, even the children knew that things couldn't get much worse. In a fit of temper Maggie threw in her ironing job, saying she couldn't bring herself to iron damask table-cloths and serviettes any longer for the rich bitch whose husband had pushed farmers with little kids off their properties. Grandpa said he was only doing what his bosses in the city banks told him to, and if he didn't he'd be out on his arse too, but that didn't cut any ice with Maggie; she said she was sick of ironing anyway, and she'd find something else to do. That was the worst night of Skeeter's life, lying awake in her bed, convinced that within a few days she must confess and relinquish her hoard.

But the very next day the publican's wife knocked on the Ryan front door, and told Maggie she'd heard she wasn't ironing any longer for the bank, and could she see her way to doing the table linen for the hotel, two days a week, she did such a lovely job, and bring little Davey along too, and because it might take up the time she ought to be cooking the meal for her family, there would be a hot dinner to take home for them Tuesdays and Fridays, and a pound a week. Maggie gave the publican's wife a cup of tea and a scone, and said she thought she could manage it, and Skeeter nearly cried with relief when she came home from school and heard the news.

Grandpa didn't take it the same way. "Not right, Maggie," he said, "working at the pub, and all the ratbags in town sniffing round."

"For God's sake, Pa," snapped Maggie, "I'll be working in the laundry, and not in the public bar, and you don't mind a bit of sniffing round yourself when the mood's on you, if I'm told right." She plonked down the plate she was rinsing so sharply that it snapped in two on the tray, and one piece fell on the floor beside Skeeter's feet. Skeeter picked it up quickly and ran outside to the bin, but then she came back and listened at the kitchen door. If Grandpa wrecked her plans she'd die, but then he was only Grandpa, and not Maggie's husband; he couldn't really stop her. She needn't have worried. Maggie flung down the dish-cloth and advanced on Grandpa. "If I was going to worry about what the people in this dump say about me, I've got enough going for me already, with two bastard kids. But I'm going to feed them kids, with or without your help, and give them an education too, and if I need to be a barmaid to do it, then I'll do that too."

"Maggie, Maggie, love," protested Grandpa.

"Anyway," Maggie ignored his plea, "I'll be going in the back way, and coming out the back way, and I'll never get near the front bar. I'll be keeping meself to meself out in the laundry, with Davey along. A pound's a pound, all said and done, and you're not the one to tell me different!"

Skeeter felt a bit sad for Grandpa, for she guessed that he was feeling bad because he didn't earn as much now as he usually did, and she felt rather irrationally that Maggie had been hard on him. Grandpa went out on the back verandah, and played his harmonica softly to himself, and Maggie snapped at Skeeter to take Davey to his cot and get to bed herself. As she fell asleep Skeeter could hear the murmur of quiet voices on the back verandah, and she knew that Maggie would take the job, and that everything would be all right in the morning. And so it turned out.

In bitter July the late rains came all at once, and the river flooded, and for two days Grandpa was caught on the other side where he had been working, and a little girl from one of the farmers' camps was washed away and drowned. The water came right up into the main street, through the shops and the pub, and the school was closed for three days. When the water receded and the bridge re-appeared Grandpa borrowed a horse and rode home. Once he was assured that Maggie and the children were all right, he said that it was an ill wind, because now there would be quite a lot of repair work for him to do at the shops and some of the flooded houses. Skeeter had had a fine time, paddling in the mud, and poking about in the old shed where Grandpa kept his tools and feed for the cow and chooks. Maggie had told her to make herself useful and tidy up the shed, and she had discovered, scratched deep into a brick on the side wall behind the bench, the name Fred Ryan above the date 1901. Grandpa was George, so who the heck was this Fred? She meant to ask Grandpa, but by the time he returned home she had forgotten about it in all the current excitement.

After the flood the whole countryside changed to green again, and Spring came early with warm days and wildflowers such as Skeeter had never seen before. There were kangaroo paws and leschenaultia under every gum tree and flannel flowers and the little blue orchids along the roadsides, and the spider orchids and piano orchids among the blackboys. Grandpa said it was always like that after a flood, and showed Skeeter how to press the orchids between blotting paper to make a collection, and one day when she was rabbiting, she found three of the rare and beautiful enamel orchids. Everyone in Mudjinup seemed to get a new lease on life after the flood, including the long-faced postmistress, who suddenly left her husband and ran away with one of the bank clerks. Grandpa came home and told Maggie he'd heard that she had cut the legs off both pairs of her husband's trousers while he was asleep, so he couldn't follow them, and the milko had heard him roaring in the morning, and had to go and find someone to lend him a pair of pants before he could come out in the street.

Skeeter's eleventh birthday and Davey's sixth, two days apart, came and went, and Skeeter was top of standard five at the end of year examinations. Then one night the wireless news announced that the king who hadn't yet had time to get his head on the back of the Australian pennies had abdicated, and his brother George was now the king. Maggie told Skeeter that the eldest of the two little princesses was only half a year older than she was, and that night Skeeter dreamed that she too was a princess, and Maggie was a queen, and woke up in the morning quite disappointed to find the she was still plain Skeeter Ryan.

On the last day of school before the summer holiday, the children were dismissed early, because there were bushfires in the bush to the west of the township, and some of the children's homes lay in that direction. Skeeter was not really apprehensive, though the billows of smoke, which engulfed her at intervals as she ran, made her cough and her eyes sting. She could see the blackest columns of smoke roiling up behind the low hills of Mean Johnson's farm, and idly wondered whether the fire would burn into the farmers' wheat crops experimentally planted after the floods on the few farms which had not been abandoned or taken over by the bank. But as she neared her home she was surprised to see Grandpa and Maggie, and a man who turned out to be a passing tramp, all beating with wet bags against the orchard fence-posts and the clumps of thick grass which were alight along the roadside. They were racing backwards and forwards to the cow's water-trough to souse the bags as they dried out and threatened to catch fire, and Grandpa shouted to Skeeter, when he saw her standing open-mouthed, to get more chaff-bags from the shed and wet them, and run them to the fire-fighters. It was a hectic hour before all the burning grass had been beaten out, and the fence was saved. Some posts were destroyed, and Grandpa poured buckets of water at their bases to put out the coals, and more on the still-smoking old logs, all except one. He sent Skeeter to the house to wash a dozen big potatoes and bring them to him. These he poked deep into the coals of the log and raked the hot ash over them. "Your mother left her job early when she saw the bushfire, and forgot to bring our Friday tea," he told Skeeter. "Now she'll be too fagged to cook us any, so I'll get tea tonight," and, turning to the grinning tramp, "we'd be pleased if you'd join us."

The tramp said he would, and Skeeter ran up to the house to rescue her school-bag from the yard where she'd thrown it, and to help with the evening jobs. While Maggie milked the placid old cow, Skeeter fed the chooks and sent Davey to fill the woodbox, and refilled the old black kettle which had almost boiled dry on the stove.

Grandpa and the tramp were still inspecting fence-posts, and as she worked she could hear Grandpa calling out inquiries to groups of men riding back into town from where they had gone to help the farmers. No crops had been fired, and no stock lost, but it would have been a different story in a normal year if all the fields had been planted, they said. The fire was still burning in the range, but with the wind change there was no longer any danger to the settlements.

The sun sank through the haze like a great crimson ball, and the acrid smell of smoke changed to an overlay of eucalyptus mixed with what was almost a tantalising perfume.

"That's sandalwood," explained Grandpa, "there are still a few odd trees in the bush, the stumps left by the sandalwood-cutters. They used to send it to China to make joss-sticks, and when I was a boy we often burnt a sandalwood log in the fire-place."

The tramp, whose name was Jim, said he'd smelt it round the Chinese joss-house in Darwin, and sometimes up in the Peninsula.

It turned out to be one of those enchanted evenings. Grandpa said his tea had to be eaten in the open air to be appreciated and Maggie agreed that the house was like an oven, so they spread rugs on the back lawn, and Maggie made the tea in Grandpa's work billy and brought it out with enamel mugs, and Grandpa raked the potatoes from the coals and threw them onto a sugar bag to cool. Then he rubbed the ash from them with a clean bag, and Maggie split them and dropped a great lump of butter into each one, and they feasted in the guttering light of a kerosene lamp on a box, eating with their fingers, and dribbling butter down their chins, savouring the crisp cracking skins and the soft rich insides, and the grown-ups washed theirs down with tea, and the children with mugs of milk.

"A meal fit for a king," said Jim, "but one a poor old king would never get." Skeeter's last lingering desire to be a princess immediately dissipated, wiped out by the certain knowledge that potatoes baked in the coals would be a pleasure that princesses could never know.

With the coming of true darkness the backdrop of the hills sprang to life, with winking, glowing lights where tree-stumps still flared or fell in red cascades of coals. And then the yarns came, and she listened entranced as Grandpa and Jim told of other bushfires in other places, not always with a happy ending, and then Jim talked of places the others had never seen, of the pearling fleets up north, and the great plains where the bushfires ate up a thousand square miles of country with no-one able to stop them, and the animals fleeing before them, with the scavenging hawks diving on the smaller creatures as they fled in terror before the flames.

Davey fell asleep on the rug, but Maggie allowed Skeeter to stay up until all the yarns were done, and the grown-ups decided on another cup of tea.

In the morning Jim was gone, and Skeeter spent the day in a dream, treasuring his stories and rehearsing them to herself. Mean Johnson called in and asked Grandpa if he could give him a hand repairing fences, and Grandpa said give him time to fix his own, and he'd be on hand the next day. Skeeter, in an old straw hat of Maggie's, offsided for him, and that was how she came to spy out more likely rabbit warrens on the farm, and ear-mark them for later investigation. There was a week's work on the job, which brought them up to Christmas Eve, and Skeeter wrote out the docket for Grandpa instead of Maggie, and Grandpa said she'd been such a handy offsider that ten bob of it was wages for her. She had expected nothing, and the enormity of the sum, the equivalent of forty pairs of rabbits, made her think briefly of her land savings. But the thought was followed immediately by the realisation that it was Christmas Eve, and with such a sum she could buy presents for everyone.

They had early tea at five o'clock, and then, decked in their best clothes, they joined the throng of townspeople and farmers in Mudjinup's main street for the joys of Christmas Eve shopping and good fellowship. Skeeter had never seen such a crowd in the town before, for this was the first time the Ryans had been rich enough to buy anything more than the extra food luxuries, and Maggie refused to have her nose rubbed in their deficiencies, arguing that unless you could be in it up to the hilt it was better not to go and watch others doing what you couldn't afford to do. Skeeter had seen Grandpa hand Maggie some money after he had given her the crisp ten-shilling note, and she noted with satisfaction that this year the Ryans *were* going to be in it up to the hilt.

With promises to meet at the Post Office at half past eight, the family split up, and Skeeter rushed eagerly to the newsagent-cum-toyshop, where she had seen three bright toy motor-cars resplendent in the window. Two of them, including the middle-sized one she wanted for Davey, were still there, and she waited in an agony of suspense to be served, afraid that the customers before her might chose Davey's car. But at last it was hers, wrapped in bright red paper and coloured string, and she still had seven-and-sixpence in her pocket. Firmly she set her feet towards the expensive shop, that half of the chemist's which doubled as the jeweller's . For Maggie she bought green and gold ear-rings, nestling on brown velvet in a little box, and for Grandpa silver-coloured cuff-links, also in a box, but set on more masculine dark-blue card, and she paid the outrageous sum of threepence extra to have them wrapped in gold Christmas paper, and tied with the finest of gold string. Sixpence of her trove remained, and she thought fleetingly of the ice-cream vat packed in salt which had arrived on the train. No, the sixpence must go into the Lactogen tin. She begged a large brown-paper bag from the grocer to hold her purchases, and he gave her a newspaper cone of boiled lollies and a pat on the head for Christmas, and then as an afterthought called her back and added a tin of peaches for her Mum for being a regular customer through the year. Skeeter yelled hullo and Merry Christmas to schoolmates as she made her way finally towards the Post Office, where she could see Maggie and Davey waiting. People were walking not only on the footpath but right in the roadway, and some of them had arms linked together and were singing, and the man whose wife had run away with the bank clerk was embracing a lamp-post, as drunk as a monkey. Then Grandpa pushed through the throng behind her, with four ice-cream cones, two in each hand.

Skeeter's ice-cream lasted nearly all of the two mile walk home in the moonlight, with Grandpa carrying Davey pick-a-back. She had seen everyone she ever knew, and they had all been happy. All except Mean Johnson. He hadn't been there, she was sure, or she'd have seen him. She supposed he was too mean to buy Christmas presents. But then, maybe he didn't have anyone to buy presents for, and, come to think of it, it was his money that had enabled the Ryans to get into it up to the hilt, as her mum would say.

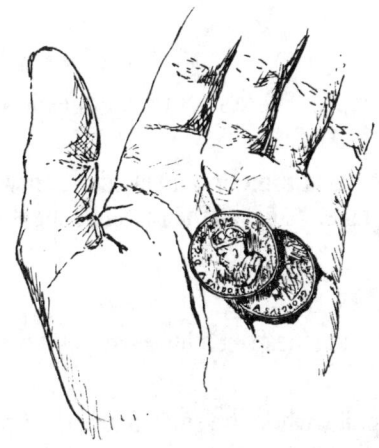

Chapter 3

An unexpected ally

For two years when the rabbits were populous there, Skeeter had surreptitiously trapped them on the Johnson farm, carefully avoiding its owner, quite unaware that he often saw her or the evidence of her visits, and was just as careful as she was to avoid confronting her in case he frightened her off again.

So he was quite surprised when one day, not long after Christmas, she appeared on the farm house doorstep and asked abruptly if she could talk to him.

Skeeter had thought about the Christmas bonanza more than once in the days following, and had admitted to herself that of course he must know about her exploitation of the farm warrens. She decided that perhaps he wasn't mean after all, but only hard-up like everyone else, and if that was so, her proposition might bear fruit.

She came to the point straight away.

"Mr. Johnson, I'd like to come to a business arrangement with you. Can I lease your warrens?"

The man straightened up and regarded her soberly. "What did you have in mind, Ginger?" he asked.

"Well," said Skeeter, "I could pay you tuppence a week, and come when I wanted to, and you mustn't let anyone else come but me."

"Sounds fair enough," said the man, "you're pretty young for a share farmer, but I reckon we can do a deal. But that's going to cut into your savings, isn't it?":

"Mmm," agreed Skeeter, "but I guess it's what Grandpa would call an overhead expense, like buying traps and all that."

Mean Johnson appeared to ponder.

"There is another way," he said, "but it would mean more work for you. I need the rabbits cleaned out now I'm putting the crops in, so I could give you a contract. You can still pay me your lease, but I'll pay you sixpence a week to do the job if you think you can handle another half dozen traps. There's some old ones in the back of the shed you could use."

Skeeter did some rapid mental arithmetic, and liked the answer, but could she manage the extra time the job would take. " I get all the rabbits?" she queried, struck by a sudden thought.

He nodded.

"Sounds fair," she agreed, and stuck out a little paw, and they shook solemnly on the deal.

Ralph Johnson felt a little guilty when the small figure disappeared with her burden of extra traps, but he reckoned that if she was really dinkum about her land there were a lot stiffer pressures waiting for her in the future, and the one he had imposed on her early rising could be considered part of the toughening-up process.

Skeeter reported her business proposition at home, and Maggie then suggested that if she was prepared to get up half an hour earlier she ought to be allowed to keep half her earnings for herself. With her job at the hotel she could manage without the extra money. Skeeter, who had never really liked deceiving her mother, was overjoyed. She could now put her money in the bank, where it would be truly safe, and bit by bit she could add the contents of the Lactogen tin and cover up her earlier subterfuges. The only drawback was that Maggie's knowledge of her savings might finally lead to her suggestions as to what it should be used for, but Skeeter knew that her mother's strict standards of right and wrong would restrict her to suggestions only; it would be Skeeter's money, and Skeeter would have the last say over it. Besides, that all lay in the future, and as Grandpa would say, there was no need to jump her hurdles before she came to them. In the meantime she would concentrate on Johnson's rabbits.

At school her world continued to broaden. Her sixth standard teacher, Mr. Bartlett, was no martinet, and when Skeeter arrived after second bell, flushed and puffing from her run, he did not punish her with the cane around her legs, but told her she must make up the time after school. It was those extra ten minutes after four o'clock that led to Skeeter's introduction to the world of children's literature. Mr Bartlett began to lend her his books, which she devoured at playtime, lunchtime and in the hour between tea and bedtime after her rushed homework. Skeeter liked the adventure stories best, and her only regret was that none of them were ever about Australian children.

She confided this fact to Mean Johnson one day in his farmhouse kitchen, when they had just completed the ritual of his acceptance of the weekly two pennies, and then paid her the contract "tanner." Skeeter had firmly rejected his suggestion that they deduct the twopence, and he pay her fourpence; it somehow seemed less businesslike to her, and he understood her need to hand over the actual money to him.

"Do you like poetry too, then? " he asked suddenly. When she nodded he opened the door from the kitchen to an adjoining room, where Skeeter saw, against the far wall, two shelves, loaded down with books. He reached down a volume and handed it to her.

"Here's some Australian stuff for you, then, Ginger. The Banjo should be just your cup of tea."

If there had ever been any possibility of Skeeter's resolve waning, her introduction to the Australian outback poets ensured the opposite. The nebulous land of great empty stretches in the school atlas suddenly became peopled with men and women and blackfellows and wild horses, and drovers with nicknames, and even a priest or two.

Skeeter had never given much thought to religion; she presumed that the Ryan's disregard of church had something to do with her not having a real father, and that Sunday school was like birthday parties and school picnics where only "little ladies" were invited because of the end-of-year Christmas party. She knew all the Bible stories from her weekly school Religion classes, and that there were two sorts of Christians, Catholics and Protestants. When she asked Grandpa which lot the Ryans belonged to, he had laughed and said they were Bush Baptists, and didn't have a church.

So Skeeter was mightily intrigued when old Father Riley, from the Catholic Church, was transferred, and a new younger priest arrived, with such a missionary vigour and a bulldog tenacity to round up the flock, that the whole town reverberated from his efforts.

He turned up at the Ryan's house one afternoon just after Skeeter had arrived home from school, and strode uninvited into their kitchen, announcing heartily, "I'm Father Regan. I've been here a month, and I haven't seen you at Sunday Mass yet. You must be Catholics with a name like Ryan. So I want to know why you are neglecting your religious duties, and what are we going to do about it."

Maggie turned from the stove, flabbergasted. Skeeter paused from stuffing bread and jam into her mouth, and regarded the apparition with interest. But Grandpa, who had been sitting at the end of the table, engaged in pouring hot black tea from his large cup into the saucer to cool, suddenly stiffened as if he had been shot. He put down the saucer slowly, so as not to spill the tea, and then rose to his feet and placed both hands wide apart on the end of the table, his head thrust forward, and his great grey walrus moustache bristling.

"Mister," he said slowly and clearly, "we are not going to do anything about it. This particular branch of the Ryans are not Micks, and not ever likely to be. And I may as well tell you why. We haven't been ever since we come to Australia, and that's since me grandfather's time. He come out to Swan River colony in the hold of a convict ship, and all because of a Catholic priest just like you, me boy."

Father Regan began to stutter, but Grandpa cut him short. "Me Grandfather, Danny Ryan, borrowed the priest's horse one night, back in Ireland, just to go and visit his girl. The horse was back in the field before morning and none the worse for it, but the priest dobbed him in for a thief, and he got sent to Swan River, and lost his girl for good." But Father Regan, his chosen path before him, and his eyes agleam, was not to be put off by this explanation.

"But Mr. Ryan," he began, "surely a man cannot blame the Church for one of its priest's shortcomings so many years ago."

"The Ryans can," stated Grandpa firmly. "The Church made convict stock of us, and the Ryans don't forget easy. A man's been hit once is a fool if he goes back to the same place to be hit again, so I'll say goodday to you, and mind the step as you go!"

"Goodday to you all," said the priest as he went, "but I'll be seeing you again, I'm sure."

Skeeter had to leave to set her traps, but after tea she pestered Grandpa for the story of Danny Ryan and his adventures in Swan River Colony, and out of the blue she remembered the brick in the old shed, and asked who was Fred Ryan, 1901? "He was my older brother," said Grandpa, with a little sigh, "and a direct descendant of Old Danny, I'm thinking. He was a bit of a lad, and wouldn't settle to a trade like I did. Got in with an older bloke, and went into the horse-trading business, and a bit of jockeying too on the side. Me mother never did like the other fellow, but Fred thought the sun shone out of him, and then there was talk around about the older bloke being none too straight about some brand or other, and there was rows at home, and then one morning when we got up Fred was gone, and the older bloke too, we found out later, and we never seen either of them again. And that's thirty years or more ago."

Skeeter fell asleep that night quite delighted with her new knowledge. It wasn't everyone who could boasts two horse-thieves in the family, almost as good as a bushranger, like everyone whose name was Kelly claimed as their own.

All the year the news on the wireless became more and more gloomy. It was not that people were poorer than they had been, or that jobs were scarce. In fact, the opposite was true. Australia was slowly but surely recovering from the Depression. But the news from overseas was increasingly about Hitler and Mussolini, and the inevitability of another European war. And a war which involved England automatically involved an Australia which still had clear memories of the last one.

None of this affected Skeeter, whose days were so full that she had little time to think of anything but her schooling, her jobs, her growing bank account, and how to snatch time to enjoy the story books which Mr Bartlett now supplied to her regularly.

In the Spring Mean Johnson's farmhouse changed overnight from a bachelor establishment to a family home, with the arrival of his widowed sister, and her six-year-old grandson. Skeeter knew they were coming before they arrived, for the lonely man could not disguise his pleasure when she called to settle-up. "You'll like Melly, Ginger," he told her, "she's bossy, but, bugger me, she's got a good heart. She's had a rough time with her drunken old man, and her daughter dying of T.B., and I'm glad there's a home here for her. She's coming on Tuesday's train."

"Well," said Skeeter, looking matter-of-factly at the untidy kitchen, "I reckon we'd better do something to clean up this mucky place before she comes."

So on the Sunday Grandpa minded Davey, and Skeeter and Maggie went up to the farm, and in its owner's words, washed hell out of the whole place. They worked all day, denying entry to Ralph Johnson to all but the back verandah, and he occupied himself by killing a sheep and sweeping the yard clean. Maggie would accept nothing for their work, so he insisted on giving them half the sheep for their labours, and so tired were they at sundown that if Grandpa and Davey had not come to meet them they would have been almost too exhausted to carry it home. " I don't know why people call him Mean Johnson," said Skeeter, "Mr. Johnson's one of the best people I know."

"Yes," agreed Grandpa, "it's just that he was careful when he had to be, and he lived like a dog to keep that farm of his. Others that weren't so good at it, and lost theirs, were the ones that give him that name, and it stuck. But he's a fair man, and I'd as soon him for a friend than others I could name." Skeeter agreed vehemently, and even Maggie nodded her head. They did not notice her fleeting secretive smile.

On the following Sunday the Ryans were all invited to the farm for lunch to meet Melinda Lewis and her little grandson Bill, the first time in Skeeter's memory that they had ever eaten a meal away from home. This memorable event heralded the beginning of a social as well as a business relationship, and Maggie, so long deprived of the company of her own sex, lowered her defences against Melly's determined advances. Davey and Bill were mates immediately, and the two women became firm friends. Melinda, as her brother claimed, was kind-hearted and practical, and her hard and sad life with a weak man who had sought solace from the bottle, had neither permanently soured her, nor affected her innate nature.

The farmhouse was not long in showing outwardly that a woman was in residence. The windows now sported curtains, and the yard became a garden as Melly bullied her brother into digging flower beds and carting flat rocks from the gully for pathways. It was this garden which inspired Skeeter to her next business venture, for, under her determined onslaughts, the rabbit population of the farm was decimated to such an extent that Skeeter began to find herself walking long miles with little to show for it. On the day she terminated her contract with Ralph Johnson, she had already planned her next venture.

The Ryans had always grown their own vegetables, but now the beds of flower seedlings were already pushing through, and Skeeter, whose sharp eyes had watched all Melly's ministrations in the farm garden, had already made a list, beginning with the hotel, of possible buyers of regular fresh flowers. She had planted iceland poppies, sweat-peas, chrysanthemums and petunias, and on Melly's advice, borders of zinnias, which Melly said were so tough that they grew by themselves, and survived when all else failed.

Maggie watched her with interest, but said that she preferred the bush flowers herself.

"So do I," said Skeeter, "but nobody buys them."

"What on earth are you saving for?" Maggie wanted to know. "It's not natural, Skeeter, now the real bad times are over. You don't have to do it any longer. You ought to be having fun with the other kids now."

"Just habit, I suppose," said Skeeter, "and they are pretty, aren't they?"

With December and the end of the school year, the problem of Skeeter's continuing education had to be faced. She had now completed her primary schooling, and there were two options open to her until the compulsory school-leaving age of fourteen, three years away. Those who could afford to board their children in a hostel sent them to the larger town, forty miles to the north, where they attended the High School, and returned home by a school bus for the week-end. For the others, the primary school offered a combined standards 7, 8 and 9 class taken by the headmaster, which supposedly allowed children to sit for the coveted Junior Certificate, but only with the basic subjects, no science, no languages. Only the very rich, of whom there were a handful among the long-established landowners of the district, and one or two of the businessmen, could consider the ultimate of college in Perth.

Skeeter herself gave little thought to the matter, for she presumed she would stay on at the local school, and when the headmaster sent a message home to ask her mother to call at the school she supposed that it must have something to do with her secondary enrolment.

"What'd he want, Mum?" she queried, when Maggie returned.

"Well, you're going back to school here next year, but Mr. Giddons says you're clever enough to win a scholarship. It has to be in the year you turn twelve, and it's on the standard six work which you've already done. He wants to coach you at school, and then you sit for the scholarship at the end of the year, and if you win one, it means five years school all paid for by the State, board and all. There are fifty places, and he thinks you could get one of them, Skeeter."

Maggie was clearly excited about the prospect, and Skeeter's interest was roused. She had vaguely regretted that she would not be going with some of her schoolmates to the neighbouring High School, but this seemed even better. Mr. Giddons had said that it was the best High School in the State, and it was in the city too, which Skeeter had never seen.

Skeeter did win a scholarship, but she did not get to the best High School after all. And that was Maggie's fault. After all the congratulations and the back-slapping, Mr. Giddons threw a spanner in the works when he explained to Maggie that it was not a boarding school, and that she would have to find somewhere for Skeeter to board, some relation perhaps, and the board and the bus fares would be duly paid by the State.

Maggie was adamant that no daughter of hers was going to board God knows where in the rotten city from the age of twelve to seventeen. She knew what happened to country girls in the city who boarded with strangers, and she knew it from first-hand experience, and that was that. Nothing that Mr. Giddon's explanations or Skeeter's pleadings could say could change her mind one iota. A boarding school, yes; private boarding, no, and that was that!

Skeeter bawled, and privately considered running away up north, and Maggie went tight-lipped and silent about the house. Grandpa sympathised secretly with Skeeter, but they both accepted that there was no point in his speaking-out. The end of the school year approached, and Mr. Giddons told Skeeter to ask her mother if she might be allowed to board at the C.W.A. hostel in the neighbouring town with the other children who had gone to the High School there, for the State would pay the fees for her. Skeeter said she would, but she didn't bother. For a year she had dreamed of college in the city, just like the school stories she had read, and if she couldn't have that, she didn't want a substitute. She told Mr. Giddons that her mother had said no, and the disappointed man left town with his family for his summer holidays.

Just after the miserable New Year, Father Regan knocked on the Ryan front door, and Davey answered the knock and led him through to the kitchen were Maggie was sewing. She looked up with a surprised frown. For the past two years they had nodded to each other in the street, but she had never had a conversation with him since Grandpa's confrontation in this same kitchen.

"I've not come to convert you, Miss Ryan," he began, "but if you'd like to offer me a cup of tea, I believe I could possibly be of some help to you and the little girl."

Maggie, somewhat mystified, but aware of the requirements of normal hospitality, asked him to sit down, and reached for the teacups.

"I've heard about your daughter's scholarship from Mr. Giddons," he said, "and I've been doing some checking around, for it's a real shame if the child can't take advantage of it."

"You'll not make me change me mind, Father Regan," said Maggie firmly, "I'm surprised you'd try. What's it to you, anyway? We don't belong to your Church, as Pa made pretty plain to you."

"Ah," replied the man, "that's so, and I respect it. But we still might be able to help each other. My older sister is a nun, and she's the head of the best Catholic Girl's College in Perth. I was down there for a couple of days after Christmas to visit, and we talked about your daughter. Now it's been hard times for the schools the last few years, and the ones with the best results in the public exams are the ones that attract the parents with money to spend on their children's education, and that's where your Marion comes in. The State scholarship can be transferred to St. Mary's, and your daughter would get the education she deserves, and good results for the school, and the good nuns to watch over her into the bargain."

"But," stammered Maggie, "we're not Catholics. Aren't the schools only for Catholic children?"

"Well, yes, in the good times. But in the last few years we've had as many as twenty percent of the pupils non-Catholics, just to fill the empty places. Our fees are lower than the other church schools, because we don't have to pay for the teachers, and the education is first-rate, so there are plenty of non-Catholic parents who want a good education for their daughters who can't afford their own schools, and send them to ours instead. Sister Francis knows that Marion is not a Catholic; that would be no obstacle."

One side of Maggie's mind was groping with the possibilities, and the other was registering that the priest had rather nice black curly hair, though what that had to do with the matter she couldn't think.

Her hand was almost trembling as she reached out to refill his cup.

"She's illegitimate!" she burst out suddenly, and was almost un-nerved by the sudden compassion in his eyes.

"Sister Francis knows that," he said gently, "and if you don't mind calling yourself Mrs. for the sake of the child, you see - then there's no call for anyone else to know. Your business entirely."

Maggie nodded, but did not speak.

"Education's a grand thing," the man said quietly. "I though if being a Catholic school stuck in your neck, there might be a chance you'd consider a Protestant school, so I phoned a couple of them, the better ones. They're stricter about the religion, I'm afraid, and I think they might buck at the birth certificate. Will you give St. Mary's a try and think it over?"

Maggie steadied the teapot with her other hand. "No need to think it over, Father Regan. We'll take it. It sounds a fair bargain to me, and better. There's no future in a place like this for Skeeter - Marion - and as long as I know she'll be safe..."

"Safe, my good woman," laughed the priest, "the dear nuns practically lock them up like jailbirds. You'll hear nothing but complaints about it for the next five years."

And so Skeeter's miserable summer changed in flash from the worst to the best, and Maggie, Davey and herself had their first holiday by the sea, a whole five days of it. Grandpa produced the money from somewhere, and the Ryan children travelled on a train for the first time in their lives, and saw the sea they had only read about and seen at the rare picture show. They stayed at a boarding house right close to the beach, and Maggie took the children on a bus to the school amid lawns and playing fields near the wide river, and Skeeter met Sister Francis, who seemed to know all about her. Another Sister showed them over the school and Skeeter thought it was just like a story in one of her books, and she'd wake up soon.

Then they went back to the boarding-house, and down to the beach to swim in the new bathing costumes Maggie had bought. The next day they caught another bus to the city, and the children regarded their mother with new eyes. Maggie knew just where to go, and she bought underclothes and shoes and socks and pyjamas and hats and materials to make the uniforms, and a beautiful suitcase, all from a list the Sister had given her. She told the smiling saleslady to have it delivered to the boarding house, and asked for the discount for cash and paid for it all from a roll of notes which made Skeeter gasp with amazement. She didn't dare ask where it had all come from, and if she had Maggie would not have told her. Grandpa had borrowed a deal of it from Ralph Johnson, interest free, and pay it back when you're ready.

Then the wonder of lunch in the shop's cafeteria, with little plates of real ice-cream with strawberries, to take down from the shelf onto Maggie's tray beside the plate of sandwiches with a sprig of parsley, and a glass of lemonade each for the children, and a cup of tea for Maggie. Maggie allowed the children to eat the ice-cream first, before the sandwiches, in case it melted, because it was a holiday, and Skeeter couldn't remember when she had seen her mother look so pretty and happy.

The last two days of the holiday went so fast, and yet they seemed to last forever, there was so much to see and do. The Ryans walked and swam and fished and watched the sideshow and discovered strawberry ice-cream cones at a kiosk. On the last evening as they were walking home from the beach a car drew up at a boarding house a couple of doors down from their own, and Skeeter was surprised to see two children from Mudjinup climb from the car with their parents. She called out in excitement, and the girl looked over.

"What are you doing here?" cried Skeeter.

"We come here every year for our holiday," replied the child in a bored voice, as her mother, with a sharp glance at Maggie, pulled at her arm.

"So do we," yelled Davey, and Skeeter, on the impulse, poked her tongue out at the whole family, now occupied in unloading suitcases. As she glanced back at her mother, half-expecting a thump on the back for her rudeness, she saw that Maggie's tongue was out too, as far as she could get it. Then suddenly all three Ryans were giggling together as they skipped lightheartedly up the boarding-house steps.

Chapter 4 *Two pounds a week and all found*

February 1944. The small plane laboured its way northwards hour after hour, and Marion's mind, on the verge of giving way to a half-sleep, flitted between past incidents, and expectations of what lay ahead. The plane had already landed three times since the early morning take-off, and each descent onto the tarmac had resulted in an increasingly hot and dry blast of air, such as Marion had never before experienced. But the pilot and three children and their mother and the two aboriginal stockmen hardly seemed to notice it, the pilot busy with unloading mailbags, while his passengers made for the white-painted opensided shed where tea and sandwiches awaited them.

Marion's lips twitched as she remembered Ralph Johnson's surprised comment at their Christmas celebrations just six short weeks ago.

"Well, bugger me, Ginger, you really are a 'young lady' now!" She supposed she was. Only Davey still addressed her as Skeeter, and five years at St. Mary's had refined her country drawl and imposed a degree of sophistication which she used according to the company in which she found herself. She had submitted to five years of Maggie's beloved music lessons, she could speak passable French, and she had lived up to Sister Francis' expectations of excellent scholastic results, as well as gaining kudos for the school on the sporting field. She had only pained Sister Francis once, and even Sister admitted extenuating circumstances, and said that perhaps it had been for the best, all things considered. The War had entered its third year, and when the first early morning air-raid alarm sounded before the school had its shelters built, the Sisters and the prefects had hurried all the children from their dormitories into the ground-floor assembly hall, the children half-asleep and not sure of what was happening. Sister Francis climbed to the stage, and no sooner had the eerie sound of the siren died away than she announced loudly that they must all pray hard, and immediately began to do exactly that herself. Then sudden emotive hush and the single loud voice triggered a scream and a sob from a nervous child, and instantly the frightening panic began to spread from child to child like a ripple widening from a dropped stone in a pond. Marion, standing beside the piano on the stage, acted on impulse. She flipped the lid, seated herself at the Baby Grand, and began to belt out the tune of a school hymn, but the words she bellowed as loudly as she knew how were an extremely bawdy version brought back to the school by one of the girls whose brother had learned it from the Yanks. Half the girls in the Upper School knew it, and with delighted grins they began to join in. The others regarded them with astonishment, none more so than the assembled nuns, and by the time the last naughty verse died away the moment of panic was over.

"Do you know any more?" hissed Sister Joseph, disregarding the flustered Sister Francis.

Marion did, though none quite so outrageous, and while the sing-song progressed, and little girls learned songs their parents might not quite approve, Sister Joseph and the prefects risked the prospect of Japanese bombs and went to the kitchen to make cocoa for the whole school. When the all-clear sounded Sister Francis caught Marion's arm as she was filing out of the hall. "That first - er -song, Marion. I've taken into account that you're a non-Catholic, but the tune, dear, the tune was an unfortunate choice!"

"Yes, Sister," said Marion dutifully, "but I had to choose one they'd all know, and it did the trick, didn't it?"

Sister Francis could only agree, but Marion thought it would probably be some time before Sister Francis chose that particular hymn to sing on Sunday nights in the school chapel, and she was right.

Marion had enjoyed her five years at boarding school. She gained a measure of popularity because of her sporting prowess, but she somehow still remained a loner, and the holidays, mostly spent working on the Johnson farm, were still the high-points of the year. "Still aiming for the station, Ginger?" Ralph asked her once more, and she assured him adamantly that she was.

Mudjinup was as changed as Marion was. The war, and the presence of an Army Camp nearby had seen to that. Suddenly the Depression was only a bad dream, and there was money around. Grandpa had work and to spare, and he bought himself a second-hand utility which he drove the same way as he drove a horse and cart. The need for a receptionist at the hotel saw Maggie promoted from the laundry to the front desk, to share the job with the publican's wife, and Grandpa's fears were allayed when he saw that any liquor salesmen or Army officers who came "sniffing around" were dealt with frigidly.

Farm labour was so scarce, and the need for farm produce so great, that Marion, Davey and young Bill were kept occupied for any holidays they could spare; they mustered sheep, drove tractors, sewed up wheat bags, and willingly carried out any task set them. Ralph Johnson insisted on paying them the same wage he would have paid a man if he could have found one. But the Army had got in first, and taken all the men, and by the time Marion sat for her last exam, and plans were made for Davey and Bill to go to the neighbouring High School, he would have been in dire straits if the Government hadn't sent him two Land Girls.

During her last year at school it had been taken for granted that Marion's future lay in becoming a teacher, and she had accepted that it was as good as anything; she had no stomach for nursing, and any profession that might promise the money she coveted demanded long years of training at University. Two years at the Teachers' College was the best she could think of.

She saw the advertisement by chance in the newspaper that carried her Leaving results in early January, and she knew with absolute conviction that Fate had taken a hand in directing her future. It had already been arranged that, as soon as the exam results were out, Marion was to go to Perth for an interview before making application for the Teachers' College. Ralph Johnson, who had business to discuss with the Agricultural Department, had offered her a lift in his car, powered, like most that year, by a charcoal burner. Marion, phoning friends for mutual congratulations, was invited to stay with one of the girls in the suburbs for the few days, and Ralph Johnson booked in at a city hotel after delivering her there.

Marion could hardly wait for the next morning, despite the celebration party organised for the evening by her friend, Annette, also an aspiring teacher. When Annette's father dropped them off in St. George's Terrace just before nine the next morning, Marion made an excuse of prior shopping and agreed to meet Annette at lunch-time, by which time both of them should have been interviewed, though not, as Annette supposed, by the same person. In her handbag Marion had the folded newspaper page with both her results and the advertisement, and she lost no time in making for the Stock-agent's large central office.

When she said that she was inquiring about the governess job in the Kimberleys, the desk clerk asked her to wait while he phoned, and twenty minutes later she was re-directed to the small hotel, where, coincidentally, Ralph Johnson had booked in the day before. Mrs. Burton and the three children for whom she wanted a governess were guests there, and Angela Burton would interview the applicants herself.

"You're the first," she told Marion with a smile, "and maybe the only one. Not too many girls might like the prospect of going north to an area from where most of the white women and children have already been evacuated down here."

Marion liked her on sight, tall and slight, dark-haired and tanned, and with a down-to-earth manner of speaking that reminded Marion of Maggie. The children had been taken to the zoo for the day by another couple from the hotel, so Marion did not meet them.

"They are eight, ten, and seven," said their mother, "and I have no intention of sending them away to school at that age, or of taking a house down here, and staying with them. Our home is on Delroy Springs, and that's where we belong, and I'll teach them myself if I have to, but it would be a lot easier for me if I could find a suitable governess, because there are plenty of other things for me to fill my time."

She was delighted with Marion's obvious academic ability, but anxious that the girl had some idea of what she was taking on. "There's still talk of Japanese invasion, and you know that Darwin, Wyndham and Broome have been bombed. But we don't think any more of that is likely now. The station owners who took their cattle inland and even talked of burning their homesteads a couple of years ago, have mostly come back. But I suppose it is still a remote possibility. Worried about it?"

Marion shook her head vigorously.

"Then there won't be any company your own age, just the family and the men who work for us, and the blacks, and most of the time it'll be the kids and me, because the men are away in the stock-camp for most of the year."

Marion nodded.

"No shops, no doctor, no phone, mail once a month if we're lucky, holiday once a year, during the Wet, weather-permitting, two pounds a week and all found."

Angela took a cigarette from the pack on the small bedside table in her room, struck a match, burned her finger, and said "Damn!" She re-lit the cigarette, and continued, "In case I haven't already put you off, there are no roads to speak of, crocodiles in the river, snakes and dingoes, and the sandflies in the Wet. And never any spare time. But the climate in the Dry is the best in the world, and the scenery is wonderful. Still interested?"

Marion said thoughtfully, "There were a few girls from up north at school, and all of them, every single one, all they ever talked about was the station and getting home again for the holidays. Oh, we all did that, but not the way these girls did. It was as if they were only marking time, and nothing else mattered. I think I'd like to see for myself what made them feel that way."

Angela Burton smiled broadly at her and said, "Well, you'll have every chance to do that. But go away and sleep on it, and phone me in the morning. I'll have to wait here and see if anyone else turns up, but remember, if you do decide you want the job, it means you'll be a year at least away from your friends and family. It's a long time at your age."

When Marion knocked on Angela's door the next morning they greeted each other almost like long-lost friends.

"There were two others yesterday," laughed Angela, "but they both thought better of it before I'd even got to the crocodiles. Now, meet the children, and then we'd best get cracking - there's a lot to do."

They spent an hour at the Correspondence School collecting lesson papers; two hours at the warehouse ordering clothes, to be sent north by boat, for the station store; a quick lunch at the hotel, and then, as they were leaving the dining-room, Ralph Johnson appeared in the foyer. He thought at first that Marion had come to check up on their departure time, but she soon put him right. She introduced Angela as her new boss, and Ralph began to say "Well, bugger me," but stopped himself in time and said, "Pleased to meet you." He invited them all, and Marion's friend Annette, to have dinner with him that evening, before the return to Mudjinup the next day, and Marion knew, by the end of the evening, that she had a friend who would help smooth things over with Maggie and Grandpa when she got home. Annette said she was crazy, but hadn't she always been a bit that way, and wished her luck.

Angela told Marion that there wasn't any chance they could get to the station in the next month because of the wet season river heights, but she hoped that by early February they might get through, and Ralph gave her the farm phone number so that she could keep in touch with Marion. On the three-hour drive back to Mudjinup he told Marion that if she changed her mind, or needed money, she only had to send him a telegram, and she confided that she had a savings account that stood at the princely sum of 260 pounds, but she'd remember his offer. Then she told him how the town used to call him Mean Johnson, and he said some of them still did, but that was how he came to be in a position to offer her a loan if she needed it, and they both laughed, and Marion said she guessed they might call her Mean Marion too if they really knew how her mind worked.

Maggie and Grandpa took the news a lot better than Marion had expected, and Davey was highly excited.

"After five years in uniform, you'll need more clothes," said Maggie, especially if you can't get any for a year," and she took Marion's clothes ration book and bought as much material as she was allowed and made two light cotton sundresses and a pair of shorts.

When Ralph Johnson delivered the phone message that the Burtons would leave by plane in the second week in February, Maggie announced that she was taking a couple of days off work to accompany Marion to Perth to meet the family for herself. Grandpa said he hadn't been to Perth for years, and Davey anxiously commented that he hadn't either.

"And you won't be going this time either," said Maggie, "because Melly and I are taking you and Bill across to Rockton this very Sunday, as you well know, to get you both settled in at the hostel before school starts."

But Grandpa had come. He'd asked Ralph to lend him a land girl to milk the cow and feed the chooks while they were away, and he'd clipped his moustache and donned a white shirt, and produced the cuff-links which Marion had given him so long ago.

The train journey had been long and hot but, despite all the servicemen and Yanks vying with them, Grandpa's country whistle had got them a taxi straight away to take them to the hotel.

Marion was glad the two families had met; she decided that Maggie and Angela were rather alike in some ways; they didn't fuss, just went ahead and did the things that needed to be done. The last day in Perth had been a busy one. Marion had taken the children to the Correspondence School to meet their teachers, now returned from holidays, and then she had bought herself what she estimated was a year's supply of complexion cream on Maggie's advice. Her hair, the year she had begun school at St. Mary's, had darkened considerably and taken on a curl, and the freckles of her childhood had now disappeared, but she still sunburned easily.

Grandpa gave her a present of a leather writing case and fountain pen, and Maggie showed a flash of unexpected sentimentality by asking a street photographer to photograph the three Ryans together.

And now that was all in the past, and the unknown North she'd yearned for so long was coming closer by the hour. By late afternoon they were due to arrive in Derby, and it was already nearly three o'clock.

Marion, seated directly behind the pilot, was fascinated to see the great stretch of coastline spread below with, as far as she could see, no sign of human habitation apart from the tiny towns where they had landed.

The pilot shouted to her over the roar of the engine, "Better fasten your seatbelt, and pass the word to the others. Looks like a bit of dirty weather ahead!"

On the horizon to the left, Marion could see a faint line of dark grey drawn like a pencil line between the blue of the sea and the blue of the sky.

"What is it?" she shouted to Angela.

"Might be a cock-eyed bob," shouted Angela, "we won't make Derby, if it is!"

The pilot grinned over his shoulder. "Don't worry, I'll go inland if I have to, got plenty of juice. We'll be able to skirt around it, with luck, if it's only a small one."

The atmosphere grew increasing turbulent for the next hour, and all of the passengers began to look squeamish. Marion felt her stomach lurch, and it was only by sheer will-power and by keeping here eyes closed tight and not moving a muscle that she resisted the violent urge to throw up. They were flying blind in grey cloud now, with the rain belting against the windows, and Marion wondered, if this was skirting around it, whatever must it be like right in the middle of it. "See, no worries," yelled the pilot suddenly, as the buffeting diminished, "she's well south of us now. Derby in about twenty minutes!"

As the plane began to make its descent towards the small collection of tin roofs and the long jetty reaching out into the sea, Marion could only breathe a sigh of relief. It had stopped raining, but all the horizon that she could see from her small window was patched with thunder clouds and jags of lightning played between them. The town itself steamed in bright sunshine, and at the end of the runway a battered-looking green truck was waiting beside a light-coloured, equally battered utility.

Chapter 5　　Introduction to The Wet

Marion didn't get to see much of Derby that trip, just the end of the runway and the very outskirts of the township. As the relieved but weary passengers climbed from the plane one of the two lanky figures who had been squatting on their heels in the long shade of the truck elongated himself and strode over to the family. Dark-haired, lean and tanned, he appeared to be in his mid-twenties.

"G'day, glad to see yer back. Good holiday?" Then without waiting for an answer he shouted over his shoulder to the black stockman, who had now risen to his feet. "C'mon, Alec, get cracking, grab those ports and sling 'em on the truck!" Then again to Angela, "We gotta move, Mrs. B. We had a bastard of a trip coming in, and if that storm catches us, just another half inch on the track the way she is, we've got Buckley's chance of making it!"

Only then did he become aware of Marion, standing a pace or so behind Angela. "Righto, Mick. Marion, this is Mick Hardy, our head-stockman - Mick, Marion Ryan. Kids, go and help Alec get the right cases, and there's a parcel, Mick, that big one wrapped in hessian there."

The pilot, engaged in unloading the luggage, grinned and greeted Mick and the man in shorts and singlet who had been sitting in the utility. The children, chattering excitedly to Alec, ran back and forwards to the truck. "I brought your swags," called Mick, "and an extra one like you said, and we got a good tuckerbox in case we get stuck. The boss said you'd probably want to stay in town overnight, you'd be flat out after the plane trip, but I reckon if you do it'll be more than overnight, that's for sure."

"You could be right, Mick," agreed Angela. "We'll leave now. Give us five minutes. Those two ports, Alec, leave them till last. Now, Marion, grab a pair of slacks and a shirt, and flat shoes, and come with me." As she spoke she was rummaging in her own suitcase for similar items. Marion did the same and followed her quickly to the weird-looking squat tree just off the runway, big enough to shelter them both behind it.

"We'd ruin our good clothes, so change quickly," ordered Angela. "The kids are all right. I didn't put them in good things to travel."

Back at the truck, Rob, Anne and Terry had already divested themselves of their shoes and socks, and a green canvas sheet of the same dusty and grubby appearance as the rolled swags was being roped down over the paraphernalia on the back of the truck in such a fashion that a fold was left free to be pulled if need be over the nest made with swags between the two large drums roped at the back of the cabin. Here the two younger children burrowed down, and Rob and Alec fitted themselves into a hollow in the very middle of the load on top of a folded swag-cover, which they could use to cover themselves if the rain caught them.

Marion was never to forget that first trip, her initiation into the outback. There would be others just as strenuous, and worse, with bogs and breakdowns, and long walks, but by then she was broken-in and they all became just part of the day-to-day life, the sort of thing that happened sooner or later to everyone who chose to live in outback Australia. But none of them was as memorable for sheer undiluted discomfort as that first trip between Derby and Delroy Springs.

She sat the long night through, squeezed in the cabin between Angela and Mick. After the first few miles in the waning daylight, the road deteriorated quickly. It could hardly be called a road, for it was merely a two wheel track in a sea of grass which reached as high as the doorhandles of the cabin on the sides, and only slightly less high between the two tracks. Periodically it descended into creek-beds, sometimes paved roughly with stones, sometimes not, and most of them with running water. Mick drove confidently, for he and Alec had driven the same track the day before and had detoured or corduroyed round the worst stretches, and had built a crossing over the worst creek.

Then suddenly it was black dark, and the headlights picked up only the waving grass, and Marion thought maybe there was no track at all. Her legs and back began to ache from the cramped position, and she lost all interest in the animated conversation of her two companions and dozed in snatches. A rough passage over a limestone ridge jerked her awake to an even fiercer ache in every part of her, and again later she was startled out of a fitful half-sleep by a sudden hammering on the cabin roof above her. The truck ground to a halt, and she almost cried in relief. The children wanted to relieve themselves, so everyone got down and took turns to go round to the back of the truck while the rest stood in front of the headlights and stretched and massaged aching muscles. Mick and Alec rolled cigarettes and Angela produced a packet of tailor-mades from the pocket of her shirt. Marion suddenly became aware of hunger pangs and though longingly of the sandwiches she had refused at the last touch-down before Derby. Mick began clearing grass-seeds and insects from the piece of flywire fixed in front of the radiator, and Alec went back into the darkness and re-appeared with a bucket of water, which he poured over the still-running engine to cool it off.

When they climbed back in to resume the journey Angela took the wheel and Mick got into the passenger seat and fell asleep in seconds, after instructing Angela to be sure and wake him at the Big Boab. How could he sleep like that, Marion thought resentfully.

Twice more during the long, long night, the truck stopped for the drivers to change places, and then it was piccaninny daylight and the truck stopped, and the engine was switched off, the rain was behind them, and it was time for breakfast.

Alec soon had a fire going, while Mick rummaged on the back and handed down equipment to Rob. Angela produced a bottle of oily, strong-smelling stuff from the glove-box and began applying the contents to the faces, necks, legs and arms of the younger children, and then dabbed it on her own face and hands. She passed the bottle to Marion, "Home-made citronella mixture for the sandflies. They're not too bad out here, but they'll eat us alive down by the creeks. It takes about a month to build up an immunity to them, so slap it on, Marion, or you'll be sorry." Marion didn't like to say that she was already sorry, because her ankles were itching intolerably from her short walk through the grass from the truck. The meal was quick. Four calico bags of varying sizes were hauled out of the tucker-box, containing tea, sugar, bread and salt beef. They ate strips of the meat on slabs of town bread, which Mick had bought the day before, and drank sweet black tea from enamel pannikins.

"There's a tin of condensed milk in the tucker box if you take milk," offered Mick, but Marion was too hungry to bother, and she washed down great lumps of food with gulps of the tea, far stronger and sweeter than she had ever drunk before. She thought it was the best meal she'd ever had; it restored her flagging spirits; momentarily she forgot that she was tired, dirty, sweaty, itchy, and so far out of her depth that she half expected to wake up soon from a dream.

Then Mick, squatting opposite her across the campfire, suddenly stared past her, and leapt to his feet. "Hell! Look at that! We're going to run right into it! We'll be up the Creek without a paddle if we don't get to Steep Creek before that hits!" The monsoon thunder cloud boiling over the range to the north told its own story. Behind them the weather was coming in from the west, and ahead of them a storm loomed directly in their path.

In less than a minute they were all aboard again, and Mick was driving with a new intensity, and a speed that was, in Marion's eyes, foolhardy in the extreme. She was bounced and thrown around, and began to wonder how the passengers on the back were faring, or if they actually were still on the back. Angela, with hands braced against the glove-box to steady herself, was staring fixedly at the approaching menace of boiling grey cloud. A hectic twenty minutes later they reached the steep banks of a creek which Marion, at first sight, believed was a quite impossible task for any vehicle to attempt. But the built-up stone crossing was still visible. Mick stopped the truck, and peremptorily ordered everyone off.

"Get across quick, and, Alec, get the stones ready!"

Everyone slithered and scrambled down, across, and up the opposite bank, except Alec, who positioned himself half way up the bank, with one arm clutching a tree trunk to steady himself, and some smallish boulders at his feet, obviously left there for a purpose.

Mick began to back the truck away, and then, when he thought he had enough of a run-up, he gave it full bore and came hurtling down into the creek bed, across, and up. So steep was the cutting that by one third of the ascent the truck's speed was halved and slowing every second. The engine roared; the watchers from the bank held their breath. The vehicle laboured past Alec, and he ducked quickly and shoved a boulder in the track, and then grabbed another and darted across to the opposite wheel-track and shoved it down too.

Still the truck laboured on, almost stopped, roared again, and kept coming. Nearly there. One last supreme effort, and then Angela was at the driver's side of the cabin, and Rob at the passenger side, shoving their hearts out for the last few inches which meant success. What a cheer went up, Marion yelling as loud as any, when the vehicle pulled to a steaming halt on flat ground. Alec replaced the stones, and came labouring up with a broad grin.

"You beat 'im that time, Mick!"

"What are the stones for?" Marion whispered to Anne.

"When the truck slips back. You stick the rocks there, and sometimes they stop it."

"Not when there's a big load on, though," chipped in little Terry. "Then we have to unload the truck over there, and carry the stuff across, and then load it up again over here. Nobody likes that," he concluded sagely.

Back in the truck.

"Here," said Mick, thrusting a tobacco tin at Marion, "roll me a smoke, will you. I need one after that!"

Marion opened the tin tentatively, and looked nonplussed at the dark tobacco and the packet of papers squashed inside it.

The Angela saw her expression and laughed, "Here, give it to me, and watch. You'd better learn, whether you smoke or not. It's often the passenger's job to roll the smokes in this country."

She deftly rubbed up the tobacco, holding the paper on her bottom lip. Then she poured the tobacco onto the paper, spread it long with her fingertips, and rolled it into a neat cylinder. Taking a tin of wax matches from the glove-box, she extracted one, tucked in one end of the cigarette paper with it, then scraped the match on the back of the tin and lit the cigarette, which she passed, with the tin, back to Mick.

"Townie, is she?" was Mick's only comment.

"Yes," laughed Angela, "but I think she's the sort that'll learn fast."

The blinding rain struck them two miles from Steep Creek. By the time they reached Delroy Springs in the late afternoon Marion had learnt the first great survival law of the outback - if it has to be done, you have to do it yourself. She had also learnt that the priorities of cleanliness and meal-times were non-existent on certain occasions, that these tough little bush kids might be a different proposition to the polite meek children she had first met, and that the human body had far greater reserves than she had ever believed possible.

She staggered down from the cabin of the truck into a torrential gust of rain that almost swept her off her feet, was dimly aware of welcoming shouts and verandah steps with half a dozen tight-trousered, booted legs standing at the top step. Hair and clothes plastered to her, mud streaked up to her thighs, across her knuckles and, unknown to her, daubed across one cheek from where she had tried to wipe the sweat from her eyes with the back of her hand, she climbed up the steps and was introduced to the boss, the cook, and the saddler.

"Remember that first impressions count," Sister Francis had impressed upon her charges; if she could only see her star pupil now, thought Marion, as she shook the proffered hands.

Jim Burton, a shortish, nuggetty man, grinned at his new employee and said, "Have they warned you that once you drink the water of the Delroy River, you'll never be able to leave the country?"

Marion replied with some spirit that, as far as she could see, it was more likely to be the water on the road than in the river that would stop her leaving, and she'd be quite happy to stay rather than face something like that again.

They all assured her that it wasn't always like that, and while she dripped mud and water onto the wooden verandah she was formally introduced to Sam, who was the saddler, and Brownie, the cook. They didn't seem to have any surnames. Then it was a shower, clean clothes, and a meal with the family by lamplight, which Marion and the children, half asleep, could barely finish. Angela escorted her to her bedroom, warned her to tuck in the mosquito net round the bed, and bade her good-night. She fell asleep almost instantly, with the rain still drumming heavily on the tin roof.

She woke refreshed to bright daylight to see little Anne standing beside her net bearing a steaming tea-cup, and the greeting, "The rain's gone, but we had four inches last night, and the river's up, nearly to the horseyards. Wanna see?" Marion did, she wanted to see everything, but first there was breakfast, this time not in the house where they had eaten the evening meal, but in the dining-room attached to the kitchen, a fly-wired, verandahed complex about twenty yards from the main building. Everyone helped themselves from a mountain of steak, smothered it with black sauce, and helped it down with toast and copious draughts of tea. Angela suggested that, as she had a great deal to do, perhaps the children could show Marion the run of the place, and they'd defer school until the next day.

Rob disappeared with his father, but the two younger children took Marion in hand to show her what seemed at first to be a small village rather than the single homestead she'd pictured in her mind. The main house itself, up on stumps, and with verandahs all round, contained the bedrooms, a bathroom, a big open room in the middle furnished with a punkah, cane chairs and lounges and the table where they'd eaten last night, and leading from it the station office. At the very end of the building was a room set up as a schoolroom, and all the outer walls leading on to the verandahs were made of a clever arrangement of louvres, optional windows or walls according to the season. All the doors were the double glass doors which Marion knew as French windows,

The kitchen, with its huge cooking range and ovens and a series of Coolgardie coolers on its verandahs, opened into a dining room with a scrubbed wooden table bigger than any Marion had yet seen. Brownie explained that most of the homesteads had kitchen and dining room under a separate roof from the rest.

"The kitchen's always stinkin' hot," he grumbled. "At least a house without a kitchen ain't so bad. Don't burn down, neither, if the kitchen goes! And that's happened more than once, I can tell yer!"

By the time Marion had seen the meat house, the store, the saddler's shed, the workshop with adjoining men's quarters, the station garden, the windmill and tank, and the large set of yards, she was beginning to get in inkling of how independent of outside help the people of this part of the world had to be. A quarter of a mile away was the blacks' camp.

"We won't go there now," said little Terry. "There's nobody much home anyway; they're all on walkabout. And you hafta wait until you're invited. Dad said it's rude not to, if you're a kid, and I spose that means big girls too."

Angela told her later that there were only three old and infirm pensioners left in the camp, who weren't able to walk the long distances the walkabout involved, and every few days the old people walked up to the station to collect rations. When Marion asked why Alec hadn't gone on walkabout she was told that he was not a full-blood, but had a white grandfather or great-grandfather, Angela wasn't sure which, but anyway it was enough to bar him from complete acceptance by the tribe. He could not be given the full manhood status, or ever become a dreaming boss. Some tribes, Angela said, were not as strict as this one, but Alec didn't seem to mind. He could have gone with them if he'd wanted and taken a minor part in the Big Sunday corroborees, but he seemed to prefer to stay at the station, and he was certainly handy to have around.

Marion thought about Alec occasionally in the days to come. She wondered whether he really did mind, not belonging to either one or the other. Perhaps he was a loner, like she'd been in her childhood. But her life was so busy that she didn't have much time to ponder on the subject. The day's routine began with breakfast at six, and a start on lessons at seven or half-past. It was too hot and humid to work the children in the afternoons, and after the midday meal everyone retired for a siesta for an hour or more. After that respite the station work began again after smoko and continued until sundown, when the gong rang for the evening meal which they called "supper". "Except," explained Angela, "when we have visitors, and then it's dinner."

Supper or dinner, everyone showered and changed before the evening meal, and the men appeared in white shirts and white trousers, mostly tight-legged just like the stockman-cuts they wore during the day, and the women in cotton dresses. Jim Burton sat at the head of the table and carved the meat and Angela served the vegetables from covered tureens at the other end of the table. Marion found the formality a far cry from the Ryans' mealtimes, but it wasn't so unlike her boarding school experience. There were certain rules of etiquette to be followed, both in the homestead and out in the bush, and in the stock-camp, and in the next few months Marion would learn most of them. An unconscious infringement of outback etiquette labelled its perpetrator as a "silver-tail", a visitor from down South who couldn't be expected to know any better, who might fit an office chair okay, but would never fit the outback way of life.

She was to learn that the blacks' rules were even more rigid, and their employment at the station had to be made to fit within their rules. Marion would always remember her first faux-pas, which occurred one morning when she directed the butcher-boy to carry the hefty forequarter of beef through into the kitchen when he asked her "Where I puttim this one, Missus?"

The next minute there was a wild shriek from the kitchen, and the butcher-boy dropped the meat on the threshold, and stumbled backwards so fast he nearly knocked Marion over. He wheeled around and disappeared and Marion ran into the kitchen to find a very fat black woman cowering in the corner on her haunches with her face buried in as much of her skirt as she could get over her head. Marion thought she must be hurt in some way, but all she could get out of the woman was a wail of "Can't look, Missus, can't look!"

Just then Brownie came back from the store with an armful of tinned goods, saw the meat on the floor, and started to swear until he spotted Marion. Then he burst out laughing, placated his muttering off-sider and told Marion that the woman was mother-in-law skin to the butcher boy, which meant that they could not look at, speak to, or acknowledge the existence of each other, or anyone else belonging to that skin, on pain of punishment by death if they did so.

"Somethin' to do with their marriage laws," he explained. "You'll soon get to know 'em all, and who's who, and you don't send anyone on a message anywhere they'll be likely to meet a wrong-skin person, otherwise they won't come back from yer message, which puts yer up a gum-tree if it was important to yer to get that message through."

The children knew everyone in the blacks' camp as well as they knew their own family, and they took on the job of educating Marion with the same sincerity that she devoted to educating them. It was a fair exchange.

Chapter 6
Cattle-buyers and horse traders

In the middle of March the tribe returned, forty-seven people in all, counting the five babies, two of whom had been born on the walkabout. The day before they arrived old Boodgerie appeared at the kitchen door at afternoon smoko time, and addressed himself to Jim Burton.

"Boss, tomorrow big mob come up, proper hungry bugger. Mightbe you gettin killer, puttim wood longa camp!"

"Righto, Boodgerie, I'll see to it. Mick, you could give Alec the truck to get the wood this afternoon, and the two of you could get a killer in the morning. Might as well give them a welcome home."

"How on earth does he know they'll come tomorrow?" puzzled Marion.

"That's what we'd all like to know," commented Jim, "but they will come, you can be sure of that. If you ask him he'll tell you a bird told him, or a goanna, or whatever his dreaming sign is. Must be some sort of mental telepathy. Of course the mob are due back round about now anyway. But I've seen this sort of thing happen when there's no expectation about it. Once when I was a kid we had to send one of their men in to the doctor when he came a buster off a horse. Three days later out of the blue the whole mob started to wail and cut themselves with bits of tin. It was about three in the afternoon when they started carrying-on, and blow me down, we found out later that was the exact time he died. He wasn't real bad, we thought, didn't expect that, but they knew all right. We'll see 'em all again tomorrow, you'll see."

Marion didn't see them come. Nobody did. They skirted the house and the yards, and by mid-afternoon the camp was populated again, and that night there were the pinpoints of a dozen campfires as the wanderers feasted, and then at full dark the drone of a didgeridoo, the clacking of sticks, and voices raised in corroboree, which carried on the night air to the whites sitting after supper on the verandah. It was still going on when Marion drifted off to sleep, a background music which she would hear on many a night in the years to come.

The tail end of the Wet, the three weeks between Marion's arrival at the station and the return of the blacks, were what she thought of later as her gentle easing into a way of life which was so different from anything she had known, but which she liked more and more each day. There was so much to do, she was needed, there was a place for her here, and she knew she fitted it. Not just supervising of the children's lessons, which she handled with ease, but the increasing responsibility of the many and varied other chores which cropped up, especially when, over the next two or three weeks, the telegrams began to arrive via the transceiver from the ringers wanting a job for the season, and word arrived that the ship carrying the years' stores for the station had finally berthed in Derby.

Marion also acquired a new pupil. On the morning after the tribe's return she went with Angela to the small room behind the store where the Royal Flying Doctor Medical Chest was kept.

"Sick parade," said Angela, "straight after breakfast every day, and when every one gets back, it'll probably mean a patient or two every day. Right now, we'll have quite a few. You'd better get to know the ropes, in case Jim or I aren't here in an emergency."

She explained how all the medicines went by a number on the bottle, so that the doctor, contacted on the transceiver, could prescribe treatment without fear of the layman administering them misunderstanding and mixing up the drugs."

"With the blacks it'll mainly be these," she said, indicating two large bottles, "coughin' medsin and rubbim medsin."

But that morning there was more than coughs and sprains. The new babies were presented for inspection and admiration; a half-healed spear wound was cleaned and dressed; a child with a badly burned foot in a suppurating mess was treated; and Marion was kept busy handing out bars of home-made soap to every adult, who apparently hadn't made use of such a luxury since leaving the station the previous November. Their bathhouse and laundry was a billabong behind their camp, and from the yells of delight and the chiacking that went on for the whole day on the billabong banks it seemed that bathing and washing clothes was the greatest game ever.

"Tomorrow we'll choose our staff," promised Angela. She hesitated.

"I don't know how you feel about it, Marion, but Terry's little friend is back, and he used to come to lessons sometimes last year when I was teaching the kids myself. He's a good little kid, no trouble, but if you'd rather not take him on, if the job's enough as it is, well, I'll understand. Some girls mightn't like it, I know, him being black and all that."

Marion's mind flew back to the class-room where little Elsa Kickett stood apprehensively before the hostile stares of the white pupils, and she laughed out loud.

"Of course I don't mind, Angela. Terry will be expecting him, won't he? I guess one more won't make much difference."

Angela was quite obviously relieved. "Yes," she admitted, "Terry's been asking me. Yandi's quite a bright little fellow, actually, and if he wasn't in school with Terry, then Terry would be itching to be out with him, and you don't know our Terry yet. He can be a little tiger if he thinks he or Yandi aren't getting a fair go. There isn't anyone else round Yandi's age in the camp, and none of the others show any signs of wanting to go to school, and of course, I couldn't handle it if they did. There was talk of a real Government school here for the black children - sometimes they go to the mission - but I suppose the war has altered things, and maybe they'll get back to thinking about it if and when things get back to normal."

So Yandi came to school, and the Delroy Springs school immediately became trilingual. Rob and Anne spoke English to Marion and pidgin to Yandi; Yandi and Terry used a mixture of pidgin and English to Marion and the others, and the Aboriginal language between themselves. Even Marion found herself saying You-ai instead of yes on occasions.

Three white ringers joined Mick in the quarters, and Sam the saddler moved on. Brownie had two black girls to help in the kitchen; there were two to help in the house, and another two or three laundry girls. Teddy-poor-bugger took charge of the garden; two goat-girls brought the milk to the kitchen each morning and there was a butcher boy, and an old man whose sole job seemed to be sweeping up the leaves in the house garden.

With the weekly issue of dry rations to the tribe and the additional staff the store shelves began to empty quickly, and Marion learnt the bushman's art of substitution, and marvelled at the ingenuity employed by Brownie, and suspected that her leg was being pulled when the men were yarning one night about the many and varied substitutes they had eaten in their time. She'd taken it for granted that Brownie was so-called because his surname was Brown, but Mick assured her that it was because, towards the end of the Wet when the stores were low, he never chucked out the weevilly flour when the weevils were as big as shirt buttons, but used it to make brownies and passed the weevils off as currants.

"Wait till you meet The Cookin' Game, eh?" said The Queensland Ringer. "Overland trout's his specialty, eh, and he sticks a fancy sauce over it and gives it a fancy French name, eh, and you reckon it's pretty good too, eh."

"Only one time he took a job cookin' at the Wyndam pub," chipped in Brownie. "Kitchen was a bit close to the bar, though, and the Missus told him she wanted something special for some silvertails comin' up from Perth for some do at the Meatworks. So the Cookin' Game reckons he'll give her a real flash entree, and he bribes a coupla gins to catch a half-dozen bit fat goanners. He's gonna give 'em Overland Trout with Frenchy sauce and a bit a parsley, see, but the old goat got a bottle of brandy to ginger up the sauce, and gingered himself up along with it. First two or three trout come out okay, but he left the claws on the next one, and who gets it but the bigshot silvertail's wife. And did she put on a show! Screeched so loud they reckon she cleared all the crocs away from the end of the jetty. And the Missus give the Cookin' Game the bullet right then and there. So he don't tell her that the parsley was chopped-up indigofera, or somethin' - just takes out his cheque in Bundy rum, and goes back to where he's appreciated, down Turkey Creek way, I think it was."

Jim Burton could tell yarns with the best of them in the short hour or so after the evening meal, when the day's work was done, and everyone relaxed. Some were yarns he'd had from his father; many incidents were from his own youth; others from hearsay. Marion noticed that most of them had one thing in common; the heroes or villains of the stories were all a little larger-than-life and they all went by colourful nicknames. Nobody seemed to bother much with surnames in the Kimberleys. Brownie explained why.

"Y'see, some o' these fellas ain't got the same name up here wot they was born with, so to speak, and a fella who goes by the name of Bill Smith in the Port might be Bill Somebody Else up in Darwin, and somebody else again down in Adelaide or wherever he come from. If ya call him Billy the Con then everyone knows who ya mean." A lot of these nicknames were derived from real or fancied resemblances to the animals and birds of the surrounding countryside.

Marion knew instantly who The Frilled Lizard was when she met her for the first time some months later at a race meeting. What she didn't yet know was that word of her arrival at Delroy Downs had been spread by mulga wire, and opinions had already been mooted that the Chestnut Filly showed signs of staying power. (Time would tell whether she was cut out for The Track when she decided whether or not to stay in the country after her first year's contract was up.)

By the middle of June the first mob of fats for the Wyndam Meatworks had been mustered, and 300 store steers were being tailed along the river waiting the arrival of a buyer from a station inland from Carnarvon. Many of the regular drovers had joined the Army, and Jim wasn't happy about the experience or expertise of those still available, so it was decided that Mick and the stock camp would take the Wyndham mob on the road while Jim and those of the black ringers left behind would carry on with the branding.

The arrangement for store cattle was not a new thing. Every year the Carnarvon station, Box Hill, had a reasonably good season, its owner, John Blythe, took delivery of stores to fatten for the Perth Market, and he made his own arrangements for transport. The two families were vaguely connected by marriage and had known each other for years, so the buying trip was more than a mere business arrangement, something of a social event in the land where social events were few, and fewer still in wartime. John Blythe rarely came on his own, usually bringing at least some of his family with him, and also, if he intended overlanding the cattle, the drover who would take them and probably pick up cattle from the other stations on the way for other buyers, to make up a decent mob. This was cheaper than sending the mob by sea from Derby if other buyers chipped in to pay the drover, and the wartime demand for beef to feed the servicemen had pushed up the price so that memories of the Depression were now just a bad dream.

Marion's letters home to Maggie and Grandpa were full of descriptions of the cattle work and the plans. She had described the country and the people and her job in detail in her first letters, posted whenever an opportunity occurred, either by the not-always-regular road mail service, dependent on whether the mailman could obtain enough rationed petrol, or by the occasional visitor through to town.

To Marion the little town of Mudjinup where a little girl called Skeet had once lived had already become rather like a place in a story-book, well-loved but relegated to a back shelf, and only to be taken down on rare occasions. Delroy Springs was real, but Mudjinup only came back to life when Maggie's letters arrived, and then survived only a day or two. As a child in Mudjinup Marion had been an outsider; at school as an adolescent she had been accepted, but only conditionally, because she was an agent of scholastic and sporting honours for the school; in the frontier world of the Kimberleys, on the brink of womanhood, she, like everyone else, black, white or mixed blood, was a person in her own right, and the priorities of birth or brains were of little account when the chips were down. An English nobleman with an Oxford degree and a million pounds in the bank would be great hit in Perth drawing rooms, but not worth a cracker lost in the Kimberley Ranges or out on the waterless plains to the south, where a naked black man with a spear could walk like a king and make the decision whether the nobleman should live or die. Marion, for the first time in her life, was completely comfortable in her environment, new and challenging though it was, and she knew that the instinct which had guided her northwards, triggered off by learning bush poetry in a small town schoolroom, had been the right one to follow. The Chestnut Filly was going to be a stayer.

The Blythes were driving up by road this year, and no questions asked as to where John Blythe got the petrol ration coupons for such a long journey. John had some sort of contract in the wind for supply of meat to the American Army Camp based not far from Box Hill, and everyone knew that the Yanks seemed to be able to lay their hands on as much petrol as they wanted.

When the telegrams finally arrived that the travellers were on their way Angela organised a spring-cleaning and an arrangement of bedrooms and a discussion of menus that had Marion mildly surprised. Only when all was to her satisfaction did Angela relax. She explained to Marion.

"John's a nice chap, no worries. He's the sort that takes you as he finds you. It's free and easy when he comes alone. But Mary Blythe's a different kettle of fish. I can't really take to her. Stand-offish, if you know what I mean. Doesn't say much at all, but I get the feeling she's looking for cobwebs, noticing everything. The less I like a person the more I clean up. Jim reckons it's the craziest logic he ever heard; he reckons if I don't like someone I shouldn't care what they think. Not that I actually dislike the woman; I just don't know where I stand with her. You can't get close to her."

When the Blythes arrived the mystery of the petrol coupons was solved. Besides their two sons they had an American major on leave as a passenger, a middle-aged rancher from Dakotah, keen as mustard to have a look at some Australian cattle-country. Angela quickly reshuffled the bedrooms, putting ten-year-old Tim Blythe in with Rob, and sending seventeen-year-old Peter to bed down in the quarters with The Queensland Ringer, alone there with Brownie, with his arm in a sling from a broken collarbone, left behind when Mick and the boys left for Wyndham. The Queensland Ringer was one of the greatest skites in the country, and Brownie left much to be desired as an audience, having spent much of his working life in Queensland and apt to make cynical comments. The Queensland Ringer welcomed the youthful Peter with open arms and open mouth. Peter, thought Marion, looked as if he could take it, and maybe even skite a bit in his own right.

Then she was introduced to Mary Blythe, polite but aloof. She expected that she would feel the same reaction to the woman that Angela felt, but she didn't. There was a quality about Mary Blythe that instantly reminded Marion of Maggie. "She's prickly, like Mum. Or maybe just shy," and Marion surprised herself by taking the woman's hand and shaking it so warmly that Mary Blythe was momentarily startled.

The visitors stayed for ten days in all. Jim took John, Peter and the Major all over the run, sometimes camping out and sometimes returning to the homestead overnight. Mary Blythe remained unobtrusively at the homestead, reading or writing letters, and occasionally visiting the schoolroom where Tim, who was a lone pupil back at Box Hill, was enjoying the novelty of having fellow students to work with. Marion was aware that Mary Blythe had initially raised her eyebrows at the presence of Yandi in the schoolroom, and she was glad that the Blythes' visit was long enough for the message to sink in that her own younger son's loneliness was the price paid for his parents' prejudice. Mary admitted as much to Marion at the end of the week, as the children ran off to the yards to greet the returning horsemen. She had never given a thought to the possibility of schooling any of the black children in the Box Hill camp, or allowed Tim to mix with them.

During the evenings that Peter spent at the homestead, Marion and he found that they had a great deal in common. She was two months older than he was, and they had both studied the same courses at College, and found they had quite a few common acquaintances. Both had vaguely considered going on to University, but rejected the idea in favour of a more practical life. By the third evening it was obvious from their animated conversations that something more than merely following the dictates of polite socialising was taking place for both of them. Marion found herself looking up expectantly when she heard a step on the verandah and experiencing a vague feeling of disappointment if it wasn't Peter. She told herself severely that it was merely the fact that they were of an age that made them more attractive to each other, and that if they'd met at a party in Perth they would probably have not got beyond a few commonplace remarks to each other. She certainly hadn't intended to let him kiss her in the garden in the moonlight, or to respond so ardently when he did. But then, what made her agree in the first place to go there with him so he could point out the constellations in the night sky, when she knew every one of them, probably better than he did, thanks to Grandpa's tutelage when she was about eight years old.

Before she fell asleep that night, she accused herself disgustedly of being just as underhand as the silliest boy-mad girls back at school, and then grinned to herself and admitted that she had enjoyed the moment inordinately, and would certainly endeavour to repeat the experience at the earliest opportunity. In a few days he would be gone, and that would be an end to it.

She fell asleep with the thought that she supposed she ought to put some time in to finding out what made boys tick, while making sure that she was never side-tracked from the ambition which had guided her life almost as long as she could remember.

Marriage was a trap which Marion had long ago decided must be avoided at all costs, and nothing in her reading, her studies, and her observations had done anything to change her mind. Once you were married you were a goner, back to being like a kid again, being told what you could do, and what you couldn't, with someone else to make all the major decisions in your life for you. Being single meant you were treated like a real person, even if you were pitied as an old maid if you were still unmarried at thirty. The few single women that Marion knew didn't look as if the fact worried them at all; and public opinion hadn't worried her in the slightest as a kid, so it wasn't likely to influence her now. Anyway, she had years ahead before she reached that point, and by then she expected to be far too busy doing what she wanted to do.

The next day the drover arrived with his plant, and after a couple of days' spell was on the road again for the long trip south. Peter went with the drovers for the experience, three quid a week if he was useful, and his tucker only if he was a passenger. His father had arranged it all with the drover before he left home, with the strict proviso that the drover was to forget that Peter was the boss's son. With one exception the other ringers were all blacks. Marion and the children rode the first couple of miles with them, amid the dust and the bellowing, and then turned for home again. Marion rode silently, but her thoughts had little to do with Peter, apart from the fact that she was wondering how she could engineer for herself just such an experience as he was now undertaking. She didn't doubt that sooner or later the opportunity would come.

Once the Blythes and the Major had also been farewelled it seemed that the station would resume its old routine again, but barely twenty-four hours elapsed before another visitor arrived, another station-owner, but, as Angela said, rather a different kettle of fish to the Blythes.

Marion had heard them speak of Old Fred, and here he was in the flesh, grey-haired, bandy-legged, squint-eyed, and mounted on a horse which even Marion, who really knew very little about horses, immediately recognised as something special. So this was the proprietor of Halley's Cut, the hideaway valley in the ranges, accessible only via a jump-up that no vehicle was ever likely to negotiate. Old Fred bred horses, not cattle, and he made his living supplying replacement stock-horses for the stock-camps ravaged annually by the Walkabout Disease which took such a toll on all the Kimberley properties. Horses bearing Fred's FST brand were agile and sure-footed and could turn on a sixpence. They had to be, to be able to get up over the Jump-up and out into the foothills in the first place. There was always a great demand for Fred's annual turn-off, and being nearest neighbours Delroy Springs got first crack of the whip when the colts came on the market.

Old Fred Halley was a small, wrinkled, nut-brown man, with a profusion of curling grey hair poking through the equally wrinkled blue shirt tethered together by only a single button. The moleskin trousers were slung so low on the bony hips that the shirt had escaped at the back, but at the front it was held in place by a broad leather belt, which was adorned by a number of home-made pouches. He wore concertina-leggings over high-heeled boots, and round his neck above the wiry grey mat a red and black printed neckerchief. The whole was topped by a bent and dusty black ten-gallon hat which appeared to be prevented from descending right down over his head only by a pair of large and hairy ears whose upper halves obligingly bent over to form platforms to support the hat. "My God," thought Marion, "he's a leprechaun!"

Fred dismounted and threw the reins to a black boy mounted on an equally smart looking horse a yard behind him. He bellowed a greeting to all and sundry, and then asked where the boss was. But the boss had heard him arrive, and came out of the office onto the verandah, followed by Angela, who immediately greeted him with evident pleasure and sent a house-girl scurrying for a pot of tea.

Marion met Fred at dinner-time, but she had already examined him in detail from the schoolroom window as he and Jim squatted together in the yard, and drew mud-maps in the dirt, and discussed whatever business had brought Fred out of his retreat. At dinner Marion learned that Fred's boys were holding a mob of horses in the yard a mile or so down the river, and in the afternoon Jim planned to choose about ten of them for the Delroy plant. Angela suggested that she and Marion and the children go too, and Fred said they'd be more than welcome, and it would be a great pity if they didn't, because this was their chance to inspect fifty of the finest horses bred in the Kimberleys, FST horses, FST for Fast and FST for First.

That was how Marion saw, fell in love with, and acquired Banner. She hadn't the faintest intention of doing anything more than admire the horses; the thought of a purchase hadn't entered her head. Jim had given her a station horse to ride any time she wanted in the first week after she'd arrived, which had suited her fine until the day she met Fred Halley, horse-trader, and the palomino colt, Banner.

As Jim singled out the colts he wanted to try out before making a final decision Marion watched with interest from the top-rail of the main yard, Terry and Anne beside her. The horses milled together at the end of the yard as two black boys tried to cut out the ones Jim wanted to put through their paces. Then the palomino broke away from the mob, and galloped round the perimeter of the yard, its mane and tail waving like golden banners, to skid to a halt immediately in front of Marion on her precarious perch. The horse raised its head, sniffed the air, whinnied, and then stretched its neck out to sniff, first her booted foot, then the hand she stretched out tentatively. "You beauty," breathed Marion. The palomino nickered softly.

Then out of the blue Marion heard herself saying, "Mr. Halley, what's this one worth? I'd like to buy this one."

"Hey, Marion," laughed Jim, "you don't do it that way, you try it out first. Then you make an offer if he suits you. You're no horse-trader, girl!"

"No, he's the one I want. I'll ride him if you like, but I know he'll be right. I just know."

"Might be a better horse-trader than you think, Jim," chuckled the old man. "Banner here's got a mouth like silk, and a heart like Phar Lap. He's an ambler when you want, and the chances are he could win the Cup at the races if you asked him to. The young lady knows class, Jim, and if you was buying Banner I'd say ten quid, but to her it's eight quid, and I'll throw in the bridle I plaited meself that Banner got broke in with. And he's a quiet horse, too, Miss, not a bit of vice in him."

So Banner went into the little mob that Jim had chosen and was driven to the homestead horse paddock, and after tea that night Angela debited eight pounds from Marion's credit on the station books, and Jim added that amount to the cheque he wrote for Old Fred. "You didn't have to buy your own horse, you know," he told Marion, "there's always a station horse when you want to ride."

"I know, thanks, Jim," she said, "but I just wanted him. I got a funny feeling up my spine when he stood in front of me. He sort of asked me to buy him. So I did."

"Well, I spose that's as good a reason as any, considering female logic. And if Fred says he's good, you can be sure he *is* good."

"Well," thought Marion as she walked back down to the kitchen for a last cup of tea, "that's a start. I've got a horse and a bridle. Now all I need's a saddle and a station!" All fleeting thoughts of Peter had vanished. Banner had ousted him completely.

Chapter 7   *Cook on the grog*

The perfect days of the northern winter ticked by, and Marion rode Banner almost daily, and taught him to come to her whistle and to stand and wait whenever she dismounted and dropped the reins over his head to dangle on the ground in front of him. She counted it a good investment to choose a saddle from the catalogue and to order it by mail from Perth. The Queensland Ringer plaited her a halter, and Mick, not to be outdone, plaited her a leather belt with pocket-knife pouch to show that Queenslanders were not the only ones who could plait leather. Jim said it was a pity the race meeting at the Crossing had been suspended because of the war, because Banner would have a pretty good chance of winning the Ladies' Race, and Marion secretly agreed with him.

Then Peter came back, this time permanently. At the end of his droving trip, his father had contacted Jim and asked him to take Peter on as a jackeroo and teach him the ropes of station life in the north. He inferred that Peter was too big for his boots at home, after having successfully earned his three quid a week as a drover, and anything tough Jim could throw at him would be all to the good. When Angela told Marion of his impending arrival, Marion found that she was looking forward to seeing him again, but when he arrived on the mailplane, he was only a day at the homestead before Jim took him out to the stock-camp and handed his education over to Mick, and it was five weeks before she saw him again.

This was the last big muster for the year, and this time the Meatworks bullocks were to be taken by a drover recommended by the manager of a Company station who would make up the mob with his own bullocks. The return of the stock-camp and the tailing of the bullocks coincided with holidays from school, officially a week in September, but because the children had worked through the May holidays Angela had agreed to a two-weeks spell, and Rob had disappeared into the stock-camp.

Brownie was run off his feet feeding the men, and the days were full of noise and dust and yarns after supper, and corroborees in the moonlight down at the camp. One of

Peter's string of horses was savaged by a crocodile near the mile-long Deep Hole just up the river, and the whole camp turned out to shoot the brute one evening, but no-one saw so much as a gleam of red eyes in the torchlight, and Angela put a ban on the kids fishing in Deep Hole unless some of the men were with them.

Peter and Marion fell into the natural pattern of talking together after supper, occasionally touching hands, and sneaking a goodnight kiss before he went down to the quarters, and the Queensland Ringer sulked and went off his tucker, but nobody except Brownie noticed it.

Then the drover arrived with his plant and his men, and they were still two hundred yards away from the cattle-yards when every Delroy ringer eyed one of the riders and simultaneously remarked, "It's a girl!" It was indeed a girl, and Marion, jumping down from the top rail, recognised that girl almost immediately. "Elsa!" she shrieked in delight.

"Hell's bells, it's Skeet, it really is! Dad, look who's here, it's Skeeter Ryan in the flesh."

Ted Kickett, drover, rode over with a broad grin and greeted Marion, and Elsa's two brothers joined him. Ted excused himself and introduced himself to Jim, after calling to Marion, "Come down to the camp and see Mum; she's our cook, and for sure there'll be a feed on for little Skeeter Ryan any time she looks in."

Marion, dragging Elsa with her, rushed up to the house to see Angela, to introduce her friend and to let Angela know she'd be eating supper with the drovers that evening. Then she saddled Banner, and together the girls rode to the camp by the river where the drovers' plant horses were already hobbled out and feeding along the flat.

What talk there was that night; so many years to cover; so much water under the bridge of bad times and good; and an addition to the family, Jimmy Kickett, eight, who should have been at school and wasn't, because these days the family was on the road droving for most of the time - but he could read and write, thanks to Elsa, and what more did he want? The two white boys in the camp were quite left out, but they didn't seem to mind, just sat in the firelight and listened, and grinned companionably at the girls.

That was how Marion came to go droving, as she'd always known she would, but earlier than she'd hoped. Elsa suggested it, and Ted agreed he could take an apprentice for the two weeks of her school holidays. She could go with them as far as the next station up the road, and then ride back in two or three days, ready and refreshed to start the last term's schoolwork. Marion didn't doubt that Angela and Jim would agree, but she reckoned without Peter.

It was well after ten when she unsaddled Banner and turned him out into the paddock, and, still walking on air, opening the homestead garden-gate quietly. The shadowy figure stepping out from the cookhouse verandah startled her back to reality.

"Peter," she cried, "what on earth are you doing up so late? What's wrong?"

"What's wrong?" he hissed at her. "You ought to know what's wrong. What's the matter with you, going off with those yella-fellas like that! Haven't you got any pride! Don't you know what's the done thing, and what's not, in this country?"

Marion was flabbergasted by his attack.

"What do you mean?" she whispered.

He grabbed her arms and pinned them to her sides, and pushed his face close to hers in the moonlight.

"Just this," he said coldly. "No girlfriend of mine mixes with yella-fellas like the best of mates. You can make your choice." His fingers were biting into her arms. She shrugged free, and experienced another of those rare moments when everything stood still and the slightest detail was imprinted on her consciousness for all time. She could see his white face in the moonlight, and behind him the very grain of the wood of the verandah post, and beside them the green-dark leaves of the garden shrub and the white blobs of blossom, heavy with scent on the night air.

She wondered whether she was going to hit him. Then the moment passed. She pushed him away from her and said coldly, "What a stinking little snob you are, Peter. And what a hide you've got. They're my friends of years, and I've only known you a couple of months. I'm not making a choice, you are!"

He made another snatch at her arm, but she pulled away.

"What do you mean?" he snarled at her. "Whites don't mix with Abos socially, and if you want to be respected by decent people you'd better remember it!"

"Huh!" she hooted at him. "White men don't mix socially! But they can't get a black girl into the swag fast enough after dark, can they! And then they won't talk in public to their own half-caste kids because it's not the done thing. Who do you think you're kidding Peter? Well, it's not me!"

He grabbed at her again, spitting out in fury. "You stupid little bitch. Can't you see what people will think? Just as well they'll be gone tomorrow; then maybe you'll see sense!"

"Yeah," hissed Marion, "and I'm going with them, so shove that in your pipe and smoke it!"

Whatever his reply might have been, it was cut short by a loud and irate comment from Jim's bed on the verandah.

"For Chrissake, shut-up and go to bed. Some people have work to do in the morning, so beat it!"

They parted. "Nigger-lover!" he hissed over his shoulder.

"Hypocrite!" she replied.

When Marion woke in the morning Angela was holding her own tea-cup and proffering one to Marion. She settled herself on the end of the bed, and said companionably, "What was all that about last night?"

Marion explained.

"Well, in a way he's right, Marion," commented Angela. "I suppose I ought to explain. Not every boss is like Jim, especially on the Company places. The wives are the worst. This is probably the worst place in the world for gossip, and all of it's malicious. Can you take it?"

"I reckon," grinned Marion, "I had a pretty good training as a kid. Elsa was my only mate then, so why not now? But I hope Peter comes round, because I do like him a lot, you know."

"Well, that's settled then," Angela drained her cup and stood up. "Come on, breakfast, and then we'll find you a decent swag, and you'll want a good thick jumper. Wish I was coming with you; I'd love to get out of the house for a while. Tell you what, I'll take your swag down to the camp in the ute while you ride Banner. Do you think your friends might offer me dinner if I turn up on time?"

Marion jumped out of bed and hugged her.

"Angela, you're a mate!"

"As good as Elsa?" laughed Angela.

"Could be!" grinned Marion, alias Skeeter, alias The Chestnut Filly, all agog to go droving in God's Own Country, where men were men and nice girls knew their places in the required order of things.

Marion's fortnight was as short as a day and as long as a year. It passed too quickly and yet it spun into infinity. The girls marvelled that the one short year in their childhood had cemented a friendship which jumped a nine-year gap so effortlessly.

"When you stuck up for me that first day at school, Skeet, it made me feel I was as good as any of those kids. Until then I think I was in danger of getting a chip on my shoulder, which would have been an admission that I wasn't as good. And I've never had any doubts since."

"Well, I never had any doubts, but I never had any friends either till then. I think being mates with you made it easier for me later to make friends without sticking up a barrier people couldn't get past."

After the long dusty days in the saddle, Marion stretched out in the swag and stared up into the velvet star-studded sky and exulted in her good fortune. This was a freedom she had only dreamed of. A good horse that was something more than a horse; a regular meal of salt beef and damper garnished with onions and ambrosia; a six foot square of earth on which to roll out her swag and revolve the night through with the revolving stars; and a job that had to be done, that could not be postponed, a point that must be reached by each day's end or the day be extended into the night. She thought that the self-discipline of the drover's life must be something like that which drove Hannibal to push his army across the Alps, and she wondered why she thought of it as a freedom. Why not the horse, the swag, and the tucker bag, and roam where you will - wasn't that real freedom? It had to be the freedom of knowing that you *can* discipline yourself, that you set a goal with no thought of giving up.

The absence of a daily bath; sleeping in her clothes; her bed nothing but a groundsheet and a blanket between her and the unyielding earth; and a day that began at sunrise and ended long after sunset. It was tough, but she knew that this was a good trip, nothing like some of the bad times on the road with which the ringers' yarns were studded.

Elsa told her she was an incurable romantic, but admitted under pressure that she too never wished herself anywhere else when she was riding behind the stock in her father's camp, whereas the nine to five job in the store, weekends free, that she took in the off-season, the pictures on Saturday night, pretty dresses and make-up, all of that just seemed a marking of time until the next Dry season and the drovers' camp again. "I suppose it's because nobody pushes you," she said, "you just have to push yourself, and that's different."

When the day came that Marion must begin her ride back, Ted Kickett was suddenly reluctant to let her go by herself, though that had been the original arrangement. She couldn't get lost, she only had to follow the stock-route, and with an early start and no hitches she might do it in two days. Until that moment came Marion had not thought of the prospect, and when she did she was careful to conceal the fact that she was not nearly so confident as she seemed. Ted said he couldn't spare a man to go back with her, expect for young Jimmy, who was only half a man because his mother insisted on keeping him with her in the afternoons when she drove the wagonette ahead to set up the night-camp, and once there, tried to make him study his reading books, not that she could help him much, not being able to read herself.

Marion thought about it, and then said if his mother could spare Jimmy, how would it be if Jimmy rode back with her, and then stayed at the station until they came back on the return trip. Being the last trip for the season they could easily come back that way, and Jimmy could come to school and she'd catch him up a bit with his schoolwork. She was sure Angela and Jim wouldn't mind. At first Ted and Mrs. Kickett demurred, but when Marion told him about Angela asking her to take Yandi on, they finally acquiesced, with the understanding that if it didn't suit the Burtons Marion was to send Jimmy through with the mailman to catch them up on the road.

Saying goodbye to the Kicketts was almost as bad as saying goodbye to Maggie and Davey and Grandpa. Banner seemed almost as bad. He didn't want to leave his mates among the plant horses either, and nickered bad-temperedly until he saw Jimmy's horse and the pack-horse ready to lead off. Then Marion felt ashamed of herself when she thought of the little boy, being parted from his family for three weeks for her sake, and not a word of complaint out of him. She resolved to make it up to him, and make his stay a memorable one, for she knew that Angela would be happy that she hadn't had to ride home alone, and would make the little fellow welcome, and Jim would hardly notice. What Angela did at the homestead was always all right with him.

For the two days of the ride home it seemed almost as if they two were the only real people in the world, all others just vague shadowy figures far over the rim of the horizon. There was a comfortable and easy companionship between them, not of an adult and a child, but of two equals dependant upon themselves and each other in a little world suspended in time and place. They camped early and made a meal of damper and salt beef, washed down with black tea. The horses had been watered before sundown, and given a feed carried on the packs, and then tethered out so their riders could make a quick getaway in the morning. Marion was keen on reaching the station before nightfall, and they made such good time on the second day that it was well before five o'clock when they cantered up to the station yards and dismounted to unsaddle the horses and turn them loose.

That their arrival had been watched for was soon evident as a flying little figure came racing down from the homestead verandah. It was Anne. She threw herself into Marion's arms, screaming "Marion! Marion!" and then burst into tears. Marion dropped on one knee to comfort her, aware that her brothers were now also running down the path towards her.

"Daddy's hurt," the child sobbed, "The Flying Doctor's took him away, and Mummy's gone too!"

Suddenly Terry had wriggled into her embrace too, and the tears were brimming over onto his cheeks. She hugged them both and stood up, looking questioningly towards Rob.

"Dad got thrown in the yard this morning by a colt, and he hit his head against a post. He was unconscious for a while. Mum got the plane to come, and she went with him. She said you'd be home today for sure, but even if you weren't, Marion, we'd have been all right. She said for you to call up the base at five o'clock on the wireless for a message. I called at two o'clock, and they said Dad was all right, and we weren't to worry, but they'll tell us more at five. I think it's nearly five now," he ended anxiously.

"Here," Marion ordered, "you help Jimmy unsaddle and fix the horses, and I'll run up and get on the wireless straight away."

Even as she ran she wondered where Brownie was, and in the back of her mind she noted that the kitchen, as she passed, seemed strangely quiet and empty. She switched on the Traeger set quickly, and heard the base operator call for any final traffic. She pressed the transmitter button and began calling, "QT QT Queen Tare Queen Tare," and she was rewarded with an instant response.

"Hello Marion. Glad you're home. Angela was just a little worried you mightn't get back in time to call in. She's gone back to the hospital but she said to tell you that Jim's conscious but pretty badly concussed, but the doctor expects he'll be okay again in a few days. There's a slight fracture, but nothing dangerous. You're to give me any message, and I'll phone the hospital and pass it on to her."

Marion thanked the operator and asked him to re-assure Angela that everything was okay at home, and she'd call again tomorrow for any further news. Then she signed off, and switched off the set determinedly before any curious listeners on the network had a chance to call her, and probe for details of the accident.

The four children were now running up towards the house, and she met them on the step with the report she'd just received. The relief was so great that Anne started to bawl again, and then to giggle, and then they all began to speak at once.

Marion laughed, "Come on, come on, let's get organised. Terry, Jimmy can sleep in the extra bed in your room, and what about baths, and then you can tell me all about it at tea. Now, off you run."

She saw Anne and Terry glance towards Rob, and then they dutifully took Jimmy in tow and disappeared, Rob remaining as the spokesman for something that obviously had them puzzled.

"What's the problem, Rob?" queried Marion.

"It's Brownie," the boy began hesitantly. "He was all right at smoko-time, just after the plane left. He said he'd look after us if you didn't get back, and then he told us to go out of the kitchen and not bother him while he got dinner. We could go and play, but not to go riding any horses because he didn't want another accident on his hands. So we didn't, Marion. We didn't feel like it anyway. We just sat on the verandah and talked. We talked right till dinner-time, and it got later and later but the gong didn't ring. Then all of a sudden one of the gins started screaming, and the door burst open and they both came running out yelling, and they lit out for the camp like there was debil-debils after them."

He paused for breath, and Marion grabbed his arm.

"What was it? What was wrong?"

"Well, we all got up and ran over to the kitchen to see. We thought Brownie might be hurt too. But he wasn't, Marion. He was standing by the table with his shirt all open down to his belly-button, with a silly look on his face, a silly sort of grin, and pots and things on the table but no sign of any dinner. When he saw us at the door he turned and shouted at us. He told us to bugger off or he'd cut out our gizzards. He did, Marion. We got such a shock we all ran straight back to the house and shut ourselves in Mum's and Dad's bedroom in case he followed us. He's on the grog, Marion. We watched the kitchen through the louvres. After a while we could hear him throwing things about and swearing, then he started singing, and after a while he came out and went into the store once, then he went back into his room, and he hasn't been out since. Gee, Dad'd be mad if he knew. Where could he have got the grog? Dad won't let the men have any grog on the place, 'cept at Christmas!"

Marion hadn't seen any bushmen on a drinking spree, but she'd already heard plenty of tales, some hilarious and some pathetic, and she'd heard the recipe for Kimberley Champagne.

"The metho," she said, "he must've laced something with metho and drunk it. The louse! Just because your Mum and Dad aren't here. I hope the stinker's left us enough to light the pressure lamp! Let's go and see!"

"I kept the fire going," Rob said as they walked over to the kitchen. "When he went back to his room, we came over here to get something to eat, we were starving, and I stoked up the fire in the stove too. The girls never came back."

"Why didn't you tell your mother when she called on the wireless at two o'clock?" Marion asked him, but she really knew the answer before he replied.

"We didn't want to worry her while she was so worried about Dad. Anyway, we thought you'd be back soon, and you were, so it's all right now, isn't it?"

Marion wasn't too sure. She wasn't even sure that she knew how to light the pressure light, but she needn't have worried because the bottle of methylated spirits had disappeared from the lamp shelf.

"There's a gallon in the store," said Rob. "Shall I run down and get it?"

They went together. The tin had gone. There was no sound from Brownie's room, but Marion decided against any approach. He had probably locked the door anyway. They ran back up to the kitchen and Rob found a couple of old kerosene lanterns on the end of the shelf, which they filled and lit.

It had been dusk when they walked back from the store, but by the time the lanterns had been located and lit it was almost full dark, for the tropic nights came quickly. They left one lantern on the kitchen table and walked over to the house with the other. The three younger children were clean and combed and waiting for them. The sight of them reminded Marion of how dirty and untidy she was herself, so she told them to go to the kitchen and set the table there, and wait until she and Rob had had a clean-up, and then she'd rustle up some tea for them.

Rob showered first, and then went to the kitchen, got some steak from the kerosene fridge on the verandah, and sliced it, and put it on the stove in the large frying pan. By the time Marion arrived it was almost cooked. She fried eggs for everyone, and made tea, and they finished the meal with bread and jam, and a banana each from the hand that hung from a wire on the verandah. With a good meal under the belt everyone's spirits rose accordingly, and when Anne discovered the day's bread-dough, cold and sagging now on a small table in the corner, they hauled it out, turned it out onto the table, and divided it up, a loaf for everyone, and Rob showed them how to knead it, and they all thumped and pummelled. Jimmy's kneading was quite professional; obviously he'd done it before. They greased the bread-tins and set the loaves to rise on the hob, and then sat around the table to wait. Nobody thought of going to bed yet; together they could forget their apprehension.

Marion took one of the lanterns and went to the schoolroom for paper and pencils, and showed the children how to play the scribble game, where one of them scribbled across a sheet and another had a time limit to turn the scribble into a picture. They played the game until Terry noticed that all the loaves had risen and the bread was ready to cook. Then for the next hour Marion told them stories, until the rich smell told them that the bread was ready to come out. Rob turned the loaves out onto the table to cool, and then they really were tired enough to go to bed.

"Why don't we all bring our blankets and pillows and sleep on the lounge-room floor," Marion suggested. No sooner said than done. No-one changed into pyjamas, but slept in their clothes like they did in a swag, and no-one suggested that the lanterns be blown out. Marion turned down the flames and set a lantern at each end of the room. She didn't know whether the kerosene would last until morning, but at least it was comforting to the children to go to sleep shielded from the total darkness. All right, admit it, she thought; it was comforting to her too.

They slept late. The goat girls, clattering buckets on the kitchen verandah, woke them. By the time they had washed their faces and combed their hair, the goat girls had gone again, and the two buckets of milk were standing on the verandah table. There was no sign of the kitchen girls, and there were only grey ashes in the stove. The dirty dishes of the evening meal were still stacked in the sink.

Rob lit the fire and Marion gave them boiled eggs and toast, and stowed the rest of the bread in the large wooden bread bin that doubled for a seat. Ann strained the milk and set it on the stove to heat to separate the cream, and they discussed strategies. No word to Angela of their problem when Marion called in to the base.

Marion sent Rob down to the camp to tell the kitchen girls to come up to work, and Brownie wasn't there, so they'd be safe. She didn't know what to think about the cook. Was he sleeping off his binge? Was he perhaps already in the horrors? Would he re-appear and abuse them all? She didn't know what to think, and she decided to play it by ear if he did re-appear. She only knew that she was so mad about his behaviour that she didn't care how sick or crazy he was, so long as he didn't pose a threat to them. She would have locked him in his room if there'd been a key on the outside.

Maudie and Pansy came to work reluctantly, but Marion re-assured them, and set them to work, telling them to call her at once if Brownie showed any signs of approaching the kitchen or house. She guessed they'd spend more time watching than working, but at least it was an approach to normality, and she soon made it more so by herding the children into the schoolroom, and setting them all to work. They had hardly settled down than Yandi slid in and took his seat too.

Dinner-time approached, and there was still no sign from the quarters. Perhaps he'd drunk so much he'd killed himself; well, Marion wasn't going to check up on him; he could stay there and rot for all she cared. But now she was cook as well as governess, so she'd better think of what to have for dinner. Luckily there were only five children and herself to worry about, so that shouldn't be too hard. She left the children working and went to the kitchen. The girls had cleaned up, and had set the table in the dining room, and placed a platter of cold salt and roast beef on the kitchen table. Marion sent Maudie to the garden for tomatoes and cucumbers, sliced the bread and meat, and told the girls to help themselves and then come back after dinner to wash up and to put on a boiler of salt meat from the cooler before they went home for the day. She decided against ringing the gong for dinner in case it roused Brownie from whatever stupor he was in and caused him to re-appear. Instead she returned to the schoolroom, checked the children's work and sent them to the dining room.

It was almost like normal, but they were all aware of the empty places where Jim and Angela usually sat. Only Jimmy and Yandi and Terry were their usual bright little selves. Marion found herself talking to Rob and Anne as if they were adults too; the tension wasn't very far below the surface with them, and they were still understandably worried about their father.

Maudie and Pansy returned when they had barely finished eating, an hour at least before Marion expected them. Pansy had a great welt across her cheekbone, and was snivelling as Maudie led her along. "Hell's bells!" thought Marion, "not more trouble!"

Marion sat the girl down at the kitchen table and examined the bruise while an indignant Maudie explained.

"That no-good bugger Larry bin come back, Missus. He bin fight longa that Mick and he bin pull out longa stock-camp. He bin comeup while we bin workin longa kitchen today. Usfella bin takim tucker you bin give back longa camp. That Larry bin tellim Pansy you gibbit tucker longa me, and Pansy bin say nomore, so he bin hittim, takim tucker."

"Me proper 'ungry, too, Missus," whined Pansy, flinching as Marion bathed the bruise.

There wasn't much wrong with her that another meal wouldn't cure, so Marion cut her another dinner, while Maudie, avid for a gossip, related a variety of unpleasant incidents featuring that no-good bugger Larry, including the fact that he knew that the Boss and the Missus were in Derby and Brownie was sickfella. "You watchim, Missus," she advised Marion. "Mightbe 'im come up makim trouble longa you."

"Shush," said Marion, "don't frighten the kids." She called out to them to take a banana each and go back to school, and they could get the paints and crayons out and have a drawing lesson while she organised the tea, and she heard them go off talking and laughing. They loved the drawing lessons, when they could give rein to their own free expression.

The girls washed up and helped Marion select the salt beef, showed her how to wash it, and told her to put the potatoes, carrots and onions into the boiling beef water an hour before she wanted to serve it. Maudie volunteered to make a jelly and custard, and neither girl seemed to want to leave to go back to the camp although it was long past the normal time that their day's work was finished. It seemed they were more frightened of Larry than of Brownie. When there were no more chores to do Maudie made a cup of tea for them all, and Marion toyed with the idea of sending a messenger out to the stock-camp with a letter for Mick to come back to the station. But he was doing the job the station depended on, and if he left the stock-camp to its own devices maybe they'd fall apart too; he'd already be short-handed because Larry had pulled out. It did not occur to her that Peter would be with him, and could probably carry on. Anyway, only Larry knew exactly where the stock-camp was working, and he wasn't likely to tell her even if she did ask him, and who could she send, anyway. She decided against that move.

She went over to the house and called in on the three o'clock session and picked up a telegram from Angela saying that Jim was much better and Angela would be returning with the mail-man in two days' time. Only two days. Surely she could manage the situation for two days. Angela's cigarettes and a box of matches were lying on the table beside the transceiver. Marion picked up one and lit it, and as she smoked it she felt the tension go out of her. Of course she'd manage. She stubbed out the cigarette, and strolled up to the schoolroom to admire the children's efforts. Jimmy, who'd never had crayons before, was greatly excited, and he certainly had a wonderful eye for colour.

Marion was helping them to clean the paint boxes and put away their crayons when a plaintive shriek from Maudie silenced them all. Marion ran out of the schoolroom and Maudie and Pansy were both on the house verandah steps pointing towards the kitchen.

Brownie was staggering onto the kitchen verandah, and there was no doubt about the mood he was in. Muttering and swearing, he blundered inside, and they could hear him shoving things around, pushing and searching. Marion was puzzled. He mustn't have found the metho tin in the store, she thought, otherwise he'd be choked down for a week; he must think it is hidden somewhere in the kitchen. The same thought must have struck Rob, because he yelled suddenly, "You won't find anything in there, old man; we couldn't even light the lamps, thanks to you."

Maudie, with the courage of numbers on her side, added her piece: "You go siddown quietfella, ole man; nomore makim trouble longa usfella."

The man's angry face appeared, his hands clutching the sides of the doorway for support.

"All right!" he roared. "You shut up, you black bitch! It's the ginger bitch that's hid it, I know. I'll fix both of yers, I will!"

Marion had had enough. She was scared, but most of all she was angry.

"For crying out aloud!" she yelled at him. "Have some bloody sense. There's nothing here for you, so get the hell out of it!"

The tone of her voice must have penetrated the man's befuddled consciousness. He disappeared inside without a word, re-appeared a moment later with a loaf of bread under his arm, and lumbered off towards his quarters, muttering to himself.

"Poor old cow must be hungry," thought Marion, "but serve him right. Hope he chokes on it for all the trouble he's caused."

"He's taken our bread, Marion," Anne pointed out. "Will we make some more?"

"No," said Marion, "we'll ask Mum to bring some back from town. How about we make some scones now."

They all helped. It was a motley result, but nobody minded, and they tucked in with a will and sampled each other's efforts, chattering all the while. Yandi ate enough for half a dozen little boys, and then grinned his goodbyes and set off for home. But it was obvious to Marion that Maudie and Pansy weren't going to return to the camp of their own volition, and the more she thought about it, the more she realised that it might be some comfort to her to have their company during the long night ahead. Nothing was said, but they seemed to read her mind. There were spare blankets in the bathroom cupboard, and room for two more on the lounge floor.

Maudie said she'd go feed chooky-chook and gettim egg, and Rob said somebody ought to water the vegetable garden, and so he and Jimmy went to do it. Pansy and Anne set the table for an early tea, and Marion refilled the lanterns, and as an afterthought carried a bottle of kerosene up to the house.

Despite all the scones they'd eaten the children made a hearty meal. Maudie and Pansy were at first reluctant to sit down at the table with them, giggling with embarrassment when Marion insisted. Having always eaten their food with their hands before this, there was much hilarity from the younger children at their efforts to manipulate a knife and fork at first, but they took it in good part, soon got the knack of it, and played to the gallery.

When the dishes were washed, they all repaired to the house with the lanterns, rolled out their blankets and sat around in a circle while Maudie, a born raconteur, told stories of animal legends that had been passed down to the children of the tribe. Marion was utterly fascinated, quite as much as the listening children. Maudie transported them to another world, relating the stories in her inimitable pidgin, but interlarding them with aboriginal words and phrases and little songs that were hauntingly beautiful. Then at last they all rolled into their blankets, Marion last of all. She had taken a walk around the darkened verandah, staring out into the blackness. The only sound she heard was the far-away eerie call of a curlew.

She did not know how long she had slept when she felt the light tug at her shoulder. She sat up in the instant.

"It's only me, Marion," whispered Rob. "I got up to go to the toilet, and I think I heard somebody in the store. You come and listen."

Together they crept out onto the verandah, ears straining. Rob was right; there was somebody there, more than one person, and they weren't really making much effort to disguise their presence. Marion could hear low voices, and then the sound of somebody bumping against the stacked boxes in the dark.

"It's Larry, I'll bet, and somebody else too," whispered Marion. She wished she'd locked the store yesterday, but she hadn't thought of it, as it was usually left unlocked for easy access, for neither the blacks, nor anybody else, had ever been tempted to steal from a boss who always acceded to any reasonable request for the goods stored there.

What was she to do? Rob decided it for her. He had disappeared, but in a moment returned bearing the shotgun from the office. She did not know what it was until he thrust it into her hands.

"Be careful," he said, "I loaded it. I took a lantern into the office and loaded it okay. Put a shot over the roof. That'll give 'em hurry-up!"

"Yes, indeed," said Marion, "why not!"

She hadn't the faintest idea how one fired a shotgun, but she supposed it was the same as the .22 she'd used back on Johnson's farm. She tucked the barrel into her shoulder and pointed it in the general direction of what she calculated should be well above the store roof. Then she squeezed the trigger. There was a flash of light, a blast, and the recoil which sat Marion back on the verandah floor. They heard the rattle of shot against galvanised iron, and then all hell seemed to break loose. A long wailing half-scream, half-shout, other shouts, banging of overturned tins, bashing against walls, the bang of a door, came from direction of the store, and behind them other startled screams from the lounge room.

"It's okay, it's only me," called Rob, and then exultantly to Marion, "That put a bend in 'em, didn't it?"

But poor Marion was appalled. "What if I killed someone? I meant it to go high. I didn't mean to hit the store!"

"Nah!" said Rob, "couldn't kill 'em at that distance. Too far. Probably didn't even go through the wall. But you shifted 'em, Marion, you shifted 'em!"

Quite evidently they, or at least some of them, were still alive, because the shouting and yelling was still going on as the intruders retreated at full speed towards the camp.

Nobody at the house was going to sleep after that. Rob was all for taking a lantern and going to the store to see if there was any blood spattered around. He seemed hopeful that there would be. But Marion, shaking with delayed shock, wouldn't let him. It was Maudie who took charge then.

"You needim cuppa tea, Missus," she ordered. So they all, draped in blankets, repaired to the kitchen, stoked up the fire, and Maudie made tea and found a tin of biscuits. She sat Marion in front of the fire, while Rob related over and over again to the admiring children and Pansy how he had heard the intruders and loaded the gun for Marion.

Then suddenly it was piccaninny daylight. The children dropped their blankets and ran en masse to check out the store. The shot had peppered the walls, but they couldn't find a drop of blood. There were tins and packets where the loot had been dropped in haste, but not a corpse to be found. They came back and reported to Marion.

"And Brownie was growling in his room!" reported Anne.

"Oh Lord," thought Marion, "I'd forgotten all about Brownie."

But Brownie was packing his gear. He came out from his room with a swag, still unsteady on his feet, but determined enough to carry the swag and dump it into his old ute parked at the rear of the store. He went back inside for a suitcase and boxes and loaded them too. Then he came half-way up the path and yelled to them.

"I ain't stayin' around this loony place no longer. You can tell the boss to send me cheque to Halls Creek." And with that he got in the ute and drove away.

The blacks were gone too. Maudie and Pansy sneaked off towards the camp which was strangely silent, and came back to report that not a soul, not even Yandi, was still there.

Cheerfully they breakfasted round the big kitchen table, and then Marion went up to the office to send a telegram to Angela.

"Please bring bread, one gallon metho, and new cook."

Chapter 8

Visit to Halley's Cut

Marion hung over the verandah railing and counted heads. "Where were you all when we needed you!" she grinned to herself. The bell for afternoon smoko had brought them all forth; the stock-camp ringers from the quarters, Old Fred with them, where he had been yarning to Mick since dinner time. Jim and Angela from the office; all converging towards the kitchen-dining room building where a fat and jovial half-caste woman now held sway in Brownie's stead.

Carla Dawkins had taken the job conditionally, to help Angela out. She had a ten-year-old daughter, Katy, and was quite willing to take on the cooking as long as Katy didn't miss out on her schooling. So the verandah classroom was now stretched to capacity, although it would probably lose Jimmy Kickett tomorrow, for Maudie had told Marion conversationally at dinner-time that "drovers come-up tonight, Missus." The tribe had returned shame-faced a few days after their disappearance, Larry, Teddy-poor-bugger, and another youth no longer with them, and any inquiry as to their whereabouts merely elicited a vague faraway stare and a scratching of a black toe in the dust. As Marion said to Angela, it was not only as if the individual being questioned did not know where the three had gone, it was as if they had never even known them, in fact never even heard of them. Even little Yandi had merely given her an owlish look, ignored her question, and begun to read from his reading book in a sing-song voice.

"They'll turn up in a few months as if nothing happened, and I suppose we'll act the same way - with Teddy and the boy anyway. They were just led on by Larry. He's a trouble-maker, but he's a darn good stockman. Mick's never had any real trouble with him before, but he's one of those fellows with a chip on his shoulder, and they're all the same, black or white. Sooner or later there's a barney."

But Brownie was another kettle of fish. Jim swore that he'd make sure that the man never got another job in the district. He'd probably hang about in Halls Creek until his cheque turned up, drink it out, and then make his way into the Territory; he'd know he was finished in the Kimberleys. The Burtons knew of his weakness for the grog, which was why Angela had, before she left, taken the tin of methylated spirits from the store and hidden it in her wardrobe, believing she had removed the temptation. The bottle in the kitchen contained only enough for the lights for a few days, and she hadn't really thought he'd touch that. Not when they'd left him in trust with the children. Alone, yes, but even the most mongrelly of white men could have been expected to rise to the occasion in an emergency where a girl and young children depended on him. There would have been no trouble from Larry either, if Brownie had been sober.

"Still, you handled 'em okay, Marion," grinned Jim. "The story will go round the country, with a bit tacked on every time it changes hands, so don't be surprised at the yarns that'll come back to you. First you go droving, and then you shoot up cooks and blackfellows. Half the country will want to shake your hand, and the other half will dodge you like a bait. And in the meantime, you'll probably never have any trouble like that again; they'll all be leery of you!"

Peter's reaction had pleased Marion, and made her forget the lingering irritation she'd felt about his attitude to her friends. He was proud of her, and at the same time appalled that he had been so close and yet so far during the ordeal. He felt guilty too, and admitted to her that it had been he, and not Mick, who had fought with Larry, and Mick had taken his part because two white men had to stick together when there were only two of them. If he hadn't had that fight, Larry wouldn't have been in at the station. She assured him that it wouldn't have made much difference, because it was Brownie they were frightened of, not Larry, and maybe if she hadn't taken the shot at the store which made Brownie pack up and leave, well maybe he might have given them worse trouble. Peter allowed her to re-assure him, and promised that he'd give Brownie the hiding of a life-time if he ever ran across him. Marion didn't want that. In retrospect she felt nothing but pity for the old man and his wasted life; he had been friendly and likeable for all the months she had known him before his outbreak. The poor old bugger was his own worst enemy.

The Kicketts arrived and made camp in the early afternoon, and Jim asked them all up to the evening meal. Peter behaved like an absolute gentleman, and joined after tea in a card game with Marion, Elsa and her brothers, and the two young drovers, while their elders yarned on the verandah. The next day, before the drovers left, Marion and Elsa exchanged promises to write, and Marion made up a packet of books and lessons for Mrs. Kickett to carry on Jimmy's education during the off-season. Elsa said she'd probably take a job in Carnarvon while her Dad and the boys were horse-breaking, but if she didn't, then she'd see to Jimmy's lessons. Jimmy didn't look at all appreciative. It was easy to see he'd rather be with Dad and the boys, but he knew the right thing to do, and he thanked Marion gravely for her help with his reading, and she thanked him just as gravely for his company on the ride from the drover's camp to Delroy.

Then they were gone, and Old Fred was the only visitor still at the station. He stayed for a couple of days, waiting on the mailman for some apparently important mail. The mail run did not take in Halley's Cut, for the rare communications did not warrant a service. Only once or twice a year did Fred receive mail, and that always came addressed care of Delroy.

"Maybe I oughta join yer school, Marion, so you can teach me ter read," he said, "but I reckon it's a bit late now. But I spose I'll stick to me horses, and give the books a miss. I done all right without 'em so far!"

When the long official envelope arrived in the Delroy mail-bag, the old man stayed only for a quick smoko and then rode off with the packet tucked inside his shirt. It occurred to Marion later that he'd gone off with it unopened, and obviously it was quite important to him, but what was he going to do with it if he couldn't read it. She said as much to Angela.

"Oh, I thought he might have told you, he's taken such a fancy to you," said Angela. "Junie can read. She writes a beautiful hand too. Educated on the mission."

"Junie?" queried Marion.

"You won't ever meet her, unless you go to Halley's Cut," said Angela. "She's his wife, but she's black. Well, maybe they're not legally married. The Department doesn't allow it, so nobody talks about it, and nobody that's not a good friend of Fred's ever goes to the Cut. She's been with him ever since Jim and I have known him, but even with us, if we visit, she goes down to the camp with the other blacks while we're there."

"Did they have any children?" asked Marion curiously.

"No. There aren't any half-castes on Halley's Cut. Maybe Fred couldn't have any children, or Junie made sure there weren't any. Sad, in a way, but the Government's strict on co-habiting, Fred would go to jail if they knew. I suppose it's a good law, made to protect the Aboriginal girls, but in some cases it doesn't quite work out that way, and Fred's and Junie's case is one. But there's no evidence, so they couldn't prove anything against him."

"Gosh, even up here, people's lives get interfered with by silly rules of society," said Marion indignantly.

"Particularly up here," added Angela firmly, "so you don't say anything about it to anyone, not even Peter who you're so chummy with."

"Particularly not Peter," laughed Marion.

But she thought about Fred later, and was glad he had someone, and she was glad she wasn't like Peter, whose reaction she could easily guess. She could thank Maggie for her open mind, taking people as they really were underneath their skins. Her attitudes came from her family background, and she supposed Peter's came from his. She was lucky with Angela and Jim, who judged people on their merits; not all station whites were like them, she knew, even from the little experience she'd had in the country. But Peter was coming round. He'd changed his attitude to Elsa already; he'd laughed and joked with her the other night, and her brothers too. She thought maybe she was a bit in love with Peter, and so it was important he started thinking for himself. Very important, if they did fall in love. Then she would have to tell him about not having a father and Maggie not being married. So she'd better make sure she didn't fall really in love with him before she was quite sure how he would react. She'd just keep her mind on her ambition to own her own land, and that ought to keep her feelings about Peter in check so she could handle them.

Gradually the year began to wind down, and the hint of summer to infiltrate the bright dreamy days of the dying Dry season. The stock-camp had taken rations for a month, loaded the packhorses, and departed from the homestead for a last round of branding at the furthest end of the run, and Marion's eighteenth birthday was celebrated quietly in their absence. At the beginning of December, Peter would also be eighteen, and he had talked about joining the Air Force, but what war-news filtered through to the outback suggested that the war might soon be over, and Angela said it probably would be by the time it took to train Peter for the pilot he wanted to be.

"I don't think they'd take you," said Jim thoughtfully, "seeing your Dad's a property owner. Grazing's a reserved occupation, and we've got to stay on whether we like it or not and raise bully beef to feed the army. They won't even let Mick go, because he's a head-stockman, so the chances are, Peter, that you'll be allocated to your Dad's place, seeing you haven't got any older brothers. They might let you come back here at a pinch, if your Dad's not short of men, but I doubt they'd let you join up."

"And after the war, I don't suppose it will be much different for a long time," said Angela, "because then we'll have half of Europe to feed. That's why we're rationing food in Australia now, trying to get as much as we can through on the convoys to Britain."

"We don't know how lucky we are, do we," mused Mick. "Beef three times a day if we want it, some but not enough in the Australian cities, and bugger-all for the poor old Pommy civilians. But if you get stuck with it, Pete, you don't want to go poking your nose into the city once you're eighteen. Like as not, some old duck would shove a white feather at you, or ask you why you aren't in uniform. No way I'm going south again until it's all over!"

"Well," rejoined Jim, "at least the Government appreciates what you're doing, Mick, even if the general public doesn't. You're better off than the black ringers; nobody gives them a mention, and if we counted them all up, there'd be a lot more blacks than whites working in stock-camps round the country without a thank-you, kiss-me-foot!"

"Yeah, true," admitted Mick. "We couldn't do without 'em - the one's Pete don't knuckle up to, that is - but look at it this way. They love the job, gives 'em something to do, bit of excitement in their lives. Better than sitting on their backsides in the camp. In the old days they hunted, but now you feed 'em, Jim, so they'd be bored stiff. They're great riders, good cattlemen as long as they've got a good man over them to work 'em, and they take a pride in the job too."

"Couldn't one of them, a real smart ringer, take charge, instead of being 'worked' as you call it, Mick?" asked Marion.

Jim answered her, "Maybe one day, Marion, but never while they're still tribalised. Say I've got a black ringer just as smart as Mick here, and I put him in charge of the camp.

He's got a position in the tribe, and he's got to do what he's told by every man in the tribe who's superior to him, and that's most of them because he's still a young fellow. He's got to pay whatever his skin-uncles ask of him, and if he gets an order to join a kadaicha party he's got to down tools, drop everything and go, leave the cattle, leave the stock-camp, tell nobody. Even say he's somewhere away from the influence of the elders, he still can't take charge. They're all tribesman first, and ringers second, and they're all equal standing. He can't give orders; they won't take it from him. Sure, he knows the orders to give just as good as Mick does, better than Peter, because he's a smart man and he's been at the game longer, but I could give the job to Peter and they'd follow him, while if I put a black ringer in charge they'd argue and refuse to do what he told them."

"That's the way it is," Mick assured her. "Alec's as good a man as I am, but the only chance he's ever got of being a head-stockman is Buckley's. In the tribe his status is the lowest of all, because he's got a touch of white, so no black ringer would take orders from him. And if you had a white stock-camp they wouldn't either because he's black. If he was a full half-caste he'd be all right, because the blacks reckon that's near enough to white, and I reckon most of the young white fellows think the same."

"It's not fair, is it?" said Marion.

Mick looked at her and grinned.

"Who ever said life was fair?" he said quizzically. "As the Froggies say, 'C'est la vie'."

"So we've all got to go on with our lives within the bounds somebody puts on us," contributed Angela. "Alec can't get to be head-stockman, and Peter can't get to be an airman, and unless I go to bed now, I can't get up in the morning, so goodnight all."

As the days grew warmer Marion started lessons earlier. The children all had examinations to finish the year's work, just like any other school, so Marion planned on their revision lessons before the heat of the day drained them of energy. They finished the day's schooling at dinner-time, and in the afternoon, after the siesta hour, Marion helped Angela with pre-Wet season odd jobs, or exercised Banner in the company of one or more children on their ponies. Much as they would have liked to go swimming, Deep Hole was still out of bounds because of the Old Man Croc, and the smaller waterholes had dried back and were muddy and uninviting. The children compromised by stripping to their shorts and hosing each other on the lawn, and sometimes Marion put on her bathing suit and joined them. Carla kept up a supply of cordial ice-blocks for them, which she made daily by freezing cordial in the metal moulds which she had brought with her. There was barely room in the freezer compartments of the kero fridges for the ice-cream which was another of her specialties. Terry told his mother that Carla was a children's cook, while Brownie had been a grown-ups' cook. But Carla was both; she loved cooking, and Angela secretly hoped that Carla's stay would be a long one. She seemed happy enough, and everyone showed their appreciation of her efforts. She had cleaned out the larger store-room adjoining the kitchen and turned it into a bedroom for herself and Katy, and when the weather grew warmer, she put their beds out on the kitchen verandah.

The Wet Season loading arrived, three truckloads over two days, while the stock-camp was still away. But there was no lack of willing helpers to unload it.

Marion didn't ask where the coupons came from to cover all the stores and clothing which she knew were rationed down South. The supplies were to last a year, but, like everybody else, black and white, she spent lavishly in the excitement of all the new goods stacked on the store shelves. The cotton materials mainly earmarked for the lubras' dresses were a gold-mine. She chose dress-lengths for herself and some to take to Maggie for Christmas, and bought new boots and hat and check shirts for next year, for it was already understood that she would be returning after her holiday. They didn't discuss it in so many words; it was just taken for granted.

The much smaller Halley's Cut loading had come as part of the Delroy loading, and Jim sent one of the black boys over with the message to tell Fred of its arrival. When Fred turned up a couple of days later with a string of packhorses, he revealed that the big square box contained a Traeger transceiver, and Marion was delegated to show him how to operate a transceiver on the Delroy set. His call-sign was the same initials as Halley's Cut, 9HC Howe Charlie, and he was as nervous as a cat the first time he spoke to the Derby base operator. A smaller box held a Flying Doctor medical kit, which Angela went through with him.

"Never know when a fellow might get crook, eh," he mused, looking sideways at Angela. "I got a fair sorta mob of blacks at the Cut now too." He appreciated that bottles and packets were numbered as well as labelled, a forethought on the part of the suppliers for bushmen like Fred who could only read figures.

Jim suggested that Fred might like him to come over to help him set up the aerial for the transceiver, and the old man accepted readily.

"Long time since you been up to my place, Jim, coupla years, ain't it. Tell you what, why don't yer bring Angie and Marion too, make a visit of it, like."

So that was how Marion first came to visit the Cut. Angela did not make the trip, but offered instead to supervise the children's examinations in Marion's absence. Marion recognised that she had been particularly honoured, for few outsiders beyond the Burtons and Mick had ever been invited, and as she saddled Banner and watched the pack-horses being loaded up early the next morning, she felt that she was finally accepted into that elite brotherhood of the bush, those who "belonged" and called the wild ranges and steep gorges and lush valleys home, and never wanted to be any place else. She would not have changed places that morning with the King himself. She experienced a gush of warmth towards the wiry little man with his springy step and his bawling voice and the great floppy hat balanced on his ears, and all that silver and gold day she rode along pandanus-lined creeks, over the rocky foothills, and finally to the Jump-up, oblivious of her sweat-streaked shirt and the little black flies. She caught the spell of mounting anticipation from Banner, who knew he was going home again, and trotted along with no need of urging, no matter how steep the incline or how rough the terrain.

The sheer awe and grandeur of the ranges and the seemingly almost-impossible ascent of the Jump-up took her breath away, but not so much as the beauty of the valley spread out below them when they had finally laboured up the narrow and dangerous track to the top. The whole cavalcade paused there for breath, and Fred moved to Marion's side and pointed down to where a tiny cluster of buildings shone in the late afternoon sun on a rise not far from the tree-lined banks of Halley's Creek.

"She ain't a big run," he said proudly, "but I reckon there ain't any better horse country anywhere in the world."

Then he whistled shrilly, and saddle and pack-horses set off as one down the comparatively easy descent into the kingdom of a man called Fred.

The building materials of the Cut homestead were all local, except the nails that had been used in its construction; roofing iron and larger items could never have been ferried in over the Jump-up. In the late afternoon the building's colours were gentled into blues and greys and creamy-beige. Marion wished she was a painter; her camera could never do justice to the scene that lay before her.

"Gee, isn't it beautiful?" she said to Jim Burton, riding beside her.

"Sure is," agreed Jim, "not all the mod cons of city living, of course, but comfortable enough, you'll be surprised."

The three-roomed dwelling with wide verandahs all round was built of bush timber and mud-brick walls, with a space of about ten inches between the tops of the walls and the roof for coolness. The roof, pitched quite steeply, was made of layer upon layer of paperbark, inches thick, and inside the three rooms were ceiled with white-washed hessian tacked to the wooden framework. At one end of the living room was Fred's masterpiece, a mud-brick fireplace divided roughly into two sections. An ant-bed oven with a thick wooden door and a flat top which formed a hob took up one section, and the other had the firebed as its base with a row of iron bars eighteen inches above it, each one set into the oven on one side and the side of the chimney on the other. A large kettle and a camp-oven were both simmering gently over the glowing coals.

All the furniture was hand-made with axe, adze and plane, from the table and stools in the centre of the room, to the bunks and chairs laced with greenhide in the other two rooms. Marion marvelled at the cupboards in the kitchen and the small bedroom that Fred offered her.

"Me father was a carpenter. Learned a bit from watchin' him when I was a kid," he volunteered, when Marion admired his work.

On the verandahs the excited blacks were laughing and chattering as they stacked the goods unloaded from the pack-horses, but there was no sign of whoever had provided the ample meal awaiting them in the camp-oven, a savoury stew whose odour suddenly reminded Marion of how hungry she was. How did the blacks know Fred would be back on this particular evening? That mental telepathy again, she supposed. Well, after this Fred would have his transceiver, and could send and receive messages like everybody else, so long as there was someone there to receive them. She idly wondered how he was going to re-charge the battery needed to operate the wireless, but no doubt he'd find a way, he'd certainly managed well with everything else he needed.

She found a bucket of water and a tin dish on the small table in the bedroom, with a rough towel and home-made soap beside the dish - that really was telepathy now - and had a quick wash and dragged a comb through her dusty red hair.

Fred and Jim were still shifting packages and talking on the verandah, so in the fading light she found plates and knives and forks and set the table for three. Like the dining table at Delroy the centre of the table was graced with pepper, salt and black sauce as permanent fixtures. She wondered if Fred had a light, or whether he went to bed with the chooks, as Maggie used to say about Grandpa. There was a light. She found a pressure lamp and bottle of kerosene and a smaller bottle of methylated spirits with a filler attached on a shelf which ran the length of the kitchen on the side opposite the door.

Thanks to Angela's tuition, she now knew how to light the thing, and when the men came in after their quick ablutions somewhere on the verandah, she had already set it on the hook suspended from the ceiling between the fireplace and table, and had found teapot and tea-leaf and was pouring boiling water from the kettle to make the tea she knew they'd be craving. Fred fetched milk from a Coolgardie cooler on the verandah, and sugar in a pannikin from a bin at the end of the cupboard. Then he produced fluffy-textured bread wrapped in a sugar-bag and served them great plates of stew, which both the men doused liberally with black sauce.

It was not until her appetite was assuaged that Marion realised how tired she was after the long day's ride. Fred gave her a torch and pointed out the outhouse, and promised he'd show her round on the morrow, and then she said goodnight and fell into a dreamless sleep between the rough grey blankets on the horsehair mattress in the little bedroom.

The butcher birds woke her in the morning with a cascade of sound, and she rolled out of the blankets with the zest of youth and a hunger to go with it. Old Fred was frying steak at the fireplace, and the steaming tea-pot was already on the table. Jim was outside assessing the possibilities for erecting the aerial, and considering whether the tall slender gum-tree at approximately the right distance from the roof-ridge would do instead of setting in a pole.

In the end they did choose the gum-tree, but Marion had nothing to do with the installation, for she was being escorted by Maria, a shy giggling fourteen-year-old, clad in trousers, check shirt and Williams boots similar to her own garb, to see the horse-yards, the gardens with a variety of vegetables, the goats, and the grove of bananas and pawpaws close by the waterhole which served the homestead. Maria spoke surprisingly good English, not the pidgin variety which was the lingua franca of all the other blacks Marion had met. Curiously, she asked Maria where she had learnt it, for she was fairly certain that the girl had probably never left the valley except on walkabout, where she would only hear Aboriginal languages spoken. Maria told her that Junie, educated at the Mission school, spoke proper English, and bossed all the kids until they did too. There were only about thirty tribespeople, five families, and they all worked for Fred with the horses and the station jobs. Sometimes the young fellows took outside jobs after walkabout time, but mostly they came back. Not like the girls. They had to go to their promised husbands when all the tribe met at Big Sunday.

"What about you, then? Shouldn't you be gone too?" asked Marion, who knew that the little girls were passed to their husbands' camps at about the age of eight to be trained by the older wives.

"Junie's my sister," replied Maria. "She was brought up at the Mission, where our Mummy was working. Junie wouldn't go to an old man. She kicked up such a fuss that in the end he wouldn't take her anyway, said she was allasame white rubbish. Me too," she grinned. "Our Mummy died when I was a little fella, and Junie took me, and we come here. We don't go walkabout with the others; stay here with Fred."

"What about your father then?" asked Marion. These were the very first emancipated black women she'd ever heard of, and she had some idea of what the defiance of tribal laws must mean.

"Dunno," said Maria, leading Marion further along the bank to where an ingenious fish-trap was set up. "Don't remember 'im. Junie said he had 'nother young wife and other kids, and they all went away when our Mummy died."

Marion wondered whether she was going to meet the elusive Junie, but there was no sign of her when they got back to the house. Jim was testing the wireless, and chiacking Fred, who still regarded it warily as if it was a snake that might bite him. By lunchtime Fred had made his first hesitant call to the base, and been welcomed on to the network.

It was too late to ride back to Delroy that day, so Fred said that after lunch and a siesta he'd run in a few horses for Jim to look at, for he had some promising colts coming on for the next year. They could get an early start on the morrow, and even call up Delroy on the galah session to let Angela know their exact plans.

"Looks like you'll never get off the air once you've got the hang of this thing," laughed Jim.

"Dunno about that," rejoined Fred. "Seein' I ain't got a battery like you fellas, and I gotta pedal while I talk to keep the power up to her, then I ain't goin' to be talking more than I hafta!"

So that's how it's done, thought Marion. The old-time pedal radio that was the forerunner of the modern model would serve Fred well; all he'd need was enough breath to pedal and talk at the same time. She examined the equipment with interest.

After lunch Marion insisted on washing-up the few plates, and the men retired to the beds on the verandah on the shady side of the house. It was a hot day but the insulation of the paper-bark roof kept the inside rooms reasonably cool. Marion had never got into the way of sleeping after the mid-day meal, because she did not begin work as early as the men, and she had so far not experienced the cruelly enervating midday heat of the tropical Wet season. That was still to come. The first storms and the thick clouds that kept the humidity imprisoned at ground level were only weeks away, but now, although she dutifully lay down on the bed in the small room, she was not sleepy. At Delroy she always read for a while after dinner while the others rested, but here there was nothing to read. Her eyes drifted round the small room with its two small wooden-shuttered but glassless windows. The space between wall and hessian ceiling filtered in enough light for her to examine her surroundings in more detail than she had done the night before when she was so tired.

The washstand that held the tin basin was a simple affair, but she could see that the cupboard was more complicated, quite a well-made piece of furniture really, with two drawers at the top over two doors with carved handles to the compartment below. She got up and wandered over to examine it, idly wondering what local wood had produced it. It was the most natural thing in the world to pull open first one drawer, then the other. There was a collection of ledger type books, pencils, a couple of steel-nibbed pens and a bottle of ink in the first drawer. This must be Junie's "office", she thought, where the paper-work which all station men seemed to hate so much was done. The washstand could easily double for a table, and there was a chair beside the bed. The other drawer held paperwork too, envelopes and their contents, store lists clipped together, a catalogue or two, she saw at a glance, and she was about to push the drawer back when her eye fell on a snapshot half protruding from beneath the other papers. She pulled it out without thinking, sepia-toned and not very clear in the dull light.

It showed two young men leaning over a fence on either side of a gateway where an older woman in an ankle-length dark dress stood staring into the sun with one hand on the open gate. Marion was about to drop the snapshot back into the drawer when something familiar about the gate arrested her. Just like the gate at home. And the front of the cottage behind the three figures. It was as familiar as if she had known it all her life.

She had known it all her life. The same verandah posts, and just caught on the edge of the picture the shadow of what could only be the big gum tree in the yard. She stared hard at the tiny faces, and knew with certainty that she was looking at Grandpa in his youth, and beside him, two people who could only be his mother and his brother, Fred. The realisation hit her like a bolt from the blue. Fred Halley was Fred Ryan, jockey, horse-thief, the prodigal son who never returned, her own great uncle. She quickly dropped the photo back where she had found it and pushed the drawer in guiltily, suddenly aware that she had committed the unforgivable crime of snooping.

She lay on the bed again, overcome with her discovery. Fred must have known long ago that she was his relation; she'd talked about Grandpa and Maggie and Mudjinup often enough in his hearing. Now she knew too. Suddenly she began to giggle.

Chapter 9 — *Christmas down south*

An early Wet Season storm delayed Marion's departure from the station, but the mailman got through five days before Christmas, and she and Peter both returned to Derby with him, where they were able to connect up with a south-bound plane after only one day's delay. Peter left the plane at Carnarvon, where John Blythe was waiting to meet him, but Marion had been unable to contact Maggie, and the best she could do on her arrival in Perth was to phone the Mudjinup hotel to leave a message for Maggie that she would be on the evening train.

Marion's mixed emotions surprised her. Pre-Christmas Perth, servicemen everywhere, noise, and an appalling rush of homesickness for the station, battled strangely with her excited desire to see her family again. She had the strangest feeling that Delroy Springs did not really exist, and that she had awakened with a sense of loss from a very pleasant dream into an environment where she no longer belonged. She was still light-headed from the long plane trip; it must be that which contributed to the extraordinary let-down feeling she was experiencing. She pulled herself together, cloaked her luggage at the station, and made her way to the stock-agent firm's office to change into cash the cheque Jim had given her. She'd almost forgotten what it was like to handle real money again. She spent an hour in a Department store buying presents. A bag of crabs and oysters, smelling sea-weedy just like the Derby mud-flats, completed her purchases, and she returned to the station with only time to retrieve her luggage, buy a ticket, and find a seat on the already crowded train. It was almost dark when the train left; and it would be after midnight before it reached Mudjinup. Marion fell asleep to the jolt of the train wheels, hoping that her mother had received her message and would be at the station to meet her.

Maggie was there; Grandpa was there; and Davey was there; and in the background Ralph Johnson was grinning and picking up suitcase and parcels.

"Well, bugger me, Ginger, where's your spurs and big hat? Not even a blue heeler. You ain't changed a bit!"

She had really, but in the excitement of the welcome home she forgot all about it. They talked, and interrupted each other, and cracked crab-shells and prised open oysters to eat with fresh bread and butter and a dash of vinegar round the big kitchen table, just as they had done on other occasions, because shell-fish all the way from Perth might go off it they were left until morning after six hours off the ice. It was nearly dawn before Marion fell asleep on her own familiar bed.

Christmas was busy, and so was New Year, with Ralph's sister Melly's wedding to a quiet middle-aged Army major, who had owned a farm until the Depression and had spent much of his leave-time on the Johnson farm. Young Bill approved highly of his new stepfather, but decided, after collaboration with Davey, that his place was on the farm with Uncle Ralph, who would once again be left to his own devices when Melly moved to Perth with her major.

Marion brought to the surface with a slight shock of realisation the fact that Maggie and Ralph were more than just friends, and had been so for some years, when she thought about it. While they were washing the dishes one evening, she asked her mother conversationally, "When Melly goes to live in Perth for good, are you going to marry Ralph?"

Maggie laughed. "Oh, what big eyes we've got all of a sudden. No, my dear, I'm not. I like my job. I like my independence. Ralph did ask me years ago, while you were still at school, but it saved us both a lot of problems when I said no. Melly lived there then, and she would have felt she ought to go; two women under one roof never works, no matter how good friends they are. Besides, there's Pa to think of. I know he'd say go and live with Ralph, but wouldn't he just rattle around in this place with all of us gone. He stuck by me when I needed a home, so I'll make one for him as long as he needs it." She wrung the dish-cloth reflectively, and then grinned conspiratorially at her daughter.

"Ralph and I survive okay, Marion. The town's long since got over talking about me, the old dears have had much more interesting scandals since the Army camp moved in; I doubt we'd rate a mention these days. Or care."

"Good for you, Mum!" smiled Marion, but she was then momentarily surprised when Maggie took an altogether different tack.

"Good for me, but don't get any ideas about yourself, Marion. It's not good at all when you're young. I hope you and this Peter..."

"Aw, heck no, Mum! Peter's so straight-laced it wouldn't occur to him. Peter's a "gentleman", Mum, best school, women on a pedestal sort of thing!"

"Ha!" said Maggie grimly. "So was your father! Don't let that fool you, my girl."

"Oh Mum," laughed Marion, "you don't have to worry about me. I might even marry Peter in a couple of years' time when we're twenty-one. I like him a lot, and I know he likes me more, but there's a lot of other things I want to do first, before I think of settling down. And I've got my head screwed on right, you know."

"Well, as long as you remember," said Maggie, and quoted, somewhat inappropriately Marion thought, "in your life there will be moments, and for those moments don't give your life!"

Marion sneaked down to the shed and had another look at Fred's brick. She did not mention her discovery to Grandpa or Maggie, but she took a roll of film of the family and the home which she would show Old Fred when the opportunity presented itself. Melly's major had managed to get three rolls of film for her, even though they were strictly rationed, and she had taken two rolls at the wedding, with quite professional results. Her portraits of Maggie, Grandpa and Davey were equally good, and the cottage had a homely charm.

Marion's days were full, during January. She helped Davey and Bill on the farm with the end of wheat-harvest chores, talked long hours with Grandpa in the summer evenings, took a four-day visit to Perth with Maggie to choose and consign the items on the special list Angela had given her, and she visited the Correspondence School to collect the sets of lessons she would take back with her. They went to Perth by train, but Ralph met them there on the last day in his car, and took Maggie out to dinner while Marion looked up her school friend. Annette had reconsidered her career, and had spent the past year at University. Marion suspected, before they even met, that they would have very little in common now, and she was right. They spent a reasonably pleasant evening, but Marion knew that neither of them was at all interested in the other's chosen way of life. She said as much to Ralph and Maggie on the way home.

"It all seemed too superficial to me," she confessed. "I don't belong down here any more. Annette and her friends don't seem quite real. Not like Angela and Jim, or Mick and Peter, or even Pansy and the blacks."

She caught the quizzical glance that Ralph threw her, and hastily added, "Oh, Mudjinup's real enough, and you and the family, Ralph, but there's not really a place for me here, either, is there?"

"Spose not!" agreed Ralph. "Not with the things you want out of life, Ginger. A jumping-off place, say. Incidentally, when are you jumping off again?"

"End of the month, if the weather's right. Angela's going to send me a telegram when the road's likely to be open, and I'll go out with the mailman from Derby."

As January drew to a close Marion could not help laughing at the difference between herself and Davey in their attitudes. While Davey whined about the proximity of his return to school she found herself counting the days to the possibility of the telegram bidding her return.

"I can't put a finger on it, Mum," she confided to Maggie. "It's not really the people I miss. There's nobody can take the place of a family like you and Grandpa and Davey. It's not the place either. Derby's an awful place if you compare it to Mudjinup, flies and dust, and houses just tin roofs and walls and cement floors mostly. There's flies and dust at Delroy too, and mosquitoes and sandflies. But there's something else that seems to make up for all that. The silly thing is that the one thing I notice most is something that hardly registered with me when I was up there. When I get into bed at night-time there's no sound of blackfellows' corroboree in the distance, and I notice it isn't there. At Delroy I didn't even notice it *was* there, most of the time, but when it's not I miss it. Silly, isn't it?"

"Can't say it makes much sense to me," commented Maggie. "But it's a good job, and you like it. The people are nice, and you can save all your pay, which you can't do anywhere else. And as long as you're happy there, that's the main thing, dear."

"Well, I fit there, which is more than I ever did anywhere else. Come to think of it, we might all be a bunch of misfits up there, because I don't really think any of them would fit too well down south. Peter, maybe, but none of the others. That's it; that's what I like about it. It's a big enough country for there to be a place for everyone who wants a place there."

"Well, I can't say I'd fancy it myself," shrugged Maggie, "too hot for my liking, and all those blackfellows. Not my cup of tea."

"Do me, though!" laughed Marion. "I think the blacks must have sung me. That my country now, that one!"

The telegram came, and goodbyes were said.

The plane touched down in Derby in a repeat of Marion's arrival the year before - hot, humid, and lowering grey clouds rolling in from the sea. She had been the only passenger all the long afternoon from Carnarvon, and both she and the pilot were ready to call it a day. The mailman's ute pulled alongside just as the pilot had finished anchoring the plane down and unloading mail bags, parcels and Marion's suitcase.

"Probably make a run for it tomorrow," he assured Marion. "Got a couple other passengers, now you've arrived, too."

The other passengers turned out to be Carla and Katy. "Wasn't going back without you was there; a real good job, Delroy is, but Katy's gotta have her schooling," announced Carla. Marion pointed to the parcel wrapped in sacking, and assured Carla that Katy's lesson papers were there along with the others, and felt a glow of satisfaction that she was so obviously approved of by this half-caste woman of ample proportions and definite ideas.

They didn't make a run for it the next day, or the next few days. Six inches of rain fell overnight, and more was reported from Delroy and all the stations along the track. Marion kicked her heels in the hotel for a week or visited the young nurses at the hospital on their time off. She wished Mick would turn up to pick them up, and privately thought the mailman was being a bit too cautious. When they finally did leave town a fortnight later she realised that, if anything, he'd erred the other way. With an overload on the truck of all the mail which had stacked up since the pre-Christmas run, herself, Carla and the mailman crammed into the truck cabin, and Katy and the two young ringers and a dog sitting up on the load wherever they could find a perch, it was a hell of a trip, punctuated by bog after bog. Marion said as much to the mailman, who merely shrugged and said it was pretty much the usual wet-season run.

It didn't rain, but it might as well have, because everyone was drenched wet with sweat, which attracted the sandflies in droves. The dog, belonging to the ringer named Andy, fell off the truck, and Andy thumped the cabin roof for the mailman to stop, but he wouldn't, swearing he'd get bogged again if he did. A mile or so further he did get bogged, and the dog had caught them up and lay panting in the shade long before they managed to dig out. Carla and Marion and Katy sat in the shade too, switching at the flies with bunches of leafy twigs; paying passengers were excused from digging when there were non-paying passengers, or not enough shovels to go around.

Whenever it was clear that digging was going to be a lengthy enterprise Carla and Marion got a fire going and boiled the billy. "A big bastard of a bog" was the factor that decided the timing of their sketchy meals; ordinary meal-times did not enter the picture. If the going was good, they kept going. The mailman had spent five weeks once bogged in the same place.

"Me and a blackfella," he told them. "We woulda run out of tucker, but we was lucky, because it was the Christmas run, and we had all sorts of flash stuff in the tucker line for the stations further out. We could see we weren't going to get out, and most of the stuff woulda gone mouldy if we hadn't et it. We had ham on Christmas Day, and a Christmas cake and all the trimmings, and a nip of rum to wash it down. Johnny run down a goanna for New Year, or what we reckoned must be New Year; we was gettin' sick of all the boiled lollies and stuff by then."

This being just a run-of-the-mill trip for February, it took only three days to get to Delroy Springs. The welcome for the first vehicle through for the year was uproarious. Marion was home again.

Chapter 10

The War ends and the outback plans a celebration

The monsoon rains deluged the country for the rest of February and most of March. The Delroy River ran a banker on three different occasions. Alec and Boodgerie reported seeing the tracks of an old-man croc near the flooded horse-yards, and Mick and Jim thought it might be the big croc from Deep Hole on walkabout for a quieter place to hole up for the Dry Season.

"Coulda been chased out by an even bigger one!" said little Terry.

Weevils invaded the flour, and even Carla was hard put to produce reasonable bread. Everything grew mould overnight, boots, saddles, even the plug tobacco Jim kept in a jar in the office. The men were tied to the homestead, but filled in their time doing saddlery repairs, and making bridles and hobble straps, for Sam the saddler had not turned up this year, and now there was no chance that he would get through to Delroy. Mick plaited a belt for Marion, and a miniature version for Anne, and after school Rob spent hours in the saddle-shop plaiting himself a halter under Mick's tuition.

Marion's and Carla's days were routinely filled, but Angela, now that Carla had taken over the cooking again, sometimes found herself at a loose end. She had long completed the usual job of making calico ration bags for the stock camp, and there was no office work outstanding, or blacks' medical needs to attend to. She fought a losing battle with insects and frogs whose one aim in life seemed to be the invasion of the homestead, kitchen and store. She wrote long letters to her friends and relations down South, with not much prospect of posting them for weeks. Her garden grew like a jungle, and she spent hours, when the weather permitted, trying to civilise it. The creepers and shrubs were a riot of colour, and the frangipani trees gave off a scent that pervaded the whole garden.

Rob's vegetable garden had long been washed out, but the pumpkin and watermelon vines pushed unrestricted over vegetable beds and fences. The seven-year beans and chokos provided the only fresh vegetables apart from pumpkins, and Carla turned chokos into something closely resembling apples by cooking them with sugar and tartaric acid. Served with plenty of custard or goats' cream, or in a pie, Marion could hardly tell the difference.

Then the monsoon trough retreated, and the country began to dry up, and through the dominion of tall green grasses and stretches of blue waterlilies the outside world began to penetrate. The tribe came back, a shame-faced Larry with them. The Queensland Ringer turned up with two packhorses and a lanky mate named Dick, who hailed from the Channel Country and wanted to put in a spell in the north. Jim put them on the books straight away, and set them to building a wing on the homestead yards in preparation for the horse muster.

Mick was still breaking in the colts when the first loading truck pulled in to the delighted cheers and yackis of children and blacks. The passenger in the cabin proved to be Peter, tanned and grinning and as full of skite as the Queensland Ringer. Marion's heart leapt in anticipatory pleasure. The marking-time of the Wet season was over, and the cattle work became the hub around which the station revolved.

Banner had been picked up in the first round of the horse muster, and when Jim had commented that it was a pity that such a likely looking horse was destined to be no more than what he termed a "house pet", Marion allowed herself to be persuaded to hand him over to Mick to train as a stock horse with his string of colts. Jim gave her a mare to ride in Banner's place, while he put in the season in the camp. Jenny was quiet, but not too quiet, and had plenty of pace, so Marion was pleased enough at the prospect of Banner's apprenticeship. This had been arranged before Peter's return, but his nose was out of joint that Marion had entrusted Banner to Mick and not to him.

"Oh, be your age, Peter!" she told him. "Mick knows all about working horses. You're just learning yourself. Anyway, I didn't even know for sure that you were coming back when we decided about it."

Peter had to be content with the inference that she might have considered him if he had been there, choosing to forget that she had made the direct comment that he was still a jackeroo.

She recounted the incident to Angela, with the comment that sometimes she felt years and years older than Peter, not just a few months. "He's like a kid, sometimes. I'm supposed to butter him up to keep him smiling."

"You're learning too," laughed Angela. "He's just an ordinary man. Keep buttering in the things that don't really matter, but stick fast in the things that do, and you'll get on okay, both of you." But Marion was still inclined to be pig-headed on the subject.

"I don't see why I should," she said. "It's not really honest. He didn't want the job of training Banner; he only wanted me to ask him first. Then he could have said Mick would do a better job, instead of me saying it."

"Exactly," said Angela. "And you both would have got what you wanted, wouldn't you?" And she left Marion to mull, unconvinced, over the pros and cons of flattering the male ego. It would undoubtedly work with Peter sometimes, or the Queensland Ringer and his mate, but she couldn't see it having much effect on Mick; he'd see through it like a shot. He was doing it for Banner, not for her, so there'd be no point anyway. An honest thank-you was all he would expect.

"I'm too much like Mum to act any other way than I do," she concluded. "We'll have to take each other as we are." And for the most part she and Peter quite suited each other in a courtship that, because of its environment, could not follow the normal procedure of dating, dressing up, and showing the best side only of their natures. It was more a family proximity, where they lived and worked together, and the flaws had to surface sooner or later. The real persons were exposed in a matter of weeks, and the test of whether they were not merely the victims of propinquity had survived their holidays and the availability of other company their own age and the opposite sex.

When the news came through that the European war had ended, it was generally accepted that it was only a matter of time until the Japanese were pushed back from the Pacific Islands where they were still fighting so tenaciously. Most of Marion's teen-age life had been set against a background of war, but it had touched her less than most, for she had no male relatives or friends actively involved in the services. She had been an onlooker to the grief of school acquaintants at the loss of brothers and sometimes fathers; there had been a few English and Dutch girls at school from Singapore and the Dutch East Indies whose families had suddenly disappeared into the oblivion of the Japanese prison camps, overnight made dependent on the charity and sympathy of the nuns; she had knitted sox and scarves for the soldiers along with the other girls. But she had lived only on the outer fringes of a situation which, child-like, had not really concerned her because there was absolutely nothing she could do to change it.

The news that the Yanks had dropped big bombs that wiped out two whole Japanese cities, and that it was all over, was announced over the Flying Doctor network, and the excitement spread like wildfire from station to station. Everybody cheered and wept and hugged each other, whites and blacks alike, though many of the station blacks had very little idea of what the great excitement was really about. But they did know how the outback celebrated, and Pansy told Marion with glee twenty-four hours before there was official confirmation, "Big race-meetin' comin' up, Missus!"

Three weeks to organise it. Men's voices replaced the women's on the galah sessions; mustering programs were hurriedly re-arranged; the Derby publican telegraphed for extra beer supplies; women sewed dresses for the Ball from homestead curtains; likely horses were galloped on improvised tracks; and everywhere the fever pitch grew.

Five days before the agreed date Jim sent Peter, Alec and the Queensland Ringer with the horses to The Crossing to help the representatives from other stations to clear the track, set up the camps and build the necessary bough sheds and exercise the horses.

"What's at The Crossing?" Marion asked.

"A race track," laughed Angela, "cut out of the bush, and railed on one side for the last hundred yards to the winning post. Before the war there was a bough shed for the Stand,

and another for the bar, and most of the stations had a bough shed of some sort in their camps. And a Ladies and a Gents made of a forty-four gallon drum inside four posts with whitewashed hessian tacked around them. But the white ants will have eaten most of that by now. The boys will have to start from scratch, I reckon."

"Don't forget the dance-floor, Angie," grinned Jim. "That should still be okay."

"Yes," she agreed. "That's a cement slab, Marion, pretty big, and we line up trucks on one side with their headlights on for lighting. Don't forget to wear a petticoat, though, otherwise everyone can see right through your dress."

"Seen some pretty wild times, that dance-floor," said Jim. "Worth a few flat batteries, though."

The race meeting was supposed to last three days, but Carla estimated the food supplies for a week to be on the safe side. She was an old hand at race meetings, and cooked and packed unperturbed, and anticipated all Angela's suggestions.

Three days to go, and Mick drove the truck over with stores, swags, and as many of the blacks as could conceivably be fitted on board. He returned to report that half the countryside was already in residence; the track was looking good; Julna station had a mystery horse; there had been a couple of fights, one of which had involved the Queensland Ringer, who was a bit burred-up but not too bad; and that Old Fred had set up his camp already next door to the Delroy Camp.

Angela was like a kid again with Marion. She and Marion had solved the new dress problem. Whether you needed it or not you had to have a new dress for the Ball. It had always been full-length all-the-trimmings-ball-gowns in the past, and would be again in the future, cement-slab and car-headlights notwithstanding; but the rationing of the war years had put a ban on the making of long gowns for balls or weddings. Angela had a gorgeous green gown which she had worn to the last Crossing race-ball five years before, and Marion had a red one which Melinda had given her, too old in style for her, and most definitely the wrong colour for a red-head, but it might have been made for Angela. They swapped delightedly. The green gown needed taking in at the waist for Marion, but that was the work of half an hour.

"Oh Lord," gasped Marion. "What do I wear on my feet? 'Lastic-sides?"

It was little Terry who came to the rescue there. Marion used the green in his water-colour paint box to transform her soft-leather white sandals into a passable substitute. Not the best, but they'd do.

Someone had to stay home from the celebrations to mind the station. There were animals to be looked after, and there'd be strangers passing through. It wasn't like Halleys' Cut, with the Jump-Up for protection, and there were thousands of pounds worth of stores and equipment. Someone had to stay. Everyone thought of it, but nobody mentioned it until Rob brought it up at the meal-table the night before departure.

"Are you going to stay home, Dad?" he asked Jim. At eleven he was already aware of the responsibilities that might fall one day upon his own shoulders.

"No, son. I have to come, to see that everybody behaves themselves, don't I?"

"I'm going to stay," said Mick quietly. "I've been once, and there's too many rowdy fellas over there for a self-respectin' well brung-up bloke like me!"

Rob's face showed his relief that the Dad he hero-worshipped was going to be with them, and Anne, who hero-worshipped Mick, nearly burst into tears.

Departure time was supposed to be four o'clock in the morning, but it was five before they got away, and the truck was even more overloaded than the first time. Its makers would have swooned in horror if they could have seen the combination of bad roads and overloading to which the poor old thing was subjected. But it wasn't, Marion noticed as they approached their destination, any different to any of the other station trucks and vehicles, and some of them had come a lot further than the Delroy complement.

A big buxom woman announced to the world in general that they'd been three bloody days on the road to do 150 miles, and she was perishing for a drink, and had the beer truck arrived. Her tall skinny husband grinned, and told her she wasn't getting near no beer truck until she'd fixed up the tucker for the mob, and she gave him a playful swipe that would have knocked down a lesser individual, and then began shouting orders to the couple of white ringers and the pack of children still tumbling off the back of the truck.

"That's Peter and Yvonne de la Roche," whispered Angela. "When the beer truck does arrive, and she's sampled enough, she'll start talking French. They both came out here as kids, but you'd never know, would you?"

There were some familiar faces, people Marion had seen in Derby, or who had passed through the station. Fred greeted them as soon as they arrived, and Peter, exercising a horse on the track, gave a wild whoop and sent his mount towards them at a gallop. The blacks hauled down their swags, and made off to join their friends at a camp further down-river. This was one time when they would not be at the beck and call of any white man; everyone was expected to do his own chores. There would be a black-boys' horse race on each day's program, and foot-races for black men and women along with the whites' races on the third day. They would watch all the races with delight, and cheer and yacki for the horses and riders from their own stations with as much, if not more, enthusiasm as any of the white residents. Only the whites bet their hard-earned money with the two bookies who had turned up; the blacks spent theirs with the hawker.

Marion had wondered vaguely what people would do about actual cash-longa-finger; all dealings that she knew of were always done by cheque. But the committee had organised a representative from the bank in Derby, and he had come to the meeting in company with two young policemen, with a gladstone bag of notes and coins, and strict instructions to have any suspect cheques authorised by a committee member.

Jim changed a cheque and strode over to the group of waiting Delroy blacks. Marion noticed that he gave them all varying amounts, but all in ten-shilling notes, nothing larger, and they all immediately made a bee-line for the hawker's van.

"Nick over there, will you, Marion," Jim whispered, "and just stand by, and see the hawker doesn't cheat them with change. I'll get Angie to relieve you in a little while."

She followed the chattering group, and looked with interest at the coloured handkerchiefs, packs of cards, pocket knives, combs and mirrors, and gaudy dresses, and saw the wisdom of Jim's hand-outs. To most of the happy blacks the difference between a ten-shilling note and a five-pound note was a mystery, in that land where real money was a rarity, and it would be simple for an unscrupulous person to cheat them. The Afghan hawker spotted Marion immediately, muttered something to his lean young offsider, and the Delroy contingent got value for its money, and some change to boot.

By nightfall Marion, with Peter now at her side, had met nearly everyone of the couple of hundred revellers. Some names she would remember, because she had heard of their owners and their exploits; others she didn't always catch. The people she remembered easiest were those who answered only to nicknames, like their own Queensland Ringer; she hadn't the faintest idea what his real name was, and she'd known him for over a year.

There was Windmill Jones and his two black boys, Sancho and Panza, an inseparable trio. He was a grizzled fellow in his late forties, and his two offsiders were in their mid-twenties, and had been together since he had come across the two little boys, about four and six, starving and emaciated, near a primitive camp at a desert waterhole out in "tiger country". They spoke no vestige of pidgin English, but the bloated corpses of the man and the lubra who must have been their parents told a clear enough story. They had been speared and clubbed, probably while sleeping, and either the children had been overlooked, or had escaped in the fracas. The murderer or murderers would not have bothered to follow them up if they had known of their existence, because it was unlikely they would survive for long in that inhospitable country.

But Windmill, poking about "looking at country" in between jobs, did find them, and, as dispassionately as he would have tended a wounded animal, nursed them back to health, and gradually taught them English. Not then, or at any time since, had they been able to tell him where they came from, or what had happened. The trauma seemed to have wiped their minds clear of any life they had lived before Windmill found them. Now they were like sons to him, good offsiders in his trade of tank-building and windmill erection. They spoke good English, and had little or no connection with any other blacks, for they had no tribal connections, and saw the world through the same eyes as any itinerant white man whose life was lived in outback places. Where they were not welcome because of their colour, Windmill Jones himself did not go.

But the races were for everyone. For obvious reasons Sancho and Panza could not make their camp with the blacks, and as the Queensland Ringer said, "if yer keep yer eyes closed, it's just like talkin' to any other white man."

The three made their camp with Old Fred, and another old chap known only as Calamity, whom Fred had known way back.

The beer truck arrived just on dark, and by the aid of pressure lamps the first crates were unloaded into the bough-shed bar, and a two-bottle limit was sold to the enthusiastic customers.

"War's over, but she's still rationed, boys," warned the barman. "We gotta make her last coupla days, anyway!"

Jim, Peter and Fred brought their quotas back to the camp, and though the beer did not last out the hour the flow of visitors from other camps did not cease until near midnight. Peter and Marion sat on Peter's rolled swag and held hands in the firelight, and listened in awe to the exuberant and exaggerated yarns which were tossed back and forth, and noted that every station represented believed that the Cup winner, the Bracelet winner, and the footrace winners black and white, would all come from their own neck of the woods.

When Marion finally stumbled off to her swag in the bough-shed bedroom she shared with Angela, Anne, Carla and Katy, she was dog-tired from the day's excitements, but avid for the fun of the coming days. The men and boys had all laid out their swags in the open; there was no need of privacy for them. As in the stock-camp, all they took off were their boots and their hats, and most of them had worn their hats right up till that moment, although sundown was six or more hours behind them.

Chapter 11

Race-meeting at the Crossing

Hilarious and hectic, the first day of the races. Bright colours of clothes, the brightest of all among the blacks; sounds of loud cheerful conversations and bursts of laughter; the smells of frying steak, of dust and leather and tangy woodsmoke of cooking fires; it was the combination that could only belong to an outback race meeting.

The bar opened at two o'clock, despite the plaintive pleadings that had gone on all morning. The races had started at mid-day, and Peter had already come in third in The Maiden, and Delroy had its first ribbon. Old Fred won the big race of the first day by a short head, and by evening the betting on the Cup was evenly divided between his mount and the Julna horse. The old man was so elated that he began celebrating somewhat unwisely at the bar, and Angela began to worry whether he'd be in a fit state the next day. Jim said he'd keep an eye on him, and Angela privately decided she'd better keep an eye on both of them herself.

Marion and Peter were inseparable. It was a thirsty day, and there was plenty of lolly-water served from one end of the bar counter, bottles only. Despite the police attendance, nobody seemed to worry about the 21 years age limit for alcohol sales, and while Marion chose to drink the lolly-water, all the young ringers decided it as fit only for the kids.

The dust of the last race had barely settled, and the groups of people began to break up and head towards their camps, when a tattoo on the horn of an old flat-bed truck, and a stentorian yell of "Bath-time, girls!" alerted Marion to the fact the she certainly did need a bath to wash away the sweat and the red dust of the day's hectic events.

"Where?" she said curiously, as Marion thrust a largish ration-bag towards her, and said, "Here, stick your towel and undies and clean stuff in that. Anne, here's yours! Now, hop up on the truck!"

Most of the women and girls, all with bags of some sort, were soon loaded, and as the truck drove off ponderously Angela explained amid the laughter and chatter that the waterhole a couple of miles up-river was reserved exclusively for the ladies' ablutions, and a similar one down-river was for the men. The earliest arrivals at the race-track had the job of making sure that the lily-studded waterholes were untenanted by crocodiles, and if there did happen to be an unwelcome saurian in residence, the hunt was on.

The truck followed barely-defined wheel tracks along the river bank and pulled up on a stony open flat above the paperbarks and pandanus that lined the river bed. The noisy passengers disembarked and stripped in the shade of the trees. The splashes, shrieks and giggles that ensued outmatched the raucous shrieks of a dozen white cockatoos disturbed from their late-afternoon reveries. One only of the ladies deferred her bath. The stout and genial driver descended from the cabin, hoisted herself and her equipment first onto the flatbed and then on to the cabin roof. Marion, standing up to her waist in water rinsing the redder dust from her red-gold hair, was astounded at the silhouette of a stout woman in shirt and jodhpurs, sitting cross-legged on the truck cabin roof with a 22 rifle across her lap supported by one hand, while the other held above her a bright floral sunshade.

The middle-age woman soaping herself a few yards away followed Marion's open-mouthed gaze and commented dryly, "Hullo, I'm Mary Taylor, and that's Shirl you're looking at. Sure-shot Shirl, makin' sure none of the bastards sneak up on us. You're the Delroy girl, aren't you, the one they call the Chestnut Filly?"

"I'm Marion Ryan, yes, from Delroy," Marion stammered. "But who'd sneak up on us - the men? They wouldn't, would they?"

"With a few rums under the belt, o' course they would, sneakin' goanners! But not with Shirl up there, they don't! She'd put a shot up their tails, soon as look at them, and don't they know it."

Anne and Katy engaged Marion's attention by diving at her legs to duck her, but she was no sooner out and towelled dry than a hoy from the truck roof was directed to her.

"Hey, you there, the Delroy girl. How about relieving the guard? I hear tell you can handle a gun when there's human goanners around!"

So while Sure-shot Shirl bathed and the stragglers came out of the water, Marion found herself on sentry-go under the floral umbrella, giggling at the thought of what the good nuns from school would say if they could see her now.

Those who had missed the ride on the truck came straggling along in utilities, and all shouted a greeting to her, sitting like a queen under her bright sunshade. Then, clean and refreshed, everyone made back to their camps and the evening meal.

"No grog till after!" said Jim firmly to his contingent. Fred, cleaned-up and nearly sober, nodded his head owlishly, and everyone, churchgoer and bush baptist alike, made for the large Julna camp, where the A.I.M. padre was to hold a service in thanksgiving for the ending of the war which had sobered their lives for so long. It was a moving service under the stars with the congregation seated on improvised forms or swag-covers spread out on the ground, and there were tears in more than one eye for the memory of those ringers who had once revelled here, but were now buried in some foreign grave.

The "branding" came next, when six bush children were christened, including a leggy kid of about seven, Shirl's boy, who didn't seem too keen on the idea and had to be cuffed into place by his mother.

The supper provided by the ladies was a wizardry of cakes and biscuits and dainty sandwiches, and Marion marvelled that so many artistically iced cakes could have survived the long distance they had come.

"We have the big supper tonight," whispered Angela, "while everyone's still fit enough to appreciate it. A lot of them won't make it through the Ball, and this way, the kids get to come, too!"

They were still eating when a couple of the men spread a swag in front of the padre and called for quiet.

"We're having a calico muster for Paddy Doonan's Missus and the kids," one of them announced, and threw a couple of notes onto the swag. Immediately others followed suit, and the pile of notes and cheques mounted up.

"Kathy Doonan's working at the pub in Derby, ever since she got the telegram that Paddy wasn't coming home again, and the Padre here will see she gets the money, and thanks to you all," said the big, genial man who had been the bookmaker at the course. "And if you bet up big tomorrow, folks, she'll get a bit more, because I'll split my winnings with her."

"Should be plenty," yelled a wit from the back of the crowd, "considering the lousy odds yer givin'!"

Marion, as she and Peter walked back to their camp, could not help but feel warmed by the generosity of these people, some of whom she had just met, but with whom she felt as one as she had never done before. As she threw her own pound note onto the pile she had noticed that many of the older men were dropping three or four notes, tens and twenties too. Peter was impressed also.

"When you marry me, I hope they don't ever have to have a calico muster for you," he said.

Marion looked at him, startled, but they were then right at the camp, and the Queensland Ringer was bawling at them to come and have a pannikin of coffee, and the moment was passed.

The second day of the races was the big day, and Carla's cheerful voice calling "Daylight!" had everyone out of their swags while the birds were still heralding the dawn. Carla wanted breakfast over and the camp cleaned up early so she could have most of the day to herself. Old Fred, exercising Faugh-a-ballagh on the track, returned barely in time to be served with fried curry and toast to keep up his strength for the big race.

"Faugh-a-ballagh, that's an Irish war-cry, isn't it?" laughed Marion, as Fred tucked in. "My grandpa says his ancestors used to yell it at the English when they fought against Cromwell."

"And yer ancestors always knew a good horse, Marion," said Fred, with the straightest of faces, "so you be after putting yer money on this one this afternoon."

"He knows I know," thought Marion, and with an impish grin, she replied, "I sure will, Uncle Fred!" Fred winked a wrinkled eye-lid, and laid a finger across his lips, and Marion winked back at him.

Faugh-a-ballagh won the Cup, and Peter de la Roche's horse won the Bracelet for Yvonne, and Shirl won the ladies' race on a clumper, with Marion in the middle of the field on Peter's horse. At the end of the day Delroy's position improved when Jim won the Jumbo stakes, and Alec won the Blackboys' Race, and there was much elation in their camp as they all made ready for the Ball. Marion hadn't expected to win her race on a borrowed horse, and in such exalted company, but she had much higher expectations for the footracing on the Gymkhana Day which would end the meeting tomorrow; she'd do her bit for Delroy there.

Jim insisted on driving Angela, Marion and Carla, in all their finery, to the cement block beside the race-track winning post, so their shoes and the hems of their dresses would not be soiled in the dust if they walked. It was only a few hundred yards, and they rode in state on the back of the truck to the whoops and cheers of their own menfolk and others they passed on the way.

Vehicles were already lined up with headlights blazing around the perimeter of the dance-floor, and the orchestra was tuning up - two guitars and one squeezebox. The Julna manager, as Master of Ceremonies, had already overcome the disappointment of losing the Cup and the six months' salary he had bet on his horse, and was exhorting all and sundry to step up for the barn-dance.

Peter grabbed Marion and swirled her onto the floor, and soon she passed from partner to partner, all fresh-shaved, white-shirted but tie-less, and tapping their feet in their high-heeled boots with a tireless energy. Marion had never enjoyed herself so much. She didn't miss a dance, and she lost count of her partners, except for Peter, who claimed her for every third or fourth dance. Carla, rotund in red, did not sit out a dance either, with Windmill Jones as a constant escort. Yvonne de la Roche was cheerfully tight before the evening was half under-way, and all her partners were "Cheri" until one accidentally stood on her toes, and then it was something else which Marion could not understand, being limited to schoolgirl French. Angela danced sedately by with the Queensland Ringer, who was maudlin, but not too maudlin, and was without doubt the best dancer on the floor, drunk or sober.

One of the guitar players began to pick out a corroboree rhythm and his partners hotted up their accompaniment; high-heeled boots began to stamp and male voices to chant; and a spontaneous and improvised dance evolved on the instant. Shirl's skinny husband spun onto the floor with arms rigidly outstretched and became a blackfellow before their very eyes, stamping out the rhythm of a totemic dance, and the dancers made way for him and began to clap the rhythm with hands instead of boomerangs. Marion was deliriously excited. The stars, the rhythm, the revelry about her combined in such a crescendo that when Peter, arm about her shoulders, whispered suddenly, "Why don't we get engaged?" she answered, "Yes, yes, let's!" without a second thought.

The M.C. announced it, and everybody cheered, and everybody drank their health. Marion found herself standing by the bar in a laughing, singing group and heard the barman say, "Well, that's it, folk. Last case opened. Then the grog's off!" She suddenly thought of Mick, all by himself back at Delroy, and grabbed Jim's arm, and said, "Lend me a quid, Jim, please." The barman handed over the two large bottles to her, and she ducked away with them to where the Delroy truck stood in the moonlight, climbed on the back, and hid the bottles in the toolbox, wrapped in a piece of hessian. She'd get Carla to pack them in the tuckerbox before they left for home.

There were some who did not seek their swags until piccaninny daylight, and others who did not find them at all, but collapsed where they stood, or rather, leaned. When the gymkhana began at midday, one lanky ringer, propped against the judge's box, slid down and passed out at Marion's and Pansy's feet, and Pansy commented, "Poor bugger - too much 'e bin eatim beer!" She had been persuaded by Angela to represent Delroy in the Lubras' Foot-race, and despite her protests that she was "nomore skinny fella, allasame racehorse," enter she did, and came flying home first, to make a Delroy double with Marion winning the Ladies' Sprint by five lengths. The Queensland Ringer would undoubtedly have won the Men's Foot-race too, if Sancho Jones, barred from entering by a ricked ankle but betting big on his brother Panza, hadn't sooled his blue heeler onto the Queensland Ringer in the heat of the moment. A cranky ringer named Dick had bet on the Queensland Ringer, so he took a swing at Sancho, who forgot about his ankle and hit back. The bookie jumped in and took bets on the fight, which was good while it lasted. Panza bet on Dick and won five quid, the same that Sancho had won by backing him in the race, but in the camp at tea-time the brothers got into an argument because Sancho reckoned Panza should have backed his own brother whether he reckoned he'd win or not, the same as he had done.

When they broke camp next morning, the Delroy contingent was no more and no less elated, sick, burred-up or self-satisfied than any other station camp's complement. Whatever their personal state, they all agreed it had been a mighty race-meeting, and they'd all see each other again at The Crossing in a year's time.

At Delroy Mick had had a busy time. He had cleaned out first the saddle shed and then the store. He had spring-cleaned his room in the quarters, washed his blankets and dug a couple of new garden beds just on the off-chance that Angela might want them. Anything to stop the flood of newly-fledged but persistent thoughts which sneaked up on him every time he took a breather.

"I shoulda gone, and blow saving my pay from the bookies! I shoulda thrown my hat in the ring with young Pete! He's too young for her; a bit of a lightweight too! But she might reckon I'm too old, not much fun. I bet I coulda won the Bracelet for her, though!"

He made and drank countless mugs of black tea, alternately congratulating himself for sticking to his saving plan and cursing himself for not taking advantage of the race-time atmosphere to court the red-headed kid who, he now saw, wasn't such a kid after all.

Chapter 12   *Weddings, planned and impromptu*

When they got back to Delroy, Mick met Jim's inquiry of "How was it?" with a monosyllabic "Quiet!" and thereafter became known as The Quiet Fella to all the district, with the exception of the blacks, to whom he had always been Mikardi and always would be.

"Marion and Peter got engaged! Marion and Peter got engaged! They're going to get married!" chanted Anne and Terry. No-one noticed the sudden start in Mick's dark eyes or the momentary tightening of his jaw.

When Marion produced the two bottles of beer intact from Carla's tucker-box with an exaggerated flourish, he accepted them with a quiet "Well then, I'll drink to your health." Marion hardly had time to register that the friendly hug she'd half expected was not forthcoming, when she was upstaged by Anne and Katy, who had each bought him a bright neckerchief from the hawker's van, a blue one from Anne and a red one from Katy.

To Marion, the rest of that year fled by on wings. She did not see all that much of Peter, because the mustering camp was away from the homestead three and four weeks at a time, and then home only long enough to hand over the bullocks to the drover, to repair gear, change horses and stock up the tuckerbags. The stockcamp delivered the final mob for the year to Wyndham, and when they returned it was nigh on Christmas, and the end of Marion's stay at Delroy. She and Peter were to fly south to Carnarvon, where she would spend a week with his family before going on to Mudjinup for Christmas. The wedding was tentatively set for sometime late in January in Perth, when Jim and Angela and the family would be there on a holiday and to settle Rob into boarding school. And to find a new governess, said Angela wryly.

Marion had even hoped that Old Fred might have been at the wedding too. She had given him the latest photos of Grandpa and his old home, and elicited from him his permission to tell her family of his existence, though they agreed there was no need for anyone else to know. But if he considered making the trip it was not for long.

"Halley's been me name a lot longer than Ryan, Marion, and I got me a family, all me blacks, up here now. More better you just tell George to come up and see me, eh. I could show the young fella a few horses'd make his eyes stick out, I reckon!"

Marion had written to Maggie about her engagement, but she did not mention Fred; that news could keep till Christmas. Maggie's reply had been almost non-committal, but Marion could tell she was pleased.

"She won't have to struggle like we had to, Pa," she told Grandpa, and proceeded to the one-and-only uncharacteristic deed of her life.

"I'm not going to muck up things for Marion with her in-laws," she told a delighted Ralph. "We'll get married quietly as soon as you can arrange it."

Grandpa was equally pleased, and made no bones about Maggie's proposed shift to the farm.

"I've batched before, and I can batch again," he said, "and I'll come up to you for a feed on Sundays."

As it happened he was not to batch alone, because Davey seized on the opportunity to push his case to leave school now that he was fourteen. He wanted to become an apprentice to Grandpa, who was whole-heartedly on his side, and Maggie, who had till then been doubtful about Davey leaving school, was soon persuaded to agree.

Marion got all this news in a rare letter from Davey, who attributed the success of his pleadings to Marion's pending marriage, but she did not know that one of the factors that had influenced Maggie was her realisation that the wedding certificate would require the name of Marion's father, and that was something she had no intention of revealing. Ralph's name as step-father would do very well instead. When she told Ralph this he grinned delightedly, dug her in the ribs and chuckled, "Well, when it comes to Davey's turn, it'll be true, won't it! When we get married I suppose we ought to tell him. You were so damn proud, Maggie, you'd never let me do anything for my own kid, so it's nice to know I'm going to be of some use to Ginger now!"

Marion, although she had sometimes thought about it, had never got around to telling Peter about her background; the moment had never seemed right. She knew it wouldn't make any difference to him, but she was not so sure about his family. "Marion, daughter of Miss M. Ryan," on the wedding invitation would hardly meet with the same approval as "Daughter of Mr. and Mrs. Ralph Johnson" in the eyes of the landed gentry round Carnarvon.

And she realised just how right her supposition had been when she and Peter arrived at Box Hill in December. Mary Blythe was charming, and John Blythe obviously accepted her as a fitting bride for their older son, but there was none of the family warmth of the little cottage at Mudjinup. Peter escorted her round to the homesteads of family friends, but at none of them could Marion imagine being greeted as Ralph might have greeted her, or Angela and Jim back at Delroy. Peter, who knew of her intention to seek out the Kicketts some time during her stay at Box Hill, was openly relieved that the whole family was absent on seasonal work in some other district. Marion could see that she was never going to become really close to any other members of Peter's family, but then, they didn't really seem very close to each other.

Peter took her riding over the run in the early mornings, and she enjoyed these sojourns far more than the evenings with the family. One day they visited the adjoining property, which was also owned by the family, but managed by a young couple with two small children. Yalunga had been purchased some years before for Peter, and it was there they would live when they were married. Marion loved what she saw of the place immediately, but she could not help wondering what would become of the people who lived there now, and asked John Blythe after dinner that evening.

"Oh, I suppose he'll find something else. He's always known the place was Peter's when he married, though I don't suppose any of us thought it would be so soon. You're both very young, you know."

He went on to explain that his employee wasn't really a manager, because Yalunga was being run as an outstation of Box Hill, and naturally, would continue to be. All the important decisions were made by himself at Box Hill. Marion wasn't really keen at the sound of that, but Peter didn't seem to mind that Yalunga was to be their place only in name. She consoled herself that he would grow into the responsibility in time, though the old man had a pretty tight rein on the properties, and his family too, as far as she could see, and Peter might have a job ahead of him prising his independence from his father's hold.

The two families would not meet until the wedding, which the Blythes had firmly decided that they would organise when they learned that Ralph Johnson was only Marion's new step-father. "We can afford it," John said, "and we've a lot of friends who ought to be invited to Peter's wedding, and we wouldn't feel right about the expense with you only wanting a handful of guests."

"I don't want a big wedding," she whispered fiercely to Peter, but he wasn't much help.

"You go down and organise your dress and all the trimmings, and don't worry about it. You'll love it when the day comes; all the girls do."

When Maggie and Ralph and Grandpa and Davey met her at Mudjinup station the first thing Ralph said was "Well, bugger me, Ginger. You've got your block already. Took me till I was nearly forty, and you're only nineteen!"

She showed them photographs of Peter and his family, and Box Hill and Yalunga and they were suitably impressed. A photograph of Old Fred winning the cup on Faugh-a-ballagh was also in the box of loose photos, and this seemed just the right time to tell them all about their long-lost relative, who also owned a station. All thoughts of Peter and Box Hill were instantly relegated to the background, and they yarned well into the night about Fred and Halley's Cut, and Grandpa could hardly contain his excitement. He'd never thought that he would ever know what happened to the brother who had left home so long ago, and here he was, a station owner in his own right, and a cup winner to boot.

"He's got the best horses in the district, Grandpa," Marion assured him, and Grandpa nodded his head with a tear of remembrance in his eye, and said "That'd be Fred, that'd be Fred!"

In the days that followed there was little time amid the Christmas preparations for Marion to really talk to Maggie. There was a subtle difference now between the old Maggie Ryan and the new Maggie Johnson, who seemed to be as approving of the traditional wedding the Blythes had planned as the old Maggie would have been doubtful. She even volunteered to travel to Perth in the New Year with Marion to help her choose the wedding gown and accessories, but Marion explained that she would have to see her friend, Annette, and ask her to be bridesmaid, and she would probably be a week at least in Perth. Perhaps the dress would have to be made by a dressmaker; if she needed Maggie's help she would phone her at the farm, and Ralph could drive her down for the day.

She went to Perth by train the day after New Year, knowing that she could phone Annette and immediately be made welcome at her home, but feeling the need to be alone for a little time at least. She booked a room at the hotel where she had first met Angela, and by chance was given the very same room in which the interview had taken place. That made her think of Delroy, and she lay on the bed and snivelled a little, and wondered whether the Wet had come in for Christmas, and whether Old Fred had made it across from The Cut, as they said he always did unless the rivers were running bankers. She pictured her old room opening on to the wide verandah, which she was never likely to see again, and felt a violent surge of jealousy towards the unknown girl who would, in a few short weeks, take her place there. It was only mid-afternoon, and Marion must have spent an hour indulging herself in the misery of home-sickness for the north and her friends there. Then she decided she was being childish and silly, she, who had always known what she wanted, was acting like a little kid. She would wash her face, go downstairs and buy a packet of cigarettes, come back to her room and make her plans for the morrow like any sensible young woman about to be married to one of the most eligible young men in the country, who loved her and whom she loved. Oh, but did she really?

She got into the lift and pressed the button for the ground floor. She had seen cigarettes for sale at a kiosk near the office, so she would get a packet there. The door slid open, and she stepped out. At the office counter a man was bent forward, obviously signing the register, and a cigarette swag was leant against the counter beside him. The silhouette of broad shoulders in blue shirt, and tight stockman-cut trousers above high-heeled boots was so familiar, but it was the broad-brimmed hat lying on the counter with its unique curl on either side that made her heart leap in her breast.

"Mick!" she shrieked, and next moment, oblivious of the startled glances around her, she had thrown herself into his arms, and was bawling her heart out against his chest.

Mick patted her shoulder, slapped his hat on his head, and hoisting his swag with one arm, he put the other around her and led her back towards the lift. She thrust her room key at him and wept copiously against him until the rolled-up sleeve of the blue shirt was soaking wet. When he dropped the swag to unlock her door, she was still crying and clinging to him. He shoved the swag inside and kicked the door shut with his foot. Then he picked her up and carried her gently to the bed, and sat, cradling her in his arms until her sobbing eased.

"Oh, Mick," she whimpered, "it's all gone wrong. I don't want to marry Peter. I want to go home!" and she burst into a fresh bout of tears.

"Home is where the heart is," said Mick softly, and took the blue neckerchief which Anne had given him from his pocket and wiped her face with it, and kissed her firmly on the lips. "Marry me instead, little Ginger, for I love you like nobody ever got loved before!"

"Oh yes, oh Mick, oh yes," she whispered. "Why didn't I know? Why couldn't I tell?"

He took her hand and eased Peter's ring from the finger and put the ring on the bedside table. Then he kissed her again, and there were no doubts, and there never would be. The room faded, and a million lights burst and shattered in a blaze of gold.

"I was coming to Mudjinup to tell you myself," he said. "I got your address from Angela. Every night, like a little blackfellow, you kept callin' me. So I came."

"But, Mick," she said wonderingly, "I never thought of you at all; I only thought about myself, and why I wasn't happy when I thought I had everything."

"Yeah," said Mick patiently, twining a red-gold curl around a calloused finger, "I heard you."

She suddenly began to giggle.

"I wanted a smoke, so I went downstairs to buy some, but you drove it out of my mind. So put your pants back on, boyo, and roll me one now."

"It's coming up two years since I taught you to roll a smoke," he said, fishing for the tobacco tin in the pocket of the discarded blue shirt, "and I don't carry any lightweights in my camp. But, seeing it's a special occasion, I'll make an exception this time."

She threw the pillow at him and knocked the open tin spinning so that the tobacco spilled out onto the carpet. There might have been carpet fluff included when he finally built their smokes, but if there was they didn't notice.

Marion wrote the letter to Peter that night, when Mick had finally gone to his room, and packed the ring and the gold watch Peter had given her for Christmas to be registered and posted at the GPO the next morning. It was easier than she thought. She didn't mention Mick, only that she had realised they weren't right for each other, and she was sorry for all the inconvenience to his family. Once the letter was posted she forgot Peter entirely. There was a lot to do. After all, she had a wedding dress to buy. Mick helped her choose a green voile summer frock and shoes to match, and when he bought grey gaberdine stockman-cut trousers and a white shirt she added a tie, and over-rode his protests that he hadn't worn one since he was a kid. They filled in forms at the Registry Office and were told to come back at four the following afternoon with two witnesses.

Mick's time down south was limited; he had to be back in Derby to meet Jim and Angela by the 14th, so they could have their holiday as planned while he took the truck back to Delroy and managed the station until their return.

"I didn't plan to stay on after that," he told her. "Reckoned I was due for a change. Thought I might poke over to the Territory, and maybe look at a bit of country. Like the idea?"

She loved it. Between them they had saved almost two thousand pounds, for Mick had been north all the war years, with only the occasional trip to Derby or Wyndham, and not even a race meeting where he could blue any of his savings. They decided to go straight to Mudjinup the day after they were married, and then to have three or four days on Rottnest Island before catching the plane back to Derby.

Marion made the excuse that she wanted a store-bought haircut for her wedding and said she'd meet Mick back at the hotel. She managed to visit the hairdresser, and also a doctor, because if it wasn't already too late, she didn't want to get pregnant. She wanted Mick all to herself; there wasn't any place for a baby in their lives just yet, that would come later.

When she did meet Mick at the hotel he had found the witnesses for them. He'd gone to the pub which he'd been told the unattached ringers from up north considered their watering place, and there he'd found not one, but three, acquaintances, one of whom was chatting up the barmaid, who happened to be off duty the next afternoon, and all four of them had happily agreed to come along.

After dinner Mick told the manageress their plans, and she smilingly agreed to shift them to a double room the next night. Then they went to the pictures and saw the film "For Whom the Bell Tolls" and held hands like a pair of kids.

By unspoken mutual agreement Mick did not come into her room when they got back to the hotel, but kissed her outside the door, and whispered "Tomorrow, Ginger!"

The little group waiting for them outside the Registry Office had obviously already taken aboard a number of preliminary toasts, and were drawing the amused glances of the passers-by and the occasional wowserish sniff of disapproval, but once inside they quieted down temporarily while the Registrar performed the ceremony. Mick and Marion had bought the ring that morning, a simple gold band. Mick had easily fielded the jeweller's attempts to sell him an engagement ring as well with the comment that he'd buy her a pearl-handled pocket-knife instead, which would be a lot more useful. They spent as much time choosing the pocket-knife as the ring, and it went to the wedding in her bag along with her hanky and comb.

Mick paid the fee and received the marriage lines, which Marion folded and tucked in her bag; everyone kissed everyone else; and then they were out in the street again. That was when Barbie, the barmaid, took over.

"Back to the pub, all," she ordered, "for the wedding breakfast, dinner, or tea, whatever youse like to call it!"

She, with the help of the boys, and the publican, who had a soft spot for his northern clientele and their free and easy attitude to spending up big, had bought a wedding cake, given orders to the cook, and turned over the pub dining room. All the current guests were invited, and the staff by the end of the evening had all joined the party too. Some, knowing the plans, had even bought presents. Marion enjoyed her wedding reception even more than she had enjoyed the Crossing Races. Apart from Mick, she had never met any of the people there, but that would also have been the case with most of the guests if she'd gone ahead and married Peter.

Mick had got his tie off and stuffed in his pocket long before they opened the first bottle of champagne. Marion had never tasted champagne before, and the bubbles got up her nose. She liked it, and pronounced it "proper-flash lolly-water." The Quiet Fella, aware that his bride was under-age, and not sure whether the city constabulary would be as accommodating as their northern compatriots, kept a wary eye on her glass. Somebody called for a speech from the groom, and Mick, the man of few words, obliged.

"Thanks, everyone, from both of us." He stopped, and turned to look with dancing blue eyes at Marion. "Yer know," he confided to the expectant faces, "it gets mighty cold out on the plains in the Dry. I reckon she's gunna be worth about six dogs in a man's swag!" The guests cheered.

"Speech from the bride!" they yelled.

Marion was beginning to notice a sort of golden haze towards the back of the room, but she shook her head and focussed on the faces in front of her, and said impishly, "I wonder what he reckons I'm worth in the summer-time!"

"Hey," said Mick, grabbing her arms, "I'm taking you home," and to the laughter and cheers he steered her to the door.

"Let's find out," he grinned, as he helped her into a taxi. They did.

Ralph met them at Mudjinup railway station. He had only expected Marion, and when she introduced Mick he grabbed his hand and shook it and roared with laughter.

"You didn't hang onto that block for long, Ginger," he chortled, "but looks as if you've got something good in its place."

He shepherded them into the car, explaining that he'd dropped Maggie off at the cottage with some cooking she'd done for Grandpa and Davey. He was still chuckling when they pulled up outside the cottage.

"Hey, Maggie," he called, as she came expectantly out onto the verandah. "I got you under false pretences, love. She's not going to marry Peter; she's already married. This is Mick!"

It was just as Marion had assured Mick it would be. They were all delighted with him, especially Grandpa, who was thrilled as a kid to meet someone who had known his long-lost brother Fred for years, and was full of anecdotes about him. Maggie, aware of the delirious happiness of her daughter compared to the quiet, almost-introverted girl who had left home a few short days before, accepted her son-in-law immediately. It was a grinning Ralph who explained to him how Maggie had succumbed to "responsibility", and asked him whether his family would have expected the same. It turned out that Mick had grown up in an Adelaide orphanage, and knew nothing of his family. The matron had commented that the baby dumped in a basket in the orphanage foyer was a hardy little fellow, and that was how he got his surname. The Michael part of it came about because unknown new arrivals were named alphabetically as they arrived, and M was next on the list. He'd been fostered out to a farmer in the Adelaide Hills at twelve, who'd overworked and underfed him, and resented the few hours away at school each day, so that Mick, at fourteen, had run away and worked his way north. He was twenty-eight, and his birthday was the first of August, give or take a few days.

"Same as the horses' birthday," said Grandpa, "easy to remember!"

When they got back to the farm it was well after midnight, but Ralph insisted on drinking their health, and produced a bottle of whiskey and glasses, and they sat around the kitchen table. "Oh," said Maggie, "a letter came for you yesterday, Marion. I'll get it."

It was a letter from Peter's mother, enclosing a proposed list of guests for Marion's approval and possible additions before the invitations were sent out. When Marion tossed it down the table Maggie idly picked it up and began to scan down the list. The next moment she was choking on her drink, and whooping and coughing, and Ralph had to thump her on the back, and produce his handkerchief for her to wipe her streaming face.

"Well, I never!" she said, still half laughing and coughing together.

"What's all that about?" queried Ralph.

"Marion's father," she giggled. "Marion's father and his wife, they're on the list. Imagine his face when he saw me, and realised I'd had the baby after all. Looks like you might have saved an embarrassing situation all round, Mick."

Marion looked for the letter to scan the list out of curiosity, but only the envelope was there. Maggie helped her look for it innocently, still giggling, and Marion knew that she wasn't even going to be able to limit the mystery of her paternity to a possible fifty or so, not if Maggie knew anything about it.

"What's it matter, anyway?" grinned Mick, when she grumbled to him later in bed. "We're both in the same boat, and it's the future that counts."

They didn't get their short honeymoon on Rottnest Island after all. They spent the whole week on the farm, or at the cottage, and Mick and Ralph had long yarns together, and Mick, who had been secretly afraid that Maggie might have been upset, knew that he had been unconditionally accepted into the family and was happy for Marion's sake.

They had only a day in Perth before they caught the Derby plane, and most of that was spent at the saddlers, ordering packs to be made and sent up on the first boat, and at the Army Disposals store, where Mick chose two Army trunks, jackets and hats for them both, and other assorted gear, all to follow them by boat. Mick was especially pleased with the stout canteens and a leather rifle scabbard to fit a saddle.

"This stuff will be perfect for when we make the Grand Tour," he told Marion, "and it's a quarter of the price we'd pay for new stuff."

He also chose the camp ovens and billy cans, but when they were all packed and paid for, Marion's eyes fell on a stock of enamel plates and pannikins, and the owner of the shop gave her two of each and two sets of cutlery, and one trunk was opened to squeeze them in. When Marion told him they were just married he became even more expansive and offered to loan Mick his utility to take the trunks to the shipping office in Fremantle, and when Mick demurred and said he'd never driven in traffic before, the owner called his wife down from upstairs to mind the shop, and insisted on driving them to the port himself. Although Mick had spent nearly fifty pounds, it was still a nice gesture, and they capped it after the trunks were finally consigned, by buying cooked prawns from a roadside kiosk, and shelling and eating them all the way back to the city in the late afternoon. They were on first name terms long before they parted, and Jeff had admitted to a season as a meatworker in Wyndham when he was still single, and told Mick that if he ever wanted any gear sent up on the boat he only had to write and let him know. Though Mick would never have any time for big cities, he reckoned, as cities go, Perth would have to be one of the best.

As the plane made the approach to the Derby airstrip the vivid green of the terrain and the intermittent sparkle of sunlight on stretches of water told the passengers that the Wet season rains were well-established, but they could see the Delroy truck like a toy at the end of a strip with a tiny figure squatting beside it.

The expression on Jim Burton's face when Marion followed Mick off the plane was, in Mick's words, that of a stunned goanna, but his recovery was immediate and he drawled laconically.

"G'day, you two. How long you been gone, Mick? Two weeks? For a quiet fella you must have done a wing of talking!"

"Nope, just the usual," grinned Mick, "and I've got an offsider now to do most of it for me!"

Back at the pub the more perceptive Angela was not at all surprised; she had known the reason for Mick's sudden decision to take a break down south, and the result was no less than she had expected. The kids were delighted.

"Peter's nice, but Mick's better," confided Anne. "I was going to marry him myself when I grow up, but he's a bit old, I spose, so I don't mind you having him, Marion."

The family was to catch the plane on its return trip the following day, and Mick booked into the pub for the night with Marion. The evening meal was a quiet celebration in their honour.

"I'm pretty-well cleaned out till the boat gets in," said the publican. "I ain't got any champagne, but there's a bottle of Russian plonk on the back of the shelf. Vodka, they call it. Like to try that?"

Jim said they would, and Angela put a dash of it in lemonade for the children.

Jim gave the toast -

"To the Chestnut Filly and the Quiet Fella. In the land where only the best of us come out even, may they have more than a fighting chance!"

Part 2
Serendipity

Chapter 13

The Grand Tour

As soon as the family had been farewelled on the plane, Mick made haste to collect the few items from the store, which Angela had listed, and Marion sought out Carla in the little cottage where she and Katy spent their holiday with her old mother, a little old black lady of great dignity, and her sister Mitzi, who was a wardsmaid at the hospital.

Carla didn't seem all that surprised to see her. Her plump face wreathed in a self-satisfied grin, and she said, "Thought you'd come to your senses before it was too late. You done a lot better for yourself, Marion, than you deserved, wasting all that time on that uppity young fella!"

Marion managed to persuade her that Katy's schooling would not be neglected under a new governess, and Carla offered to teach her a few tricks of the trade of station cooking when she returned to Delroy with the Burtons, before Mick and Marion left, and she dictated her foolproof bread recipe, which Marion scribbled on the back of an envelope, to carry her through the next few weeks.

The trip back to Delroy was average for the early Wet season; they got bogged once, and had a few near-misses. The rain threatened but held off during the two-day trip, and neither of them really noticed the steamy heat in the plans they made for the future. They were dirty, sweaty, and deliriously happy. At Delroy Sam the saddler had been batching, and Alec, who had not gone walkabout with the tribe, was offsiding for him and learning a few of the finer points of saddle-repairs. They greeted Mick and Marion with broad grins and open arms, and when Marion saw the state of Carla's kitchen, she could guess why.

For all that there were only four of them, no blacks, no children, no stock camp to worry about, the days were full enough. Cooking and cleaning without the usual assistance of the black girls was a full-time job for Marion, but Maggie's early training stood her in good stead. Mick answered the wireless, made the weather reports, and wrote up the station diary. He lost no time in calling up Howe Charlie and telling Fred about the wedding, to which news Fred responded by promising them two of his best colts for a wedding present as soon as the road was clear after the Wet. Mick asked him to break-in another four young horses while he was about it, which he'd like to buy, to add to the dozen or so he already owned on Delroy.

The monsoon rains settled in, the creeks ran bankers, and the grass grew inches overnight. Mick telegraphed weekly reports to Jim, and Marion, in exchange for washing-up the dishes after midday and evening meals, spent an hour or more after supper each night at her old job. Sam had admitted that he'd never been to school and felt the handicap of not being able to read and write, and was almost embarrassingly grateful when Marion offered to teach him.

"Can't leave Alec out in the cold," said Mick, "you may as well teach him too."

So despite the flying insects round the light on the big kitchen table, the pupils sat down to master their letters from the primers from the school-room, and both were elated at their easy mastery of the new skill. By the middle of February, Marion knew that both of them had enough basic knowledge to get by, and that she had opened up a new world to them. Unbeknown to her, Sam fashioned a pair of leggings and a plaited belt, and Alec made her a redhide bridle and a saddle-bag, as payment for her labours.

As the time approached to make the trip in to Derby to pick up Angela and Jim and Anne and Terry, Mick was obviously reluctant to leave Marion on the station, although she assured him she could handle any situation which would be likely to arise in the few days he would be away. Then Jim wired to say that they would be returning by boat, and that he'd bought another vehicle for Delroy, and they'd get home under their own steam. Mick lost no time in wiring him to collect the trunks which should also be in the cargo, and Marion organised her willing helpers in a welcome-home spring-clean, with special attention to the kitchen, knowing that Carla would be returning too. Mick shifted their belongings into his old room in the quarters, and put in a day in the laundry boiling sheets and towels in the copper, which he said ran rings round the creek and a flat rock any day.

The next day the tribe came home from walkabout, and Marion had a full day's work ahead of her tending their minor ills, and issuing rations and clothing to replace the multitudinous rags they had swapped or gambled during their sojourn away. When the hauntingly familiar overtones of corroboree reached her as she lay in Mick's arms that night, she murmured, "It's more than home, up here, up north, isn't it, Mick? This is my country."

"It's more," said Mick, in that poetic flash which is second nature to the bushman. "It's my blood's country. Anywhere else is exile, okay for walkabout, but you don't feel a real person, not complete, until you get north again."

"We tick the same way as the blacks now, don't we," mused Marion. "Our blood's country, I like that. We've got a closer bond with them really than you could ever explain to whites down south."

"Well, we *are* closer to them than we are to those whites; you live close to the land for long enough some of it's got to rub off on you. All I know's I feel right up here and wrong down there."

"And poor little Rob, he's in exile right now, Mick. Gee, I'll bet he'll hate it."

"Same for the black boys his age, Honey. It's the end of being a kid and the making of man ceremony. Only lasts six months for the black kids, but it's sure a hell of a lot tougher. Toughens them up for the dry creeks to come, I guess."

Although Marion knew that the Burtons in their new vehicle could not arrive much before sundown, she imagined she heard the sound of the vehicle coming a dozen times that day. But when it finally did arrive she did not hear it, only Pansy's joyous shout from the verandah, "Truck comin', Missus!"

What a wealth of talk, and swapping of experiences and yarns, and admiration of the new truck, and savouring of good rump steak such as the travellers hadn't tasted since they left. Carla resumed immediate control of the kitchen, and the children recited their exploits to Yandi, and greeted their excited pets.

Marion saw at once that Jenny Wilson, the new governess, was going to be a stayer. She was a tall, good-natured farm girl from south of Perth, obviously very practical, and Marion felt a twinge of jealousy to see how readily the children had accepted her, as if she herself was now a thing of the past. Which, of course, she was, she had to admit. Her future lay elsewhere now, with Mick, and in a few days their time at Delroy would end.

The Grand Tour began with much the same preparations as for the stock-camp starting out for a six weeks' muster. Mick's horses and Banner were shod; Marion was introduced to the correct way to pack and load the pack-saddles, and stores and salt-beef were donated courtesy of Delroy Downs. The tin trunks were packed with the gear they could not take with them, the good clothes and wedding presents, and left in the Delroy store.

"We'll send for them," laughed Mick, "when we've got a homestead to put 'em in."

"I still think you're leaving too early," cautioned Jim, "the Wet's not over yet, and there's a lot of rivers and creeks between here and the Territory."

"We got new camp-sheets to keep the rain off," replied Mick, "and I reckon there might be a lot of fellas making for the Territory now the war's over. There's a bit of country I'd like to look at I reckon I could get a grazing licence on. But we gotta be there first up to get a look-in."

They had barely retired to their room for their last night at Delroy when there was a discreet tap at the door. In the shadows Alec stood hesitantly, and Marion heard the low rumble of conversation between him and Mick, but could not make out what they said.

She heard them bid goodnight to each other, and then Mick came to bed and told her that Alec had asked to come with them. "Sorry I couldn't say yes to him. He'd be a good man to have, but he's a key man here for Jim now that I'm going; couldn't take him away from Jim. Besides, can't afford a man yet, until we've got a place and some cattle and some money coming in; that's a fair way off yet. I explained to him and I think he understood all right."

When they said goodbye at piccaninny daylight next day Alec was not there, but Marion did not notice his absence among the hugs and well-wishing and last-minute advice from all the others. When Anne's tears began to trickle Marion felt her own eyelids prick, and she was still snivelling a mile down the track. They made Halley's Cut by sundown, and unloaded their packs on Fred's verandah. Junie sat with them for the evening meal, and after supper Marion pulled out the packet of photographs from Mudjinup which she had carried all day in her buttoned down shirt pocket. Fred accepted them with pleasure, and commented that Maggie was the spitting image of his mother as he remembered her. They stayed the next day at Halley's Cut, and put the new horses through their paces, and then it was goodbye again, and out through the foothills and down into the plains country, just the two of them and twenty-one horses, take your turns with the packs, boys, you're jacks of all trades now, no favourites, saddle-horse one day, packs the next, and a couple of days running free; hobbles every night and no going back now. The only horse which showed no sign right from the first of wanting to return to his beat was a big black gelding which Marion had named Excelsior.

Sometimes they followed roads, and sometimes they cut across country. Most days they made a good thirty miles, and for the first week they did not meet anyone, black or white. A camp routine was soon established, but the best time was lying together in the swag, looking up into the great field of stars above them, hearing the muted tinkle of the horse-bells as the feeding horses spread out, and planning together what the future might hold for them. Mick was not one for wasting words in the daylight hours, apart from instructions and explanations, and for the most part they worked and rode in companionable silence; but after nightfall, sitting round the campfire, he became poet and dreamer, and Marion realised that her formal education was but a pale shadow to that which he had gained over the years of observation and quiet thought in lonely places where the basic truths of nature were evident for those who cared to see. She was very much the student, dependent upon Mick as her teacher, and she loved every minute of it. Loners by nature, both of them, they melded day by day into a unit that neither of them would have ever dreamed possible.

The Northern Territory had been, until the war, isolated frontier country, a settlement on the northern coast at Darwin, and another at Alice Springs, and between them a thousand miles of rough track, where tributary tracks led off to the great Company cattle stations, and lesser tracks still to the homesteads of the few battlers and the camps of the prospectors. But now all that was changing. From Alice Springs to Darwin a gleaming bitumen all-weather road followed the Overland Telegraph line, built in haste by the Government to rush troops and equipment north against the possibility of Japanese invasion. Now there was access where there had been none before, and the word had gone through the north that, by taking up a grazing licence on an area of Crown land, a battler could come eventually, if he made a go of it, to lease his own bit of country and build a station on it. It was not a challenge for the faint-hearted, but to Mick and Marion it was the opportunity to have a go. Maybe they'd find a block, maybe they wouldn't, but they never once doubted that there was any other road to follow.

They camped one night at Peter de la Roche's Avignon, and spelled the horses for a day and washed their clothes. Marion was vastly amused by the sprinkling of French oaths which interlarded the pidgin conversation of Yvonne's housegirls. The station buildings were primitive compared to Delroy; the de la Roches were still very much battlers. But their hospitality was warm and genuine and Yvonne pressed a bar of fresh bread and a rich fruit cake upon the travellers as they packed up to leave, the same wrapped in two calico ration bags imprinted with a fleur de lys. "Did it with a potato cut and Indian ink," smiled Yvonne.

And so the days passed, riding always into the morning sun, Marion with the widest-brimmed hat in the Kimberleys and her shirt-sleeves buttoned to the wrist, and Mick picking out the night's camping places as the shadows of their mounts lengthened before them. Sometimes they met other travellers and stopped to yarn about the track ahead or behind them, or to share a billy of tea; sometimes they rested for the midday spell by pandanus-lined creeks if the mosquitoes weren't too bad; and sometimes they threaded their way across jump-ups and through gorges where the horses' hooves struck sparks from the rough and stony ground.

At Halls Creek, a mud-brick settlement where once thirty thousand gold-miners had toiled, reduced now to a population of about thirty, Mick applied to the local policemen for a permit to take his horses across the border and they allowed themselves the luxury of a drink at the pub, where the refrigeration unit, waiting on spare parts from Perth, was temporarily substituted by wet bags thrown over the beer crates behind the bar.

From the town they followed the road to a station near the border, good grass all the way, and brolgas dancing in their hundreds on a broad plain one late afternoon, and cattle-pads winding towards windmills on the horizon.

"I guess we've crossed the border now, "said Mick. "We'll camp tonight in the Territory," and to celebrate he picked a camp-site not too far away from a waterhole in a timber-lined creek and hobbled the horses out early. While Marion made a damper he strolled across to the waterhole with a fishing line and came back in an hour or so with a large catfish.

After the meal they sat in companionable silence. Beyond the campfire the bright moonlight cast shadows almost like daylight. Somewhere a horse neighed, and another answered it from along the creek. Then another.

Mick straightened up from his seat on the rolled-up swag where Marion leant against his knee.

"Someone coming!" he announced briefly.

They scrambled to their feet as the silhouettes of two riders approached the campfire, and Mick walked forward to meet them. The two figures dismounted and stood hesitantly beyond the firelight.

"Hell's bells!" exploded Mick. "It's Alec! Alec and -- and Pansy!"

"We been followin' you, Mick, one day behind, campin' in your camps. Nobody seen us. We kept outa sight," Alec announced simply.

"We comin' with you, Missus," contributed Pansy to an amazed Marion, as she staggered slightly with weariness.

Marion boiled the billy again and cut slabs of damper and slices of beef, while Alec turned out the two horses to join their erstwhile companions from Delroy. When Marion handed the food to Pansy the skinny black hand trembled with eagerness. It was obvious that neither she nor Alec had eaten a decent meal for some time, and it was not until the pair had eaten and drunk their fill that Mick began to question them.

"I stole the two horses, but the saddle's mine. We took it in turns to ride bareback," said Alec. "Pansy, I stole 'im too. Mightbe you can't send us back, Mick, them blacks at Delroy kill us if you do!"

He reached over and took the tobacco tin Mick handed to him. Pansy squatted in the firelight and looked up at him admiringly.

"We been mates long time, Mick," he went on. "You steal this girl," (with a nod towards Marion), "from that Peter, and you go looking for new place. I reckon, why not me too. No place for me in the tribe, and Pansy got an old husband got two wives already. She like me long time, eh, Pansy? So I tell her, fetchim swag and we go. By Christ, Mick, you travel slow alright. More better we get a move-on, okay?"

So they did. The honeymoon trip was over, and the job beckoned. Mick sent a wire to Delroy from the first Territory station they came to, and waited for a reply on the next day's session. He could not ask for a sched because the transceiver there was not on the Derby network. He reported that Alec and Pansy were with them, and asked for a price for the two horses. Jim's reply came back on the first session next morning.

"Not surprised tell Alec Pansy keep horses bonus good workers stop spears sharpened not safe they ever return stop good luck all Jim."

The station manager was on his own with the blacks, his wife down south with the children on an extended holiday, and he enjoyed the company of his unexpected visitors. The place was owned by some bigwigs down South, he told them, pretty tight with the money and no white staff except himself and his wife, they didn't pay her, anyway. Out of the way place too, didn't get much company. He produced a bottle of rum after the evening meal of steak and onions and seemed set to yarn for hours. When Marion began yawning he offered her a bed on the verandah, and he and Mick sat up yarning long after she fell asleep.

"Daylight!" Mick's cheerful voice woke her, as he pushed a steaming cup of tea in a big white china cup underneath the net to her. "We're staying a couple of days," he told her. "Bill's offered us a job too good to miss!"

Bill, it seemed, ran a few head of cattle of his own on the station, a concession from his employers to keep a regular manager there.

Mick caught Marion's quizzical glance, and laughed. "None of our business, Hon. Maybe a couple of silvertail Sydney doctors could be that stupid. Anyway, Bill's got a share with his brother on a battler's place over near The Bitumen, and he wants to shift a couple of hundred head over there. Been trying to work out how he could do it, when we came along like an answer to a prayer. We're going that way, we got the horses, and now we've got the men too. He'll pay us in cattle, fifty head of mixed steers and heifers, and I give the receipt for them to his brother when we deliver the rest ." He pulled his notebook from his shirt pocket. "I got a mud map here, and the fellow's name and description and his brand and particulars. Bill's made a map of the way to go, not the regular stock-route, but with a small mob and such a good season should be a cup of tea!"

Marion sat up and took her tea and grinned at him.

"So I'm going to be a drover's wife, eh?"

"More like a drover's cook, me darlin' girl. And first up, a ringer. We put in a couple of days helping Bill get his mob together, they're handy enough, he says, and well-handled."

At this stage Bill had called them to listen to Jim's telegram on the transceiver.

As she pulled on her boots Marion considered that life in the outback wasn't so slow as people might imagine. In the space of forty-eight hours the Hardy partnership had expanded to include a workforce and a potential nucleus for the cattle herd on the block that was yet to be.

Chapter 14   *A virgin block beckons.*

Marion's fears about the legitimacy of the undertaking turned out to be ill-founded. Bill's employers, two brothers, Sydney doctors, asked only that he turned off a certain number of saleable cattle each year and ensured that there were breeders enough to maintain the numbers; in a good season he could brand calves for himself; not so good, fewer calves. In return they didn't want to be bothered with requests for more than the bare necessities to keep the station running, and Bill considered it fair enough. They paid for his wife and kids to have an annual spell away too. Something to do with their income tax, not that they paid any tax on income earned in the Territory. Owners didn't, only the poor bloody working men. But Bill intended in time to be a full-time owner himself.

"I don't really hold with these absentee-owners, Mick," he explained, "but you gotta admit that they got the money to open up a bit of new country, and by working for them a fella does get a chance to get a start eventually himself. It's just good common-sense that they give a man a share of some sort, so's he'll make sure the place is run the best it can be."

"Not like the big English Company places, though," said Mick, "they're pretty lousy with their managers and their blacks, so I've heard!"

"Well, now," grinned Bill, "might be so, but I reckon a lot of them managers has got a share whether the bosses know it or not!"

Bill was agreeable to lend them the extra saddle they needed for Pansy, to be left with his brother, and he filled their pack saddles with dry rations from the station store, and fresh salt beef from his last killer. When his mob was yarded at last he added a couple of killers for the journey. They didn't, Marion noticed, carry the same brand as Bill's mob.

It was an easy start to the trip because the mob was, as Bill claimed, well-handled, and he and three black boys accompanied them for the first day and a half. Marion didn't after all, have to cook. Alec doubled as horse-tailer and cook, and ex-governess and ex-housegirl were Mick's ringers, making up for what they lacked in experience with enthusiasm and anxious desire to follow the boss's instructions to the letter. Pansy was not exactly a newcomer to the game. She had worked in the stock-camp in her early teens, until her old promised husband had claimed her and forbidden a job where he could not keep his eye on her.

Marion had never worked such long hours in her life, and for the first three days it was a case of mind over matter to keep herself from dropping asleep in the saddle, especially on the night-watch. Mick had wanted to spare her the night-watch at first, but she had insisted, knowing that he would take her two hours on top of his own three, and by the end of the week she no longer noticed any hardship. She fell asleep as soon as her shoulders touched the swag blanket, and developed a facility for taking momentary catnaps on dinner-camp.

The mob got a good variety show when it camped each night. Alec and Pansy corroboreed; Mick ran through a repertoire which included mournful bush ballads, yodelling, and Banjo Paterson recitations; Marion sang a combination of popular wartime songs and old classics she had learned in the school choir. Audience reaction was good, for the mob was never restless at night, a fact that the ever-vigilant Mick noted with relief. Bill's mud-map was easy to follow, and better going than the stock-route to the south, notorious for its patches of drummy ground and frequent cattle rushes.

"You couldn't bring a big mob this way, more's the pity," explained Mick. "The natural watering places are only enough for a small mob, and then only after a real good season, like this one."

On occasions they watered the cattle at station bores, where Bill had sent telegrams asking permission to pass on a certain date. At least Mick supposed he had, for they were never challenged.

"It's a good trip to cut your teeth on," Mick told Marion. "They don't often run as sweet as this one. Small mob, happy camp, good boss, eh?"

"Tucker's a bit rough, though," grinned Marion cheekily, but quickly withdrew her comment when Mick said she could take over the cooking herself if she liked.

Fortune has a way of smiling at first upon individuals who seize an opportunity and take up a challenge, some say to reward them for their enterprise, and the cynics claim to get them in too deep to be in a position to back out. Whatever the truth of the claims, so it was with Mick and Marion. When they finally delivered the mob to Bill's brother, Ernie, and cut out and crossbranded their own fifty with a wire-brand X for the time being, Ernie told them of the disposal sale proposed for the big ex-Army camp a mere seventy miles up The Bitumen.

"They're letting the locals in first, jeeps, weapon-carriers, fuel, even huts if you're lookin' for a homestead. Plenty of good tools too. Five quid seems to be the going price. I'm going up tomorrow to pick out my lot, why dontcha come with me!"

It was an opportunity too good to be missed.

Mick's savings had been ear-marked mainly for the purchase of some breeders to get started. His plans certainly did not run to a vehicle at this stage, and while there was no family to consider, they both thought in terms of a shed for a camp with Marion out on the run most of the time with Mick. Excited, they discussed the new prospects. Ernie, a battler himself, dismissed the fact that they didn't even have any land yet.

"You got the block picked out, of course they'll give you a grazing licence on it. The Government's so keen to get blokes on the country after the fright the Japs give 'em, they 'll bend over backwards to encourage you. That's why they're giving away all this Army stuff so cheap. Give blokes like you a good start. Look, I'll tell yer what I'll do. You get the stuff you need, and you can leave it here, and your cattle too, while you go up and check out yer block and then go up to Darwin and fix up about it. Yer blacks can stop here too, with mine, and maybe give us a bit of a hand while yer away."

"Ernie, you're a trump!" grinned Mick, grabbing the man's calloused hand in a spontaneous gesture.

Marion's eyes danced with excitement.

"Aw, one o' these days you'll do as much for me," mumbled Ernie. "You already done us a favour, bringing the mob across from Bill's. Anyway, I might come up and look at the block with yer for a day or so. Good to see a bit o' different country for a change. How did yer get on to it, anyway?"

"Well, I haven't seen it for the last four years now, "admitted Mick, "but I did a bit of prospecting there with an old fellow for a couple of months between jobs. Just before I went to Delroy. I'd been working my way up north, up from Adelaide, ever since I was a kid, working on stations. Reckoned I'd join up at one stage, but somehow there always seemed a real important job to be done and no-one else there to do it if I left right then. Fact is I was about to turn around and head for Adelaide again when I met this old fellow and decided to have a bit of a spell before I joined the Army. He was looking at the rocks, but mostly all I could see was the Mitchell and Flinders grass plains and the permanent holes in the creeks. I reckoned it'd do me if I ever got the chance. We went back into Felix Creek, and I went to see the Government bloke there to see about a fare down to Adelaide, instead of the Army they sent me across to Delroy, said I could help feed the Army instead. And that's where I've been ever since."

"Rough country, then?" queried Ernie.

"Yeah, pretty rough, but some good plains; about nine hundred square miles I'd reckon, big private place to the south of it, and Arnhem Land Reserve and Mission to the North. Too small an area to interest the big fellas, but looked pretty good to me. I been dreaming about it ever since, and what a fellow could do there with a bit of hard yakka."

"And yer got a keen little off-sider there too, by the look of 'er," grinned Ernie.

"Gosh, what terrific luck," breathed Marion, "seems too good to be true! "

"Not luck," commented Ernie, "just a matter of bein' in the right place at the right time. There'll be plenty times when it aint the right place to be, when there's a drought on, like. Yer take it as it comes!"

They left with Ernie at daylight in his old truck, Alec and Pansy with them. Pansy had declared herself too much frighten stay longa strange blackfella, and when Alec had approached Mick to take them along Ernie had jumped at the chance of Alec driving his truck back for him when he acquired a jeep. He admitted he couldn't split himself in two, and as none of his own blacks could drive, Alec would fill the bill nicely.

The old truck was no speedhog; it took them two hours to reach the old Army camp, though fifteen minutes of that had been spent at the small hotel on the way to pick up two dozen bottles of cold beer, with which they planned to clinch their bargains. The half-dozen personnel left on site had one idea between them; to get the stuff disposed of as quickly as possible. Mick had expected, when he planned his enterprise, to have to pay at least two hundred pounds for a suitable shed, but now, for less than half that, he found himself the owner of a Sydney Williams Hut, a smaller two-room verandahed building, a weapon carrier, a jeep, a load of forty-four gallon drums of fuel for the vehicles, six cyclone beds and horsehair mattresses, and a large box of assorted tools. The buildings had to be dismantled and carted away, and Ernie, who had also bought a Sydney Williams Hut suggested that they all set to on his first, cart back what they could fit on his truck and the weapon-carrier, and he'd bring back a couple of his boys to give a hand with the rest.

By lunch-time on the second day, Ernie's plunder was all back on his run, and a start had been made to pull down Mick's buildings. The camaraderie established during the work on Ernie's buildings, plus Marion's foresight in suggesting that they number each sheet of corrugated iron as they pulled it off, so they could put it together again in the same order, prompted Ernie to make the suggestion that Mick had thought of himself, but didn't like to broach.

"How far from here d'yer reckon your place is?" asked Ernie.

"A good 150 miles, north-east, I'd reckon, according to the map, but I dunno what the track's like."

"Well, why don't yer take yer jeep, and have a look at it, and if yer reckon the truck would make it, we may as well take it there for yer, instead of goin' back on our tracks to my place. You supply the fuel for the trips, and give me a hand to put up my Sydney Williams when yer pick up yer cattle and gear there and I'll help yer cart all this stuff out."

One of the soldiers, an interested onlooker, who said he knew the road part of the way, volunteered to go with Mick, and sought and received permission from his commanding officer. It was the evening of the next day before they returned, weary but elated. It was fair going for the first 100 miles, but the next stretch of thirty or so was a real rough track, and the last twenty-five just a set of wheel-tracks, one of half a dozen sets they'd made in an effort to find the easiest way. Without the soldier and his compass, Mick didn't think he could have found a road, would have had to go up to Felix Creek and go in on the in on the track he knew, but they'd finally got into country he recognised, and come right on to the site he'd picked years ago as the best place for a homestead. He'd camped there with the old prospector, and the signs of the campfire were still there. Two sandy creeks to cross, which might mean unloading the truck unless they corduroyed the crossings first, but otherwise, if not clear going, at least possible.

Marion would never forget that trip; she went on the weapon-carrier with Mick, in the lead of the truck with Ernie, with two black boys perched on top of his load, with Alec and Pansy bringing up the rear with the jeep loaded with swags, fuel and water canteens. At the first creek crossing, she boiled the billy and made a meal while the men chopped down trees to augment the embedded logs already there. For the most part it was plain country, but the going was rough because of old ant-bed bases hidden in the long grass, and they camped the night at the second crossing, ready to tackle it when they were fresh in the morning. Alec found a better crossing a few hundred yards downstream, not so sandy, with flat plates of rock, but joltingly rough in the clefts between the rocks. They soon came into foothill country, which slowed them almost to a crawl. With no protection from the sun in the open vehicle they sweated, but if Marion noticed the heat, it was evident that Mick did not. He drove with complete concentration on the track, his goal still miles ahead, but in imagination he was already there.

It was early afternoon before they finally drew up on relatively open ground on a slight rise about two hundred yards from the bank of a wide lagoon fringed by blue waterlilies.

"This is as good a place as any I've seen," said Mick. "Any closer to the water, maybe we could get flooded out."

Ernie pronounced the site as more than adequate, and Marion said it was beautiful. Alec gave a broad grin and hastened to fill a bucket of water from the lagoon to boil the billy for a quick meal, after which, with one accord, they rolled out their swags in the shade for an hour's siesta.

Then the vehicles were carefully unloaded, Mick directing where each stack should go. Pansy announced that there were plenty fish in the lagoon, and was delegated to catch some for supper. Her efforts were successful, and they cooked them blackfellow fashion in the camp-fire while Marion toasted bread and laid out pannikins on the square of canvas that was her tablecloth.

After the meal, the men planned on an early get-away before the first light, and it was decided that Marion and Pansy should stay behind. Pansy, apprehensive of strange country, needed some persuading, and demanded that Mick leave his rifle with Marion.

"Mightbe some strange blackfella come up!" she announced.

Marion giggled as she thought of the last time Pansy had seen her handle a rifle, with dire results for the wall of the Delroy store, but Mick said it was a good idea and fetched it from the weapon-carrier along with a box of cartridges.

"One more trip should do it, and anything more we'll get when we go back to Ernie's for the rest of the camp gear," said Mick. "See you about two days' time!"

It was still pitch-dark when the men rolled their swags, Mick and Alec splitting theirs to leave blankets for Marion and Pansy, who had already dragged two of the cyclone beds close to the camp-fire.

"This way we don't need swag-covers," Marion explained when Ernie chiacked her, "only one cover for a married-man's swag, and they need them, so we're doing this to help, see!"

"Too much proply-good mattress, him help little bit too," smirked Pansy, smoothing her blankets in the firelight.

The girls were both asleep again before the growl of the receding engines had died away.

The next two days on their own, in a situation which was stripped of any of the superficialities of a civilised life-style, reduced all differences in their backgrounds and placed them on a footing in which each was able to see the other as she really was, rather than an example of a particular social level. Neither girl was typical of her kind, both were individuals. Marion had always been an outsider, by reason of her birth, and somewhat of a loner by inclination. Pansy, by defying the laws of the tribe and running away with Alec, had thrown away any chance of tribal status and risked physical retribution also if she were caught; hers was an act of extreme courage, knowingly exiling herself from the only life she knew and sacrificing all the ties of kinship that were such an important part of Aboriginal life. Their two days of exploration together was the beginning of a genuine friendship which was to endure for many years. Circumstances had thrown them together, and the basic similarity of their characters made it easier to forget the rules of their societies and adopt those of common-sense. Each had something to give the other, and both subconsciously accepted that fact.

Marion woke first, and stirred up the fire. Pansy, with the coming of daylight, had dismissed her fears of the evil spirits which populate the darkness, and could hardly wait to begin exploring the creek and savanna flats around the camp. Marion thought it more important to get the camp straightened out first, to choose a more permanent camp-site for the period while the buildings were being erected, to set a batch of bread against the men's return and build a wind-break for each couple's sleeping quarters. They compromised, mixed up the dough, and put the boxes of stores in the shade on one of the cyclone stretchers, and then set off upstream along the pandanus and ti-tree creek, of which the lagoon was an obvious anabranch. There were long waterholes at intervals, all with fish, but when Marion suggested a swim, Pansy demurred with the comment "Mightbe crocodile, more better wait longa twofella men lookabout!"

"This far inland they'd only be fish crocs," objected Marion.

"Youai," agreed Pansy, "fish croc mightbe littleone, but he gottim teeth allasame razor, indit?" They decided against a swim.

One of the waterholes, which they estimated as about six miles from the homestead site, had a fairly wide sandy approach to the water on the inside of a wide curve in the creek's course.

"Gee, good white sand for cement, when we need it," said Marion, but Pansy's sharp eyes had registered more.

"You seeim track!" she pointed excitedly.

They tumbled down the slope, and there were the clear imprints in the sand.

"Big mob cattle bit water," stated Pansy. At that stage in her life Pansy's counting ability ended at "one, two, three, big mob," but Marion estimated that there could be ten or twenty in the mob; there were certainly cows and calves, and a bigger track that could only be an old bull.

"Scrubbers!" she yelped delightedly, "cleanskins!" They could see a clearly-defined pad leading off into the savanna country, but no actual sign of any cattle.

"This one cheeky fella, night-drinker," announced Pansy, still examining the tracks.

They spent an hour lolling on the bank in the shade, and then retraced their steps to the camp. Marion's house-wifely urge had resurfaced, and the sweaty smell of the clothes she was wearing reminded her that there was washing to be done. They carted water from the lagoon and set it on the campfire in a big steel bucket, into which Marion shaved slivers of bar soap with her pocket-knife. She boiled the shirts and her undies first, and then the dirty trousers, and then Pansy did her lot. They carried the laundered garments in smaller buckets to the lagoon to rinse, Pansy carrying hers effortlessly on her head, and then decided to risk any fish crocs and have a bath in the lagoon. They stripped off and splashed among the water-lilies.

"We're going to have to drink this," laughed Marion, "but I suppose one bath won't hurt, or a little bit of soap. I s'pose we'll have to cart the bath-water in future, though, when Mick rigs us a shower."

Hungry after their ablutions, they unearthed the camp-oven from the coals and turned out a crisp-crusted cartwheel of bread, the aroma of which sent their taste-buds tingling. They broke off a triangular wedge each, as soon as it was cool enough to touch, and plastered it with golden syrup, and washed it down with tea lavishly sugared.

Marion decided then and there that the two greatest things she appreciated in the bush was a feed when you were really hungry, closely followed by a wash when you were really dirty. She fell asleep that night contented and happy, to the call of a curlew on the flat, and the light hum of the trees, which can be heard in the night-silences of the bush by those with ears tuned to the sounds of nature.

The second day the girls explored about four miles upstream from the camp, taking with them a parcel of bread and salt meat for a picnic lunch. They saw plenty of wallabies, and surprised an emu with half a dozen striped chicks, but saw no further signs of scrubber cattle. Neither of the two waterholes they passed were easily accessible for larger animals; the steeply sloping banks were tangled and overgrown, and too likely to harbour snakes for the girls to venture too close to the edges.

As they half-expected that the trucks might return that night, they went back to the camp in mid-afternoon, but it was not until nearly midday the next day that they heard the welcome sound of vehicles labouring over the rough ground.

"Throw another perentie on the fire," shouted Mick as he drew up, "we're starving!"

"Got the lot!" announced Ernie, climbing down from his truck. "Double the load the blokes who made the truck reckon she'd carry. Slowed us down a bit though; didn't want to break an axle out 'ere!"

The men ate ravenously, had a short siesta, and then unloaded, after which they disappeared towards the creek for a clean-up and change of clothes.

Before they left the camp the next morning Mick and Alec placed their stores and smaller items on one of the cyclone stretchers, attached ropes to each end, and hauled the stretcher up almost to the fork of the big gum tree.

"Don't want the dingoes poking around in our stuff while we're gone,' he said.

"Or any of them scrubbers the women seen," added Alec laconically.

"Time enough for them," laughed Mick, "we'll get 'em in good time, but first there's a coupla buildings to attend to! All aboard for Ernie's place!"

Chapter 15

Post-war Darwin.
Mick stakes his claim.

Ernie's Sydney Williams Hut went up in three days, and he talked of putting in a cement floor, glass windows instead of shutters, adding a verandah, and moving into it as the homestead. It was certainly six times as roomy as the two-room wooden structure that presently served that purpose.

Mick, anxious to consolidate what he called a slippery holt on his block, decided to go straight to Darwin to organise his application. At first Marion was to go with him, but then Alec suggested that they may as well start off with the cattle, the three of them should be able to handle fifty no trouble, they could do it in a fortnight. Mick agreed.

"Right, Alec's in charge as far as the cattle go, and if any smart-alec bails you up on the road, Honey, you're the boss. You better keep the gun. There's fellas'll try to push a blackfella around might think twice about a red-head with a gun in her hot little hand!"

Marion mimed a stick-up with herself as heroine, and Mick slapped her bottom.

"Anyway," he added, "I should be able to meet you about half-way. I'll get the business done and pick up the stores and stuff we need, and then come back through Felix Creek. Chuck the packs on the jeep, and I'll take the truck, have to see about a petrol ration for it too while I'm there; no need to let on about what we got from the Army."

Marion wrote a hasty and enthusiastic letter to Maggie, giving, at Mick's suggestion, the Post Office at Felix Creek as their address. Then she scribbled a list of what she considered essentials for the next six months. Mick crossed out nearly half of them, breeders must take priority, no frills until they could sell their first mob of steers. Next year, maybe. There wasn't time to argue what constituted frills. With a hasty kiss and a pat on the shoulder Mick was gone.

He found Darwin a hive of post-war activity, Government men everywhere, old inhabitants returning, ringers like himself, Chinese storekeepers, blacks, and everywhere the evidence of the war-time bombing in shattered buildings and heaps of rubble slowly being cleared away. He booked into a pub, half of which was flattened, but in the other half it was business as usual. A stout woman showed him to a room where four beds barely fitted, and told him the bathroom was in the shed he could see out the back behind the kitchen.

He shoved his swag underneath the bed and then straightened up quickly at a low growl from beneath the bed nearest the window. A blue heeler, all fangs and wrinkled muzzle, was camped beside a battered suitcase and swag under the bed, doing guard duty.

"That's what I need," thought Mick, "to watch that drum of petrol on the back of the truck," and aloud he said, "all right, fella, you can watch my stuff too while you're about it!"

The bathroom was nothing to write home about, but at least he was clean and shaved when he returned to the room, and found the owner of the heeler sitting on his bed with a parcel of new clothes beside him. He introduced himself as Alan, a stockman who'd been in the Army for the last three years, now on his way back to his job down the track. He told Mick where to find the Lands Branch office, and deplored the shortage of women in town, but applauded the fact that there was plenty of beer to make up for it.

Mick took a walk and found the office, but a notice outside advised him that business hours were nine to three, too late for him to stake his claim that day. He walked back to the pub to check on his truck, and then to the harbour, busy with shipping which had to thread its way between the bombed wrecks of ships marked at intervals almost up to the wharf itself.

Mick paid for a bed he didn't use that night. The room was so stuffy, and with petrol still rationed he feared his forty-four gallon drum on the back of the weapon-carrier might be a temptation to some of the riotous clientele he could hear at the bar. In the end he took his swag and rolled it out on the back of the truck.

Breakfast was at seven, steak and eggs, surprisingly well-cooked, but then Mick had to cool his heels until nine. He drove to the office, and was first inside when the door was finally opened to the public. There were about four desks behind a long counter, and Mick stated his business to a clerk in white shirt and shorts and long socks, who called to a similarly-attired chap about thirty at a desk in the far corner.

"Mr. Cameron will fix you up," he said, "he handles this section."

Mr. Cameron produced the application form immediately, and leant chattily on the counter as Mick filled it in. On a large map affixed to the nearby wall Mick pointed out the area.

"Oh, one of the Wilson River blocks, eh. There's two out that way, was to be three, but they've been split up to make them a bit bigger. That's number one, twelve hundred square miles. Have you seen the country?"

Mick replied that he'd had a look at some of it.

"Good country, is it, good grass country?" enquired Mr. Cameron interestedly.

"All right," said Mick non-committally.

"What sort of grass does it grow?" persevered Mr. Cameron.

"Green in the Wet, brown in the Dry," replied Mick shortly. There were some fellows who could ask questions, and some who couldn't, and Mr. Cameron was one of the latter. But he didn't seem to be put off easily.

"Well," he continued jovially, "by the look of the river and creeks there ought to be plenty of permanent water, wouldn't you say?"

"I wouldn't know," grunted Mick, "hope so, but you'd have to see a few seasons through, or ask the blacks. I haven't seen any blacks."

"Well, that's it then," said Mr. Cameron, "just leave your address, and we'll let you know. Just a formality really. You'll be called in for an interview."

"But - but," stammered Mick, "I don't have an address. I thought it could all be fixed up straight away. You're the blokes that do it, aren't you?"

Mr. Cameron smirked at him, and Mick's growing dislike hardened into a gut feeling of distaste for public servants, who could push a man around while never amounting to much themselves.

"My good fellow, these things take time, you know," announced Mr. Cameron, "but maybe we could stretch a point. Come back in a couple of days, and we'll see what we can do."

Mick had to be content with that; obviously there was some red tape he didn't know about. But his disappointment rankled, and for the first time he began to feel a slight apprehension. He went back to the pub and had a beer, and then decided he'd buy the bags of flour, coarse salt, sugar (Alec was a demon for sugar), potatoes, onions, a chest of tea, and the few tinned goods he'd allowed. He thought he'd give Marion a surprise and take back a second-hand table and chairs, which she knew he'd crossed from the list, but this plan was thwarted. Second-hand, or new for that matter, furniture was not to be had for love or money; furniture in post-war Darwin was even shorter than womenfolk, for with the return of the evacuated families, any sort of basic furniture was at a premium. Many families had left their homes as they stood and now returned to find them, if they were still standing, stripped of almost everything moveable.

"What the Japs left, the Army took," said one man bitterly. "You want furniture, son, you're gonna have to make it from what you can find, or ship it up from South!"

After the weeks of the cheerful company he'd experienced out bush, Mick found that he wasn't much enjoying his spell in Darwin where everyone seemed to be either miserable or on the make. He returned to the pub with the idea of collecting his swag from the room, and driving out of town to camp on one of the beaches. Alan was there, sitting on his bed in a mood that matched Mick's. His boss had not turned up as arranged, and he'd passed the afternoon gambling at fan-tan in one of the illicit Chinese establishments.

"The Chinks've got about half me deferred pay," he mourned, "if Paul don't turn up termorra, I think I'll go croc-shooting with the fella I met this arvo. He's lookin' for a mate. I'm goin' down ter have a drink with 'im now. Why don't yer come too?"

It seemed like a good idea. Mick had no intention of throwing his money away on grog, but one or two beers might brighten him up and pass the time. They left the heeler on guard, though neither of them had even seen the other two boarders whose belongings were sitting on the beds that obviously hadn't been slept in the night before.

The bar was crowded, and the noise horrific, mainly cheerful, but with undertones of brawls to come. Alan's croc-shooter wasn't in evidence, but Mick's roving eye noted Cameron sitting on a stool at the far end of the bar deep in conversation with a chap whose cut immediately announced him as a Southern squatter, flat-heeled elastic-sides and the hat on his knee with the brim turned down all round, you could pick 'em anywhere.

Then Paddy, the croc-shooter, hallooed from the doorway, and the next couple of hours passed convivially, as all three men swapped yarns. Paddy already had a camp out of town, and had practically persuaded Alan to go with him when Mick went out to relieve himself and check on his truck and load.

He slept on the truck again that night, and fell asleep quickly despite the sounds of revelry not too far away. He woke as usual at piccaninny daylight, showered and went to the early breakfast. Then he collected his swag and said goodbye to Alan, still in bed, and the now-friendly blue heeler, and went down to the makeshift office to pay his bill. The charge was reasonable enough, but he didn't intend to waste any more money on a bed he didn't intend to use, when he had a swag and a perfectly good tuckerbox on the truck and the sea for a far cleaner bathroom than the one the pub sported.

While he was fishing in his pocket for change the man Cameron had been talking to in the bar came along the corridor towards the dining room.

"Oh, Mr. Fullerton," called the landlady over Mick's shoulder, "excuse me, Mr. Fullerton, phone message for you from Adelaide to ring this number," and she fished into a drawer full of notes and coins and pulled out a slip of paper. The man came over to the counter and took the paper and thanked her; as far as either of them were concerned Mick might not have been there. He paid his bill and was glad to get out of the place. Alec and Pansy had better manners than these townies seemed to have, who reckoned they were so much better than the blacks. Mick hoped he wasn't going to have to waste too much more time before he could get out of town.

He found a good camp above an open stretch of beach where the sandflies weren't too bad, but the tide was half a mile out and still going, so he wasn't going to be able to swim for some hours. He sat on his swag and went over his list; still had to get some dried fruit and tobacco and wax matches, and he'd need horseshoes for the rough country and some barb and plain wire. He went back into town in the afternoon and made his purchases, and asked in vain for the whereabouts of a stock agent who might be able to get on to some breeders for him.

"Gawd," said one obvious old bushman whom he'd stopped in the street, "enough big Pommy Companies hoggin' all the best country in the Territory, ain't there! Runnin' twice as many cleanskins as they got branded up; what more do yer want! The time ain't come yet when we need agents, son. Yer'd be doin' yer country a favour brandin' up some of them cleanskins that only grow up to be useless big scrub bulls. Country needs cleanin' up , get a bit of control in the herds, and it's blokes like us oughta help do it!"

Mick reflected that there was a lot of truth in what he said. Half the world was still rationed for meat while thousands of tons of beef on the hoof roamed uncontrolled, never to be marketed, on the vast English-owned North-Australian runs. Still, he'd need a bill of sale for more than the fifty head he already had to be in the clear with the Lands Branch if they enquired.

He fronted at the Lands Office early next morning, and asked to see Cameron, whose desk behind the counter was vacant. "The young clerk asked, "Mr. Hardy, is it?"

Mick nodded.

"Mr. Cameron left a message for you, sir. He said to tell you he's sorry but the block you wanted had already been applied for, prior to your application."

Mick was stunned. His face went white. It was all he could do to get himself to the truck and climb behind the wheel, where he sat for five minutes getting himself together. Then he stuck out his jaw, drove off, parked the truck a couple of streets away, and walked back to the office. Cameron was going to tell him himself, he knew the bastard was there somewhere, hiding out the back. If Cameron could see him approach through the louvred walls he could play the same game with Cameron. When a blackfellow doesn't want to be seen coming he applies the techniques that Mick now used to advantage. Within ten minutes he could see, without being seen, that Cameron was back at his desk, probably congratulating himself that he'd seen the last of Mick.

In the next few minutes the Quiet Fella belied his name. He slid into the office, vaulted the counter and hauled the flabbergasted clerk to his feet by the front of his shirt. His chair went sprawling, while three other clerks watched aghast. Mick shook his quarry like a terrier with a rat and bawled at him, "There wasn't any other applicant the other day, or you'd have said so then. You didn't even know where the block was, until I showed you on the map!"

Cameron struggled and tried to speak, but Mick shook him again.

"You picked the wrong bloke to put one over, you little mongrel. I dunno what you're up to, but I sure as hell know there's something fishy going on. You trot out the other application and let's have a look at it!"

He threw the clerk across his desk, and stood breathing fire and smoke, just as the door to an inner office was opened and a middle-aged man enquired coldly, "Just what is going on out here?"

Both Mick and Cameron started to speak at once, and the crestfallen clerk now much whiter about the gills than Mick had been half an hour earlier.

The Director held up his hand and gestured towards Mick.

"You'd better come in to my office and explain. Assaulting my clerks isn't going to solve whatever your problem is. You could be charged for that, you know."

Mick, the cynosure of all eyes, strode over to the office and was ushered inside. The Director closed the door and offered him a seat on the other side of the desk, and pushed an ash-tray towards him.

"Most of you chaps smoke, I know, so roll yourself one, and then tell me about it."

Mick did so, and the Director listened without comment or question. Then he rose and opened the door to the outer office and quietly asked the still-stuttering Cameron to bring him both the application forms.

Within minutes Cameron tapped hesitantly on the door, entered, and put the two forms on the table in front of his boss. He was about to go out again when the Director ordered, "Stay here, Cameron," and picked up both forms, glancing from one to the other.

Mick watched his face closely, while Cameron stared doggedly at the floor in front of him.

The Director glanced up.

"Well, Mr. Hardy, this application does seem to be in order, I'm afraid. It's dated a full week before yours!"

Cameron straightened up expectantly.

"Can I ask who the fellow is that's beaten me then?" queried Mick icily.

"Well, hardly, Mr. Hardy, these things are confidential at this stage, you must see that," said the Director.

"Well," grated Mick between clenched teeth, "what about I tell YOU his name, would that alter things?"

"It might," said the Director, with a new spark of interest in his expression, "particularly if you tell me the right name, and how you found it out."

"It's Fullerton, isn't it?" snapped Mick, on the inspiration which had come to him just moments before. Cameron made a choking sound, and drew the Director's attention away from Mick.

"Wait outside, Mr. Cameron, please," he said quietly, and the clerk, no actor now, slunk out.

Mick explained how he'd guessed the name, and the Director listened, seemingly dispassionately. Then he asked Mick to wait outside and called in the hang-dog

Cameron. Mick cooled his heels outside the building for quarter of an hour and then was summoned to the office again. The Director smiled at him this time.

"I think we can safely say your application is approved, Mr. Hardy, but I would appreciate it if you wouldn't discuss it too much round town, say, as a favour to me."

Mick nodded delightedly. "I'll be leaving town just as soon as this is straight, no time to talk to anyone."

"Well, the formalities then. You get the grazing licence for a year, peppercorn rental really, and you get permission from us first for any improvements you want to do. You renew your tenure each year until five years are up, and then the block will be gazetted for leasehold, a 99 year grazing lease. You understand, of course, that in effect anyone can then apply for it, but it always goes to the man on the place, except under extreme circumstances, say if he's made a complete mess of it, or fallen foul of the law, something like that. He'd have to be a really unsuitable applicant not to get the lease, and I don't think that's going to apply to you..." - he glanced at the signature on the document - "...Mick. It's your sort of stick-attedness we're going to need to open the country up."

Mick's opinion of public servants was instantly revised. He grinned openly at the director and said, "I'd like permission this year to put up a set of yards and a place to live in, maybe a smaller yard near the end of the run if there's time."

The Director nodded and wrote down the particulars, which Mick signed. He phoned through to the Mapping Branch and asked for a map of the Wilson River to be sent in to him. Then he buzzed his secretary from the adjoining office, offered Mick a cup of tea, and when the map came, pencilled in rough boundaries.

"There are survey pegs," he told Mick, "but you might have a bit of trouble finding them. You can work out the approximate mileage from this. The creek's the boundary here to the north, no trouble there. The station to the south - surveyed long before the war, boundary goes along the parallel of latitude."

Mick drank two cups of tea, signed the paper the secretary brought in, wrote a cheque for the rent, stuck the map in his pocket, and shook hands with the Director, who walked with him to the front counter. Cameron's desk was vacant. Mick glanced at it and said, "Er, don't be too hard on that poor bastard, will you. I don't hold him a grudge now."

He didn't hold anyone a grudge, the world was great, Darwin wasn't such a bad place after all.

He went to the Chinese shop and bought two bright dresses for Pansy, a two-tone blue Williams shirt for Alec, a fawn one for himself, two smaller ones, green, for his Chestnut Filly, six tins of Sal Vital, and a five-pound tin of boiled lollies. As an afterthought he saw a Chinese teapot, all gold and red, up on a shelf, and he took that too. The cups to go with it were far too small for a dinkum Australian, but the smiling little Chinese girl soon produced six of the large white standard Australian variety from a box under the country. As soon as the Sydney Williams was up the first thing he'd do was build Marion a table to put 'em on.

It was Mick's day to howl; two streets from the Chinese Shop the demolition team was at work, and sticking out of the pile of rubble was a wooden door, hardly damaged at all, the perfect table top. Mick pulled up with a screech of tyres. Sure he could have it, said the foreman, and a quid would buy him a half a dozen windows too if he wanted them. Stacked up around the back of the place, glass intact, made yer think, didn't it, one wall standing untouched and the rest of the place as flat as a board. Mick handed over a pound note and the foreman helped him wrap the windows in the roll of hessian he'd bought the day before. They packed the windows on the now overloaded truck, and the foreman winked at Mick as he drove off.

The Quiet Fella whistled all the way to Pine Creek. Even the puncture he got just north of Felix Creek didn't quell his elation much.

Chapter 16

A muster proposed and rejected.

The road from Felix Creek in to the block was even rougher than Mick remembered it, a ten-hour slog with breakaways and stretches where the road had disappeared entirely under grass. It was lucky the weapon-carrier had such a sweet gear-change, with the overtime it worked that day. Mick knew he'd have to camp if he couldn't reach the homestead site before dark, but he was in luck and made it a good hour before sundown.

He got a fire going in the rough fireplace the girls had made, and pulled his tuckerbox down from the seat where it had ridden beside him for the trip out. Stiff as he was, he rejected an impulse to stretch out on his swag, and walked, pannikin of tea in hand, to gloat over the stack unloaded while Marion had been busy getting supper on their last evening there. She didn't know about his extra purchases from the Army camp when they'd got everything loaded and it was obvious that Ernie's truck could still carry a few more hundredweight. The young soldier who'd made the first trip out with Mick not only helped him pull the six-foot windmill apart and unbolt the two-thousand gallon tank while Ernie and Alec loaded the lengths of galvanised steel piping, but he suggested the 240 volt generator too. The engine to run it was heavy, so they'd squeezed that on the weapon carrier with a couple of drums of diesel. The wire, switches, globes, and all, had already been pulled down from all the huts and were stored in a shed. They took enough and some to spare and threw it on the jeep, no charge for the wire, ten quid the lot. Mick smiled happily to himself. Most of the places he'd seen in the north still operated on pressure lights or wind-power, and he knew that Marion expected no more. But his girl was now going to start her housekeeping with water and lights laid on, and, by George, Pansy could have the same in the two-room shed he'd earmarked for them. He fell asleep that night pondering the remote possibility that he and Alec might hide the gear and get rid of the girls on the day the lights were rigged, so they could come home on sundown and see their place a blaze of light.

He unloaded carefully the next morning, first building a platform onto which he stacked the rations which were to see them through the Dry. He tied a camp-sheet over them and then used some of the sheets of corrugated iron from the building to erect a strong shelter. That done, he encircled the lot with loops of rope; that should hold until they got back. By mid-morning he was ready to leave.

Marion saw the truck coming first, out in the lead of the mob they were just about to camp for the night. She gave a whoop which would have rushed a less well-handled mob, and kicked her heels into Banner's sides. She was off the horse as quickly as Mick was out of the truck and they embraced as if they'd been parted for months rather than days. Alec and Pansy continued to settle the cattle on camp.

After supper Alec took the watch and Pansy turned in. Mick, holding Marion's hands in the firelight, enlarged then on how they very nearly hadn't got the grazing licence, and Marion's eye widened in indignation.

"Why couldn't the stinker just get his own block; why did he want ours?" she burst out.

"The way I see it," Mick explained, "he's from down South, see, and he doesn't know how to judge the country up here, whether it's any good or not, so he makes it worth this Cameron bloke's while to watch out for someone after a licence who looks as if he'd know a good place when he saw it. If it's good enough for a local bloke to want it, then it's good enough for him to give it a try without taking much of a risk. I don't go looking for a fight, but that's one I had to take on."

"Thank goodness you did too. If you hadn't won that one, Mick, there wouldn't be much point to the one I think I've got you into now!"

Mick looked at her quizzically, dropped her hand and got up to refill their pannikins from the flat-sided billycan of coffee simmering at the edge of the fire. He handed the pannikin to her and waited for her to go on.

"Well, day before yesterday," she explained, "a chap came along the track behind us in a utility, and he pulled up and asked me where we were taking the cattle. So I told him we were taking up the Wilson River block, and that's where we were heading. I was pretty dirty, I know, but he could have been more polite. He just grunted, didn't even say who he was, said, "Well, I've got cattle running over that way. I'll send the boys over to muster them up before you get there." I got real mad then, Mick. He's not going to get our cleanskins if I know it. I yelled at him, he'd already started to drive off, I said, "Hey, wait a minute, mister, you've got no permission to go onto our place when we're not there." He stopped then, and switched off the engine and got out. Lucky I was on the horse, I could look down on him. He said, "They're my cattle, Mrs. Whoever-you-are, obviously you've got none there yet, so why shouldn't I muster there?" Alec rode up beside me then, he'll tell you how nasty he was. I said, all prim and proper, "Mister Whoever-*You*-Are, if there's branded cattle of yours there, or calves following branded cows, you can have them when my husband's ready to muster. Anything else there, Mister, you know the rules, there's nothing to prove the cleanskins are yours!" He just gave me a dirty look then, didn't say anything, and drove off. Mick, he must be the manager of that place south of us. Did I do the right thing? I'm scared he'll go and muster anyway."

"Honey, you little beauty, of course you did," Mick hugged her.

"Looks like another change of plans though. It'll be a week at least before you get home, and he could work that out and send his men over anyway. He doesn't know where I am, but he could come over in a vehicle to check out whether I'm there or not, he'd know we'd have to be camped somewhere along the creek. And if he doesn't find me there, well, he can go ahead. Honey, it looks like you're going to have to finish the trip without me after all. I'd better take the jeep tomorrow and leave you the truck. Mr. Whoever-he-is isn't going to get our cleanskins if I know anything about it, either. There's enough store bread on the truck to last you till you get home, and I'll see Alec in the morning and see if he can hurry the mob up a bit."

"I always seem to be saying goodbye to you these days," mourned Marion.

"Yeah," he agreed, "and I s'pose there'll be more of it too before we're finished. But right now, you roll into your swag, I'll do your watch tonight, least I can do."

When Alec rode up to the fire half an hour later Marion was already fast asleep. Mick took the pocket-watch from him and mounted the other night-horse. Pansy got an extra hour's sleep too that night before Mick finally succumbed to weariness and rode in.

Mick saw them on their way at sun-up, and then headed back the way he had come. He was still twenty miles from home when he cut the tracks coming in from the right. He saw where the driver had pulled up to check and then driven on over Mick's own tracks yesterday. There was only one set of tracks so the fellow was still there up ahead of him. Mick put his foot down.

A jeep like his own was parked on the outskirts of the camp, and a man squatted on his heels smoking in the meagre shade thrown by the vehicle. He rose to his feet, ground out his cigarette butt, and walked towards Mick with hand outstretched.

"Paul Buxton. Parrot Hill," he said briefly. Mick shook the proffered hand and replied in kind, "Mick Hardy."

" Sorry if I upset your wife the other day. Bad mood. Just got a blast from Head Office. Put me in my place though, bit of a fire-eater, isn't she?"

Mick, who had been expecting a confrontation, relaxed somewhat.

"Yeah," he admitted. "Good mate! Look, I'll put on a drink of tea, and we can get acquainted."

Buxton said he was dry and a drink of tea would go well. When they were squatting in the shade of a tree with their pannikins Mick asked interestedly, "If you hadn't seen my fresh track and found me here, were you planning to muster my block?"

Paul Buxton laughed.

"Look, Mick, there'd have to be a few Parrot Hill cattle here. There were storms to the north of us end of last Dry when we got none, so some would have followed the storms. Head Office reckons my branding figures are down, are a bit too, not that much though, so when I saw your little mob on the road, and heard the block was taken up, first thing I thought was I'd better get our cattle off it."

"And anything else here too, eh?" asked Mick.

"Well, Mick, you could have been mugs new to the game. Worth a try. What would you have done in the circumstances?"

"Picked up everything I could find, taken 'em home, and branded 'em quick smart!" said Mick laconically, "but we aren't mugs, Paul, and the cleanskins belong to the bloke who owns the country, eh?"

"Guess so, but they would have been the progeny of our cows in the first place, you gotta admit."

"Why?" said Mick. "How about the mission up north of here; they'd have some cattle."

"Ha," snorted the Parrot Hill manager, "any cleanskins from that in-bred, run-out mongrel herd up there wouldn't be worth the bullets you'd want to stop the mickies breeding with your own cows!"

"Wherever they come from they're mine!" said Mick firmly.

They parted an hour later, having agreed that when Mick could muster, Parrot Hill would be invited to attend. But that time was a long way off; a full muster would need a big team of ringers or a good set of yards, and Mick had neither. He firmly rejected Buxton's offer to bring his whole team over to scruff and brand on the flat with a bronco panel in exchange for fifty-fifty cleanskins; that meant the man must think there'd be a worthwhile number, and Mick would like to spy out the lie of the land first before he committed himself. Besides, he still didn't have a proper brand. The application had only gone in the afternoon he left Darwin, and he still had to have it accepted, and get the brands made. He didn't tell Buxton that.

"You're a tough bloke, Mick, stretching it out so a few more calves grow up and leave their mothers, eh?"

"What would you do in the circumstances?" parried Mick.

"Okay, okay," said Buxton, "well, I'll keep in touch. Got a wireless? Our call sign's 8TZ."

"No, not yet. Have to get one some time, I guess."

"Yeah. Well, be seeing you." He shook hands again, adjusted his hat over his eyes and drove off.

Mick watched thoughtfully until the vehicle was out of sight. He wondered just how many cleanskins there might be on the run, and just how good a manager Buxton might be. Parrot Hill would have had notice to pick up any of their cattle when the Wilson River blocks were split up, and if he hadn't done so then, that was his look-out. Men were short on every place and cleanskins rife on all the big runs because of the war, but the war had been over nearly a year now. Still, it depended on what his Head Office would allow him for wages; those concerns often wanted their pound of flesh without paying anything for it. He decided against going back to the drovers straight away. Buxton could easily read his tracks and slip in behind him with his stock-camp. Depended on how big a bind he was in with his bosses whether he'd risk doing that, because he'd know that Mick would soon find out whether he had or not. But you could pick up a lot of cleanskins in a week if the cleanskins were there, and not much Mick could do it about then. No, Alec would handle the droving all right; Mick could put in his time better checking up on his southern boundary and poking around in the scrub a bit to get some idea himself of possible cattle numbers.

For the next four days Mick used a lot of petrol, but he saw a lot of country. Each day he ran across small mobs of cattle, which galloped away wild-eyed as soon as they sensed his approach, and he followed pads, often on foot in the rougher country, until he had a fair idea of the watering places. No wonder Buxton was so keen to muster, the place looked like an already-stocked holding. And all this to the south of the homestead creek, which almost bisected the property; it wasn't being optimistic to expect that north of the creek would be much the same.

Sure by the fifth day that there was no time left for a lightning raid across the boundary, Mick met the drovers only a few miles short of the home-run. The mob looked bigger.

"How many?" he said to Marion as she rode up.

"Fifteen," she smirked, "all cleanskins, though. We butchered one, and hunted all the others."

Mick threw back his head and roared with laughter. While Buxton had been sniffing round after the cleanskins on the block, the Chestnut Filly had been pinching fifteen head of his legitimate cleanskins. And this was the girl who'd worried about Bill's honesty. He said as much.

"Well, I wouldn't have thought of it if he hadn't been rude to me," she protested.

"Remind me never to be rude to you, Honey," he said, still chuckling as he hugged her. "Now what say you and Pansy take the truck and go home for a clean-up, and let Alec and me push these poddies along a bit and get 'em over the boundary. We can have 'em home in three days, I reckon."

As Mick might have expected if he had been more experienced in the ways of womenfolk, Marion and Pansy had discovered the materials for the proposed water and lighting systems, there was going to be no surprise there. As he said disgustedly to Alec, they'd worn a pad a foot deep round every stack of gear there. But Marion hadn't touched the box from the Chinese shop, which he'd specifically marked. *Don't touch! - Detonators!* So he had the pleasure of handing out unexpected presents after supper.

Marion hadn't twigged what the door was meant for, stacked as it was beside the hessian-wrapped windows, so he surreptitiously removed the teapot and cups in the darkness, and shoved them into the nearest pack-bag. Might take a trick there.

The cattle had to be watched that night, but they had camped contentedly after a long drink and a good feed. Mick had kept them off water for two days, making sure they didn't get a drink, and as a result, didn't feed out much, so that when they did get to the home waterhole really thirsty and tucked-up they'd be more likely to remember it and be reluctant to leave it. The cleanskins were a bit of a worry, though he didn't say as much to Marion. All they wanted to do was get back to their own beat, unlike the well-handled mob that had been on the road for so long. Four that repeatedly broke away he let go, but for Marion's sake he persevered with the rest.

"I did try to tell her they'd be a nuisance, Mick," said Alec apologetically, "but she wanted 'em bad to spite that bloke."

"Forget it," said Mick, "woulda done the same in your shoes."

The next day Mick and Alec put up a rough bush yard close to the camp while the girls tailed the cattle. That way they could be yarded at night, and the girls could tail them out during the day for a couple of weeks until they settled down, while the men set about the business of erecting the buildings and ensuring the water supply.

Mick had long since worked out where he wanted the buildings to be to get the best advantage of sun and wind and had marked out the areas with rocks. They put up the small shed first for, in the unlikely event of rain at that time of year, there were now stores and gear that needed protection. Two rooms with a lean-to verandah back and front and a dirt floor, it was the basic dwelling, but when Marion rode in after yarding the cattle and saw an actual building outlined among the amorphous piles of steel girders and corrugated iron she experienced such a rush of emotion that she surprised herself. This camping place was really going to be her home, the central heart of the block of country that little Skeet had dreamed of all those years ago; she gulped with the happiness of it all.

"That'll be your place when we're finished, Pansy," said Mick as they ate supper round the fire.

"You puttin' blacks' camp bit close longa homestead, indit?" she commented with a sideways grin and dancing brown eyes.

"Nomore blacks' camp, that one married couple's cottage. Got to puttim closeup for 'lectric light," said Mick, keeping a straight face.

Pansy dug Alec in the ribs. "More better us twofella get married allasame whitefella siddown longa cottage!" and she went off into a peal of infectious laughter.

"What you goin' to call the place, Mick?" asked Alec suddenly.

"Yeah, I guess we can't go on calling it The Block much longer. What do you reckon, Honey?"

Marion said she didn't know, but maybe she'd get some ideas if she looked at the map in the morning.

Mick produced the map as they breakfasted just after sun-up, and Marion brushed off the piece of canvas she'd cut the damper on, and spread the map flat and pored over it.

"Hey, Mick, what about this? Across here, near the table-land country, there's a hill marked Mount Jindit. Must be a feature to be named already. That any good?"

Alec's eyes widened and he turned his head away quickly, Pansy merely looked owlish, but Mick couldn't control himself. He burst into a hoot of laughter, while poor Marion just looked mystified at the reaction her words had caused.

Alec, always the gentleman, but with lips still twitching, touched Pansy's arm, and said, "C'mon, we got work to do!" and left Mick to explain.

Still chuckling, he said, "You're right, darling, it is a feature, a conical hill with just a knob of hard rock left on top. You can see it for miles. The prospectors poking through this country, probably the first ones through, gave it the obvious name - The Gin's Tit. Then a surveyor through here just before the war reckoned, seeing it was such an outstanding feature, that the blacks would have a name for it, so he asked his blackfellow guide, and happily wrote down on his map what he thought the blackfellow said."

"Oh, Mick, of course. Well, we can't call it that then." She started to laugh herself. "I'll think of something else."

In the end they called the station Serendipity. Mick said it sounded okay, but did it mean anything. And Marion told him yes, it did. It meant the ability to make good things happen by sheer chance, and Mick must be one of the very few people who had the gift. Like deciding to take Bill's cattle and turning up just in time to get in on the Army Disposal windfall, and deciding to have a drink with Alan and the croc-shooter just when the Lands clerk was talking to Fullerton in the bar. If he'd said no to Alan's invitation they wouldn't be here now, would they? Mick said dubiously that was just luck, but Marion firmly insisted that it was more than that, and anyway, they couldn't call the place Lucky Downs, it sounded too much like tempting Fate. Luck could change. The more she thought about it the more she liked it.

She scratched the word out with a stick in the dust and Mick had a sudden vision of it on a sign-post on the turn-off from the Felix Creek road.

"Yes, by George, that's it!" He gave her his one-sided grin. "You deserve a reward for that. I'll tell Alec to help Pansy to let the cattle out, while you grab a blanket. We'll have a quickie down by the creek."

"See what I mean," laughed Marion, "you just set in action another happy occurrence just by chance."

Chapter 17 *Homestead camp established. A trip to town.*

As soon as the stores were shifted out of the weather into the small shed, the building endeavour ceased temporarily while Mick and Alec put up a horse-paddock. Mick walked out a line enclosing about a square mile, adjacent to where he reckoned on putting the yards, with one side running just behind the buildings. He kept an eye out for trees solid enough for strainer posts and marked them as he went, while Alec followed with an axe marking trees fairly close to the line that would be suitable for fence-posts.

Mick estimated they'd need about three hundred posts, but they ought to be able to cut fifty or sixty a day each. They debated whether to cut posts in the morning and dig postholes in the afternoon, or whether to stick at the post cutting until they had enough for the full job, but decided in favour of not mixing axe-work with crowbar-work, better to keep the muscles tuned to one thing at a time; if they cut too many posts, well, they'd soon find a use for them.

When the posts were cut and stacked along the line, they exchanged axes for shovels and crowbars, and by sundown next day had completed almost a mile of two barb, one plain wire fence. Mick though the cattle were quiet enough to let go, but they may as well tail them a few more days, seeing the horses had to be tailed and hobbled out at night until the paddock was ready for them. He left Pansy with the cattle and sent Marion scouting for a fallen log suitable to be hollowed out for a water trough. She found two, one large and one small. When they took the truck to load them on the next morning she explained, "Big one for the horses, small one a wash-trough for me."

Mick axe-trimmed the big one and showed her how to burn it out to shape and then went back to the fence-line for the day. She squatted in the sun and whisked at the flies and hoped the horses would appreciate what she was doing for them.

Then at last the fence was finished, the wire gate made, and the horses escorted into their paddock, hobble-free at last. The cattle did not seem to see them go; on the first night free half of them went back to the brush yard of their own accord and camped there.

Mick had measured the distance from the lagoon to the fence line to match the piping he had on hand, but until the mill and tank were erected the trough had to be filled by bucketing the water from the lagoon. Mick and Alec filled it the first time, and Mick said the girls could keep it topped up after that.

"Uphill all the way," pouted Marion, and raised no objection when Mick suggested that they put up the mill, build a tank stand and bolt the tank together and fill it, before they went back to the job of putting the Sydney Williams together.

"We've eaten and slept out on the flat for so many months now that another week or two isn't going to make much difference," she said, but all the same she was pleased when the tank was finished and the building began again.

She had seen the Sydney Williams Huts as they stood at the Army Depot, large rectangular steel-framed corrugated-iron sheds with corrugated-iron lift-up shutters in lieu of windows, and corrugated-iron doors, strictly functional, and she expected her new home would look much the same. But Mick had no intention of following the original plan once the roof was on. They didn't need a barn, he pointed out, but they did need verandahs in that climate, he'd move the walls in under the roof a bit.

The completed building had four large rooms with verandahs on three sides, the last room opening straight onto the flat to be the saddle shed. Next to it was the store-room, then the bedroom, and lastly, the kitchen, opening onto a back verandah, with a bathroom in one corner separating back and side verandah. There were doors enough for saddle-shed, kitchen, store-room and bathroom, the others would come later. He left a doorway from kitchen to bedroom, and bedroom to verandah, and open spaces for the windows, which he said he'd put in when the Wet season came and the stock-work was over. He'd rig the lights then too. Time was moving on, and there were cleanskins to be branded. And a yard to build first. And a bullock paddock before the Wet.

He did, however, make bush timber legs and supports for the door, and produced his table with a flourish.

"Wow!" shrieked Marion delightedly, "Now I can get the tucker up out of the ants and the dirt!"

"But the chairs are up to you, my girl. Should be some boxes around."

"Yeah, for the time being, but next killer can Alec cut me some greenhide strips, and I can make 'em like those chairs on the kitchen verandah at Delroy."

Pansy was called in to admire the table, which she did very satisfactorily with a long drawn-out "Ooh-aah!" She walked over and laid her hand on the smooth surface, and then they saw a transformation before their eyes. Slim Pansy's whole silhouette seemed to change and she became stout Carla. Every mannerism was there as she mimed Carla telling the housegirls what she'd do to them if the table wasn't scrubbed down properly, and Alec, peeping around the door-way to see what all the hilarity was about, was sternly admonished by gesture to wipe his feet before he came inside.

"Won't make much difference yet, Pansy," laughed Marion, "it's a dirt floor inside same as outside."

"No matter," said Pansy, dropping her pose, "one day we gettim proper floor he gotta do it then."

Marion decided she wanted the table on the back verandah for convenience because she still had to cook in the open until they acquired a stove. The men had no sooner carried it out for her than Pansy froze, head on one side, and said "Motorcar come-up!"

Mick's first thought was that it might be Paul Buxton, but the sound was coming from the direction of the Felix Creek track. They waited expectantly until they saw the utility in its attendant cloud of dust. Then Alec motioned Pansy and they withdrew to the small shed, as Mick and Marion walked towards the newcomers. The white man's neat khakis and the badges on the hats of both white and black men proclaimed them policeman and his tracker.

"Constable Tom Roberts," the young man introduced himself with a friendly smile. The tracker squatted beside the utility.

"Mick Hardy, isn't it?"

Mick introduced Marion and invited the young policeman onto the verandah, but he returned first to the vehicle and fished in the glove box.

"Brought you some mail."

There were two letters, a slim one from the Brands Office and a thick one which bore Maggie's handwriting. Mick put them aside while he stirred up the fire to make a billy of tea.

Tom Roberts stayed the night. That was the first night at Serendipity that Alec and Pansy did not eat with Mick and Marion, but lit another campfire behind the little shed, where Toby, the tracker, joined them.

Marion and Mick liked the policeman on first sight.

"I'm policeman, stock inspector, protector of Aborigines, all rolled into one. Anything you want to know?"

They talked well into the night. Tom had to assess a petrol ration for the station, though he didn't think the rationing would go on for much longer. He also pointed out that they needed driving licences, a fact that hadn't occurred to either of them before, and under his Protector of Aborigines hat, he gave them a list of basic food, clothing and blankets they were required to supply to Aboriginal employees and dependants. That done, he filled them in on various generalities about the vast district he patrolled.

Mick opened his letter and found that the MTM he'd asked for was not available, but the second M had been reversed, and the Hardy brand was now officially MTW, with an earmark of a V out of the bottom of the right ear facing. Tom told him that he could get brands made by an old chap in Felix Creek, and offered to take the particulars back to him.

Tom left late in the morning next day, after having registered the truck and jeep, written out driving licences for Mick, Marion, and Alec, and given Mick a supply of petrol ration coupons. He commented on the absence of any dogs on the station, and said he thought he knew where he could get a couple of good heeler pups for them. Marion had read her letter and scribbled a reply, which he promised to post for her, along with the one she had written at intervals over the past few weeks to Angela at Delroy.

Mick asked him whether the single store in Felix Creek carried stocks of fencing wire, and Tom offered to take an order back so that the store could get it down from Darwin for Mick by the time he came in to pick up the brands. Then he threw his swag on the back of his utility and called to Toby. As an afterthought he fished a couple of large pumpkins off the back. "Wife thought maybe you could use these, if you didn't have any yourself." Marion accepted with alacrity, and they parted with an invitation to visit Tom and his wife when they went to town.

"What a nice chap," remarked Marion, as the utility disappeared.

"Most outback policemen are," commented Mick, "pays to get along with the locals. Except the bad-hats, poddy-dodgers and so on!"

Marion had the grace to look ashamed, and then they both burst out laughing.

Alec, too, had been gleaning information from Toby, some of which might have surprised Tom if he had overheard it. The assessment of situations and characters, as seen through white and black eyes, often carried a different perspective. "Sometimes, I see 'em two ways," he told Mick.

"That reminds me of something I've been thinking about for a long time, Alec. I ought to be paying you and Pansy wages, but until we start selling cattle, which won't be this year, well, I just can't run to it."

Alec looked surprised.

"Mick, nobody don't pay wages to blackfellas, jus' clothes and tucker and tobacco. We aren't expectin' you to. We come of our own accord!"

"Beside the point. Anyway, you aren't a blackfella, Alec, and I'm not Nobody. You're both working for me, and I couldn't do what I'm doing without you. You oughta get something for it."

"Look Mick, forget it. We both got a better life than we had any other place, or likely to have, the way things are. Pansy, she likes that Marion better than anyone else she ever know. They real good mates."

"No," said Mick firmly, "fair's fair. What I reckon, Alec, is, when we do start branding and get under way, we brand some of the steers for you, a percentage depending on what we get. We could fix up an extra wire brand, so we'd know which were yours when we got 'em in, or maybe you might even get a brand of your own in time. What d'you reckon?"

Alec could only grin widely and nod. He shoved out a hand and they shook on it, no more words said.

Mick, on Tom's estimate, had decided to drive in to Felix Creek in three weeks' time, having rejected Tom's suggestion that if he made it five weeks the races would be on.

"Maybe next year," he'd said, ignoring Marion's interested glance. "Can't afford the time."

The weeks went quickly, too quickly for Marion's liking. The girls, though they no longer tailed the cattle regularly, spent as much time in the saddle as out of it. Their own mob had split up into smaller groups, wandering further afield and finding new waters along the main creek (which now went by the name of Homestead Creek), and smaller pools in some of the tributary creeks. Each of the groups had now been joined by bush cattle, and it was the girls' job to track down the little mobs, put them together, work them a bit, take them in to water sometimes, get them used to handling. Sometimes the girls took a cigarette swag and camped out overnight. The run became more and more familiar to them. Marion reported that some of the mobs now had more cleanskins than branders in them, and there were a few strangers here and there too. She marked the waterholes that looked like lasting well on Mick's map, and he began to take more and more notice of her estimates of numbers. What she was learning about tracking from being in Pansy's company outweighed her wishful thinking and made her figures more reliable.

The men had enclosed the trough in the corner of the horse paddock in a 40 by 30 water yard, and extended it a further 30 yards, which they divided on the long side into two, to make a 20 by 10 and a 10 by 10 enclosure. It was hard and tough work. They used solid bloodwood posts, any amount to be found close by along the creek, and Alec had found a patch of lancewood for the rails about ten miles away, which had to be cut and carted on the truck, but were worth the trouble because of their superiority over any closer timber. They made the gates by sinking blocks of bloodwood with pipes in them for the base of the gateposts so they would swing as if on hinges.

When Mick and Marion finally went to town the last of the plain wire had been used to wire on rails, and Alec and Pansy were told to take a spell for a couple of days.

The road was new to Marion, and so was the settlement of Felix Creek. It was nearly dark when they got in, and the first person they saw in the one-street main street was Tom, who greeted them like old friends and insisted that they camp at his place rather than go to the hotel. Mick hadn't intended to stay at the hotel anyway, camp just out of town on the river, but when assured that Tom's wife wouldn't be put out, he accepted the invitation.

Muriel Roberts was a pretty brunette with a toddling son clutching at the skirt of her sunfrock. Marion, in trousers and shirt because all her other clothes were still at Delroy, felt a bit gauche at first, but Muriel soon put her at ease. She herself was a station girl, and needed no explanations. Marion thoroughly enjoyed the evening, particularly as the conversation no longer concentrated on cattle and yard-building.

In the morning Muriel showed her round the garden, picked some pawpaws and pumpkins for her and filled a cardboard carton with tomatoes and snake beans. She called Toby to dig out some banana suckers and wrap them in wet bags.

"The store only sells potatoes and onions, so if you want anything else you have to grow it yourself. In this climate everything grows so quickly, Marion, you can have a garden in no time."

Though Mick always maintained that as long as you have onions you never got Barcoo rot, Marion decided then and there to save seeds and put them in a garden as soon as she got home. Mick came back at lunch-time with Tom and two delightful blue-heeler pups. They'd driven to a place a bit out of town to pick them up after Mick had loaded the wire and got the brands.

"Cattle dogs, so don't make too much of a fuss of them and spoil them," warned Mick to Marion, who was doing just that.

"Pitty you can't come in for the races," smiled Muriel as they left.

"Next year for sure," called Marion, as she settled the pups beside her.

They got home well after midnight, and Marion slept until Pansy's exclamation over the pups woke her; the men had been working at the yards for hours.

Yard finished, Mick took a couple of days to accompany the girls on their track-riding, to see the prospects for himself, before he started on the bullock paddock. Home again, he said thoughtfully, "I think it might be worth while taking up Paul Buxton's offer to muster with his stock-camp and split the cleanskins. We'd get more that way than doing it by ourselves, and there's plenty there all right!"

He suggested that Marion and Pansy take the jeep and drive down to Parrot Hill with a letter for Paul, but they were saved the trip when the Parrot Hill manager himself turned up with a laughing crowd of blacks on the back of his truck, en route to the races and checking out the shorter track there through Serendipity. He made his apologies again to Marion, and accepted smoko.

"Thought you might see it that way," he told Mick, and nodded at Mick's mud-map of the proposed bullock paddock.

"Tell you what," he said, "I'd like to get into it as soon as we can. Why don't I drop off a couple of my boys on the way back from the races to give you a hand." That suited Mick.

"Want me to take your two in to the races along with my lot?" He nodded towards Alec and Pansy in conversation with the Parrot Hill blacks, none of whom had got off the truck in case they got left behind.

"Yeah, why not, they've certainly earned it," grinned Mick.

Alec and Pansy didn't take much persuading. Mick wrote Alec a small cheque.

"Enough to have a good time, but not enough to get into trouble," he said.

Pansy re-appeared dragging their swag, already attired in one of her Darwin dresses instead of the pants and shirt she'd worn moments before, and was hoisted aboard by willing hands. Alec passed up the swag and vaulted aboard.

Marion watched them go with something akin to envy - the races were the best fun of the year.

"C'mon, girl," Mick gave her a quick hug, "into the jeep, and I'll show you where we're going to put the paddock!"

Chapter 18 *Parrot Hill attends a muster.*
The padre visits.

Alec had not devoted himself purely to pleasure at the races. He had also taken the opportunity to size up the Parrot Hill boys, and persuade two of them to volunteer for the fencing job. Big Jimmy and Wally were both single boys, good natured, competitive, and could skite as good as any white fella, so the chances were they would work with the same camaraderie.

When they got back to Serendipity, Mick and Marion already had the fence-line roughly marked, extending two sides of the horse paddock for approximately another four miles, to make a five by five mile paddock with the horse paddock tucked into one corner of it. It was as good going as Mick could choose, big trees for strainers wherever possible, with only one patch of thick scrub of about a quarter of a mile to negotiate. The weapon-carrier, with a log wired in front, roared and grumbled its way slowly through the tangle of undergrowth until it finally was through into clearer going. Then he unhitched the log and reversed its position so that it now dragged behind the truck. He set Marion to driving the truck behind him as he scouted ahead in the jeep marking the line. Stretching the imagination a bit, Marion thought, you could practically say she was making a road, but it was gut-busting work, and she was glad when Mick called a spell every couple of hours.

With the return of the work force she went on to lighter duties, handing the truck over to Alec, and retiring to her old job of track-riding the cattle with Pansy.

"No good having a paddock to put 'em in, if we don't know where to pick 'em up," said Mick, "You two can keep 'em in hand until we bring up the re-inforcements."

"He had set a date with Paul Buxton for the loan of the Parrot Hill stock-camp for a fortnight's muster, and the fence-builders raced against time to complete the bullock paddock, and the days ran into one another as the posts and wires crept steadily forward. First light saw the men on the job, and the setting sun heralded knock-off time. The girls had it easier, returning home in time to make bread, cook vast quantities of beef and potatoes, and to tend the embryo garden Marion was encouraging behind the house. The pumpkin seeds had been scattered round the run any time anyone going anywhere on horseback had thought to pocket a handful.

Marion, sneaking a siesta on the verandah after dinner, was awakened by cheers as the two vehicles roared up to the homestead.

"All done," announced Mick, as the men crowded behind him. "We put a wire gate from the horse paddock into the bullock paddock, and turned the horses into it, so they'll make a pad round the fence-line before we put the cattle in. They've got to come back to the horse paddock to get a drink every day."

"Two barb, one plain," grinned Alec, "good as you'd see anywhere!"

"And the girls can help the horses tomorrow, eh?" laughed Mick. "What do you say to dragging a log behind the truck a couple more times?"

"You wouldn't like what I'd say, but I guess we'll do it."

"We're a couple of days ahead of schedule, so we're taking the rest of the day off, and tomorrow we'll stick up a check fence between the homestead waterhole and lagoon and the horse yard, so nothing can drink there. Got the holes dug already!"

Wally and Big Jim stood shyly in the yard, as Marion stirred up the fire and put the billy on, and produced the brownie she'd made the day before in the camp oven. Mick disappeared into the store and came back with a couple of tins of tobacco each for the boys and a handful of boiled lollies all round, and everyone grinned and laughed when Marion lined up for her share, and then demanded a second issue on behalf of Pansy.

There was laughter and corroboree that night, a sound that Mick and Marion realised with a pang that they had not heard for a long time.

"I guess next year we'll have our own blacks; we'll have to, to run the place," said Mick as he lay in bed with his arms around his wife, and listened nostalgically to the haunting melody.

"Where'll they come from?" murmured Marion drowsily, "wonder why we haven't seen any in all this time we've been here. Pansy and I've run across plenty of old camping-places."

"Gone to the mission, I suppose, whitefella tucker and all that. We'll have to try and lure some back."

"Mmm, good idea. Nothing like soft background music, I say!" and she giggled and bit Mick suddenly on the ear. He accepted her invitation with alacrity.

The Parrot Hill stock-camp arrived on schedule.

"Big mob horse come-up!" announced Pansy, who heard them first. The girls, who had been lazing on the verandah, hallooed to the men putting the finishing touches on the yards, and then, overcome with a natural curiosity, they walked over to the yards to greet the new arrivals. Pack horses, plant horses, three or four dogs, a white man, a half-caste, and six more black stockmen, counted Marion rapidly.

The days of the Serendipity cleanskins were numbered.

Mick, walking towards the dismounting horsemen, let out a shout of surprise.

"Alan! I thought you were going croc-shooting!"

"Nope," drawled the lanky head-stockman, "can't trust them croc-shooters no more'n the Chinks. They got the rest of me deferred pay before we even left Darwin. Something wicked at poker, they was. Paul come in time to rescue me, couple days after you left."

He suddenly became aware of Marion, hovering at Mick's elbow, and made her a low sweeping bow.

"Look what the Quiet Fella's got tucked away, hidin' you out here, all to himself. Didn't mention he had a wife when I seen him in Darwin." Then expectantly, "You *are* married to him, aren't you?"

"She certainly is!" laughed Mick, and introduced her.

"No matter!" said Alan enigmatically, shaking her hand and winking.

Marion, not quite knowing how to take him, but warming to the obvious compliment, sincere or not, disengaged her hand, and said she'd see him at supper time when they were all organised. Alf, the half-caste, was their cook, and she left Mick and Alec to talk plans for the evening camp and the next day's muster, and walked back to the house with Pansy.

"Cheeky bugger, that one!" sniffed Pansy, who had witnessed the interchange, "you watchim, Marion."

Marion promised she would, and then they both burst out laughing.

"You got big mob to watch," she told Pansy, and they agreed that one of the compensations of their isolation was the undue proportion of males to females, which could only have the satisfactory effect of making Mick and Alec appreciate their good fortune and react accordingly.

"Sometimes they don't even remember we're girls, when we're on the other end of a log they're lifting, or saddling up in the yard," thought Marion, "but I reckon they won't forget in the next couple of weeks."

They didn't. Mick said firmly that the girls would not be needed in the stock-camp, too dangerous for them, he didn't want the responsibility of having to worry about them with so much else on his mind, and when Marion pouted and looked as if she might protest, he grinned at her engagingly and told her that with the girls along the men couldn't be expected to keep their minds properly on the job at hand, and she wanted lots of cleanskins, didn't she?

"What a diplomat you are, my darling," she told him.

"Plenty for you to do, anyway, Honey. Someone's got to ride the bullock paddock fence to make sure what we put in stays in. We'd have to take a man out of the camp to do it if you and Pansy weren't here."

That was what she liked about Mick. He boosted her ego and assured her she'd be pulling her weight all in one hit.

Alan was typical of scores of ringers in the back country, competent, likeable, a master-craftsman at his job, loyal to his employer of the moment, and completely irresponsible in his private life. Money slipped through his fingers like water, what else was there to spend it on but grog and gambling; his only dependant was his dog, who required nothing more that a bit of beef once a day, and gave his all in return. Marion wondered if Alan would have been more responsible towards himself if the dog had been a girl, for instance, someone to give some purpose to his life. Probably. But what girl would throw in her lot with a bloke so obviously irresponsible. There weren't too many girls available, and they could pick and choose, and girls liked security. Still he must have met plenty of girls in his three years away in the Army. But perhaps, like other ringers she had known, he could not make the choice between the girl or the job which, by its very nature, precluded marriage. Only managers had homes; the ringers home was his swag wherever he unrolled it.

The muster began on a relatively quiet note, for the cattle accustomed to drink at Homestead Hole, and now prevented from doing so by the check-fence, hung on the water in puzzlement, and were ripe for the picking. A big percentage of them were the already-handled cattle that had walked across half the Territory and they were well-conditioned to the sight of men and horses, and they had been yarded many times. The wild cattle too had become used to the sight of mounted riders in all the weeks that the girls had ridden the run, and were not unduly panicked when the riders appeared.

"No dogs today," Mick had warned as they saddled up in the yards. "That's one thing my cattle aren't used to, so I reckon dogs might do more harm than good today."

Even the yarding up provided no more than the average excitement, for the handled cattle, thirsty and with the smell of the water in their nostrils, recalled that they had drunk from troughs before, and led the way through the yards to the water. By nightfall thirty-seven cleanskins had either been scruffed or hauled up to the bronco panel and now wore either the Serendipity or the Parrot Hills brand, and Marion had sat on the top rail in her big hat with a notebook in her hand and tallied male and female.

That was the first time that Serendipity brands had smoked on hide. Mick felt a great thrill of elation as he handed the brands back to Alec and reached for his pocket knife to earmark the first struggling victim. Marion felt it, too, as she drew her first tally stroke with a stub of pencil.

There was no notebook tally after that first day. Mick did it with a pocketful of pebbles, buttoned down in his right breast pocket in the mornings, and transferred one by one to the left pocket during the day, and then, at night, the pebbles were counted and returned to the right pocket, and the number scratched on his tobacco tin with the point of his pocket knife.

The days were long and hard, and Mick, who had never been a man for dogs, was forced to admit that without the heelers many a beast would have escaped to its native scrub.

They built brush yards where they could, ate before dawn and after dark, and hardly paused to snatch at the sandwich of damper and beef the cook handed each man to pack in his saddle-bag at dawn. The dinner-camp of the normal muster or the droving trip did not exist as such; they ate when they could, and sometimes they did not eat at all, in the wild rushes and the bellowing and the dust.

Some days were better than others, with handled cattle from either Serendipity or Parrot Hills among the little mobs. The scrub bulls, unless they went quietly, were shot. They'd never be saleable and tried to break away continually, likely to take the rest of the mob with them.

Marion never knew when to expect the cloud of dust and the bellows and shouts which heralded the arrival of another mob at the yard to be cut out or branded, and added to the growing numbers in the bullock paddock which she and Pansy must police. She handed out pannikins of tea and cooked vast quantities of steak at all hours to release the stock-camp cook as an extra hand in the yard, and offered Dettol and ointment form her small stock for the worst of the scratches and bruises sustained.

They told her how a scrub bull had treed Mick and how Alec had drawn the bull off and nearly got his horse gored in the doing of it; they skited of how many mickies each man had thrown, and jeered at each other for the ones that had got away. They risked life and limb hourly and made it sound like a game, thought Marion wonderingly. There was plenty at stake for Mick, but of the rest only Alan and the cook would be paid for their work, and not a fancy wage at that.

Two weeks Paul had allowed them, and in that time they covered about half of the run. On the last day they mustered the bullock paddock and cut out the Parrot Hill cattle, seventeen of their own cattle which had roamed north, some good bullocks among them, and 149 newly-branded cleanskins. That should make Paul happy. They yarded them for the night and celebrated, the blacks in corroboree on the flat behind the little shed, and the whites and Alf yarning on the moonlit verandah of the homestead.

"We've got a lot to thank you for, Alan," said Mick seriously, "If it wasn't for you we probably wouldn't have got the block."

"How do you figure that?" asked Alan. "I never done nothing to help."

"Well, if you hadn't been such a decent bloke I wouldn't have had a drink with you and the croc fella, and then I wouldn't have seen the Lands bloke in the bar, " and Mick went on to relate the incident.

"Done a good turn without ever meanin' to," laughed Alan, "but I never done myself much good, did I, lost three years' pay in three days."

"Yeah," continued Alf, "Paul felt real bad about gettin' held up goin' up to pick you up when he got your telegram. He had the bosses up, and couldn't get away straight off. He reckoned you'd be flat broke after a coupla days in Darwin, if you wasn't already broke by the time you got there!"

"Well," said Alan, "I dunno why he worried, because I spose I woulda done it all at the first races I got to. For that matter, I woulda done it while I was in the Army, if they hadn't kept it back and give it to me when I got demobbed."

Marion, curious, asked him why he did it if he always lost, but it seemed he didn't always lose, and the rewards were worth the risks.

"I'm lookin' for a bloke who'll stake his station when I'm on a winning streak. You're doin' it the hard way, Mick, I might even get there before ya!"

"Let's know if you do!" laughed Marion, as they parted, and Alan and Alf went off in the moonlight to their swags beside the yard full of grumbling cattle.

When they had farewelled the Parrot Hill camp the next morning Marion set about catching up the station diary which she had neglected during the muster, and Mick took out the exercise book he called his stock-book, and carefully entered up 76 females and 74 males to the numbers already there. It looked pretty good at first, but then his face grew sober, and he began figuring on the back of an envelope.

"We've got four or five years to get through before we'll have bullocks to sell, nothing younger could walk the distance into Queensland. That's how long we've got to spin out the money we've got left."

Marion looked up at his anxious face, surprised at this first sign she had seen of anything but optimism for the future.

"But we've got a lot more than we really expected, haven't we? The truck, the jeep, a homestead, and now the cleanskins, cattle we didn't have to buy?"

"Yeah, I know, but Honey, it's not much of a life for you. It's about the roughest homestead I ever saw. Nothing in it, not even a stove."

"It's got a bed," protested Marion stoutly, "and a table!"

"I promise I'll fix it up for you when the Wet comes, after we've picked up a few more cattle and branded the calves that'll be dropping soon. I'll put in those windows for you, and make a few shelves, and a Coolgardie Cooler, and so on. We could rig up some sort of ant-bed oven too."

"Yes, and I'll have the garden a going concern soon," said Marion enthusiastically, firmly rejecting the memory of the tomato seedlings the pups had scratched up.

"Mick, it won't cost us much to live; we can practically live off the land here, fish, turkeys, those strangers you put in the paddock for killers. I can get some chooks from Muriel too."

"And when the cows start calving, we'll find a quiet one and tame her for a house-cow," offered Mick, catching her enthusiasm. "Honey, you're a good little mate for a battler. We'll make out okay."

He divided the figure he had written on the envelope by five.

"We've got to live on 170 pounds a year for the next five years to be safe. And that means fuel and clothes and everything, as well as tucker. Think we can do it?"

"Easy," said Marion, not really knowing the mechanics of costing that Mick had gone through with every purchase he had made that year. "If we could run to a second-hand sewing machine, I could make our shirts and things, and that'd cut down a bit."

It did not occur to either of them that, with the assets and potential they now had, they might have been able to get a bank loan to tide them over. Their backgrounds had never included an acquaintance with business finance. If they had heard the word mortgage, its only connotations would have been dread and despair associated with foreclosures during the wretched years of the Depression. They knew that they would need a stock-camp of black ringers to help with the work when the cattle bred up, men would have to be fed and clothed, and paid at least some small wage, as Jim Burton would have paid them at Delroy and fed and clothed their wives and children. They could get by with the four of them and maybe a couple of single boys, but it would be tight, very tight.

So they did the only thing they could do; forgot about the finance and got on with the job in hand. Maggie had always said "Don't cross your bridges until you come to them," and Marion had absorbed her philosophy without really thinking about it.

They took the pups along and made a more leisurely muster of parts of the run which had been missed by the Parrot Hill camp, and came back with a small mob of cleanskin cows and a couple of their own heifers, all heavy in calf, to add to the Bullock Paddock mob. Mick was intensely relieved to find that the paddock fences were still intact, for he had worried during the few days away that scrub bulls outside the paddock may have wandered up and challenged the few quiet bulls he had pushed in with the rest. He'd never seen a fence yet that could withstand the assault of two bulls, one on either side, with nothing else on their minds but combat.

Soon there were calves to hand, scruffing them in the yard and fixing them up so quickly that they went bawling back to their anxious mothers in the next yard, hardly aware of what had happened to them.

When the weather turned hot Mick realised that he ought to make the trip to town for the Wet Season stores, and he and Marion made their list and had three days in Felix Creek, longer than they'd meant to stay, but they had to wait for the train bringing a fresh consignment of flour to the store. Tom and Muriel made a fuss of them, and appreciated the fresh and salt beef from the beast Mick had killed the day before they left Serendipity. Muriel promised to look out for a sewing-machine for Marion when she and Tom went up to Darwin before Christmas, and she loaded Marion up with produce from her garden and magazines she'd been saving for months.

"Handy to have something to read in the Wet, when there's nothing else you can do," she said, and Marion realised that she, who had always been such an avid reader, had read nothing more than jam-tin labels for almost a year. There were books in her trunk at Delroy, and she vaguely wondered when they would be able to send for them.

When they got home they found they had visitors, the Inland Mission travelling padre and his wife, who had arrived via Parrot Hill the night before, and they also proffered a bunch of magazines "for the Wet." Marion and Mick liked them both on first sight. They introduced themselves as "Bill and Pat, marriages and christenings on request, but it doesn't look as if you're in need of either."

They spent a pleasant evening together, and were almost ready to go to bed, when Alec coughed discreetly from the darkness beyond the verandah, and asked Mick if he could speak to him for a moment. Mick excused himself, and they heard the murmur of voices, and then Mick came back with a broad grin on his face.

"Looks as if we need you after all, Padre. Alec and Pansy would like you to marry 'em. I told Alec to bring Pansy to see you in the morning. Okay?"

Bill seemed taken aback. "Er, I've never married blacks before. Never been asked, actually. The established missions look after them, and we don't like to interfere in their area. We look after the needs of the whites in isolated areas. I - er - don't know."

Marion, tired from the long trip and the unexpected demand of hospitality, had experienced a rush of pleasure at Mick's words, but she was unable to handle the anger which flooded her at the Padre's reaction. So her friend Pansy wasn't good enough, wasn't the right colour to qualify for his administrations. All the buried resentments of her own childhood alienation caused by the hypocrisies of religion welled up in her, and she burst out furiously, surprising herself even more than her listeners, "I bet Jesus wouldn't knock anyone back just because they're black. You mob who don't turn a hair at white stinkers and crooks couldn't care less about whether somebody's decent or not, just as long as they're not black. You make me sick!"

"Hey, Marion, hey!" remonstrated Mick, reaching out a restraining hand as she jumped vehemently to her feet.

Poor Bill, momentarily stunned by Marion's interpretation of his reticence, also stood in his embarrassment, and it was left to his wife Pat, still complacently seated, to defuse the situation.

"You've got it wrong, Marion. Bill didn't mean he didn't want to marry them; he only meant that he didn't want to offend the local mission. They do consider the blacks their area, you know. It's a bit like Roman Catholic priests don't marry Protestant couples, and Baptist ministers don't marry Anglicans, you see. Because the bush is considered differently because of the isolation, Bill's service is non-denominational, doesn't matter what you are he can marry you. So I don't see why a black couple should be any different, Bill."

"No, no, of course not," stammered Bill.

"Anyway, I think the missions only look after the blacks that actually live there," said Mick, "and we haven't seen hide nor hair of anyone from a mission, and we got one right alongside us. Come to that, Alec's part-white, if that helps any."

"Why should it?" said Marion coldly.

"Yes, why should it?" echoed Bill a little too heartily. "Tomorrow then. We can fix it all up in the morning. It's a compliment really, isn't it, that they should ask me to marry them." He was still floundering in Marion's none-too-conciliatory presence.

Pat rescued him before he put his foot in it again.

"Shut-up, and come to bed. See you all in the morning."

The bride wore her Darwin dress, and the matron of honour put on a clean shirt for the occasion. Mick doubled for the father of the bride and best man. Pansy, overcome with shyness, had to be prompted frequently, and giggled until Marion dug her in the ribs before she too succumbed to Pansy's infectious merriment and ruined the seriousness of the occasion. They hadn't thought of the ring until the ceremony was well under way; the padre hadn't quite regained his usual aplomb, and had forgotten to mention it. He came to the part "With this ring" and looked up at Alec questioningly.

"Ring?" gawped Alec; turning to Mick for explanation.

Marion quickly slid her gold band off her finger, passed it to Mick, who gave it to Alec, who, instructed by Bill, shoved it on Pansy's small slender black finger. Pansy said, "Ooh-aah, proper flash one, eh," and held up her hand to admire it. But when she lowered her hand the ring, built for Marion's sturdier Anglo-Saxon knuckles, slid straight off into the dust of the homestead verandah and rolled towards one of the pups, now almost full-grown but still full of youthful joie-de-vivre. Or maybe he thought it was a titbit being thrown him. He pounced, flicked it up with his tongue, and gulped.

"Oh my God!" ejaculated the padre, as the matron of honour gave a despairing wail and launched herself at the half-grown heeler.

"Chain the mongrel up," roared Mick, "and nobody let him off until we get it back!"

The groom was prompt to obey, and hauled the surprised animal off to the hollow log behind the kitchen that served as his kennel.

The party re-assembled, and the ceremony was concluded without further interruption. Marion, sentimental about her ring, which had never before been off her finger since the day Mick placed it there, pulled herself together, so she did not spoil Pansy's day, and resolutely put away her impulse to break down and bawl. Bill produced his register and fountain pen, and then they struck the next hitch. Alec didn't know who his half-caste father was, and he didn't have a surname.

"No problem," stated the best man firmly. "I didn't have one either, so the matron at the orphanage just gave me one. We'll give you one. What'd you like?"

"I know," said Pat, entering into the spirit of the thing, and impressed despite herself at the friendship of these two men. "Wasn't Hardy Nelson's mate? Why not Nelson?"

"Alec Nelson - yeah, that goes together all right. How about it, Alec?"

Alec grinned broadly and said he reckoned it would do him, asked how to spell it, and signed the register. Pansy, taught by Marion to sign her whitefella and tribal skin name, followed suit with a flourish, and then they all adjourned to the kitchen verandah to partake of a light luncheon of salt beef courtesy of Parrot Hill and salad vegetables courtesy of the police station at Felix Creek. There was even a cake - well, half a cake. Pat produced what was left of a boiled fruit-cake from their tucker-box, and Pansy and Alec ceremoniously cut it into six pieces.

Then Bill produced a box camera and lined them up for a photo out on the flat, the Nelsons in the middle, flanked by the Hardys.

When, some months later, Tom brought the mail which included a letter from Pat with two copies of the photograph, there was, clearly outlined in the background beyond the smiling quartet, a hollow log with a sulky blue heeler head protruding from it.

"I bet he did it on purpose!" laughed Mick.

Chapter 19   *Cyclone and bush surgery*

    They had believed that they were prepared for the Wet, but this grey world of water and tumultuous sound was like nothing Mick or Marion had ever experienced before. The belting of the rain on the tin roof drowned out their voices so that they had to shout to each other across the table, and the strident unceasing chorus of the frogs surpassed the roar of the rain, rising and falling in crescendos like waves beating against a rock face. The frogs were everywhere. With every step Marion took a dozen small ones leapt aside; they packed into billycans; pushed under boxes and swags; and in the makeshift bathroom large green ones with deep sonorous voices blinked owlishly between utterances. In the intervals between the sheeting rain-storms the world outside the building seemed to be composed of serried ranks of frog-armies stretching back to the horizons, batallions of them chanting remorselessly a paeon of praise to their water-god. The billabong, seething with them, now lapped the posts of the check fence only fifty yards from Alec's and Pansy's hut, and Marion's garden was long gone, washed down the slope into the billabong with the first torrential downpours. Only the pawpaw trees sheltering against the verandah remained, growing six inches overnight, oblivious of the garlands of small frogs perpetually dropping from their slender trunks to join their fellows in the mud of the verandah floor.

    The frogs were not the only intruders. The first storm had heralded an invasion of six to eight inch long centipedes, hundreds of them, horrible feathery translucent bluish things, advancing relentlessly as if driven by a single mind. Marion's scream alerted Mick, and then Alec and Pansy came running, the dogs panicking at their heels. At first they tried sweeping them back outside with the brush brooms, but still they came. They spent the night huddled on the beds they dragged into the kitchen and sitting on the table, the kerosene lantern burning all night, taking turns to repulse the invaders with firesticks from the ant-bed hearth at the end of the kitchen, and dodging the occasional one which dropped twitching from the rafters above them. By morning they had gone as swiftly and silently as they came.

After that traumatic night even the snakes did not bother Marion. They came singly, mostly carpet snakes or pythons, one every two or three days, intent only on sanctuary from the driving walls of water. As long as they avoided the kitchen and the bedroom Marion let them be, though she was careful each morning to upend her boots and thump them on the ground before putting them on, after Pansy related to her how she had almost put her foot into a boot already inhabited by a carpet snake.

Mould grew overnight on everything leather or wood, and the magazines the old Arnhem-land hands had given Marion grew their quota also, so that the covers became a damp grey-green unreadable mess. Mick's instructions to save their cigarette butts in case an extended Wet meant a tobacco shortage did not go unheeded, but each butt was instantly placed into an empty tin or jar with the lid screwed down tightly. Marion remembered with disgust the neglected butts she had found one morning in the tobacco-tin ash-tray, two fat inch-long slugs swollen to twice their girth, with curling tendrils of mould waving from them. A smoke, rationed race-horse thin now, was one of the few pleasures left to them, and not to be sacrificed to the voracious mould.

Nothing at Delroy had ever prepared Marion for this. The raised homestead on wooden piles, the flywired protection from the snakes and insects and frogs, and the floors above water-level had insulated her from any understanding of what a Wet season could mean to those who lived in camps and bush shelters, and she confided her reactions to the station diary.

Mick and Alec, unable to continue any outside station work, turned their attentions to improving the buildings. The glass windows replaced the shutters, and an ant-bed oven and raised fire-bed with bars set into the ant-bed hob to make a stove-top substitute sent Marion into ecstasies of delight. It took up half one end wall of the kitchen, blocked in with sheets of tin which culminated in a chimney which drew the smoke out perfectly, more, as Mick said, by good luck than good management. He built shelves in the alcove beside the fireplace, long enough and wide enough to take all the tins, cooking equipment and plates they owned, and still room for ten times as much. Mick was a perfectionist, and he had all the time in the world to do a good job. The Coolgardie Cooler he built on the verandah was twice as big and twice as efficient as the one Marion remembered from her childhood in Mudjinup. Alec, a master of the green-hide art, worked on the hide strips saved from their killers of the past six months, and stretched them across bush timber frameworks to make chairs to replace the kerosene cases they had been using as seats.

Marion and Pansy grabbed the kerosene cases before Mick could incorporate them into his building plans and with much giggling and secretly borrowed hammer, nails and hessian, converted the boxes into rough dressing-tables with shelves for their few clothes. Nails driven into the walls were good enough for the men's shirts and trousers for the time being; they had no underclothes or socks or small items like the girls had. During a couple of days' lull from the rainstorms Pansy showed Marion how to strip the leaves from the pandanus palms along the creek, and how to weave them into circular mats for bedroom and bathroom, a little protection from the muddy floors and easily replaced when they became too dirty. Day by day the homestead became more comfortable and convenient.

Pansy, in all her twenty years, had weathered as many Wet seasons, some better, some worse, and she could not really understand the violence of Marion's reaction and her obsession with some sort of raised flooring before the next Wet came around. The Wet was the Wet; there wasn't anything you could do about it, so you just accepted what came, and waited for the Dry. She pointed out to Marion that all the blackfellow rainmakers sang up the rain for the very purpose of creating plenty of animal and bird life for the blackfellows to eat in the coming Dry; you couldn't have one without the other. Same for whitefellows; no more water, no more bullock. Suitably chastened, Marion stopped whingeing to herself about the inconveniences, and concentrated on the benefits. She began to feel ashamed of herself for the slight resentment she had been nurturing towards Mick, who, she'd felt could at least have shown her some sympathy in the predicament he'd brought her to. He, of course, exultant in the thought of a good season ahead, and appreciative of the time to do all the odd jobs to improve the living quarters, had not even suspected her attitude, and certainly would not have understood it if he had.

"It's those bloody stupid Women's magazines I've been reading," sniffed Marion, "full of quizzes about love and marriage, and soppy stories, and advertisements for kitchen appliances."

So, with the anniversary of their first year together rapidly approaching, Marion got her priorities straightened out again, mentally thanked Pansy, and used the magazines page by page to light the morning fires in the new fireplace.

There was a break in the weather a few days before Christmas, patches of blue sky, vivid green of new grass, and shriek of birdlife down at the lagoon. They took advantage of the break to cut out the cows, brand the new calves, and turn them out from the confines of the paddock. Not all of them, but enough, for some, conditioned to drinking for weeks at the trough, still waded knee-deep through water each day to drink there, and were easily picked up. No point in keeping them in the paddock to flog it out once the rains ceased; it would be years before the male calves were saleable.

But out in the Arafura Sea a cyclone was gathering its strength for an onslaught upon the ragged coastline of mangroves and long white beaches. To the south of the spinning vortex of wild winds, the rains once again deluged the sodden ranges and swampy plains, and the ragged streamers of grey cloud reached out towards Serendipity, thickened relentlessly, closed in, engulfed the tiny isolated homestead. It was Christmas Eve.

Although it was barely five o'clock the light was all but gone, and Marion, reaching for the lamp on the fireside shelf, suddenly became aware that she was being watched. She stiffened and stared. Beyond the open door and the back verandah in the grey curtains of drizzle she became aware of darker streaks of grey, opaque and indefinite, like stunted tree-trunks where no trees ought to be. They stood immobile and silent, and one of the figures appeared distorted as if he were carrying an awkward bundle.

"Mick!" she called sharply, and then repeated her call louder, over the sound of the rain on the roof.

Mick, who could no longer see what he was doing in the saddle room, had just decided to give his task away, and was halfway along the verandah when he heard her call. He saw the motionless figures twenty yards away, recognised the blurred silhouettes as Aboriginal in stance, and shouted to them, "Wotname?"

Hesitantly they began to move forward. Mick motioned them into the shelter of the back verandah, and then Marion saw that the burden the man was carrying was a child. The six men were naked but for nagas around their loins, and obviously terrified at their own temerity in approaching the white man's shelter.

"They're not blacks on walkabout," thought Marion wonderingly, "they're real wild blackfellows!"

She was not altogether right. One of them at least knew some white contact.

"Wotname?" queried Mick again, and one, seemingly younger than the rest, stepped forward and spoke haltingly in pidgin.

"Usfella bin seeim track, bin follow. Wee-ai" (he pointed with his lips towards the recumbent child) "wee-ai proper sick, mightbe close-up finish, Mummy bin finish long time. You fixim?"

Mick, stepping closer to the child, saw at once that the boy was either asleep or unconscious, and that the small arm hanging loose, the hand still partly daubed with clay and strips of bark, was grossly swollen. He walked to the perimeter of the verandah and shouted for Alec, who came running from his hut to join them. As he took the child from the skinny arms that supported it, he directed Alec to find them some shelter and give them a feed.

"Tell 'em to come back in the morning. We'll do what we can."

Marion had already brought a blanket from the bedroom and spread it on the table, where Mick laid the child down. She hastily lit the lamp, and he brought it closer. A sickly pungent odour hovered over the table.

"A basin of hot water, and some clean rag, so I can get this muck off and see what's doing," he ordered. Looks poisoned to me!"

Alec appeared again, with Pansy hovering at his shoulder, staring wide-eyed at the table and its burden. The boy, stark naked, looked about six years old, and he was not full-blood. The dark straight hair, the lighter skin, the cast of features hinted at an admixture of white and Chinese blood. He lay stiff on the table, barely breathing, but Marion, noticing the flutter of his eyelids, knew that he was conscious and probably terrified.

The stink of the wound was awesome as Mick sponged dried blood and pus into the basin. The edges of the wound revealed were greenish-black in hue and the whole palm of the hand was split open. The forearm was puffy and distended.

Mick stood back, then bent again towards the boy and sniffed deeply. "It's gangrenous!" he said quietly.

"Will he die?" asked Marion anxiously, trying the quell the heaving of her stomach.

"Probably," Mick replied.

"What can you do? Can't you do something?"

Mick's face was white in the lamplight.

"That stink, that's gangrene all right, Mick," said Alec softly.

"What'll we do?" wailed Marion.

"There's only one thing we can do," said Mick, almost in a dream, as if he were talking to himself. "We can cut it off above the swelling. If we don't he'll die. He'll probably die anyway from the shock."

The momentary indecision swept from his face and he said brusquely, "Marion, see there's plenty of hot water, more rag, the Dettol bottle, and in that carton in the bedroom you'll find a half bottle of rum I was keeping for tomorrow. Get them, and then you and Pansy get out."

Marion, barely recognising her Mick in this suddenly-stern stranger, ran hastily to do his bidding.

"Alec, you'll have to help me. Shove the tin bucket on the fire, steel up the skinning knives and put 'em in to boil, and go and get my hornsaw, and boil that too."

He took the bottle Marion anxiously proffered without a glance at her, unscrewed the cap, and poured some into a pannikin. Then he lifted the boy into a sitting position and held the pannikin to his lips. The child may have thought he was being given a drink of water, or he may have reacted automatically. The first swallow sent a violent shudder through his body, and the eyes shot open in surprise.

"More!" said Mick firmly. The boy made to resist, and then slumped weakly and took two more swallows before Mick laid him down again.

"By the time the gear is boiled enough, he ought to have passed out if we give him enough."

He noticed Marion still hovering stark-faced in the doorway.

"Marion, go and get the reins of my bridle from the saddle-room; I'll need a tourniquet. And then maybe you'd better go over to the hut with Pansy. It's not going to be nice once we start."

She shook her head mutely. "We'll stay on the verandah," she whispered. "You might want something in a hurry."

They were none of them to forget that night, though the memories of the patient himself could have been nothing but pain and rum-induced euphoria.

Alec held the small body down to the table and Mick, with knife and hornsaw, amputated the arm just above the elbow and cauterised the stump with the poker from the fire. A thin scream bubbled from the boy's lips, and on the verandah the girls clutched each other. The rain had passed, and as if in answer to the scream the eldritch call of a curlew floated eerily to their ears.

Pansy began to tremble violently. "Debil-debil comin'" she gasped, reverting instantly to her tribal background.

Marion, shocked into the realisation that Pansy was about to have hysterics, hissed angrily, "Don't be so bloody silly; it's a curlew!"

Then the odour of burning flesh reached them, and it was Pansy's turn to comfort her friend, for Marion, suddenly and without any warning, retched and vomited, long and horribly, till the tears, unbidden, coursed down her cheeks, and her whole body shuddered in reaction.

Pansy pushed her onto the greenhide-laced stool and from somewhere, produced a pannikin of water to sip. Alec slid past them to the bed on the verandah, folded it down and carried it, with the mattress, past them again and into the kitchen.

Marion, pulling herself together, jumped up, picked up the blankets he had left behind, and followed him into the kitchen, with Pansy at her heels. Her mind blanked out the blood and mess of the operation; she saw only the small still figure with the white-bandaged stump protruding from the shoulder. She laid the blankets across the bed Alec had erected near the fire and watched as Mick picked up the child and laid him down on the bed. She put a hand on the small forehead; despite the warmth and humidity of the night, the skin was clammy-cold. Mick drew up a blanket to the boy's neck

"If he's still alive in the morning, he might pull through," he said soberly.

They cleaned up. To the hole Mick had dug for the household rubbish they carried everything that could conceivably harbour contamination, the blood soaked blanket, the poor pathetic bodiless arm, and Marion's table, and Mick threw some of his precious store of petrol over the pile. As the flames leapt up with a roar, he pulled off his shirt and threw it too into the blaze, and Alec followed suit. Again the smell of roasting flesh, and this time it was Mick who gagged and turned aside. The knives and hornsaw had gone into the fire on the kitchen hearth, where the handles quickly burnt away. The steel would be cleansed in the fire, and new handles could be made.

They pulled up the greenhide chairs and sat to keep vigil beside the child. Marion thinking of making a cup of tea, noticed the rum bottle standing on the shelf beside the tea-pot. Wordlessly she took it down, poured what remained into the four pannikins and handed them round.

The curlew called again, clear on the night air, like a herald signalling the re-organised battalions of rain squalls which beat anew on the tin roof. At dawn the boy still breathed. Alec went outside to relieve himself, and came back to report that the blacks had gone without trace.

"Oh my God," Marion gasped at the sudden thought. "They would have smelt it too. They probably think we cooked and ate him!"

"Could be," nodded Alec, "I don't reckon we'll see any of them round here again for a while."

"No," said Pansy, suddenly alert. "I bin see 'im go." She stopped, corrected herself. "I saw them go. While you workin, Mick, and us on the verandah. Past the yard, sneakin' off. They reckon he goin' to die, and they don't want his spirit follow them, make trouble."

The daylight strengthened. The rain still pelted down. It was Christmas Day.

Chapter 20 — *New boss at Parrot Hill*

They called the boy Christie, because he came to them at Christmas time. For some days he lay barely-conscious in the bed on the verandah, tended by Marion and Pansy. From the day he sat up and grinned at Marion, his recovery was little short of amazing. The recuperative powers of his predominant race and his environmental training stood him in good stead, and within a fortnight he was following one or other of his four protectors like a faithful dog, and chattering away to them in a language which none could make head nor tail of. His table-manners were primitive in the extreme, but he was a quick learner and soon mastered the simple cutlery and crockery. Mick said it was just as well they didn't have a kitchen table any more, so the little fellow could learn by stages.

Pansy laboured with needle and thread and turned out three pairs of passable calico trousers, which while not exactly a good colour for the environment of Serendipity in the Wet did at least clothe his nakedness. She struck the first hitch when she tried to get the first pair off him to wash them; he wasn't going to give up his new acquisition without a fight, and she made the mistake of showing him the other two pairs and miming that they were his too. Christy promptly snatched them and in a trice had pulled on both pairs over the dirty ones. It took Mick to get them off him and replace the dirty pair.

Marion dressed the rapidly-healing wound, and he submitted like a stoic to her ministrations.

"As soon as I can get over the road after the Wet, I'm going to get a transceiver," said Mick. "I don't care what we go without, or what it costs, but we're not taking any more chances. It could have been you, Marion, or Pansy or Alec. There's no way I could have done what I did if it had been you, unless maybe there was a doctor telling me what to do."

"Or even you!" agreed Marion soberly.

"Yeah, well that does it, that settles it. We definitely need a wireless. Come in handy for other things too. You can listen to the galah sessions, and check up on what the neighbours are doing!"

Marion shied the tin plate she was washing at him, but he fielded it neatly and tossed it back and ducked out the door. She smiled to herself as she rewashed the plate, but she knew that Mick was right. They couldn't afford to be without the means of contacting a doctor in a medical emergency, especially when there was no chance of making a dash in a vehicle for the three months or more of the Wet season. Even horseback would be impossible for much of that time, and horseback was no means of transport for a suffering patient. They should have an airstrip too, so the Flying Doctor plane could land if needed, and the Medical Chest supplied free to all transceiver owners complete with the necessary instruments and medicines. What if it *had* been Mick, and she had been the only person there. For one moment Marion was overcome with a terrible fear that she would not be able to cope with what the isolation of Serendipity might mean for her. But she was young and the future held such a promise for them. She remembered Maggie's words - Don't cross your bridges until you come to them - and then Mick's way of saying the same thing - There'll be plenty of dry creeks to cross, but we'll take 'em as they come! And Mick was right, she could join in the galah sessions and make the acquaintance of whatever other women there were in this world so largely populated by men.

Within a few days Mick had knocked up a substitute table from adzed planks, and two forms as seats for either side. That was at least one advantage of the Wet season, all the odd jobs got done that would not have been possible during the busy Dry season.

Alec repaired saddles and made greenhide hobbles, and Mick twisted greenhide ropes, and Christy sat cross-legged and watched them, and learned new words every day. Mick and Alec held long discussions on how to make a bridle for a little fellow with only one hand and cut strips of leather and experimented until they were satisfied. Christy was already one of the family, and Christy was going to be a ringer like the rest of them.

When Marion wrote a letter to Maggie, to be posted "after the Wet," she did not mention the awful night and Mick's enforced surgery, but merely said "We have a little half-caste boy here called Christy," and chatted about his exploits. Even Maggie, with all her practical nature, could not be expected to understand her daughter's attachment to a land of such isolation and challenge. Marion described the storms and the flooded country and the interminable chorus of frogs. That was enough; she'd break Maggie in gently.

Then the storms weakened and there were whole days of sunshine, and they lived in a green world of tall grasses and a cacophony of birdlife round the billabong. Now Christy spoke in phrases rather than single words, and Marion began to think of clothing for him to be added to the stores list when Mick decided the track had dried out enough to get to town. There was another reason she wanted a transceiver - "the wireless" as they called it - and the Medical Chest and explanatory booklet. Pansy was pregnant.

It was three months almost to the day since Christy's unexpected arrival when Alec, siting at the table with them for morning smoko, suddenly pricked his ears and announced, "Horses comin' up!"

They recognised three of the riders within the little mob of horses long before they reached the yards.

"It's Alan," said Marion, "and Wally and Big Jim, and two other boys!"

Some of the horses still had flakes of dried mud as high as the shoulders, and they were all obviously leg-weary. There were eleven of them besides the five saddle-horses and two packs.

"G'day! Okay if I put the horses in your paddock and spell a coupla days, Mick?" called Alan.

"Yeah, sure. Turn 'em out, and then come on in, the billy's on."

Marion and Pansy were all smiles; they had seen no new faces for months, and these were old friends. Pansy took a firestick from the kitchen fireplace as she said, "I make tea my place for them boys, Marion. You fellows and that Alan want to talk."

Marion grinned, "You fellas want to talk too, eh?"

Pansy chuckled.

Marion had the pot re-filled and more scones spread with jam by the time Alan, accompanied by Mick and Alec and followed by a wide-eyed Christy, stepped under the verandah roof and tossed his hat onto the floor.

It took ten minutes for Marion to give him a graphic description of Christy's arrival and the operation, before it occurred to her to wonder why he and the boys were off their run at a time when all self-respecting head stockmen were gearing up for the horse muster to begin the year's stock-work.

"I've snatched me time," he announced. "Parrot Hill's sold; bought by a Yank, and a proper bastard of a Yank too. Elton-Smythe the Third, whoever heard of a moniker like that. Mister Elton-Smythe, you men, and don't you forget it!" Alan's voice simulated a passable Southern drawl.

"First thing he done was sack Paul, and bring in another Yank he calls his foreman. Well, he didn't exactly sack Paul, but he gives this foreman his job and tells him he can stay on as a ringer, which is the same thing, ain't it. Called us cowboys too. He don't even know that a cowboy is just a broken-down old ringer who looks after the killers and the garden."

He paused and reached to refill his pannikin, while his listeners assimilated the news. "Y'got the makings, Mick? The store under new management ran outa terbacca just after Christmas," he said bitterly. Mick passed his tin over, and Alan rolled a smoke, lit it and savoured the first draw with real appreciation.

"Thought you woulda heard about the sale," he went on. "We had to do a bangtail muster right up to the first storms. The owners come up and promised us a bonus if we could bangtail five thousand head. Done it, too. Covered three-quarters of the place before the rains come. Them rotten sods from down south give us the impression that things was going to be the same as before except just a new owner; though maybe the Yank put it over them same as us. We worked like dogs to get the job done, and then the old bosses and the new one come up in a plane, and we put the cattle through the yards and bushed 'em again, and Paul got sixty quid and a handshake, and I got fifty, and the boys a Williams outfit all round, so we got our bonus all right." He glanced slyly at Marion.

"Still got it, too, Marion. A man don't mind playin' cards with the Chinks in Darwin, they're Aussie Chinks, but I draw the line at them Yankee cowboys."

Marion got up and took a tin of tobacco and papers from the dwindling store on the kitchen shelf and tossed them across to Alan; it had to be a tough situation for Alan to make such an ultimate sacrifice as to refuse an opportunity to gamble.

"Well, they clinched the deal, and then the Yank tells Paul he's gotta move out of the homestead into the cottage because he'll be needing the house himself, he's gonna live on the place, he'll be back in a week to take over. Well, he came back all right, and he's got this foreman fella and two others with him, and then the rain sets in and we're stuck with 'em. Couldn't get off the place, never seen a Wet like it before, and nothin' to do except listen to them fellas skite about what they're gonna do. Just as well Paul's Missus and kids had gone down south for a holiday before the shit hit the fan. Now, you wouldn't reckon old Paul was a knuckle man, would yer? Paul and me, we ended up in the quarters, because Chet, the foreman ,he wants the cottage because Mister Elton-Smythe the Third he wants the house to himself, don't mix with the working men. Worse than the Poms, ain't they. The coupla cowboys wasn't too bad, but that Chet, he spent his whole time walkin' round the place saying what was wrong with things, and how it was going to be different when he got started. I dunno how Paul took it so long. Chet kept ordering us to do things like they never got done before, and he acted like he thought we was going to stay on and work there when his team of cowboys arrived after the Wet. That's how little they know about us bush blokes, Mick. Anyway, we sat it out until a coupla weeks back, when it got dry enough to get out into the horse paddock and pick up our horses. Chet tells us we gotta check fences, and we tell him we're goin' after the horses, and he starts frothing at the mouth and swearing at us. Well naturally Paul dropped him. Quick too, beat me to it! And when we got back to the yards with the horses three days later, there's Elton-Smythe, frothin' a bit too, and he reckons he bought all the horses on the place. Our horses, mind you! Paul marches up to the office and gets out the horse-book and tells him to check the brands on what we reckon are ours, the ones we got cut out in the yards. What we don't tell him, of course, is that we got half a dozen of the unbranded colts waitin' for us, the pick of 'em, in a little brush yard in the scrub. The blacks had come back while we was away, and he's got plans for them too. They're all being shifted off to a Mission, he says. The single boys come up as soon as they see us, they dunno what's goin' on. The upshot was four of 'em come with me, and four with Paul, and Paul and me collect our cheques - they was already written out of course - and Paul says seeing as how the Yanks reckon they aren't going to use our Aussie stock-saddles, they got better Yankee ones coming, we'll take one each for our boys off his hands if the price is right. Second-hand saddles, not worth that much, says Paul, and we got 'em for a coupla quid each. So we give 'im the cheques back, and he writes us another one, and tells us to get off the place in the morning, which is just what we intended to do, with them colts dancin' about in the scrub waitin' for us. So Paul asks for the key to the store to get some rations for our packs, and he comes down to see what we take, and then, Mick, Alec, do you know what the bastard done then? He asks for our cheques back again, so he can deduct the cost of the rations!"

"Strewth!" ejaculated Mick, "a fella like that's not gonna last long in this county. Just as well you got the colts to even things up a bit."

"Yeah, we picked 'em up midday the next day, camped together that night, and then Paul headed south to the Glen, where they been trying to get him as manager for the last coupla years. He wanted me to go with him, but I reckoned I'd come north. Might even have a look at Queensland again if things work out right!"

When Pansy appeared at the doorway they realised it was time for dinner, and Alec helped Pansy cut off some salt beef for the boys and went with her while Marion set out the meal for the three whites. Alan regaled them with his somewhat-biased description of the Yankee expertise in matters related to the running of an Australian cattle station as they ate, and then accepted Marion's invitation to roll out his swag on the one remaining cyclone bed on the verandah for an after-dinner camp.

It wasn't until Christy had been sent to bed and they were smoking companionably on the verandah after supper that evening that Alan enlarged on what he meant by things working out right.

"C'mon," said Mick, "you've been itching to spill something else ever since you arrived. Get it off your chest, mate!"

"Business deal. I got a fancy to be a boss drover, and I know how to get a stake to outfit me plant and take on me first job at the same time."

"It wouldn't have anything to do with Parrot Hill poddies, would it?" asked The Quiet Fella curiously.

"Not poddies, bullocks!"

"You're kidding!"

"Like hell I'm kidding. Look, Mick, it's foolproof. We only mustered three quarters of the place for the Bangtail, they was in such a hurry to clinch the deal before the Wet. We didn't touch the north-east corner, that bit of tableland country, rough as guts, but I know it like the back o' me hand. Wet like we just had, the cattle will've made for the high country. We could pick 'em up in a week. Hold 'em in a gorge that's tailor-made for the job, cut out what we wanted, big bullocks that'd walk fast, take the lot along as far as the Parrot Hill boundary, and then bush the rest so they'd walk back and cover our tracks. But we gotta move fast; we gotta do it before the Yank starts looking over his ranch when the country's dry enough, which won't be more'n a week or so now!"

"But that's stealing!" burst out Marion.

"No it's not, Marion. The Yank don't own 'em. He paid for five thousand head of cattle, and they're all bangtailed. We don't touch any bangtailers, we just take a few of the bullocks, a coupla hundred or so of the thousand odd me old bosses had to throw in to the Yank for nothin'. The Yank don't know what he's got, so he wouldn't miss 'em. I reckon me old bosses would just as soon we had 'em as the Yank, and I reckon the Good Lord would too, or he wouldn't have provided the perfect place and the perfect time - and the perfect blokes to do the job!"

Mick rolled another smoke thoughtfully, as Alan paused to let his proposition sink in.

"We need your horses to muster 'em, Mick, while mine spell here for the trip in to Queensland to sell the mob, and your brand to cross-brand 'em before we go. A coupla hundred at a tenner a head, split down the middle. I take my four boys on the road, you're sittin' cosy here. We pay the boys drover's wages, and there's enough left to set me up with a good plant, and make the difference between you stayin' here on Serendipity or havin' to walk off carryin' your swags!"

All those fears that had lain dormant in the busy daylight hours, but surfaced often enough in the dark quiet of the night, rushed simultaneously into Mick's and Marion's consciousness. For the want of a few hundred pounds in a year or so, before they had bullocks of their own to sell, all their grand dreams could crash. The Yank didn't need the bullocks they'd take, hadn't actually bought them, and didn't know he had them. It was Marion who broke the silence as she murmured, almost to herself, "The Lord helps those who help themselves - to Parrot Hill bullocks!"

"You little beauty!" exulted Alan. "Mick, she's right, y'know. What a mate you got, y'lucky bastard."

Mick still pondered. The Quiet Fella was doing his homework, but Alan suddenly feared that perhaps he had not put his case convincingly enough.;

"Maybe it's not all that straight, but what sort of a straight deal has the world give us! I risk me life fightin' for me country, and a couple of years later a lousy Yank can boot me off the bit of it I call me home. And you - you're nothin' but a bunch of strays! The world owes you nothin'! An orphan and a bastard - sorry Marion - but its true, ain't it - and your offsiders, a reject by black and white shacked up with a tribal outcast; topped off with that poor little one-armed coot, who's black and white with a dash of chink! You wanta stay on top, you gotta do it all yourselves; there ain't nobody else gonna help you!" In his vehemence Alan jumped to his feet and sent the empty pannikin clattering from the edge of his stool.

"Hey, simmer down, man," said Mick quietly, "this poor old orphan pushing thirty was just calculating how soon we could get cracking! Like maybe termorra!"

Chapter 21

Cattle-duffers in the back country

With the enforced inactivity of the Wet behind them, the Serendipity conspirators threw themselves into their preparations with enthusiasm and vigour. Any lingering doubts that Mick and Marion may have had were dispersed that night as they lay in each other's arms and discussed, strangely enough, not the fact that the path might now be easier for them, but the sudden little details of the exploit as they occurred to them.

"Aren't we taking a risk cross-branding?" mused Marion. "Anybody knows that neighbours wouldn't sell to one another. Even the Yank would know that; it'd mean a neighbour could poddy-dodge for years after, and get away with it!"

"Sure, darling. But who knows our brand yet? We haven't sold a beast. Who knows Parrot Hill's our neighbour? Nobody Alan's going to meet on the way, for sure. It's the last thing anyone would expect, so they won't be looking for it, will they? I reckon we can let Alan handle any questions that come up, but I don't reckon they will!"

"Y'know what I reckon," giggled Marion, "I reckon maybe I've got a clue to your parentage; perhaps our real name should be Readford!"

"No way!" laughed Mick. "No chance of me taking along a white stud bull to give us away. Now, let's get to sleep, there's a lot to do in the morning!"

While the men mustered and shod horses, Pansy packed the stock-camp rations into pack-bags, and Marion did the same for the Jeep tucker-box. She and Alec and Christy were to brave the track and make for Felix Creek, ostensibly for rations and a transceiver.

"We don't want anyone at home on the place for a week at least," warned Mick. "If anyone does get through on the road and call in, they'll see the note tacked on the door "Gone to Town" and naturally they'll think we're all gone, Pansy and me too. Sooner or later the Yank will come over to pay a visit, though I don't spose he'd try it this soon."

"No chance there," grunted Alan, "He's bushed everyone off the place that could show him the way, and the track's not that good, even in the Dry. He wouldn't find it for the long grass. But I see what yer mean, Mick. Someone else might come along, and if they jump to conclusions and think you're in town, they won't be lookin' for you anywhere else, will they?"

"Not unless they meet me on the road without him," put in Marion.

"Risk you'll have to take, darlin'. We'll be taking bigger ones. All you gotta do is stay away for a week at least. Might even take you two or three days to get into town anyway. Don't come back without a wireless, even if you gotta go up to Darwin to get one, which you might have to do. Get the rations we need, and some clothes for Christy, and tell 'em in town if you get asked, that I'm looking about on horseback up near the Mission boundary, checking on the floods."

Alan wrote a list of the rations the drovers would need, and admonished her to keep the tally separate. There was not enough in the depleted store-room to feed the five-man team on the road as well as for the muster, so Marion needed to time her return to coincide with Alan's departure."

"Seven days, if you can, no more'n eight!" he instructed her.

By sundown they had done all that needed to be done. Pansy, in view of her delicate condition, was to be the stock-camp cook, and Mick would take the dogs along, not to work, because they didn't want to leave the obvious evidence of dog-bites on any cattle they might muster and then turn back, but as company for Pansy alone for most of the day in the camp. Luckily Mick had killed only recently, and there was enough salt beef to see them through, hastily cooked that day. Enough too, for the tuckerbox on the Jeep, and a sugar-bag of uncooked salt beef on the back for Tom and Muriel, who would appreciate it just as much as Marion appreciated the garden produce they always gave her.

"I'll feel a bit guilty staying with them under the circumstances," she admitted. "but if I don't they'll wonder what's up, and that's the last thing we need!"

"Yeah, too right. Don't you go giving the game away like that," snorted Alan, and as an afterthought added, "While yer there, see if yer can sneak a waybill from Tom without him knowin'!"

"Oh, Alan, you're incorrigible!" laughed Marion, "we can jolly well write it out on a piece of paper like plenty of others do if they haven't got a proper one. It's bad enough thinking of the possibility that if you got caught it'd be Tom who'd have to arrest you, and us accepting his hospitality like we do, without pinching waybills as well."

"That's not going to happen," said Mick firmly. "I know how you feel, Marion, but Tom's been around this country for a while. I don't reckon it would make any difference to us being friends. He'd do what he had to do, for sure, because it's his job, but I don't think he'd hold it against us much."

"Ar!" said Alan disgustedly, "yer worryin' over nothin', Marion. For a start, we ain't goin' to get caught, and if we did, there's not a jury in the N.T. would ever find a man guilty, because I don't reckon there's twelve blokes in the whole country that hasn't done somethin' in that line himself at some time or other. Why, even the best mates do it to each other, just for the hell of it!"

"Okay, okay," submitted Marion, "but no waybill. And I suppose it's just as well we've got you for a partner, Alan, and not a neighbour, eh?"

"Could be, at that!" agreed Alan with a smirk. "Anyway, Marion, fer the record, they'll be sayin' round town that's what yer doin' out here anyway. Tom'll have heard it a dozen times in the bar, up at the store. There ain't no place like a bush country town fer gossip. People yer don't know exist know all about yer, or reckon they do, and some of the things they'll be saying'd make yer hair stand on end. Y'oughta know that by now, Marion."

Marion reflected that what Alan had said was certainly true. Some of the things she'd heard about Angela and Jim during her enforced stay in Derby had been wildly far-fetched, and the men had been worse gossips than the women, taken all round.

At piccaninny daylight next morning seven riders left the yards with plant horses and packs, and headed in a south-easterly direction towards the tableland country. Marion and Alec, with an excited little boy between them, were already on their way in the opposite direction, tuckerbox, swags, petrol and water containers, and long-handled shovel roped down firmly on the back of the jeep.

Two days, three bogs, and many detours later, the uniformly-muddy vehicle and its equally muddy passengers drew up outside the Felix Creek police-station residence; the track through to Serendipity was now officially open for the Dry. Muriel greeted them delightedly, proffering showers and smoko, while little Billy Roberts made overtones of friendship to a now over-awed Christy. Tom was in Darwin on Department business, but due home in a couple of days, and it needed only a phone call to authorise him to buy a Traegar wireless and pick up a Flying Doctor Medical Chest from the Flying Doctor Base, well-equipped to cater for the requirements of the influx of new settlers looking for land in the post-war euphoria of the frontier Territory.

"Better ask him to pick up some clothes for Christy, too," suggested Muriel. The store doesn't run to kids' clothes, only materials." A second phone call instructed him to buy trousers, shirts and a jumper for a six-year-old, and the smallest felt hat he could find. Marion's only chore was to fill the ration order at the store, to which she devoted some time and the strictest supervision. The store-keeper's attempt to foist two bags of old pre-Wet, and undoubtedly weevilly, flour upon her backfired. She turned a suspicious eye upon the bag of potatoes, claimed the bag wasn't strong enough for the trip home, and asked that the contents be transferred to another bag. Sure enough, the bottom half of the bag was filled with half-rotten potatoes.

"My goodness, Mrs. H., I wonder how that happened?" declared the storekeeper.

"You know how it happened, Sam, and so do I. And now let's have a look at the onions."

Despite the fact that it was only a small order, the back of the Jeep was loaded down when Tom arrived home two days later with the wireless and the medical chest. The timing was excellent. Allowing two days for the return trip, the week would be just up, and Marion had spent a very pleasant couple of days answering the letters and socialising with Muriel. Alec and Christy had camped down by the river, socialising in their own way with the fringe-dwellers of the Aboriginal community.

Tom helped Alec load the wireless, and laughed to Marion that he could now send a telegram to Serendipity to let them know when he was coming out, so they could bush any strangers out of the yards before he got there. Marion nearly died of shock. It took her a long, long moment to realise that he was only joking in the time-honoured way, and another to reply, "Yes, and unchain all the blackfellows before you get there!"

"Speaking of blackfellows, Mick did a mighty job of the little fellow's arm, especially without a doctor on the other end of the wireless. But it's a good thing you've got one now, Marion, I reckon it's an essential in the back country."

He promised to try and organise a short trip some time during the year so that Muriel and Billy could accompany him, and then the travellers departed on the long trip home.

As they forded the last creek and came up onto the Homestead flat all three simultaneously noted the smoke from the homestead chimney.

"Mick's home!" said Alec.

Marion's heart jumped. Had something gone wrong? He was early!

"Not beat us by much," commented Alec, pointing to the lone horse in the yard and the saddle, bridle and neck-bag leaning against a post, and the next minute Mick appeared through the doorway to greet them, wearing a broad grin.

He barely gave time to hug his wife, before he turned to the load.

"Tell you about it later," he promised, "but now we gotta move. Shove the drovers' tucker into the pack-saddles on the verandah, Alec, while I unload this lot and refuel. Marion, be a love and turn my horse out, and bring in the gear, will you. We'll take the jeep. I picked out a track as far as our boundary, bit of a long way round, but the jeep will make it quicker than horses, and Alan's going to be waiting there by tonight with Pansy, and a couple of pack-horses. Quicker they get away the better. We're holding the mob in the gorge, and if Alan gets back by morning we can start 'em up straight away."

He dumped the last package on the ground and jumped into the seat and drove over to the stock-pile of forty-four gallon petrol drums. Tucker box, shovel, and Marion's and Alec's swags were still in the back. Mick unscrewed the cap of one drum, shoved a short length of hose into it, and sucked to start the petrol flowing. Then, as he noticed Marion staggering towards the verandah with the saddle on her shoulder and the water-bag slung around her own neck, he called, "I've put the billy on. Make us a coupla sandwiches for lunch, will you, to take with us."

She had barely done so, when the jeep pulled up at the verandah and Alec lifted on the packsaddles with bags evenly packed. She filled two pannikins with scalding tea, as Mick and Alec carried in the crate containing the wireless and set it down beside the window.

"I'll borrow your swag, honey; mine's full of bindi-eyes! Thanks." He took the proffered tea, then set it down again to roll a smoke. Alec accepted his pannikin, grinned at Mick, and pulled out a packet of tailor-made cigarettes. "How far am I going, Mick?" he asked. It was the first time he'd spoken since they got home.

"Only three or four days, Alec, just until they bush the cows and calves and hangers-on. I'd like to know they got away all right. Then you come back home across country, and cover your tracks till you get to our boundary, okay?"

Alec nodded.

"I'll be back with the jeep and Pansy midday tomorrow, all going well, Honey. I'll fill you in then, and Pansy can tell you any bits I leave out, like some of the bush tucker she fed us on." He plonked his pannikin down on the table, gave Marion another perfunctory hug, and made for the door, followed by Alec.

"Oh, by the way, what's our call-sign? I'd better tell Alan, in case he wants to contact us at any time."

"8BF - 8 Baker Fox. Goodbye, darling. Goodbye, Alec."

"Cheers!" And they were gone.

Marion poured a cup of milk for Christy, and a pannikin of tea for herself. It was very quiet. The depleted cartons of stores still stood where they had been dumped. Marion could see them through the open doorway.

"Christy," she said, "I reckon there might be a packet of store biscuits in one of those cartons. Shall we bring 'em in and see?"

The little boy gave her a delighted grin, and darted out and pointed to one box. They opened it on the spot. There was plenty of time to bring in the stores later. They had a whole twenty-four hours to fill in before Mick's projected return.

Long before midday the next day Marion had begun imagining she could hear the sound of the returning vehicle. She unpacked the stores with Christy's help, and inspected the parcel of clothes they hadn't had time to open before they left town, and tricked Christy out in little checked shirt and overalls. He loved the hat, and lost no time in trying to roll the brim in a miniature copy of Mick's. But he couldn't manage it one-handed, so Marion had to do it for him. She was still at it when they really did hear the vehicle.

It's occupants were dirty, sweat-stained, but elated. The dogs, Tim and Tam, bounded off the back, and made a much more satisfactory fuss of Marion than her husband had done the day before, and almost knocked Christy over. Both Pansy and Mick insisted they wanted a shower and clean-up before they ate, and Marion was forced to wait another half-hour before she and Mick could trade their adventures of the past week.

The muster had gone like a charm. The cattle had been where Alan had said they would be, still up on the high ground, and the gorge couldn't have been better to hold the mob of if they'd ordered it themselves - water, grass, and narrow enough across the entrance to rail it off with saplings, but big enough to tail the mob inside. The buffalo flies were pretty bad, so the cattle tended to run in large mobs, and they'd picked up a good five hundred by the fourth day, some bangtails and cleanskins, but more than enough three to five year old steers to suit their purposes. Alan reckoned they had time to cut out the big weaners and take them across to Serendipity, but Mick decided against it.

"Why?" queried Alan slyly, "you reckonin' on leavin' 'em here and comin' back next year when they're bigger?"

That was the day that Wally, who was tailing the cattle, called to them to look at a big cow that was down.

"Hell's bells!" said Mick, "Marion, that's when it all looked like turning sour on us. It had pleuro, you didn't have to look twice to see that."

The boys moved the rest of the cattle further up the gorge, and Mick shot the affected beast, and drained the fluid out of the chest cavity into a cleaned-out jam-tin. Alan hunted through his gear and came up with a packet of setons and a seton knife, the equipment carried by all good head-stockmen and drovers, but they still had to work out how to inoculate their mob without benefit of yards and a crush.

This was a real problem, because although Alan knew the location of a set of yards a mere fourteen miles away they could not make use of them without giving the game away to all but the rankest of newchums who might come along; it was one thing to disguise the tracks of a mob moving off the place, but another entirely to put a mob through the yards and make it look like as if they hadn't been there. It was simply not possible.

"We stewed over it all night," said Mick, "and then we decided the only thing to do was cut out the bullocks next day and tail them separately from the rest and hope for the best. Alan's going to play it by ear on the road. If it's too late, and he finds pleuro in the mob, he sticks to the stock-route and inoculates at the first set of station yards he comes to. That way, they have to go through the Government Dip at the border, which just could be a bit dicey with too many questions asked, but not if he gets in behind one of the big mobs and shoves ours through when everyone's tired out and anxious to get the job over for the day. If the mob's clean he'll probably travel three or four miles north or south of the stock-route and then slip them across the border when the time's right. He knows that country just like he knows Parrot Hill, comes from that way originally. All we gotta do is sit tight for six weeks and wait for a telegram. Then, give or take a few days, it'll take him another two weeks to get back here with the horses and fill us in with the details."

"And split the cheque!" grinned Marion.

"Yeah, my little cattle-duffing darlin', split the cheque! Strikes me, the way you've taken to the game, it's gotta be in the blood, if you only but knew who your old man was."

"We-ell," admitted Marion with an impish smirk, "On the maternal side I'm descended from a long line of horse-thieves, I suspect, so p'raps you're right! But what about you?"

"Dunno!" laughed Mick, "Maybe I'm one of those inventions that necessity's the mother of. But we better not count our chickens too soon. Alan's got a long way to go yet!"

Chapter 22

Welcome visitors from the West

Alec rode in at the end of a week with the news that the mob had travelled well, and quickly, doing between fifteen and twenty miles a day each day until he had left them. No more pleuro signs had developed, and the drovers had dropped off the decoy cattle in dribs and drabs so expertly, claimed Alec, that not even Diamond Jim Johnson could have worked out the story of what had happened there a week or so before, and he, so the story went, was so good at the game that he could track The Holy Ghost through a thundercloud. The cows and calves had been cut out and left behind at the gorge so the mob could travel more quickly, and the drovers were off the Parrot Hill run and pointed straight towards Queensland by the evening of the second day.

Mick rigged a wireless aerial and the transceiver was set up on the verandah, because Marion had not thought to buy a spare battery to operate it, and it was easier to park the jeep with its nose under the verandah and its battery within reach of the wireless leads than to lift out and carry the battery inside every time the wireless was used. When the jeep was in use the wireless was not operative, but Marion tuned in often enough to pick up from the telegram and galah sessions much of what was going on in the district. When there was no telegram from Alan by the end of the seventh week they began to wonder why he had not made contact as arranged, and it was another fortnight before they found out why, when the horse-plant and five horsemen rode out from the scrub-line and followed along the fence to the yards just on dusk one evening.

"You remember, Mick, that night you give it ter me, I scratched yer call-sign with me pocket knife on me terbacca tin. What yer don't know is that Wally fancies himself as a budding artist, and his specialty is scratchin' pictures on terbacca-tin lids. I had too much on me mind at the time to think about call-signs I wasn't goin' to be needin' for some time, so when I finished me tin I dropped it in one of the packs for safe-keeping till I needed it. Wally finds it when he's takin' a spell at the cookin' and turns it inter a windmill and trough, all scratched out in silver, like. I reckoned then more better I brought you the news in person, like!"

They'd followed the stock-route after all, though there'd been no outbreak of pleuro to hold them up. Word had drifted back that there'd been big trouble at the Border Dip, arsenic in the dip too strong, and a number of cattle from the first two big mobs on the road had died. Other mobs were held up while new supplies of dip were procured and tested, and it was general turmoil with thousands of cattle converging on the Dip, and the overworked officials intent on pushing the mobs through as quickly as they could, no time wasted checking earmarks as long as the numbers were right.

Once camped on the outskirts of the Isa, Alan had ridden in to town, found a buyer and brought him back to inspect. Two days later he was changing the cheque at the Bank, with the smiling boys waiting outside for him.

"I didn't even get to have a beer, Marion, after that. No way was I goin' to let the boys outa my sight with all them smart-alec town blackfellas waitin' round like crows at a killer. They can tell a station boy by the cut of his jib, and they know he's got pay if he's in town, and it don't take 'em long to con it outa him, no sir. The shop-keepers aren't much better, sell 'em rubbishy things at double the price, and then hunt 'em if they try to argue. I give the boys twenty quid each, Mick, and went to the stores with 'em. They got coloured shirts, and pocket knives, and lolly water, and comics, and Wally got a sketchbook and pencils, and Toby bought some white moleskins, and Big Jim's got a black sombrero, and Nipper's got a harmonica he's just about wore out all the way home. I spent twenty-one quid on rations for the trip home, and here's what's left over!"

He pulled the roll of notes from the leather writing case he'd taken from his unrolled swag and dropped it on the table with the bill of sale.

"One hundred ninety-two bullocks at ten pounds, eighty-seven steers at seven pounds, total, two thou, five hundred and twenty-nine quid, less eighty quid for wages for the boys, less twenty-one for rations from Felix Creek, I give you that back -" he did so - "and we split what's left."

He paused to roll a smoke.

"No need to get a paper and figger it out, Marion," he grinned, "I done all that a dozen times. It's exactly eleven hundred and eighty quid each due, but I took the liberty of spending twenty quid on a set of clothes for Alec, and a coupla dresses and so on for Pansy, seein' they give us a hand before we left."

From between the folded clothes in his swag he extracted an unopened bottle of rum and the Serendipity cattle-duffers and their drover mate celebrated their good fortune far into the night.

In the raw light of the next day perhaps they had celebrated a little too well. Christy, up as usual at daylight, had to make his own breakfast, and finally, bored with his own company, wandered over to Alec's cottage where the drover-boys were regaling Alec and Pansy with exaggerated accounts of their first visit to the Isa.

No-one had given a thought to what came after the successful conclusion of their enterprise; all energies were concentrated on pulling off the exploit. Now it was time to pick up the threads. Alan had the wherewithal to purchase a full droving plant, but all the regular stations had long since organised their drovers for the year. He also needed to buy more horses and gear to make up a full plant capable of handling a big job.

It seemed natural that he should consider Serendipity his base for the time being, especially as the four boys belonged tribally to that country, so he turned out his horses and suggested to Mick that, while one of the boys went with him to buy some more horses and the necessary saddles and equipment, the other three should remain to give Mick and Alec a hand with the legitimate mustering and branding. He wanted to be ready if a late job turned up and to put the word around that he was in the game for the following year. If nothing turned up in reasonable time he'd be quite happy to return and help with the cattle-work or yard-building in exchange for his tucker and a base until the next droving season. The suggestion suited Mick and Marion down to the ground.

When Alan and Wally saddled up and rode off a few days later they left what was rapidly becoming a normal station rather than a battlers' outfit. The five men comprised the stock-camp, while Marion turned her thoughts to schooling for Christy and the re-establishment of the station garden ravaged by the past Wet season, and Pansy, now obviously pregnant, milked the two house-cows, placated the bawling calves separated from their mothers for the night, and helped with the house-work.

It was now a daily routine to listen to the wireless traffic list, and on occasions to make a sched to chat with Ernie. As all the telegrams and all the conversations were common property to anyone who liked to tune in, Marion soon learned to recognise the call-signs and voices of people over a vast distance, and to learn something of their business dealings too. She didn't make a practice of eavesdropping, but she always pricked up her ears when she heard the Parrot Hill call-sign and listened unabashed to their traffic.

She was able to tell Mick that Mrs. Elton-Smythe was now in residence, and, with much giggling, that Parrot Hill's usual drover had walked out on the job and the new owner had sent a telegram to the Stock-agents urgently requesting that they find him a substitute.

"Pity we can't contact Alan. Imagine the Yank's face if he turned up for the job," she laughed.

Alan and Wally arrived home five weeks later with a string of likely-looking horses and fresh colts and a wagonette loaded with gear and pulled by two horses which Alan explained had had to be broken in to the job on the track. Their descriptions of trying out the horses to take on the job had the Serendipity listeners howling with laughter.

Slung underneath the wagonette was a coop with a white rooster and five hens in it; Alan had brought a present for Marion.

"There were six hens, but Blue Dawg et one of 'em before I could convince 'im it weren't the done thing. I dunno whether they'll lay any eggs, bein' a bit on the nervy side, you might say, after the horses bolted with 'em underneath a coupla times, but if they don't come good, Marion, you can always eat 'em!"

Pansy was delighted to see the chooky-chooks, but cautioned against letting them out of the coop before a suitable pen was made for them, in case the station dogs finished off the job Blue Dawg had begun.

Alan's idea of breaking in his colts involved using them in the stock-camp and training them to cattle-work, and thus the branding was achieved much quicker than it would otherwise have been done, and the weaners were tailed thoroughly, so that there was little chance they would seek out their mothers again once they were let go.

Plans for a set of yards and a holding paddock at the eastern end of the block were under discussion when Marion overheard a telegram on the wireless regarding the sudden illness of a drover and the desertion of all his blackboys. The cattle were being held at a station the other side of Felix Creek. Reading between the lines, it sounded as if the drover was a hopeless alcoholic, but all the frantic owners were concerned about was finding someone to take over the mob, an unlikely event so late in the season. Marion immediately sent a telegram on Alec's behalf, and rode the fifteen miles out to where the men were camped. It was good to be mounted on Banner again, away from the homestead for a spell, and it occurred to her that with Alan and his boys gone, there would be more likelihood that she would be needed at times to give a hand with the work away from the homestead.

Alan received her news with alacrity, did some immediate figuring, and estimated that he could be on the spot to take over within the week. She was despatched back to send the telegram to this effect and to await its acceptance, while Alan prepared his plant to leave, on the almost sure chance he would get the contract. It was unlikely that there would be another drover at a loose end any closer than he was. The telegram was sent on the last session of the day, and the answer came back on the first session next morning. By midday the drovers were on their way.

"See you about November," shouted Alan over his shoulder, and once again the population of Serendipity was reduced to five - soon to be six.

Marion hadn't realised just how soon, and probably Pansy hadn't either. Marion was as prepared as she believed she could be to help her friend when the time came. She had read the section on childbirth in the book in the Flying Doctor Medical Chest, and Muriel had given her, on her last trip to Felix Creek, a parcel of nappies and baby singlets and a little jacket which had served Billy until he outgrew them. Pansy had experimented with the wood of two or three local trees, and had fashioned a coolamon, which Alec sand-papered to silky smoothness. It was light, fine-grained, and big enough to carry a baby for the first nine months or so of his life. What else was necessary?

"The baby will come at night-time; they always do!" explained Marion airily to Mick, insisting that the torch be placed handy to her side of the two beds pushed together in their spartan bedroom.

"Well, what's my job, when you go racing off with that?" enquired Mick quizzically.

"Boil some water, of course, dopey. Dunno what for, but you always have to have lots of boiling water."

"Will do. Now over and out."

Sammy Nelson, however, chose to make his appearance in broad daylight, with little fuss, and during Marion's absence with Mick on a three-day inspection of their northern boundary. Mick wanted to be sure of the permanent watering places in the Wilson River, and to estimate how many cattle would be likely to congregate there towards the end of the Dry. Rough though the trip was in the jeep, with only an occasional track to follow, the beautiful weather, the proliferating wild-life, and the regular glimpses of mud-fat cattle, most of them wearing the MTW brand, made a holiday atmosphere which turned the work into pleasure. Marion could have continued the jaunt for a week, but Mick, as always, worked to the timetable of the seasons and had other pressing plans to call him home.

Christy met the jeep almost a mile from the homestead with the two dogs racing beside him. He was bubbling over with excitement, his dark eyes dancing with an obvious secret which he wasn't going to reveal. They hoisted him aboard, and he bounced between them with glee, the dogs purling behind them in the dust and exhibiting an equal excitement.

On the homestead verandah Pansy and Alec waited, and Pansy's new silhouette announced the news.

"The baby!" screamed Marion, "The baby's come! Where is it? What is it?"

Sammy Nelson slept serenely in his coolamon, and hardly woke to be admired, a dusky bundle of perfection, with his little pink palms and soles, and a bubble of milk on his tiny lips.

"Heck, Pansy, you did it without me," pouted Marion, as Sammy curled tiny fingers round her outstretched index finger.

Pansy giggled. "Alec help me!" she said simply.

Alec, for his part, merely grinned and nodded, but there was a shine in his eyes when he looked at the baby that made Mick suddenly envy him. Then Sammy opened his eyes and his mouth simultaneously, and the moment was past.

"He's hungry," said Marion.

"Me too!" announced Christy, reckoning that the adulation of the baby had gone on long enough, and anxious for some attention himself.

"Yeah," agreed Mick, dropping his hand onto the boy's shoulder. "C'mon, Christy, we'd better throw a bit of a steak on if we want a feed, looks like these women have got other things on their minds tonight."

Sammy throve, and Pansy told Marion that his Dreaming was the frill-necked lizard, but couldn't, or wouldn't, say how she had chosen it. It just was.

"What your Dreaming?" she asked Christy, but Christy merely shook his head. He didn't remember any time before his climactic arrival at Serendipity, and no amount of questioning elicited even a faint response, neither of people nor places, and with English to replace it, he no longer used even a word of the language he had spoken in the past. Marion sometimes wondered whether the blacks who had brought him might some day turn up to reclaim him, but she doubted it; they almost certainly considered him dead. If they did come, they would find him quite alien to them, the same as any little white station boy, learning his lessons and the ways of the white men, trailing Mick and Alec, unconsciously copying their gestures, and interminably asking questions. Marion and Mick were his family now, and Marion knew they wouldn't give him up.

The weeks spun by in days of blue and gold, crisp, clear mornings and pleasantly warm days, as if Nature had repented the violent extremes of the previous Wet Season and wished to make up for it. Birds flocked to the billabong with its film of water lilies, and wallabies grazed on the flats where emus and brolgas and small groups of cattle moved at will.

Mick and Alec camped out and built a small timber yard a mile or so from the biggest waterhole on the Wilson River, to be used late in the Dry to brand the latest calves before the Wet set in.

Tom brought Muriel and Billy as far as Serendipity on his routine patrol, and left them there for a few days while he continued on to Parrot Hill, and Marion exulted over the second-hand sewing machine Muriel had finally located for her. Muriel was full of talk about the races and took it for granted that Mick and Marion would stay at the Police Station at race-time. Marion could sense that Mick didn't really want to go; it was as if he feared that Serendipity would disappear into thin air if he wasn't on hand to keep it anchored down.

"We'll have to go to town for stores some time, so why don't we make the trip to coincide with the races? Just to watch. I don't mean we take any horses in to race. Not this year, anyway?" she pleaded.

Mick conceded that might work out, and Marion assured Muriel on the quiet that they'd be there.

Tom brought the news of their Southern neighbour who, for all his arrogant ways, seemed to be making a fair fist of the place with his cowboys. He'd rethought his attitude towards the blacks, and most of them had returned to Parrot Hill from the mission. Two of the cowboys, with four black ringers to show them the ropes, had taken the sale cattle along the stock-route to meet a Queensland drover who was prepared to take them on to the railhead and truck them to the coast. Tom said Mrs. Elton-Smythe seemed very nice, but without any kids to keep her busy she was obviously very lonely, and a bit like a fish out of water. All she talked about was her home in Colorado, and the way things were over there, with or without the Big Shot. Tom had intended to suggest that they came to the races to meet the local people, but had withheld any comment after Elton-Smythe had complained long and volubly about Australian attitudes and inefficiencies.

"First time he sounded off in the bar or at the course some fella with a few under the belt would take it upon himself to straighten him out, and then I'd have a fight on my hands, and the Yank's the sort of bloke who'd want to lay an assault charge, which would muck up the week-end for me, so I thought I wouldn't take a chance," he explained.

"Aw gee, Mick," Marion remonstrated after the Roberts had left, "it's going on for two years now since you had a real break. A weekend at the races won't hurt you. Alec and Pansy went last year, so they won't mind staying to look after the place."

"Yeah, honey, I s'pose I am getting to be a bit of a death-adder. Okay. I'll take my Chestnut Filly in to show her off. If it wasn't your birthday that week I wouldn't, of course. I might even give you five bob to bet with, if you're good."

But a sudden awful thought had struck Marion.

"Oh Mick," she wailed, "I can't go. I haven't got a dress. Not even a dress for the races, let alone the Ball!"

Mick looked doubtful; he was out of his depth there.

"You look good to me whatever you've got on," he said. "There'll be a hawker there, won't there? You could buy a dress, or maybe make one now you've got a machine."

"I haven't got any material, or a pattern, and the hawkers only have gin's dresses," she said miserably.

Two days later, Serendipity, the place of happy accidents, lived up to its name. Mick and Alec were away checking the bullock paddock fence and Marion was sneaking an after-dinner siesta on the verandah bed. Christy and the dogs, with Pansy, and Sammy in his coolamon, had gone fishing to the waterhole, and Marion had fallen asleep halfway through a story in one of the magazines Muriel had left her. She didn't hear the utility pull up, or the light steps that danced across the verandah.

"Strewth, Marion, you sleep like a jackeroo on night-watch. Ain't you got a cuppa tea for a poor old bagman?"

Her startled eyes opened to take in the battered old hat balanced on the leprechaun ears and the leprechaun grin on the grizzled face.

"Fred!" she shrieked, leaping up and throwing her arms around him. "Fred, what on earth are you doing here? Oh, it's great to see you!"

"Jus' passing by, so I though I better drop off yer trunks. No, I came specially to see yer. Meet me son Johnny!"

Son Johnny? Shock on shock! Marion became aware of the smiling young half-caste man still standing beside the dust-covered utility, and mutely reached out a hand.

"He's yer uncle, or yer cousin, or somethin', ain't 'e?" said Fred.

How they talked. Marion had so many queries, so much to tell, and when Mick came home at sundown, they began all over again.

Junie had never even hinted to Fred in that first year of their relationship that she might be pregnant. She had gone back to the mission, supposedly to see her relations, had the baby there, and sworn the nuns to secrecy. They had sent the baby to one of their Church Homes in Perth and Junie had returned to the Cut. Johnny, being a half-caste, had not been adopted as he otherwise might have been, but he was such a promising young athlete as a child that his prowess had earned him a scholarship to a Catholic Boys' College and a better education than any of his fellow wards at the Home could have hoped for. When he left school he got a job with an Oil Company as a clerk, but one of his school friends, an apprentice mechanic, interested him in tinkering with motor-car engines, and together they built up an old car, and talked about one day owning their own garage. But then the friend acquired a girl-friend, and Johnny became increasingly aware that his colour disadvantaged him in many subtle ways. He was educated; he excelled at sport; but in some places he wasn't acceptable. He went back to the Orphanage and pleaded with them to tell him where he came from. At first they would not help, but in the end they gave him the address of the Mission.

Junie took the telegram asking her to come urgently to the Mission, and Fred saddled up their horses and went with her, neither of them with the faintest idea of the reason for the summons.

The Mother Superior introduced Johnny to his parents, and Father Clancy helped Fred through the paperwork involved in the now permissible marriage between a white man and an Aboriginal woman, and the little difficulties attached to the correct surname, and when everything was in order, performed the ceremony legalising the union of Mr. and Mrs. Frederick Ryan.

"The nuns give us a party, too," smirked Fred, "and the priest lent Johnny a horse to ride home to the Cut, after I promised to give him one o' mine as well when I sent it back. 'E'd never been on a horse before, but by the time we got 'ome he weren't too bad. Learns quick, 'e does."

Johnny gave his version of the homecoming. Fred told how Johnny had persuaded him that a car-track could be made over the jump-up, and they'd bought some gelignite and blasted a bit here and a bit there, and made some canny horse sales earlier in the year, so that Johnny was able to write to his friend in Perth to organise the purchase of the utility for Johnny to pick up from the boat in Derby.

Fred taught Johnny to ride, and Johnny taught Fred to drive. Fred hadn't ever had a holiday, but he'd always had a yen to see the Territory, and Junie was running Halley's Cut, and Angela had said they ought to take the gear for Mick and Marion, and if they asked at Felix Creek Post Office someone would give them a mud-map, and here they were.

Marion thought Johnny looked a little like Davey; they were the same age too. If only they'd known, he would have found a welcome at Mudjinup, and as one of the family too. Maggie had never been one for caring what the general public thought. But then, if Fred had known, Johnny would never have left the Kimberleys.

The visitors were escorted in the days that followed over as much of the block as could be easily reached, but the first visit was to the horse-paddock, where Fred shouted, and, one after the other, Banner and all the other horses foaled on Halley's Cut came galloping to greet him. It was natural that Mick should give him his pick of them to ride during his inspection trips.

"Them motor-cars is all right if yer in a hurry," Fred conceded, "but yer don't see nuthin' from 'em like yer do from the back of a horse, and they're no damn good unless you got a track for 'em to run on."

Pansy and Alec had been as pleased to see "Fredalli" as Marion was, and questioned him at length on various aspects of their "country", to which it was unlikely that they could ever return. Pansy loaded him with messages to be passed on to her relations and friends in the Delroy camp.

Fred had told Marion and Mick on the first evening a piece of news that stunned and shocked Marion. Jim Burton was no longer on Delroy. Early in the year he had simply packed his gear into the old truck, told Angela he wouldn't be back, and had gone off with the governess, Jenny Wilson.

"What!" cried Marion in disbelief. "It can't be true. Not Jim!"

"It's true all right. He ain't there now, and neither's the governess!"

Marion was appalled. "Oh, poor Angela! The lousy stinker! I just can't believe it!"

"That sort o' thing's happened before in this country, Marion, and it'll happen again. I seen a fair bit of it in me time."

Marion's mind flew back to the Delroy she had known, the place where she and Mick would have been such a help to Angela in her time of need.

Fred re-assured her.

"Angela's doin' okay. The fella who took your place, Mick, he's a real good man. Got a young wife too, been a governess one time, and she stepped in and took over the kids while Angela got things straightened out. Got Carla too. That Carla, she says if Jim ever come back on the place she'll chop out his liver with the sharpest butcher knife in 'er kitchen. She's been keepin' it sharp fer 'er own husband, 'oo done much the same thing to 'er!"

"But how could he walk out on Delroy?" puzzled Marion, "Hasn't it been in his family since the station first began?"

"No, Marion, yer got it wrong. It was Angie's old man owned it, not Jim's. Angie never changed 'er name; she was a Burton too, no relation though. Just one of them coincidences, like. She was an only child, like Johnny 'ere, and she met Jim at a race meetin'. Don't you lose no sleep over Angela, Marion. She was practically runnin' the place for 'er Pa when she was just a slip of a girl, and now she's runnin' it again good as ever."

Marion knew instinctively that Angela, who had always seemed so close to the big good-natured Jim, would be working sixteen hours a day, tiring herself out, so that she fell asleep from exhaustion and had no time for the black thoughts and self-pity which so often further reduced a wife deserted for a younger girl. But the children, what about the poor kids, they'd so obviously loved and admired their father.

"Young Rob took it pretty hard," Fred told them. "'E come home from school for the holidays, and Angie waited till then to tell 'im; she'd got into the swing of runnin' the place 'erself by then. 'E didn't want to go back to 'is school, bein' nearly fourteen, but she made 'im in the end. 'E turned against 'is father, worse'n the little girl, they say. The little fella, Terry, with 'is little blackfella mate, 'e don't seem to worry too much, though."

"What a louse! How could he do that to his own children!" snorted Marion.

"You got a bitch on 'eat, I reckon most of the dogs'll be after 'er. Angie's fault in a way; she shoulda seen the lay of the land and got rid of 'er before it was too late. Angie and the kids, they'll make out orright, Marion, but Jim, 'e might 'ave a bit of a tussle 'angin' onto 'er, from what I 'ear. They reckon 'er Ma and Pa 'unted 'er up north becorse she was playin' around causin' scandals down there, where she come from."

"That'd probably be just gossip, Fred," said Mick quietly, "you know what this country's like when they get something like that to get their teeth into."

Marion could see he was somewhat aggrieved; Jim was as close a friend as he'd ever mentioned to her.

"We don't really know much about it, and I suppose it's their business anyway."

"Well, how d'you tell the difference between news and gossip, Mick?" demanded Marion, still determined to hate Jim on Angela's behalf.

"Don't really know," admitted Mick, "but thanks to Fred bringing our gear across, you've now got your dresses, so we can go in to Felix Creek at race-time and start some about ourselves!"

She laughed, and picked up his tobacco tin and shied it at him, as he ducked with an impish grin. They did not mention the Burtons again, and the letter which Marion sent with Fred for Angela was cheerful and newsy and full of messages for the children and Carla and Pansy's mother, with just a passing reference to Jim's departure.

Chapter 23

Fight at Felix Creek.
Fire at the Homestead

Fred and Johnny had barely been farewelled than it was time to prepare for the races at Felix Creek, which turned out to be something of an anti-climax. Too many silvertails from Darwin there, and the old atmosphere of friendly rivalry that had characterised the true bush meetings was missing. Without horses of their own to race, Mick and Marion were relegated to mere onlookers with no real interest in the betting. There were more drunks around, many of whom never left the pub for the race-course at any time during the two-day meeting, and the fights were more vicious.

They had taken Christy with them, and he became the innocent cause of getting the Quiet Fella involved in a fight out at the race-course. A group of children, led by a boy of about nine, apparently incensed that a coloured child didn't know his place and had dared to wander into the area where they were playing, had yelled insults at him, and followed them up with a hail of stones. Christy, one arm notwithstanding, could throw stones with the best of them, and had retaliated from his sanctuary behind the Serendipity jeep. The ringleader of his taunters retired bawling, with a bleeding cut over his eye. He came back in minutes towing an irate father, and Mick, returning to the jeep with a carton of beer, was just in time to see the man send Christy sprawling with a blow that would have floored a bullock, and follow it up with a vicious kick. Christy screamed and tried to crawl under the jeep, but Mick, with a roar that echoed across the flat, had seized the man and spun him round to face a more formidable adversary than the whimpering little boy.

It was a good fight, and there were no bells for time out. The bookmaker was among the crowd which materialised in seconds, and he seized the opportunity to quote the odds, which favoured the boy's father, who was a known fisticuffs man. The Quiet Fella didn't waste his breath on insults and abuse like his opponent, and in the end his stamina proved too much for the other man, who sprawled on the ground and refused to get up again. Mick's win was not a popular one; he had after all been defending a little uppity nigger.

Mick was burred up considerably, and his new white shirt was ripped and bloodied. The carton of beer he had dropped was no longer in evidence, stolen by one or more of the onlookers, and Christy was still sobbing plaintively under the jeep. As Marion ran forward most of the motley crowd melted away with Mick's erstwhile opponent in their midst; someone had reported that Muriel was searching frantically for Tom.

Marion insisted on driving her injured to the hospital, despite a half-hearted objection from Mick. Christy's rib had been fractured by the kick, and the Sister strapped him up and wanted to keep him in overnight, but Marion persuaded her to let him go with them when she caught the glance of terrified appeal in the little boy's eyes. When the blood was washed away, Mick had a cut on his cheekbone which the Sister insisted on stitching, an operation which Mick claimed hurt more than the punch which had caused it. They looked a sorry pair when Marion got them back to the police station.

Muriel was already home and waiting for them, and full of commiseration.

"Oh, it's not all that bad," Marion told her when they had given Christy the sedative and put him to bed. "There's one good side to it!"

"And what's that?" asked Mick, from his seat on the living-room couch.

"This!" grinned Marion, opening her purse and tipping five and ten pound notes out onto the table. "I got mad when that bookmaker only had you at tens, so I put everything I had in my purse on you. There's eighty quid there, Mick!"

He stared at her with his mouth open. Then he began to laugh, softly at first, and then as loudly as his bruised ribs would allow him.

"So that's why you took so long to come and mop up the blood," he chortled, "collecting your winnings, were you?"

"Well, naturally," said Marion primly. Then she too began to laugh.

They waited another day in town for Christy's sake, and Marion bought the second-hand kerosene fridge she'd seen at the back of the store; it would be a godsend during the hot weather soon to come. Mick managed to squeeze a small drum of kerosene onto the overloaded jeep to keep them going until he brought the truck in for the Wet Season stores, and for the sake of Christy and the fridge, drove home as carefully as he could.

Although she was able to replace twenty pounds more than she had taken out in the tin that held their savings, she knew that next year she wouldn't be pestering Mick to go to the races; the fright and anger she'd felt over Christy's treatment had seen to that. It was good to be home again, where they all belonged in more than one sense of the word.

They had barely settled in to the old routine when their Parrot Hill neighbour finally paid them a visit. He arrived alone one day just as they were finishing lunch, but refused Marion's invitation to eat, saying he'd had sandwiches on the road. She wondered why he hadn't brought his wife if this was a social visit, but soon realised that it was purely business which had brought him.

He came to the point almost immediately.

"I"d like to buy your place, Hardy," he told Mick. "My son, my first wife's boy, has just married, and he wants a place of his own. Be here next month. I see you haven't got much of a place here yet, but I'm prepared to offer you a thousand pounds for it."

Marion could hardly believe her ears. She looked at Mick, but his face was quite impassive.

"You've got to be kidding!" she burst out.

Elton-Smythe ignored her.

"Sorry," said Mick quietly. "We're not interested in selling."

"Oh, I know all about you Australians. You like to bargain. We don't do things that way in the States, but I'll humour you this once. My top price is twelve hundred fifty, and naturally you can take the vehicles and saddles and things like that."

Marion, with a snigger, jumped up from her seat and dropped a low curtesy. "Oh thank you, Massa Sah, you'all done paid us po' white trash a big compliment, but we cain't do business no way, no sah!"

Elton-Smythe shot her a look of pure hatred, and his face darkened. "Look here, Hardy," he burst out, "I don't do business with dames. Can we talk privately?"

Marion subsided into her chair, rested her chin on the palm of one hand, and stared insolently at the Yank. Mick took his time about rolling a cigarette. Then he looked up and said quietly,

"'Fraid not. My wife is a full partner in the station, and she's given you our answer, so there's really nothing more to discuss."

Elton-Smythe's lips closed in a tight line. It was obvious that he was not used to being thwarted, and he did not quite know how to handle the situation. Then he pulled himself together and stood up.

"If circumstances change," he said shortly, "and you want to sell, will you give me first offer?"

"I don't foresee that happening," said Mick, rising also to his feet. "If I was you, I think I'd look elsewhere for a property for your son. There's probably plenty of good places on the market if you look around."

"Don't tell me how to handle my business!" grated the Yank. "Good-day!"

"Gee! What a stinker!" observed Marion as she and Mick watched the retreating cloud of dust behind their neighbour's utility. "Mick, I can see now why Alan hates him so much. He acted like he thought we'd fall at his feet and thank him for the offer."

"And you," laughed Mick, slipping an arm round her waist, "didn't actually respond like a lady, did you?"

"Ain't never been no lady, boss, jus' poor white trash," she giggled.

Mick slapped her on the bottom, grabbed her shoulders and spun her round towards the doorway.

"Off you go, woman, to your chores. I've got things to do, if we're to keep our li'l ole place out of the hands of the big bad speculators!"

They thought no more of the visit until the events which occurred three weeks later brought it sharply to mind again.

Mick and Alec had been mustering the Southern part of the block and bringing the closer cattle to the Homestead yards to brand and mother up the calves, and turn out the steers in the bullock paddock, and the girls took it in turns to accompany them. Christy, when it was Marion's turn, trailed along on Buzz, a neat but quiet little filly, each day learning more of the cattleman's art. Pansy could only go when they were mustering close enough to the homestead for her to leave Sammy in Marion's care for a few hours, and they were the days when Christy's schooling took precedence. It was all hands to the leg ropes and branding irons once the bawling calves were separated in the yards, and then Christy became Sammy's nursemaid, squatting beside the coolamon under the nearest big shady tree.

But when it came time to muster to the Wilson River yards Mick made plans for them all to go.

"We'll camp there six or seven days, I reckon. Ought to clean up most of the young stuff up there, and then we can have another hit at it just before the Wet when Alan's back."

Swags were rolled, and the tuckerbox packed, swags, saddles and ropes and brands stowed on to the jeep.

"Alec and I'll take the horses, and you and Pansy and the kids can follow us up in the jeep. We'll camp back a bit from the waterhole, so we don't stir up any cattle coming in to drink."

The two men got away just after daylight, but Marion, wanting to give them time to reach the dinner camp before she arrived, waited to listen to the wireless session and sent Pansy to give the vegetable garden and young trees a good soaking and leave food and water for the chooks. She emptied the kerosene fridge and blew out the wick; the kerosene wouldn't last for more than three days, and she knew that more than one homestead had been burnt down by kerosene fridges smoking and then exploding in their owners' absences. As an afterthought she and Pansy disconnected the wireless aerial and lifted the wireless into the bedroom. Not likely that any traveller would come by who would be likely to interfere with it, and she couldn't lock the building, but without any humans around, and the dogs gone, it was just possible that a horse or a beast might poke in under the verandah for shade. She cast a last glance towards the bed under which the tin containing their cash stake was buried in the dirt floor.

The girls left the homestead about ten after a quick smoko. Pansy had run down to the pumpkin patch near the billabong for a pumpkin to add to their rations, so Marion called to Christy to put out the fire in the stove. They would travel slowly because the track was new and extremely rough, but Marion estimated that they should catch up to Mick and Alec in about three hours, and then Mick could take the jeep on to pick the camp site while she or Pansy rode with Alec. There was a real picnic atmosphere as they jolted along across the yellow savanna grassland and past red rocky outcrops under the widest blue sky in the world.

"This is the Big Country, and I love it," thought Marion as she drove with the wind nipping at her hair, "I know just how the blacks feel about it, being part of it, and Mick and I are lucky enough to be part of it too. Don't care what it does to us, I'll always feel this way." Far away, in that other world, what were her family and acquaintances doing? None of them could be so completely contented as she was in this country of her adoption.

Mick and Alec were waiting for them by the crossing of the Wilson tributary they'd named Nelson Creek. They had the billy boiling and the horses were feeding out. While Pansy sat cross-legged on the ground to feed Sammy, Marion retrieved the bread and meat from the tuckerbox for their late lunch. From the way they attacked the loaf Marion began to wonder whether the batch of bread she'd baked for the trip was going to see the distance.

It was Alec who pointed out the rising column of smoke back to the south.

"What is it, Alec?" queried Marion, shading her eyes in the time-worn gesture to see more clearly. "Is it blackfellows making a smoke, d'you think?"

"Nomore, too much smoke for blackfella."

Mick was examining the horizon intently, and from his expression Marion felt a sudden wave of apprehension.

"Did you put out the fridge, Marion?" he said sharply.

"Yes, I did, of course, I did!"

"And the fire?"

"I told Christy to do it."

Christy protested that he had done as he'd been told.

"Oh, Mick, you don't think it's the homestead, do you?"

"It's in the right direction!"

"It might be a bushfire starting."

"No dry storms yet. No lightning around to start one!"

Mick began pulling tuckerbox and saddles from the back of the jeep.

"Alec, you stay here and tail the horses, Christy, you wanta stay too?" The little boy nodded. "I'm going back for a look. Might just be close to the homestead, and we ought to burn a break. Be back tonight or early tomorrow if it's okay."

The drive home was nothing like the leisurely journey of the morning, and Mick did it in half the time. Nobody spoke, but concentrated all their energies on merely hanging on. By the time they had encompassed half the journey Marion knew with certainty that the smoke, now diminishing into a mere smudge, had indeed been fuelled by the homestead. If it had been a bushfire it would have been increasing, not dying away. Mick's face showed her that he too feared the worst. Had Christy really put the fire out as she'd told him? How could it have happened anyway? Could some freak willy-willy have blown open the door, scooped coals from the firebox and dropped them where they could start a fire; it hardly seemed possible.

Suddenly the jeep was running along the eastern fence-line of the bullock paddock and the trees cut out any view of the lingering remnants of smoke. They rounded the corner onto the southern boundary of the fence, still faster now on the better, more used track, and in minutes burst through from the treeline in a flurry of dust. Marion shouted aloud. The homestead was still there, or most of it was. There were men grouped around the kitchen end, which was charred and collapsed now in an ugly twisted mass, and one of them was playing the garden hose against the still-intact bedroom wall. It was Toby. Nipper and Wally were standing near the beds and Marion's little dressing table, which they'd obviously dragged clear of the building, and over in the Yard Big Jim was unsaddling horses.

At first it was hard to tell which of the group was Alan, they were all equally black with soot and ash stuck to the sweat of their labours.

"Insured the place, did'ya, and tryin' to put one over the Insurance mob, eh?" he greeted them.

Mick's face lit up with relief. "Thanks, fellas!" Marion echoed him.

"She was well alight when we come along," continued Alan. "We couldn't've done nothin' if the water 'adn't been close-up, beyond gettin' a bit o'your stuff out. Ten minutes later, and she'd all been a goner!"

The relief and the reaction was almost too much for Marion. She was close to tears.

"I c-can't offer you a cup of tea," she wailed suddenly. "I haven't g-got any tea, and the k-kitchen table's gone again!" She fell into the shelter of Mick's arms.

"No worry," commented Alan. "Hey, Toby, stir up some o'them good coals the kitchen table's made, and put the billy on. There's tea in me saddle-bag."

Toby grinned, and began to walk across to the yard where the saddles were now ranged on the top rail where Big Jim had hoisted them. Big Jim, already on his way back to join the others, had stopped and was staring thoughtfully at the ground in front of him. He gestured to Toby, who stopped in mid-stride, and obediently dropped his eyes to where Big Jim pointed. The others, puzzled now, watched them.

"Hey, boss," called Big Jim, "you come look dis-one track!"

Alan and Mick both went to join the two black boys.

"Williams boot nomore wide-one cross foot allasame dat one," Big Jim commented.

Mick printed his own boot in the dust and compared the two marks. The clear track that had drawn Big Jim's attention was indeed fractionally wider across the instep.

"Fresh one, too," he murmured.

Mick was suddenly galvanised into action. He straightened up and began to issue orders.

"Toby, you check around and see which way them track go. Marion, d'ye reckon you could find me a blanket and calico and roll me a cigarette swag'll go up behind me on the horse, and Alan, can I borrow a fresh horse from your plant, most of ours are out with Alec, and a saddle too?"

"Plant horses ain't here, sorry, Mick, but what about the ones in the yard?" Alan had immediately guessed Mick's plan "Would you like Toby to go along with you?"

"Yeah, good idea. But I'd like fresher horses. Could Wally run in what's still in the horse paddock? We'll take a couple of them. And a bit of tucker for the saddle-bags if y'got any to spare."

Alan gestured to Pansy and then to his pack bags still over by the yards, and Pansy hoisted Sammy on her hip and obediently made off.

"What is it, Mick? What are you going to do?" Marion had never before seen such an expression on his face. She ran along beside him as he strode purposefully towards the saddle-room, and reached down the leather ex-army rifle holster, made specifically for attachment to a saddle.

"Those tracks were made this morning," he said, "after you left. And it wasn't any Australian ringer who made 'em. I think someone watched you leave, and I don't think he's all that far away yet!"

She followed as he went to the jeep, took the twenty-two rifle from the brackets he'd fitted for it, and then ratted in the glove-box for the box of cartridges, which he transferred to the button-down pocket of his shirt.

"Now, roll me a swag, there's a good girl, and see how Pansy's doing with a bit of tucker."

In half an hour Mick and Toby were gone, swallowed up quickly in the belt of trees to the south of the homestead.

"What do you think Mick's going to do?" Marion said anxiously to Alan.

"If he catches 'im? Kill 'im, I suppose. I would, the bastard!"

He saw her appalled face, and was immediately sorry.

"No, Marion, I was only kiddin'. The Quiet Fella ain't like that. 'E's just took the gun in case they're away a few days and need a bit more tucker. Shoot a roo, or somethin'." He scratched his chin. "But all the same, Marion, a man with guts like Mick, 'e's not goin' to take this lyin' down, is he? A man's got a right to protect his home and family!" He patted her shoulder. "Now, c'mon kid, we got cleanin' up to do!"

She stared round her, not at the devastated kitchen, but thankfully at what still remained intact.

"Lucky for us you came along just in time to save most of the place, we won't ever be able to thank you enough, Alan."

"Yeah, we seen the smoke go up, and done the last coupla miles in record time."

"And left the wagonette and gear behind, and the plant horses? Well, I guess someone better go back for 'em, and the rest of us work out where to start the clean-up," Marion remarked.

Alan gave her a sideways glance, and said slowly, "There ain't no gear and horses, Marion."

"Oh no! You didn't! You didn't gamble them! Alan, you didn't!"

"Done the lot," he admitted ruefully. "Me pay for the job too. The boys own their horses, and I got the same and Blue Dawg, and the packhorse and two packsaddles. Got a job lined up for next year, too. Dunno 'ow I can take it now."

Marion shook her head slowly from side to side. What could she say.

"Anyway, not your worry, old girl. Now we better get stuck into workin' out what to do 'ere. Pansy's still got a fireplace, so yer c'n cook 'n eat there. Nipper 'n Wally 'n I c'n leave in the morning and take the jeep out, seein' yer got no packs there, 'n give Alec a hand to do the musterin' while the Quiet Fella's otherwise engaged. I'll leave Big Jim ter give a 'and with the clean-up."

The kitchen, back verandah, and bathroom were entirely destroyed, and Marion could only imagine what guts it must have taken to rescue the furniture from the bedroom with the roaring inferno behind the dividing wall. Thank God the store was safe, they could still eat reasonably well. Alan set the boys to building a brush wall round the tank supports and digging a channel from it to the vegetable garden.

"It'll do for yer bathroom fer the time bein'," he said. "Yer can stick the hose in at the side and syphon the water when yer want a bogey."

They could not begin the clean-up of the razed kitchen until the next day; by then the heat would have gone out of the twisted metal and charred lumps that had once been a refrigerator and a stove. Until Mick could rewire the rest of the building there were no lights, and the lamp was gone too.

"We better all have a clean-up before it gets dark," said Marion, surveying the substitute bathroom, "and Pansy and I'll put a feed on over at her place."

"You're a little trump!" grinned Alan, slapping her on the back. "Mick's a lucky fella. Wish I 'ad one like yer. You'd keep a man away from the cards, I'll bet!"

They ate by firelight in front of Pansy's cottage, and went early to their beds. There was much to do on the morrow. Marion fell asleep wondering whether Mick too was in his meagre swag, or whether he had already caught up with his quarry. She had no way of knowing.

Chapter 24

Christy's future at risk

"We followed the tracks," said Mick, "straight up to Unicorn Rock on the rise. He had a horse planted there, and he'd rolled out a bit of a swag the night before. He could watch the whole homestead from there, and not be seen, as long as he didn't light a fire. It was as if he knew we were all going to be away."

"I got on the galah session the other day," admitted Marion, "and Mrs. Deegue said something about maybe she and her husband taking a run over this way, and I said we'd all be away for the week doing the muster. Anybody who was listening in would have known we weren't going to be here!"

"Well, somebody did listen in," continued Mick, "and there's no prize for working out who. The horse tracks went straight across country towards the Parrot Hill road, double set, coming and going. No trouble finding 'em, seeing we knew what to look for. He cut the road just south of our boundary hill, rode down the road for about five miles, and then the ute met him. We stayed off the road on the side, but the tracks were so fresh it was easy to read 'em. He let the horse go there; you could see where he'd unsaddled it. Then he got in the ute, and the ute turned around and went back the way it'd come. Whoever it was picked him up didn't even get out of the ute."

A thought struck him.

"You haven't been on the wireless, have you?"

"No. I didn't give it a thought. Not while you were away."

"Well, don't! The Base doesn't expect us to call in for a week, and I reckon I know what that bastard's next move'll be. He'll believe the whole place, wireless and all, is gone, and he'll reason that maybe we won't even know about it for a week or so, if we missed the smoke. There couldn't be a better time for us to take a decent price and get out, if we got the right offer. You can bet Mr. Elton-Smythe the Arsonist will just happen along in a week or ten days' time, going through to Felix Creek, say, all prepared to get a big surprise at our misfortune, and then to make another offer on the spur of the moment."

The Yank turned up just as Mick had guessed he would, and by that time they had effected the homestead repairs and finished the muster as well. Where the kitchen had been a wide bough shed now took in the whole area that had once been kitchen and surrounding verandahs. It was partly walled by plaited pandanus and already furnished with a bush timber table, and greenhide and timber stools, with a Coolgardie cooler against the smoke-stained bedroom wall. There were rough shelves against the remaining wall area, most of the original kitchen shelves in fact, which by a quirk of fate had escaped the fire.

Elton-Smythe was too smart to make any offer, but his curiosity, and the normal practice of stopping to pass the time of day when passing through a neighbour's property, ordained that he pull up beside the building. The men were working cattle at the yards, and Marion was supervising Christy's lessons at the bough-shed table. Marion, following Mick's instructions, played it dumb.

She politely offered tea, which he declined, while staring around at the new aspect of Serendipity homestead.

"We were lucky not to lose the house. Must have been the kero fridge, I suppose, or a wax match, or something. If the drovers hadn't seen the smoke in time we'd have lost the lot." She couldn't resist rubbing it in. "Then, I guess, we might have been tempted to sell out. Me, anyway." She didn't risk looking at his face in case she couldn't control a smirk or a giggle. "But every cloud has a silver lining, Mr. Elton-Smythe. I don't know why we didn't think of it earlier; it's miles cooler under the bough shed rather than that hot little kitchen, and I've got stacks more room to work. The roof's weather-proof, too, and it'll take a cyclone to blow the rain right under when the Wet starts."

The Yank muttered something about being sorry they'd had a setback, and said he'd be on his way, and Marion rattled on about the advantages of the big bough shed. She watched the cloud of dust as the ute continued on along the road to Felix Creek on what was probably an unnecessary trip but had to be taken to keep up the farce.

"Hope you stake a tyre, you bastard," Marion sang out happily after the retreating vehicle.

Safely out of sight, Mick and Alan came down from the yards to hear her report.

"We don't ever leave the homestead with nobody here; wouldn't put it past him to have another go!" Mick ordered. "I don't reckon he'll give up that easy; not somebody who was prepared to burn down a homestead to get what he wanted. Somebody's got to be here all the time. With a gun handy, too. If the bastard tries his Wild West tricks here again, we'll give him a run for his money!"

They had agreed that, as soon as the Yank had made his reconnaissance, Mick and Alan would leave in the truck to pick up the Wet Season stores in Darwin.

"Nothing flash this time," Mick warned. "We might have a few steers to sell to the Felix Creek butcher next year, but we have to go easy for a while yet."

Marion counted out the notes from the tin, and reminded Mick that now she had a sewing machine she'd need material for clothes for herself and Pansy and the kids, so he'd better not cut that off the list. She was glad he was going to Darwin; he could buy dress materials there; the Felix Creek store didn't run to a wide choice in that line.

Alan was going to try and get a loan from the bank manager to set up his plant again. It hadn't even occurred to him until Mick suggested that, as he had the guarantee of the droving next year, there was the chance the bank manager would listen to him. With his record of gambling maybe not, but it was worth a try; he had the job lined up, and he had the men. If that failed, Mick said he ought to go out to the station which had booked him and put it to the owner to set him up with what he needed and take the cost of it out of the final payment for the job. Good reliable drovers weren't all that easy to come by, and the station owner would have to find someone else if he didn't stake Alan to the new plant. There was a third alternative, but Alan wouldn't hear of it. There was no way he would borrow money from Mick and Marion.

"I'd as soon cut me throat, and Blue Dawg's, too!" he stated adamantly. "If anything happened, and I got killed or somethin' before I finished the trip, the bank could stand it, and the station bloke, but Serendipity couldn't, so ferget it, old man!"

For the second time that day Marion and Christy stood and watched the dust trail of a departing vehicle.

"School finished today?" enquired Christy hopefully, and when she nodded he bounded off gleefully to station himself on the top rail of the yard where Alec and the boys were mothering up the calves they'd branded in the morning. Marion, on a sudden impulse, went into the bedroom and fished the hard-covered foolscap-size diary from the trunk where she kept it along with it's already-completed companion volume begun when they had first arrived. She recorded the date and Elton-Smythe's visit, and the fact that Mick and Alan had left for Darwin. She began to re-read some of her earlier entries, bare sentences which her memory suddenly clothed in detail, incidents she'd almost forgotten which came vividly back to life. She was very glad the diaries had survived the fire. Perhaps one day there would be children who might like to read the story of Serendipity from its very beginnings.

The hot weather burst suddenly upon them. One day it was pleasantly warm, and the next the ground was too hot to walk on with bare feet, and the waterbag suspended from a bough-shed rafter had to be refilled constantly. Pansy found and killed a snake in the cool darkness of the improvised bathroom under the tank-stand, and announced that she and Sammy would take their baths that day in the waterhole in the creek. "Too much mightbe that snake gottim mate proper cheeky-bugger!" Christy elected to join them.

"By the time you walk back from the waterhole you'll be just as sweaty and dirty as when you started out," Marion pointed out, but she went with them anyway. The water was cool under the shade of the overhanging trees and blue waterlilies dotted the placid surface near the upstream sandbank. A frill-necked lizard eyed them warily from his position half-way up a tree-trunk jutting out of the water, and then scrambled away in fear as Christy shot up the trunk in chase like a little yellow-brown monkey. The lizard escaped, and Christy took the easy way down by jumping with a yell into the water below. They splashed and ducked and tossed the chuckling baby to each other, and lay on the sandy bank on their backs and gazed up at the slivers of blue sky between the canopy of leaves.

The sun was well down when they walked back to the homestead, where, as they approached, they could see Alec talking to a khaki-clad figure standing beside a utility.

"P'leeceman!" said Pansy. It was indeed Tom. Marion greeted him with pleasure, but wondered momentarily why he hadn't sent her a telegram announcing his arrival and asking whether there were any errands from town, as he usually did. She led Tom into the bough-shed, asking Pansy to make a cup of tea from the camp-fire billy as she did so.

Tom sat down at the rough table and stared around.

"I knew you'd had a fire," he said. "Mick told me on the way through. Not a bad set-up you've got here though. Pity about the fridge though; you didn't have that for long."

"Could have been worse," Marion told him, "We would have lost the lot but for Alan and his boys." She wondered how much Mick had told him, and decided to say nothing of their suspicions unless Tom obviously already knew.

He was suddenly serious.

"Off the record, Marion. This isn't an official trip. I came on the spur of the moment. In fact I left about eleven o'clock last night. Muriel reckoned I ought to let you know, you and Mick being so fond of the kid and all that."

Marion was puzzled. "The kid?"

"Yeah, young Christy. I'll start at the beginning. I went down to close up the pub last night, 'bout nine-thirty, time to have a beer myself before ten. Fellow from Native Affairs there, young patrol-officer. Stopping there for the night, and I got yarning with him."

He paused as Pansy slid two pannikins of tea onto the table, and Marion asked her to fix the evening meal. Then he went on.

"I don't know if you know about this latest caper of Native Affairs. They're collecting up all the half-caste kids from round the camps and putting 'em in a home in Darwin. Bringing 'em up white, they reckon, giving 'em a better chance in life. Not a bad idea, I suppose, in the long run. Proper schooling, and all that. A bit tough on the poor mothers, though, but it's the law now, so they have to give their kids up."

Outside the shadows were lengthening; Marion could see Christy playing with Sammy while Pansy busied herself at the camp-fire.

"I knew all about it, of course. I'm a Protector, being a policeman. But I never thought about it affecting Christy, seeing he's with you. Anyway, this young patrol-officer, one of the ones who has to go around picking up the yella kids, well, he tells me the Department's had a letter from someone round Felix Creek about a little yella-fella at

Serendipity, so he's come down to get him, and he asked me to give him a mud-map of how to get here."

Marion opened her mouth to protest, but Tom went on.

"Yeah, I know. It'd be that fella Mick had the fight with over Christy. Well, I had to give him the directions. He said he had a bit to do in town in the morning, and he'd leave after dinner. Now, that ought to get him here some time tomorrow. When I got home I talked it over with Muriel. Actually, she said if I didn't come and tell you she'd take the ute and come herself. Reckoned you'd work out what to do. But don't tell me, will ya; I'm a Protector of Aborigines. I might be asked to check up on you, if by any chance the patrol officer doesn't find anyone at home when he calls."

Marion laughed.

"You're a mate, Tom. Now, what about a feed. I'll set the table while Pansy dishes up!"

"Yeah, thanks. And I won't stop the night this time, Marion. I'd like to get back up the road a bit, and get onto the Mission turn-off before the Native Affairs bloke comes along. He might start scratching his head if he meets me on this stretch of road coming back, when he only said goodnight to me at the pub last night!"

When Tom had been farewelled, and Christy was safe in bed, Marion called Pansy and Alec over from their hut and explained the situation to them. Officially they too would be wards of the Government, she knew that much, but so far the Government didn't know of their existence, and what the Government didn't know wouldn't hurt it.

"We could go up the Wilson River yards and camp there for a while," suggested Alec.

"I dunno," mused Marion. "He might decide to look around himself, and I couldn't stop him. More better you go somewhere there ain't any roads, I reckon."

"What say you take us that far in the jeep tomorrow, and then we go walkabout up the river a bit, and you meet us back at the yards say three or four days time?"

"Other boys too?" queried Pansy.

"Yeah, the lot of you, I reckon. We'll get away straight after early breakfast. He could get here by tomorrow dinner-time if he drives as fast as Tom did, and I've got to be here when he comes."

"What about Mick said we don't leave the place with nobody home? Say that Yank comes back, Marion?"

"I don't reckon he'll come back this way so soon, Alec. He'll go back to Parrot Hills down the bitumen for sure. Anyway, it's a chance we'll just have to take; it'll only be for a few hours."

"You sure you all right - by yourself - three-four days?"

"Course I'll be all right, Alec. I'll have the dogs here. And Mick left me the 22. You roll your swags early, and fix a bit of tucker. Goodnight."

She went to bed, but not to sleep immediately. She still had to work out a story to tell the patrol officer. One thing she knew for sure; she and Mick would have to find some way to adopt Christy. She'd never thought about it before, but she knew quite definitely that there was no way she'd give him up. He was part of the family, and the big bad Government wasn't going to get him, not if she could help it.

There was a real holiday atmosphere about the grossly-overloaded jeep as its chiacking occupants clung on wherever they could, while the girl in the big hat coaxed the maximum speed out of the vehicle that the rough track allowed. Overloading vehicles in the back country was an occupational trait; everybody did it. That didn't worry Marion.

If a spring broke she could always cut a sapling to take its place to limp home. But she was anxious to get back to the homestead as quickly as she could. There was no loitering once they reached the Wilson River yards. They unloaded swags and tucker bags quickly, and Marion told Alec she'd be back for them any time after three days; if they weren't there she'd light a smoke to let them know she'd arrived.

She had a quick and uneventful trip home, but the chained dogs greeted her as if she'd been away a week. She released them, and they followed her into the bough shed and flopped down in the shade. It was as if they knew perfectly well that, although the bough shed was normally out of bounds for them, the next few days were going to be an exception.

Marion thought she heard the sound of an approaching vehicle a dozen times before the patrol officer turned up just before dinner-time. He introduced himself as Viv Akers, and was a polite and conscientious young man, but he had public service written all over him and Marion had long ago absorbed the bushman's natural suspicion of anyone and anything remotely connected to government - any government. The bushman's individuality and public service adherence to the letter of the law were poles apart. She greeted him warily with the politeness reserved for those who were strangers and would always remain strangers. He accepted her invitation for a meal.

He was disappointed to find her the sole inhabitant of the station, and she parried this comment by asking why he hadn't sent her a telegram to let her know he was coming. This embarrassed the young man, because both of them knew perfectly well why he hadn't advised of his proposed visit. It was Department policy to arrive unexpectedly; station people advised beforehand had time to make arrangements regarding their Aboriginal populations, which were not always in Departmental interests.

"Er," he stammered, "I - I didn't think of it!"

"A pity," said Marion, "it would have saved you a trip. There's only myself and my husband, and Mr. and Mrs. Nelson and their little boy, and young Christy living here. It's a new station, so we don't have a blacks' camp here, not yet, anyway."

(She knew he would assume that Pansy and Alec were a white couple by the way she had spoken.)

He brightened.

"Actually, it's young Christy who I'm come about," he told her, and went on to explain the new legislation designed to give all coloured children living on stations an equal opportunity to those in the town.

She explained that Christy was away on holiday with the Nelsons, and she wasn't quite sure when they'd return.

"He's not exactly like a little boy living in the blacks' camp; he lives with us, and I'm teaching him his lessons. Wouldn't that make a difference?" she asked him.

He wasn't sure; he thought perhaps it would, but she and Mick would have to make an application through the right channels. She asked him what the right channels were, but he didn't seem to know, but promised to find out when he got back to Darwin.

"If he'd been here, I'd have to have taken him with me," he explained. "He's a ward of the Department, and we're responsible for him, you see. I don't know how long it would take to arrange for you to foster him, but I can assure you he'd be well looked after. We've got cottages with house-parents for the children, and they get the best of attention."

"I don't know exactly when they'll be back," said Marion vaguely. "They might have told my husband, but he's in Darwin. Christy's a favourite with the Nelsons too. He's got a good home here."

"Wow," she thought to herself, "maybe that was the wrong thing to say." The bough-shed, the dirt floor, the smoke-stained far wall, and the improvised furniture weren't exactly what the Department might consider a good home.

"Well," he said, "if you'll let us know when he comes back, then, Mrs. Hardy. In the meantime, I'll find out about the fostering."

The tone of his voice, and the way he looked around, wasn't really encouraging.

"Why don't they understand, these people?" she thought bitterly. "Christy's just a name on a list to them. They wouldn't even know about him but for some interfering busybody. Like hell I'll let you know, mister!"

Aloud, she murmured non-commitally. Then he went on to explain to her the Department's requirements for employment of Aboriginals, and gave her a printed copy of ration and clothing lists for such time as they might require it. She thanked him politely, and said she didn't really expect that they'd ever have a camp here like the big established stations had, but it was on the cards they'd need to employ some blacks when their cattle numbers built up.

He was doing his best to be friendly, but he was such an earnest young man. Marion mentally compared him to Mick and Alan, and wished he'd hurry up and leave. She was quite sure he'd believed it was just bad luck he'd missed out on Christy this time, and she let him unconsciously patronise her without once resorting to the sharp retorts that came to her mind. She noticed the ice-box on the back of his utility, and offered him some rump steak from the cooler and some fresh eggs for his evening meal and breakfast on the track, and assured him that no, she didn't find it lonely out here, especially when she had Christy for company when Mick was away working. She turned on a winning smile, and asked him if he'd mind dropping off a letter at the Felix Creek police station on his way back. May as well soften up the poor dope as much as she could. There was only one word in the note she hastily addressed to Tom and Muriel - "Thanks!"

She waved goodbye to him, satisfied she'd done a fair job in getting patrol-officer Akers onside. If he wasn't worried about how poor Christy might react to being taken away from the only home he remembered, he would at least be sympathetic towards the nice young woman on that lonely place who needed a little boy for company. She giggled when she thought of what his reaction would be if he only knew that little more than four hours earlier Serendipity was anything but lonely, with eight of his so-called wards shouting and laughing as they loaded their swags on the jeep.

Chapter 25

Alan gets his break

Alec and his party returned to the Wilson Creek yards on the third day, and waited there for another two, but still no Marion. Of them all, Alec was the only one who was at all perturbed. The interlude was a pleasant one, and time no longer seemed relevant.

"That fella gone by now," Alec said, "Mightbe we walk back, eh?"

Mick met them about half way in the truck, and immediately set Alec's unspoken fears about Marion's welfare at rest.

"The jeep packed up," he explained. "She couldn't get it to start, so she started pulling the carby to bits. Job for you when we get back, Alec, putting it together again!"

He didn't tell them that Marion had greeted his arrival home with a tirade of abuse at the hardy little vehicle which had let her down for the first time, and then a flood of tears because she hadn't been able to repair it.

They wanted to know if Alan had returned with him.

"No more. He's picking up some more horses for your droving next year, boys. Packhorse camp this time. Got some second-hand packs in Darwin, and I brought 'em home on the truck. Looks like you fellas might be busy riding some colts straight after the Wet unless he can buy 'em already broken-in."

He had told Marion of Alan's lucky break as she helped him unload the truck before he set off to pick up the hikers. They had pulled in for a drink at the Felix Creek pub on their way up to Darwin, and who should be there but the owner of Sotheby Downs himself, the very man Alan planned to see if the Bank turned him down. Mick excused himself and went to see Tom, while Alan explained his predicament over a beer, with Blue Dawg sitting at his feet with his head cocked on one side. It didn't take Aaron Duncan long to decide to take the chance and give Alan a letter stating that Sotheby Downs would foot the bill for purchase of horses, gear and stores. Most competent drovers had a peccadillo or two, he knew, and he rightly assessed Alan as being the sort of man who, though he might gamble his own money and belongings, would not be likely to do it with another man's trust. Alan's inquiries in Darwin had located a drover who had just taken delivery of his first truck, and was only too pleased to get rid of his packs at a reduced price. Mick had left Alan in Felix Creek on the return trip to go about his horse-buying, and Tom had mentioned the reason for his flying trip to Serendipity.

"Don't lose any sleep because you're not much of a mechanic, Honey," Mick comforted Marion. "We'll fix that in time. You did the main part of the job with flying colours, and that's what counts."

They both made a great fuss of Christy at bed-time that night, and although Mick had said there was no money to spare on extras that year, Marion noticed that his purchases had included a large toy truck, which he hid in their bedroom with the comment that they'd give Christy a better Christmas this year than he had last year. The box contained a smaller truck too. Sammy was toddling now, and he'd want one too. Marion wondered whether that little boy in the Adelaide orphanage had ever had such a truck of his own, and her heart went out to her big thoughtful mate. They made love, and it was as perfect as it had ever been. Then they lay together in companionable warmth, and swore that, whatever happened, Christy wasn't going to be parted from them.

Then Alan wired asking that two of his boys meet him in Felix Creek as soon as possible with three saddles, and Mick sent them with Alec and Pansy in the jeep. The Nelsons hadn't had a break for the races that year, so Mick gave Alec a cheque and told him to take a few days off. Marion sent an explanatory letter to the Correspondence School, and asked to enrol Christy in the second grade the following year. Although his schooling had been haphazard he could already read and count reasonably well, so she knew from experience that he would cope well.

Alec returned with a bundle of mail and a box of second-hand books that Muriel had collected for them, most of them labelled "Please Pass On" and some decidedly the worse for wear. It was all Marion could do to decide to ration them out over the Wet, rather than begin on them immediately.

Alan returned with thirty-five new horses, and the days were divided between breaking in the few colts and building another small yard near a drying waterhole on Serendipity's south-western boundary. They used Alan's horses for a last muster and branding for the year, and turned out the Serendipity horses for a well-earned spell.

The days were hot and breathless now, with little respite when the sun went down. Each day the humidity increased, and it became increasingly difficult to work physically after mid-morning and before late afternoon; humans and animals seemed sapped of energy, and it was as if the whole of Nature's world was poised in patient expectation, as indeed it was. Marion watched the blue sky daily, searching for the cloud build-up which must herald the first storms. But it was not until the week before Christmas that her vigilance was rewarded, and Mick and Alec were able to forego the anxious policing of those waterholes which had dried back to mere mudholes and were a trap for the unwary or weaker cattle, which waded out through the mud to the clearer water to drink, and then with the extra weight of the water inside them, became bogged and would die a lingering death if they were not pulled out. They had rescued one obstinate cow three times from the same hole. Once more, threatened Mick, and he'd put a bullet in her.

With the first refreshing storm the cranky tempers and long silences vanished like magic. Alan's boys developed wide white grins and prepared for walkabout, and nobody was surprised when the group of blacks from Parrot Hill materialised one day. Toby had told Mick the day before that they would come, and the four boys were all ready to go along with them, laughing and chattering, to a pre-arranged gathering of the tribal groups somewhere in the north. Alec and Pansy and Sammy had been invited to join them, but despite Pansy's evident yearning Alec had decided that they should stay on Serendipity country, maybe go bush for a couple of weeks after Christmas, look about a bit, and chase a few goannas. Alec had not been on a ceremonial walkabout since he was a small boy; the Kimberley tribe had never accepted him. He had no tribal status, and therefore no legitimate claim to a wife. On the other hand, Mick and Marion, Alan too, treated him as one of themselves. Because of his parentage Sammy would never have any tribal status either, but he'd be okay. Marion would teach him like she was teaching young Christy. He tossed his chubby young son in the air, and asked Pansy what she'd do if the little fella got crook, like Christy last year, and they were a hundred miles away in the ranges and had to footwalk for help. Pansy gulped and rolled her eyes and snatched the chuckling toddler in her arms.

"More better we stay!" she agreed vehemently.

The storms rolled in, in an almost ordered procession, a couple of hours of lightning and thunder in the late evening, with an inch or so of rain each time, and the thirsty land soaked it up and responded with a green flush of button grass within days. The creeks had not yet run, but there was surface water for the stock, and the threat of bushfires was past.

Marion and Pansy laboured over the camp-oven Christmas cake, a monster containing twelve eggs, which Pansy insisted the chooky-chooks had donated specially for the occasion, and Alan had commandeered the copper to make a home-brew with ingredients which had travelled from Felix Creek to Serendipity by pack-horse. He had sent Alec hunting for bottles for the promised bottling ceremony a week later, and bemoaned the fact that, even with the empty tomato sauce and black sauce bottles, they were still going to be short.

"Something will turn up, before it's ready, I'll bet, and you'll have enough containers," said Marion, watching him skim his bubbling cauldron one morning.

And so it did. One of the new horses found a break in the horse-paddock fence where a lightning-struck tree had fallen over it, and poked through and up to the homestead during the night. It drank almost a third of Alan's brew before they found it at dawn staggering against the wall of Alec's cottage in equine inebriation.

"See," grinned Marion. "You've got plenty of bottles now!"

"Tole yer it packed a punch, didn't I?" replied Alan, catching the unprotesting animal to lead it back to the yard to sleep off the effects.

Three days before Christmas Marion picked up a telegram from Tom.

"Business at Mission stop will camp turn-off tomorrow night stop have your mail will meet you there."

Marion was sorry for Tom, because he was obviously going to miss Christmas with his family, but elated at the unexpected chance of Christmas mail from the outside world. Mick debated making the trip in the jeep. If the storms held off he could do it, but on the other hand if he went on horseback he'd have to leave as soon as Alec could run the horses in. They searched the horizon, and decided to take a chance on the jeep the next day. Alec and Alan went too, more manpower, Mick said, if they had to push the jeep out of a bog. Marion cut a slab of her Christmas cake, and Alan rolled four bottles of his precious home-brew in a bag "to cheer up the poor bloke, havin' to work over Christmas."

The rain held off till Christmas Eve, and the jeep skidded and slid home in a downpour. The girls had weathered their own minor drama that morning when they'd discovered that one of them would have to kill the rooster. Pansy had finally done it, and they'd barely got it in the camp-oven and buried in the coals when the rain started and threatened to deluge the fire. It was still there under a sheet of tin, and Marion almost forgot it in the excitement of the bulging mail-bag wrapped in a camp-sheet.

It was a good Christmas, made all the better with the delight of the little boys with their trucks and the bag of lollies Tom had thoughtfully pushed into the mailbag. Most of the mail had been for Marion, with a fat letter from Mudjinup, and another from Angela with news of Delroy and the Cut and even messages for Pansy and Alec. The home-brew was potent enough to stimulate a sing-song, beginning with carols sung by those who knew them and hummed by those who didn't, and ending in an impromptu corroboree led by a giggling Pansy. The Serendipity dogs and Blue Dawg, surfeited on scraps, sneaked further into the bough shed out of the rain, and thumped their tails appreciatively. The roofed leaked onto the table, but nobody cared.

"In the scrub," said Alan, "yer lucky to get one Christmas in four, what with bushfires and bogs, or bein' camped out by yerself and fergettin' the date. This is as good as any I ever run across." They all agreed.

January and February passed in a series of grey and blue days; the creeks ran and the swamps filled, and the homestead billabong was once again a teeming riot of bird-life. Marion filled her days alternately at her sewing machine and learning from Pansy the intricacies of plaiting pandanus fronds into a protective wall for the side of the bough-shed which received most of the onslaught of the rains. Mick and Alan carted loads of ant-bed periodically and experimented with the addition of ash and water to floor the bedroom and bough-shed with a mixture which, if it wasn't exactly concrete, was at least an improvement on the straight dirt floor it had replaced. Marion transferred the tin containing their savings to a new hiding place in the store.

Mick looked forward to making his first sale of Serendipity steers. He had arranged with the Felix Creek butcher on his way back from the Darwin trip to send a small mob of thirty with Alan on his way through to Sotheby Downs to pick up his mob. They were already in the Bullock Paddock, growing fatter by the day.

"We're over the hump," thought Marion. "Serendipity is here to stay!"

It was hard to imagine any other sort of life now. She was supremely contented.

She was queen to Mick's king in a little principality of their own, and the spirit of the little ginger-haired kid was still there; she would fight to the death for them both.

Ever since they had decided that, come hell or high water, Christy belonged to them, Marion had become aware of a subtle new yearning. Until then, though she had cuddled Sammy often, she had never envied Pansy, been aware only of the physical restrictions that a baby placed on a mother's lifestyle. Now, in her quieter moments the thought sometimes sneaked into her mind; she wondered what a child of Mick's would look like, and a hazy picture began to take shape. One of the baby-spirits that Pansy believed in had obviously singled her out.

Big Jim and the boys came back from walkabout "glassy-eyed and stinkin' of goanna," as Alan put it, but he was very relieved to see them. For a fortnight the station was a hive of activity as the drovers made ready for the road, and Mick and Alec put the steers together to go with them.

There was a tinge of envy in every heart the day the drovers left. The true bushman, black or white, is semi-nomadic, and at times, without rhyme or reason, the urge to roll the swag and travel hopefully is almost irresistible. Since piccaninny daylight the smells of leather and horseflesh, the sounds of milling cattle in the yard and guttural Aboriginal voices, the ring of metal canteen again metal stirrup or girth-buckle, and the sight of the five rolled swags lying together on the ground waiting to be hoisted up and tied down across the packs had reminded those who were staying behind of what they were missing.

"I hate saying goodbye," said Marion crossly.

"Only because you ain't the one that's goin'!" laughed Alan. "Blue Dawg an' me, we ain't got no objection to yer comin' along too, yer know. Yer could leave the Quiet Fella to look after th' place, and share yerself around a bit!"

Marion laughed, and slid an arm round Mick's waist.

"Well, thanks for the offer, Alan. Can't make it this time, though. Tied up here at Serendipity for the next, say, thirty-forty years."

Alan shrugged. "C'n only try! Well, see yer round October, then."

That night Marion told Mick she was almost sure she was going to have a baby. He embraced her warmly, and then said, "I reckoned you might be. For the last week you've been going around purring to yourself like a cat with a saucer of cream."

"Oh, Mick," she pouted, "I think I've got a secret, and you go and spoil it all. You're supposed to be absolutely stunned with surprise."

He chuckled. "Fair go, Honey. I am surprised. Surprised we didn't get around to it earlier, the way I feel now you've actually told me."

They lay awake and planned for a long time. Mick was sure that baby would be a little girl, a little replica of her mother, but Marion was equally certain it would be a boy. Mick had the last word before they fell asleep.

"Law of averages," he said. "Got two boys on the place already, time for a girl."

It was surprising how quickly Serendipity slipped into its Dry Season routine. Mick and Alec, sometimes alone, and sometimes with Pansy's and Marion's help, branded calves, handled cattle, and, on Mick's insistence, marked out an airstrip and cleared it of shrubs and anthills.

Christy's first batch of school lessons had arrived with the Christmas mail, and Marion had started him off in the middle of January. It had been Tom who had organised a regular mail drop for them, when he suggested they put up a mailbox at the Mission turn-off so that the mail-contractor could leave mail there for them on his monthly run to the Mission, and collect any mail they wanted posted on the return trip. The need to supervise the lessons three or four hours a day helped to fill Marion's time as she became increasingly tied to the homestead, both because of her pregnancy and their decision not to leave the homestead unguarded for any length of time. Though they rarely referred to it, the memory of what lengths the Yank was prepared to go to force them to sell out to him was always just below the level of consciousness.

"It's not over yet," thought Marion. "A fellow like that, who's always got what he wanted, isn't going to give up so easily. Maybe next time he won't be so obvious about it, but, sure as eggs, he'll try something if he gets any sort of chance."

Knowing that her presence at the homestead was so necessary helped to quell her momentary envy of the others when they rode off from the yards in the morning, or rolled their swags for a job further away on the run. It was something she'd have to get used to, anyway, once the baby arrived; there'd be less bush work for her then.

Unexpectedly, Viv Akers of Native Affairs did send a telegram to announce his second visit, but Pansy and Sammy were the only ones home on the day he sent it, so Marion didn't pick it up until a few hours before he was due to arrive. She and Christy had taken a day off to run some supplies in the jeep up to the Wilson River yard, leaving Pansy to hold the fort.

When Viv arrived Marion greeted him like an old friend and introduced Christy. When he produced the papers for her and Mick to sign to foster Christy her assumed friendliness suddenly became real. Christy, who hadn't the slightest idea that his future had been a bone of contention, warmed to the nice man who was so interested in his school work, and showed not the slightest sign of shyness.

Marion dropped her guard and chattered away as she made the ritual cup of tea for visitors.

"Last place I called in the black girls working in the house made the tea," volunteered Viv. "Doesn't Mrs. Nelson help you?"

Marion's jaw dropped. Viv burst out laughing at her expression.

"Surely you know everyone in this country knows everyone else's business sooner or later," he said. "I did a bit of checking up on what I'd heard with your friend, the policemen, at Felix Creek. I brought some more papers to sign with me, in case the Nelsons want to apply for exemptions from being wards of the Department. I'll have to meet them though. I have to be sure the husband really can read and write and so on. Can't always rely on what some people tell us, you know!"

Marion had the grace to look ashamed.

Mick and Alec were due home at the week-end, and as Viv had a routine call to make at Parrot Hill and the station south of it, he arranged to call in at the week-end on his return trip.

"You're a lucky little fella," he said, ruffling Christy's hair, and when he produced a bag of lollies from his glove-box Christy thought that was what he meant by saying he was lucky.

"Don't forget to save some for Sammy," called Viv, as he drove off.

"I suppose I'm lucky, too," thought Marion, "to strike a decent bloke like that. After all the lies I told him, he's gone out of his way to help us. Just goes to show they're not all paper-work and no heart." Mick would like Viv, she decided, and Alec and Pansy certainly would. Viv would very likely become a friend, as Tom and Muriel had.

She would never know just how much of an argument Viv had put up before his superior had finally agreed to his recommendations; nor would she know that his picture of the red-headed girl in the bough shed was not the pathetic one she thought she'd created. Viv had decided that with that colour hair and that set of jaw he'd rather be on her side than against her. If she wanted the kid that much, and if what he'd been told about the husband getting into a fight over the boy was true, then obviously the kid would be better off with them. He could imagine that if Christy were taken away, she'd probably come up to Darwin and pinch him back, and cause a heap of trouble. She was in the right, anyway. He, too, felt that he'd made a worthwhile friend.

Chapter 26

The law steps in

The dust had settled and the calves were mothered-up. Mick and Alec squatted on their heels in the shade of the coolabah tree a few feet away from the main homestead yard, and Mick drew in the dust with his forefinger a rough map of the Mt. Jindit area, discussing with Alec the possible approach to a muster there.

Alec cocked his ear suddenly.

"Vehicle comin', Mick. From the South. Might be Parrot Hill, eh?"

"Can't see them paying us a social visit," grunted Mick, rising to his feet and staring in the direction of the now-audible revving of an engine negotiating the sandy creek-crossing just beyond the tree-line at the end of the air-strip.

The utility, with a policeman in front and two black-trackers on the back, had indeed come via Parrot Hill, and it was not a social visit. Mick and Alec strolled over to the bough shed as the vehicle drew up.

"Sergeant Vickers, from Eversham," the middle-aged policeman introduced himself. His trackers climbed down to stretch their legs.

"Come in and have a cup of tea," invited Marion, who, with Christy peering behind her, had stepped outside to see who the visitors were.

"I don't know whether you'll feel like giving me a cuppa tea when you hear what I've come about!"

Mick, arriving just in time to hear this comment, interjected, "Well, whatever it is, we'd be better discussing it sitting down in the shade, so you may as well come inside outa the sun, eh?"

The policeman gestured to the trackers to wait, took off his hat, and entered the bough shed. He was obviously ill at ease. Marion, her curiosity heightened, hastened to make the tea, and she had her back turned reaching for the biscuit tin when he spoke.

"You're Michael Hardy? Well, I've got a warrant here for your arrest on a charge of poddy-dodging eleven calves from Parrot Hill Station."

"What!" Marion swung round, and the biscuit tin went flying.

Mick, still standing, echoed her exclamation.

"I've just inspected the evidence at Parrot Hill. Eleven of their cows with calves on 'em with your brand. Got 'em in the yards there, and I've impounded them to go in to town for the trial. The Magistrate's due down in a fortnight."

Marion felt a wave of nausea, and the next minute Mick was leading her to the table and pushing her onto a seat.

"I reckon we all need a cup of tea after that," he said quietly, and poured a pannikin and thrust it to Marion. He poured another and passed it to the policeman, who sat down awkwardly, muttering that he was sorry to upset the little lady. Marion gulped a mouthful of black tea, and shook her head to clear it.

"What's it mean, Mick? It's another trick to get us out, isn't it?"

Mick patted her hand.

"Simmer down, Honey. I'll go along and see what it's all about," he said quietly. He turned to the policeman. "Okay if I talk to my offsider for a minute? Give him a few instructions for while I'm away?"

"I'll have to come with you." The sergeant was pleased to get away from Marion. He was used to women who burst into tears or screamed abuse at him, but not to ones who just stared white-faced at him as if he wasn't there. She was either a wonderful actress, or she didn't have a clue what her old man had been up to. He scrambled to his feet and followed Mick outside.

Mick called Alec, and explained tersely to him. "Stick around the house, Alec, and don't leave it except to check the bullock-paddock fence now and then. We need another trough in the horse paddock this end. You could put that in to keep you busy. We can't worry about tailing the cows and calves now; just let 'em go."

"Sure, Mick." Alec shook Mick's hand. There wasn't much else to say.

It took only a quarter of an hour for Mick to roll his swag and grab a couple of changes of clothes and his cheque book and writing case.

He kissed Marion. "Chin up, Honey. And don't sell the place while I'm away, will you?"

By now she'd regained her composure, and that made her laugh. She didn't want Mick worrying about her, and maybe the baby, when he had other things on his plate.

"I'll be right, Mick," she said. "And send me a telegram when you want me to come in, or if you want anything done." She kissed him again, and went quickly inside, with her arm around Christy. Mick got in with the driver, the trackers climbed on the back, and the utility drove off the way it had come.

Pansy and Alec slipped inside as soon as it had gone, and found Marion in tears, but they were tears of rage.

"Mick's never been near Parrot Hill since he tracked that fellow last year. And if he had, there's no way those calves would've got back to their mothers, would they!" Alec grinned his agreement.

"So it's a frame-up to try and get us off the place, so that stinking Yank can get his hands on it. I knew he wouldn't just give up!"

"The Quiet Fella don't give up easy either," Alec assured her. "I've known him longer than you, Marion. He think of something."

Pansy dumped Sammy on the floor, and started to pick up the biscuits that were still scattered around. She caught Christy's eye and pointed with her lips to the outside fireplace. Another cup of tea. It was the universal antidote in times of stress.

"How would they do it, Alan?" queried Marion.

"Easy, I reckon. Throw one of ours, or shoot it, and take a pattern of the brand from the hide. A big station's got a blacksmith, could make a brand easy. Then all they gotta do is put it on their own calves, yard 'em up with their mothers, and then call the cops. That musta bin how they done it!"

"And if Mick goes to jail for it, we don't stand a chance of getting the lease when the time's up. The Lands Department wouldn't give it to a bloke whose been in jail for poddy-dodging."

"Bit hard to run the place properly without Mick, too," agreed Alex

"That's the way the Yank's thinking. But we could do it if we got two or three more boys to help you, Alec. Just keep ticking over. Not much use, though, if we don't get the lease in eighteen months time."

Marion spent a miserable and almost sleepless night. She knew very little about the law, apart from what she had read in stories and seen at picture shows. There had to be evidence, and the Yank had the evidence. It didn't matter what anyone said about what might have happened; you had to prove it, and you couldn't prove words. Just like Grandpa's grandfather who borrowed the priest's horse and got sent to Australia for stealing it. She dreamed vaguely of bawling calves with a big brand of Exhibit A stamped all along their sides, and woke up half-believing a mad plan she'd dreamed for her and Alec and Pansy to steal the calves from under the noses of the Yank and the cops and do away with the evidence.

For the first time she felt a tiny movement in her abdomen, and then a second, a quite definite little kick. The misery fled her face, and a little smile quirked the edges of her lips.

"So you're awake too, baby," she murmured. "Okay, we'll get up then, and we'll keep our fingers crossed for your Dad!"

At that moment Mick was stirring up the campfire almost a hundred miles away, watching the policeman pulling bread and meat from the tuckerbox on the back of the utility. Their swags were already rolled, and when they had breakfast there remained only fifty miles to go to the township of Eversham, a mere fifteen miles further up The Bitumen from the Army Camp site which had offered such a good start to Serendipity three years earlier. The dirt road joined The Bitumen at the Army camp, so the last fifteen miles would be speedy, and they should reach the town by mid-morning. Eversham was Parrot Hill's town the way Felix Creek was Serendipity's. The Yank would be well-known there, and Mick a stranger under a cloud. There were better ways, Mick thought, of making an entrance into a small town for the first time, but at least he wasn't going to be handcuffed to the cop.

He'd noticed the handcuffs on the tray below the glove-box as soon as he'd got into the ute.

"Use them much?" he asked the policeman.

"Sometimes," Vickers had replied. "Use my discretion."

The handcuffs hadn't been mentioned again. The men had sized each other up in silence for the first half-hour. Then the policeman had broken the silence.

"You want a lawyer, Hardy? You can get one from Darwin, y'know. Elton-Smythe's already got on to the best fellow, I've heard, but there is another chap there who's supposed to be all right, too."

"Lawyers cost the earth, don't they?"

"Pretty pricey, I reckon, but they're smart with words."

"Not much good if the other one's smarter. I'd lose the case and owe the lawyer money as well."

"There's no law that says you have to have a lawyer, I s'pose."

"The way I see it," Mick had said, "is that a lawyer could only tell things that I'd tell him first, so I may as well tell 'em myself. I haven't got the money to spare for a lawyer, anyway."

"Well, let me know if you change your mind, but you'll need to do it quick because there's only a couple of weeks till the case comes up."

They ate breakfast quickly, the two trackers squatting on their heels at some distance from the sergeant and his prisoner, speaking gutturally in their own language. Then Vickers nodded to them to load on the camping gear while he and Mick went their separate ways to relieve themselves.

The first face Mick saw as they drove past the Eversham pub was a familiar one. Ernie spotted him at the same time and yelled a greeting. By the time they pulled up at the Police Station Ernie was only a few yards behind in his jeep.

"I s'pose," said Vickers with a wry grin, "I'd better return the compliment and ask you in to meet the wife and have a cuppa, before I show you to your quarters. You coming too, Ernie?"

Mrs. Vickers was a little bird-like woman, with grey hair pulled back in a bun, one of the kind that always liked to have everything right, and she was a bit of a martinet with the two trackers' wives who served as her housegirls. The smoko was ready and waiting. Mick couldn't help wondering how she knew which prisoners would be invited to smoko, and which ones wouldn't, but he found out later that it was a customary ritual for all white and half-caste prisoners, because both she and her husband staunchly upheld that "everyone is innocent until he is proved guilty." The contrast between the Serendipity black tea in enamel pannikins and Mrs. Vickers' bone-china cups and saucers with matching milk jug and sugar bowl, flanked by a plate of scones wrapped in a muslin cloth to keep them warm, struck him as a reversal of what really ought to happen. The "goodie" gets a pannikin, while the "baddie" gets a flash cup and saucer. But nobody else noticed any anomaly; they were too busy talking, except for the sergeant, who leaned back in his chair, and sipped his tea, and listened impassively.

Ernie filled Mick in on the local gossip. Nothing quite so interesting had happened for years, not since the case of the soldier at the Camp who got speared by a blackfellow for alienating the affections of the blackfellow's missus, and the soldier ran screaming back into the Camp stark naked with the spear still stuck quivering into one buttock, and the blackfellow racing behind him with another spear at the ready and the obvious intention of making a symmetrical job of it.

There seemed to be some doubt as to the number of calves Mick was supposed to have lifted. Some said fifty, and others reckoned a hundred or more. Others had heard that he'd come over from the Kimberleys with a reputation for the same thing, but he'd been smart enough to leave before they could pin anything on him. Some of the ladies round town knew for a fact that he had two wives he'd brought with him, one white and one black. Ernie roared with laughter as he recounted each story.

"Worst thing is, Mick," he chuckled, "you're so darn cheeky about it, naming your place Serendipity, which is blackfella for Takim-little-calf-allabout."

Mick was glad Marion hadn't accompanied him, as the sergeant had suggested she might want to do. With her touchy Irish temper, a couple of weeks at the pub with those sorts of yarns going round would probably land her more fights than feeds. Mick was already notorious; one in the family was enough. He hoped the Jury would be as level-headed as the Vickers seemed to be.

It wasn't a bad two-weeks spell for Mick; bit of a holiday really. Mrs. Vickers was a great cook, and every compliment seemed to inspire her to greater efforts. She had a good library too, and Mick was able to catch up on two or three of the classics he'd heard Marion mention but had never read himself. His mornings were saved from boredom by his offer to the sergeant to break in and work the couple of colts in the paddock at the back of the police station, which Vickers hadn't had the time to attend to himself. The sergeant offered to pay him for the job, but Mick laughed and said he'd do it for the free board he was getting. His "room", one of a pair of sparsely furnished but meticulously clean cells, was only locked at night, but the sergeant asked him not to leave the environs of the police station during the day, which was no imposition on Mick.

Ernie came back into town and took a room at the pub three days before the trial. He brought a couple of bottles of beer up to the police station and sat with Mick in the shade of the poinciana tree in the backyard.

"Thought Marion might like a back-up when she gets in, so I came in a bit early," he said.

Mick told him about the baby, and they swapped stories about how their respective stations were coming along. The subject of poddy-dodging wasn't mentioned. Ernie probably thought he had pinched the calves, Mick thought, but hoped to hell he'd get out of it some way. He hoped so himself; the future of Serendipity would be pretty bleak if he didn't.

By the time Marion arrived there Eversham had taken on a gala atmosphere exceeding even that of race-time. The publican had saved a small single room for Marion, even though Mick hadn't thought to book one for her; the Hardys' dilemma was likely to increase his annual income by forty or fifty percent, and he was duly grateful.

The pub was built of stone, in four one-room wide sections around an inner quadrangle with a well in the centre, an architecture dating from the days of less admirable relations between black and white. Long verandahs protected both inner and outer walls, and the internal courtyard sported a lone poinciana and a struggling lawn, ideal as a repository for swags in times of overflow.

Elton-Smythe and his foreman had a room at the opposite end of the building to Marion's, with his lawyer next door. The magistrate and his clerk had a room to themselves, but after that the number of people to a room depended solely on how many beds could be fitted in. Jurymen and their families, mostly from out of town, had to be accommodated, and it seemed as if everybody in the district who could conceivably leave their stations and camps had come as interested spectators.

Marion washed the dirt of her travel off, and went immediately, escorted by Ernie, to visit Mick at the police station. After the initial embrace, he held her away from him and gazed in approval. Marion had not wasted her time in apprehensive fears. She had made herself two new dresses on the old machine, to accommodate her increasing waist-line, and she wore one of them now. Mick thought she had never looked so beautiful.

"Did you bring the diary?" he queried. There was just a chance that she might not have understood the disguised request in the telegram he'd sent. She nodded. He gave her the sheet of note-paper on which he'd listed a number of points.

"Go through it, Honey, and copy out exactly the dates and entries for these times on separate paper. Then bring it back to me, and the diary too. Wouldn't want to lose that.

I'll get Mrs. Vickers to look after it for us. But don't let anyone see you with it; that's important. Shove it in a case or something when you come back."

Then Mrs. Vickers appeared with the morning-tea tray in all its bone-china splendour, and served it at the table in the shade of the tree. When Marion produced the parcel containing the trousers and shirt Mick had worn to his wedding Mrs. Vickers offered at once to have one of the housegirls iron them for him.

"They're a cool pair," thought Ernie, but he wondered privately whether Mick was doing the right thing by not having a lawyer to speak for him.

"The town's already taken sides," he told them. "Swung around a bit now, Mick. They got the cattle down in the sale-yards with the trackers watchin' over 'em, and everybody's been down to look. A lot of 'em reckon if its only a lousy eleven head it's hardly worth the hullabaloo, but others say that maybe eleven got away from you, but lots more didn't. Anyway, yer got all the blacks in town onside, since they heard about yer black missus; makes you some sort of 'lation to 'em all."

Marion brought Mick up to date on the situation at home. There had been no visitors at all since his departure. She had left Christy in Pansy's care, and Alec and Pansy were going to move into the homestead in her absence. Alec had the 22 if he needed it. He was going to listen in to the wireless twice a day for any messages, and if anything untoward happened at home, he had strict instructions to send her a telegram at the pub. She had already sent one to him to advise of her safe arrival at Eversham.

They did not waste much more time in talking; there was work to be done. Ernie drove Marion back to the pub, where she locked herself in her room and sat down to copy out the extracts. They had debated whether to risk making the phone call from the Eversham Post Office, but Ernie thought not. The Post-master's wife on the exchange would have to get the number for them, and would be likely to recognise it, and unlikely to be able to resist the temptation to listen in to the conversation. It was forty-five miles up the Bitumen to the next roadside store with a phone box. Ernie reckoned he could drive up there, make the call to Tom and get back to Eversham before anyone had missed him. They were all far too busy swapping rumours anyway, with the trial due to begin the next day. Ernie's input into the rumours would begin then. It would all be a matter of timing.

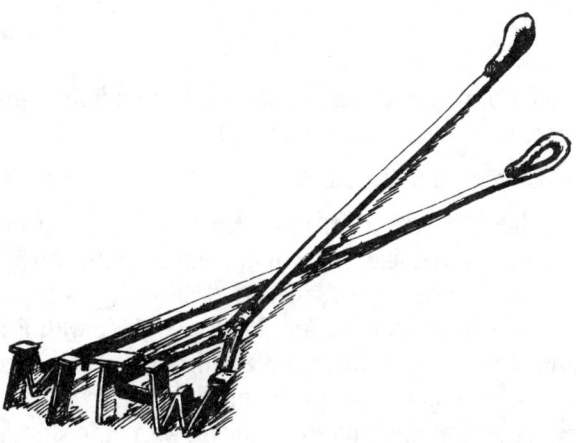

Chapter 27   *Trial at Eversham*

The Eversham Hall-cum-Court-House owed its existence to the same Army source as the Serendipity homestead, but was without benefit of verandahs, so that by nine o'clock the heat of the late September sun reflecting on the corrugated iron walls was already beginning to make itself felt inside. On the wooden dais at one end, normally reserved for the pianist and any other musical performers on offer at the local dances, tables and chairs had now been arranged for the performers in what promised to be one of the big events of the year.

Anticipating a bigger audience than could be accommodated on the wooden forms which lined the sides of the hall, the school-master had, the previous day, offered the use of the chairs from the two-room school and delegated his assistant and bigger pupils to carry them across to the hall. He had no option then, as he explained that evening in the bar, but to close the school for the duration of the trial. His Department superiors in their offices over 1600 miles away in South Australia would not know of it unless he told them himself, and in certain circumstances in these outback postings it was more important to co-operate with local needs than to follow Department instructions to the letter. The Inspector had already made his annual visit for the year during the more salubrious winter, as Inspectors always did, so there was little likelihood that he would be caught out.

By nine o'clock the schoolmaster was co-opted to take an even more important part in the proceedings than he had earlier intended. One of the jury-men, on his way into town the previous afternoon, had rolled his vehicle on a sharp bend, and was now in the hospital with a broken leg. The school-master was sworn in to take his place.

Marion had breakfasted early in the hotel dining room with Ernie, but not early enough to avoid the Yank and his lawyer, who entered the room just as Marion and Ernie stood up to leave. The Yank said something to his companion, and they both laughed. Ernie squeezed her arm, and the half-caste waitress, who had over-heard the comment, shot a sympathetic glance to Marion.

"Win or lose, that bastard's not going to put me off Serendipity," she muttered fiercely to Ernie, once they were outside in the courtyard.

"That's the style, Ginger!" muttered Ernie.

The Magistrate, who had arrived in town late the afternoon before, had advised Sergeant Vickers that he would like to begin hearing the case at 9:30, so Mick, in white shirt and stockman-cut gaberdine trousers and elastic-side boots, newly polished, was escorted there a quarter of an hour earlier. Marion, waiting with Ernie in the shade of one of the pepperina trees, felt her heart surge with pride. He looked almost debonair; there wasn't a touch of the hang-dog appearance usually associated with wrong-doers. On the other hand, Elton-Smythe, a bit over-weight, with his coarse face and little piggy eyes - it was easy to imagine him as a crook. Marion called and waved to Mick as he went through the doorway, and then, turning back, caught Elton-Smythe's eye for the second time that morning. On the impulse, without Mick there to stop her, she poked out her tongue.

When Sergeant Vickers indicated that the public could enter the hall there was a rush for seats, but as if by mutual agreement space was left in the front row for Marion and Ernie, and on the other side of the aisle for the Yank's foreman, Chet Wildean, and another lean-faced fellow who looked as if he'd stepped out of a cowboy film. He had a dark, saturnine face, and the blue shadow of a day-old beard. Marion glanced involuntarily down at his boots and hated him on sight. She guessed instinctively that this was the man who had been delegated to burn down their home.

Within minutes there was standing room only, and outside, under the pepperina trees' shade, vacated by the whites who had now moved inside, Eversham's Aboriginal population squatted comfortably, piccaninnies and all.

The formalities were quickly over, and the audience warned that any interjections or shouted comments would amount to contempt of court and be fined accordingly. The Magistrate had been on the outback circuit for some years, and was noted for his strict adherence to the rule and the severity of his fines. Nobody wanted to miss the fun. There was immediate silence.

The plaintiff's lawyer outlined the case, and called Elton-Smythe as his first witness. In response to the questions, the Yank explained how his foreman, Chet Wildean, had come to him a month earlier with some concern about the number of calves turning up wearing the Serendipity brand.

"I know it happens accidentally sometimes, when branding is carried out on the flat, as they say here, but that would only account for two or three misbranded caves perhaps, not eleven, and possibly more we haven't picked up yet."

Mick, asked if he wanted to question the witness, nodded his head and stood up.

"Mr. Elton-Smythe," he asked, "did you visit the Serendipity homestead on September 25th last year with an offer to buy the run?"

"Objection - irrelevant!" the Yank's lawyer was on his feet.

"M-mm, dunno. It might be. Objection over-ruled. Let him answer."

"Yes," said the Yank shortly.

"And did you again visit Serendipity on November 10th last year, without any particular stated reason for the visit?"

"I was just calling in on my way through to Felix Creek, like everyone does to their neighbours," replied Elton-Smythe angrily. His lawyer looked puzzled, but quickly regained his aplomb, and called Chet to the witness stand when Mick indicated that he had no further questions.

Chet gave evidence that he and his stock-camp had recently carried out a muster of the northern area of the Parrot Hill run adjoining Serendipity boundary, and had taken the mob to their nearest set of yards to brand the calves and separate the weaners. He repeated that he had not been unduly perturbed at the first two wrongly-branded calves, but as more turned up he became increasingly suspicious. He decided to hold those calves and their mothers in a separate yard, and to ride in to the station to ask Mr. Elton-Smythe what he should do about them. He left the rest of the men to get on with the branding while he did so. Mr. Elton-Smythe then accompanied him back to the yards to see for himself. In answer to the lawyer's question, he replied that, as it was not a clean muster, he would agree that there could very likely be more wrongly branded calves. He estimated that they had only picked up about a third of the cattle running in the area.

The Magistrate then adjourned the hearing to the sale-yards, so that the jury could inspect the evidence for themselves, and directed that, having done so, they take a lunch break, and the Court would resume at two o'clock.

Marion could see no point in going out to the sale-yards again, so she elected to walk back to the hotel with the aim of having an early lunch before the crowd got back. Ernie said he'd go out again anyway, and watch the reactions. Most of the jury-men had already checked out the brands some time in the past week, but it might be interesting to watch how they reacted as a group, rather than as individuals. Apparently most of the onlookers thought the same way, because a steady stream of vehicles headed for the sale-yards, and the hotel was almost deserted when Marion got back there.

For a few minutes she sat thoughtfully on the bed fingering the unaccustomed string of coloured beads she wore around her neck as an adornment to the new dress she had made. Then she pulled out the top drawer of the dressing table, and held it open. It contained two small piles of underclothes, a couple of handkerchiefs, and the writing pad she had used to copy out the diary entries for Mick.

Then, with a grin, she tore a sheet from the writing pad and put it on the dressing table, and replaced the pad on top of the underclothes. Then she took off her beads and deliberately broke the string, catching the dozen or so beads which rolled off into her hand. She dropped the broken necklace and the beads casually into the drawer and pushed it shut with a jerk. Some of the beads hit the front of the drawer with little pings of sound. She re-opened the drawer very slowly and carefully and then sketched the positions of the different coloured beads on the loose sheet of writing paper. She loosened another eight or ten beads from the string and placed them with the necklace in the middle of the pad, and then closed the drawer as carefully as she had opened it. If anyone opened that drawer in the normal casual way she would know it; she rather suspected they might, and she had every intention of giving them the opportunity. Although her door would be locked the top half of the window would not be, and after the afternoon hearing, the Serendipity jeep would be parked outside the police station until long after dark. It would be quite natural for Mrs. Hardy to visit her husband, after the turn of events the afternoon would bring. She grinned again, a little smug about her ploy, and went to wash her face and hands before lunch. The sketch was neatly folded and snug beside the little mirror in the zip-up pocket of her handbag.

By two o'clock the Eversham hall had really heated up, and the press of people within did not improve the situation. Some of the ladies had brought along Chinese hand fans, the sort Marion had seen on sale in Derby, and were vigorously fanning themselves. There were wet patches under the arms and across the backs of all the men's shirts, and the odour of sweating bodies in the confined space made Marion feel a little sick. But she had no intention of leaving the hall.

Mick was called to the stand. The Parrot Hill lawyer was poised for the kill.

"What is your brand?" he demanded imperiously.

"Don't ya know yet?" riposted Mick, and a slight titter ran through the Court.

"Answer the question!" said the Magistrate sharply.

"My brand is MTW," Mick answered dutifully.

"Do you acknowledge that the brand on the calves in the sale-yards is your brand?"

"Yair."

The lawyer turned to the Jury with an air of triumph.

"That, gentlemen, should be sufficient evidence to convince you of the guilt of the accused."

"Hang on," called Mick, "I haven't said I put it there!"

"That," said the lawyer coldly, "is for the Jury to decide. No more questions."

Now it was Mick's turn.

"I admit that MTW is my brand; everyone knows it is. But I do not admit that the branding irons used to brand those calves are my branding irons; in fact, I can prove that they are not!"

There was a hum of interest from the body of the hall, and the lawyer was on his feet shouting "Objection!"

"Oh sit down," said the Magistrate testily. "You're like a jack-in-the-box, man. That's a perfectly legitimate statement." He turned to Mick, a gleam of interest in his eye. "Go on, let's hear you. How can you prove it?"

"Thank you, Sir. Gentlemen of the Jury -" he turned towards the Jury, as he had seen the Yank's lawyer do - "you will have noticed that all the brands on those calves are three letters, spaced perfectly evenly. They have been made with a single branding iron with a three-letter motif." He paused for effect, and Marion, watching the Yank's face, noted a genuine air of puzzlement. He hadn't worked out what Mick was on about.

"Because I like to brand my calves as young as I can get 'em, and because there's not always room on a little calf's thigh for a big brand, I don't use a three-letter branding iron. I use two irons, one with a TW on it, and the other with a single M, and if I ever turn out anything as neat as the brands on those poddies down in the yard, I sure give myself a pat on the back!"

There was uproar. Shouts of "Good on yer, Mick!" indicated the sympathies of some of the listeners, and a couple of catcalls echoed from the back of the hall. The Magistrate banged his gavel furiously, and threatened to clear the hall. Everyone subsided immediately. At their table, Elton-Smythe and his lawyer looked decidedly concerned. Mick went on.

"I would like to put it to you that someone has deliberately branded some of the Parrot Hill calves with my brand with the sole aim of getting me a conviction. And I think I can give you the motive. I would like to read you some extracts from the Serendipity station diary..."

"Object..." the lawyer was on his feet again, roaring.

"Siddown, mug!" yelled Ernie, despite all his good intentions.

"Contempt of Court!" said the Magistrate firmly, and poor Ernie was escorted to the door by Sergeant Vickers.

"These entries were made by my wife, and I will read them exactly as they are written."

Mick looked over to the Magistrate, who nodded to him, and leaned over his table with interest.

"Sept. 25th last year. Elton-Smythe called in smoko time today. First time we've met him. Came straight out and offered us one thousand pounds to buy us out because his son wants a station. Said no thanks, and he upped it to twelve hundred and fifty. This place is worth twice that, not that we'd sell anyway. Told him definitely no, and he went off with a flea in his ear."

Mick flicked over to a second sheet of notepaper.

"Oct. 29th. Yesterday the house nearly burned down. Lucky it didn't all go, or there wouldn't be a diary to write in. We all went out to muster at Wilson's Yard, Mick and Alec first with the horses, and Pansy, me and the kids in the jeep. I put the fridge out, and the fire, before we left. At dinner camp we saw a smoke and came straight back. Lucky for us Alan and his boys turned up just after the fire got started, and managed to put it all out except the kitchen part. The kitchen table is gone again, and my new fridge I was going to have for the summer. What a mess. Then Big Jim called us to look at some tracks. They were not made by a Williams' boot like we all wear. Mick and Toby took swags and tucker and fresh horses and left straight away to follow the tracks. They went up into the hill behind the house. They have now been gone twenty-four hours. I'm scared."

Mick paused only to turn the sheet over.

"Oct. 31st. Mick and Toby home last night. Horse tracks went south to Parrot Hill. They camped when it got too dark to see, and went on in the morning. Found where the men had camped. Followed tracks to the road. Saw where ute had been waiting at road junction, and where rider had turned horse loose and got in ute. They came home straight across the country. Very glad to see them back."

"Can you tell all that just from tracks?" enquired the Magistrate interestedly.

"Yes, Sir, no problem to a good bushman, white or black."

"Any more?"

"Yes, Your Honour. I told my wife not to get on the transceiver about the fire, so she didn't. The Base wasn't expecting us to call in because my wife had told them we'd be away mustering for a week. I thought we might get a visitor."

"And did you?"

"Yes Sir. I'll read the next bit. Nov. 10th. Elton-Smythe called today. Said he was going to Felix Creek. Said he was sorry about the fire, but did not ask if we wanted anything from town. He's never been through this way to Felix Creek before. - That's all. Gentlemen of the Jury, maybe this is circumstantial evidence, but the certain person who had easy access to the calves, and wanted to buy Serendipity, would have a darn good chance of getting the lease when it comes up next year. Lands Branch wouldn't be likely to give it to a fellow doing time for poddy-dodging. That certain person had a motive, and any station blacksmith can make up a brand, and any ringer can ear-mark a calf with a pocket knife, when the ear-mark is a simple V like mine." Mick sat down.

The hall was dead silent. Everyone was looking at the Yank, but if they expected to see any tell-tale signs they were disappointed. His face was completely impassive, his lawyer's the same.

The lawyer began his summing-up in an almost conventional manner. He reminded Marion of a big, purring tom-cat, claws sheathed, but only for the moment.

"You are here to deal with the facts," he told the Jury-men, "and nothing but the facts. You are not here to deal with wild flights of fancy. The first fact is that you have seen Parrot Hill cows with calves branded MTW. The second fact is that MTW is the accused's brand. The conclusion is so obvious that I do not expect it will take you long to decide that the accused is guilty of the attempted theft of those calves. However, you have been presented by the accused with a fiction - and a rather clever fiction, too - which may have introduced an element of doubt into your minds. The accused has told you that his brand is slightly different because he uses two branding irons. He has *told* you this, but he has not produced any evidence to support his claim. The calves you have seen in the sale-yards represent a *fact*, but you have not seen any calves with this so-called slightly different brand, and I put it to you that you never will, because the difference exists only in the mind of the accused. The accused is, by his own admission, a desperate man. He has told you that he stands to lose his claim to his property if he is found guilty of the theft of a neighbour's cattle. The fiction you have heard, gentlemen, is the action of a desperate man, and he has compounded it by a malicious attempt to provide a motive and to incriminate my client, who is already his victim. He has read what he claims are extracts from a diary, but where is that diary? He asks you to believe what is written on those loose sheets of paper - scribbled out no doubt in the last day or so - but you have not seen the diary they purport to come from. You have not *seen* any *facts* to support his claim, because there *are* no facts. He has told you that my client offered to buy his place, allegedly for his son. My client admits that he did indeed make such an offer over a year ago, and the accused has seized upon this fact to build his flimsy story around it. What he does not know, gentlemen, is that my client, in January this year, in collaboration with his son, purchased a ranch in Illinois, U.S.A., where that son is now living. The son has no further interest in a property in Australia, and it follows that my client has no further interest in a property in Australia, at Serendipity or anywhere else. There is therefore no motive to discredit the accused, and the accused has produced not one fact to support the tissue of lies you have just heard. The accused is guilty, not only of the theft you are here to consider, but also of an even greater crime, that of attempting to throw doubt upon the good name of my client. I ask you to do your duty; to consider the facts, to ignore the fiction; and to bring down the only fair verdict - *guilty*."

For one dreadful moment Marion thought that the jury was going to dutifully withdraw. She had watched the variety of expressions on their faces during the lawyer's speech. The school-teacher, the publican, and the storekeeper would not really understand Mick's claims about the two brands; they wouldn't be able to visualise the difference. Had Mick estimated correctly the jury's reaction, knowing as he did that there were cattlemen among them? There was some whispering and discussion among them. She held her breath. The schoolteacher, who had been appointed by the others as their foreman, asked leave to speak to the Magistrate. Marion couldn't hear what he said, but she saw the Magistrate nod. The foreman sat down again.

"The jury has requested," announced the Magistrate, "that before they attempt to make a decision, the accused be asked to produce the evidence to support his story. They wish to see some of the cattle he claims are branded with two irons, and they wish to see the actual diary entries." He turned to Mick.

"Are you prepared to produce such evidence?"

Marion exhaled slowly. Mick's gamble had paid off; the trap was baited. The Yank couldn't do a thing about the brands, but he'd have to make a try to get the diary; a man who'd burn down a homestead wouldn't hesitate to steal a diary.

"Certainly, Sir."

"Well, how do we go about it? How far is it from here to your run?"

"The road's not too bad now - about seven-eight hours."

The Magistrate pondered.

"Have you got anyone out there could put some cattle together for the Jury to see?"

"Yessir - my head-stockman's there, and his wife. I could send him a telegram to pick up whatever's close to the yards at the homestead."

"How long would that take?"

"Well, I guess he could do it in a day."

"Hm-m. Let's see. Today's Monday. You write the telegram now, and my clerk will send it from the post office. Jury can inspect the cattle Wednesday. Take 'em Thursday to get back to town, I suppose. You'll have to remain in custody, but no doubt, if the diary does contain the extracts you claim, your wife will be prepared to bring it to you."

"Of course, Sir."

The Magistrate did some quick pencilling on his blotter. Then he looked up. "I didn't expect this case to run over more than a day. I have a commitment down the Track on Wednesday, but I'll make it my business to be back. The Court stands adjourned until 9:30 am Friday."

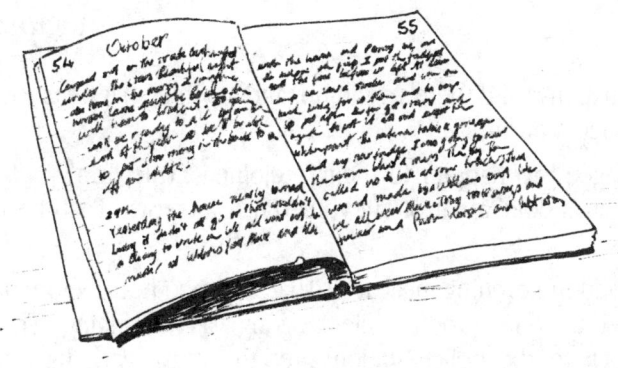

Chapter 28

New Evidence:
Injun Joe meets his match

It was an anti-climax for Marion, sitting on the lawn outside the cell with Mick and Ernie. She felt quite washed-out, much more so than the baby, who kept giving her hearty jolts under the ribs. Mrs. Vickers, like an excited but bossy little sparrow, brought the tea tray with its bone china complement herself, instead of sending the house-girl with it. If her husband had to remain neutral there was no law to say she had to, and she was now very definitely cheering for Mick. She had also guessed that the parcel she'd been asked to mind probably contained the diary.

"Don't tell the sergeant you've got it," begged Marion. "Just keep it for me till I ask you for it."

Mrs. Vickers loved being part of the conspiracy; she assured Marion with almost a simper that she had it in a safe place where her husband would be most unlikely to discover it accidentally. Then she said that she knew they must have things to talk about, and she'd leave them to it. Mrs. Vickers was a lady.

"You'll go with Marion, won't you, Ernie?" enquired Mick anxiously. "When they don't find it in the room - that's if they look in the room - they'll reckon she's gone home to get it, and if they don't have a try before she gets there, well, their last chance'd be on her way back into town. I dunno, Marion, maybe you'd better not go. Jesus, I wish I wasn't locked up here like this!"

"Somebody's got to go, and it's got to be me, or they'll start to wonder," said Marion serenely.

"Sure thing," nodded Ernie. "I won't let her outa my sight, Mick. Anyway, we'll give 'em time to search the homestead. They'll reckon on Alec and Pansy being out after the cattle tomorrow from hearin' what His Nibs said, and we'll make sure that everyone at the pub knows we're not leaving till the morning."

"I'll never forgive myself if there's a slip-up, and anything happens to Alec or Pansy or the kids," said Mick mournfully.

"Nothin' ain't goin' to happen to them," rejoined Ernie firmly. "I got it on good authority that Tom's doin' a patrol out your way tomorrow. Fact, he's probably there right now!"

The hotel served the evening meal at six sharp, a good hour before dark, and Marion and Ernie entered the dining room while the gong was still ringing. They planned to be seen driving back to the police station after the meal, and that anyone who was particularly interested should have ample opportunity to see them leave and to know where they were. No one had yet made any search of Marion's room, but that was not unexpected, given that it was still broad daylight.

Guests and hanger-ons alike wanted to talk to Marion and Ernie about the new course of events, but Marion was a stranger to the town, and no-one knew her well enough to start up a conversation while Ernie guarded her like a bulldog, and he would not be drawn himself. The curious had to content themselves with the snippets they could garner from the discussions of the jury-men's proposed visit, how they'd go; when they'd leave; who would pay the expenses.

Marion made a point of calling the publican's wife over to the table to let her know that she would be leaving early in the morning, but would like to re-book the room for Thursday night and Friday. The publican's wife told her to look in at the kitchen when she was ready to leave, and there'd be a hot breakfast ready for her. Marion told her that she was driving home with Ernie, and the publican's wife said that Ernie was welcome to breakfast too.

It wasn't yet seven when she got into the Serendipity jeep to drive back to the police station. Ernie called to her that he'd be along later to pick her up, because she was going to leave her jeep in the police station yard in her few days' absence from town; they'd make the trip in Ernie's jeep.

When Ernie arrived just before nine he was able to report that the twelve jury-men had finally decided to leave town in three vehicles very early on Wednesday morning, and ought to arrive at Serendipity some time during the afternoon. The school-teacher had been like a dog with two tails at the prospect of a bush-trip much further than he'd ever seen before, but his offsider had been pretty glum at the prospect of handling a double quota of kids all by himself. Ernie's second piece of information interested Mick more.

The publican's wife had mentioned to him that Mr. Elton-Smythe and his party were also leaving in the morning, going back to Parrot Hill for the intervening days before the trial resumed, but they hadn't mentioned an early breakfast, but then, they didn't have as far to go, did they? What she hadn't mentioned was that one of the party had already left, the dark lean fellow who'd sat next to Chet in the hall. He'd left about half an hour ago, come out of the Yank's room, gone quietly to one of the Parrot Hill utilities, and driven off.

"If we're reasoning right," Mick said, "the Yank now knows that the diary's not in your room, and Injun Joe's going to have to drive all night to make a surprise visit to Serendipity before you get home. Looks like you can go back now, Honey, and get a good night's sleep before you head off in the morning."

"Good thinking," said Marion. "All in all, it's been quite a day." Then as an afterthought she added, "Must be something about September, Mick. Our month for unexpected happenings. Do you realise that it's a year, almost to the day, since the house nearly got burned down?"

"Yair," replied the Quiet Fella non-committally.

Ernie accompanied Marion to her room, and they went inside and shut the door. It didn't escape either of them that this action would probably start a few tongues wagging, but under the circumstances Marion didn't care two hoots. She withdrew the top drawer of the dressing table carefully, and they both stared in. There were no loose beads now on top of the writing pad, and the pattern that Marion had sketched was subtly re-arranged. Nothing was obviously disturbed, and unless she had been expecting it, Marion would not have suspected that her room had been searched.

She said goodnight to Ernie light-heartedly, and bet him that she'd be up and running before he tapped on her door in the morning. Surprisingly, she fell asleep almost as soon as her head touched the pillow.......

Tom Roberts and Police-boy Banjo arrived at the homestead not ten minutes after Alec had picked up the telegram just before the end of the late afternoon session. Alec was still scratching his head and pondering the significance of the message. His face cleared as he recognised the visitors.

"Glad to see you, Tom. Y'heard about Mick, I s'pose? Pansy, what about a cuppa!"

Tom nodded. "I don't know all that much, Alec, except that the trial's been on today. Get a telegram, did you?"

"Yair, but it don't tell me much. Looks like it's still going. All the telegram says is that Mick wants me to put some cattle, any cattle, in the yards tomorrow."

He showed the exercise book to Tom in which he had laboriously copied the telegram, but neither of them could work out much from it, except that the trial was not over. Mick would certainly have told Alec the results if it had been.

Tom had decided that it would be wiser to let Alec and Pansy think that his appearance was just coincidental, but that left him with the problem of how to explain his need to hide the police utility from sight. If what Ernie had said about a probable attempt to search the homestead for the station diary was true, there wouldn't be any attempt made with a police utility parked out in front. Ernie had explained that Mick was going to plead that he had been framed, and to catch someone in the act of trying to steal the diary would corroborate his claim. Non-one need ever know that Tom's presence at Serendipity wasn't anything more than a routine patrol.

Pansy gave him the opening he needed. Too shy to speak directly to Tom, she spoke instead to Alec.

"Take twofella to get the cattle, Alec. Christy can look after Sammy orright, but Mick tell us before he go, don't leave the house in case them fellas come while nobody here. I don't like to leave the kids, mightbe they try burn the house again."

"Why can't I help get the cattle too?" put in Christy, with a bit of a whine in his voice.

"Why not!" agreed Tom heartily. "Tell you what. Why don't I mind the pic for you; got a little boy of my own not much bigger. Then Christy can go with you; get twice as many cattle that way, eh, Christy?"

"We take the dogs too, Alec?" exulted Christy.

Alec was no fool. While Pansy was getting tea, and Banjo unloading swags, he said to Tom, "You *are* expecting a caller tomorrow, ain't you! No reason for you to stay over, otherwise. Well, more better you hide the ute, Tom."

Tom had planned to do exactly that as soon as they had left in the morning. Banjo could plant it in the trees to the north of the homestead before sun-up. This made it easier.

"I don't want to scare Pansy. Maybe no-one will come, Alec. If I leave the ute in full view, then for sure they won't. But if I catch someone in the act that helps Mick, and shows me a proper smart policeman too, eh? Where is the diary, anyway?"

"Marion took it with her. No worry there. But what about Sammy, Tom? Pansy not scared, but say you got trouble and that baby get hurt?"

Alec had worked out for himself why Tom was so keen for Christy to be out of the way.

Tom had seen the meatsafe cot under the bough-shed.

"Look, Alec. Before you go in the morning, we can take the cot back over to your place, and Banjo can mind Sammy over there, while I stay here. Then, if anybody comes, Banjo can lock Sammy in the cot, and then give me a hand if I need it."

"They'll come all right, if they reckon the diary's still here. Maybe that's why Mick says to get some cattle together, to get us out of the way, make it easier for them to have a crack at it. They tried to burn the place down all right. You'd be sure too, you'd seen those tracks, but we couldn't prove nothin' then. Anybody, includin' us c'd make a set of tracks."

Banjo drove the ute back the way they had come, and hid it in the scrub. Tom had long since taught both his trackers to drive, in case he was ever incapacitated while out on a patrol, but they didn't often get the chance to get behind the wheel. The two-mile walk back to the homestead was well worth the pleasure to Banjo of being in sole control of a white man's vehicle. He could dream for a short while that one day he might have one of his own.

They ran the horses in at daylight, and Banjo saddled Buzz for Christy, while Tom watched with Sammy on his hip. They stuffed their lunches in saddle-bags. Though Alec had reckoned they'd have a good chance of picking up a lot of the cows and calves they'd bushed only a fortnight before, because they were still watering at the homestead creek, Tom had told him to stay away until well into the afternoon.

In the event that it was safe to return any earlier, he'd fire a shot in the air to let them know. Pansy, shyness forgotten, admonished Tom to look after Sammy properly; she sounded just like Muriel.

Tom had made only one mistake. From what Ernie had told him of the planned revelations of the trial, he had calculated that it would be mid-morning at least before anyone could cover the distance between Eversham and Serendipity. The move had to come from there, and not from Parrot Hill, because Elton-Smythe's only contact with his station was by telegram, and every telegram was public to anyone on the network who liked to listen in. He estimated that, considering the distance involved, mid-morning was about the earliest he could expect a visitor. He did not know of Marion's deliberate circulation of her intention to leave Eversham early in the morning, which limited the time when an attempt could be made, because of the possibility of either her unwanted arrival or of meeting her somewhere on the road between Serendipity and the Parrot Hill turn-off.

Unknown to Tom, Injun Joe, alias William Hale, was already in the position of surveillance from which he had once before spied on the activities of the homestead. He had driven all night; the reward that Elton-Smythe had promised him if he got the diary, and his own interests in preventing the true story of the fire coming out, had spurred him to super-human efforts. The Parrot Hill utility was planted in the bush about three miles south of the homestead. He had arrived there towards 4 am, but he could not afford to drive any closer in case the sound of the vehicle woke anyone at the station. The walk through the bush and the climb to his vantage point was difficult going in the half-light, but he reached it before there were any stirrings from the homestead. With a panting of satisfaction he eased himself down with his back against the rock and dropped his head onto arms folded across his knees. He could doze there safe in the knowledge that the sun would wake him in an hour or two. Much as his body craved sleep, he could only afford to catch a short spell.

It was Christy's clear voice shouting a goodbye which woke him, and he was on his feet in an instant. He did not see Tom's figure, which was almost hidden from view by the homestead building, which he had nearly reached, but Banjo, with Sammy riding astride his shoulders, was only half-way across the intervening space between the yards and Alec's cottage. He watched the man with the child disappear into the cottage, and registered that the three mounted figures were moving towards the line of trees which bordered the creek. For a moment he considered giving up the attempt, but then he thought of the payment he'd been promised. The diary would be in the homestead, and with a bit of luck the nigger would stay put in the cottage with the kid. With care he could get into the homestead without being seen or heard, but he'd have to work fast.

With a quick glance to see that the riders were nearly out of sight, he planned his approach. By working around further to the south he could keep a line of trees between him and the cottage while he was on the slope, and then he could cross the open area with the homestead between him and the cottage. He began to ease himself around the rock, and the rising sun flashed for an instant on the ornate metal belt-buckle he wore. Pansy, glancing back for no particular reason, caught the momentary flash of light. She whistled softly to Alec and pointed with her lips. Together they saw the tiny figure disappear behind a tree.

"Tom ain't expecting him on foot," muttered Alec. "I think more better I go back. Look, Pansy, you and Christy go on a bit up the creek. I'll catch you up."

He did not ride directly back, but moved around to the east, still hidden by the trees. Two could play at this game. He would cut the bullock paddock fence and follow it back, and give the fellow time to reach the homestead without alerting him.

In quarter of an hour Injun Joe had safely reached his goal. He stood under the shelter of the verandah near the saddle-room, and then began to ease himself catlike along the front verandah. He knew the layout; he'd been here before. The diary was probably in the bedroom, rather than the bough shed; if she hadn't taken it to town that would be the most likely place to look - wasn't much place else in this little dump. He slid inside through the door that opened on to the verandah, opening it with barely a sound.

Tom, sitting in the bough shed with his ears tuned already for the sound of an approaching vehicle, had planned to hide himself in the bedroom to catch the intruder in the act. He stiffened suddenly, thought he heard a slight movement from the bedroom, relaxed, then heard it again. He leapt for the door and flung it open. Injun Joe was still on his knees before Marion's trunk with the lid wide open, but was on his feet again before Tom could reach him. For a moment they stared at each other, then Injun Joe's eyes flickered sideways towards the open verandah door. Tom jumped, but the man was too quick. Tom's outstretched hand brushed the cloth of a shirt-sleeve, clutched, but Injun Joe broke away, wheeled, and his booted foot caught Tom in the groin. Then he was through the door and running like a hare. It flashed through Tom's mind as he doubled over that Banjo was too far away to be of any use. Then gritting his teeth against the pain he tried to force himself to give chase, but his quarry had too much of a start.

The four hundred yards between house and the sanctuary of the trees was all Injun Joe needed to cover before he had a fair chance of escaping his pursuer, and Tom was losing ground with every stride, strain as he might to force out that last ounce of speed.

Then Tom heard the pounding of hoofs behind him and a wild halloo, and Alec went past him at a gallop. Injun Joe didn't even look over his shoulder, but with a hundred yards to go, he didn't have a chance. Alec launched himself from the saddle and caught the fleeing man with his full weight and bore him to the ground with a crash. Injun Joe screamed, but before he could roll over, Alec, astride his back, had wrenched his arms around, whipped the bull-strap belt from his belt, and lashed the wrists together. His mare, well-trained, stood quietly by.

"You beauty!" panted Tom, all pain forgotten.

Alec stood up and surveyed his handiwork.

"I've throwed plenty of beasts in my time, Tom," he chuckled, "but that's the first time I ever throwed a man!"

Banjo came running. Tom turned the quarry over.

"Face is a bit burred-up from smacking into the ground like," commented Alec. "Could be an improvement though, eh? Nasty lookin' bugger, ain't he!"

Injun Joe spat out an oath, but was thereafter silent. Tom's attempts to question him were to no avail. They dragged him to his feet, and hauled him back to the house.

Tom substituted handcuffs and gave Alec back his bull strap.

"Well, I got a job to do. See ya later!" Alec tucked the thong in his belt, mounted and rode off.

Tom surveyed his prize thoughtfully. "I'd like you where I can see you, you shifty bastard. Banjo, see if you can find a rope!"

Banjo produced the length of rope he had seen on the back of the weapon-carrier, and Tom tied one end between the handcuffs and the other round one of the posts of the bough shed. He shortened the tether to about six feet. Injun Joe squatted down with his back against the post, licked once at the blood round his bruised lips, and closed his eyes.

"Bring the kid over here, Banjo, and then go and get my ute."

"Youai, Boss."

"Then you can have a look around for this fella's vehicle. It'll be planted not too far away. You find it, you can drive it back to Felix Creek." Banjo beamed widely. "Sooner we leave the better. We'll get going as soon as they get back with the cattle."

Injun Joe slept soundly all the morning, stirring only once when Banjo drove the Parrot Hill ute close to the bough shed and parked it beside the police vehicle. Tom made a rough meal at midday, and fed Sammy. The prisoner would not eat, but accepted a pannikin of water from Banjo and drank thirstily.

At two o'clock Marion and Ernie arrived. They had seen the tracks of the vehicle turning across the windrow three miles back, and the tracks back on to the road where Banjo had backed it out.

"That's him!" Marion, tired and dusty as she was, danced elatedly to Tom and hugged him. "I dunno his name, but I'm sure he works for Parrot Hill. He was in the Court all yesterday."

Injun Joe glared malevolently and suddenly spat at her feet.

"You dirty mongrel!" roared Ernie, enraged, but Injun Joe calmly spat again, this time at him.

"Shove him in the saddle-room; it's got a lock. Then we can talk," suggested Marion.

No sooner said than done. Instead of the rope, Tom attached a second pair of cuffs to the set the prisoner wore and locked them around the saddle horse. Then he locked the door and ordered Barney to stand guard outside. Tom felt a little bit guilty about the near-escape of the morning, and he wasn't taking any chances this time.

Marion introduced Ernie, and it took a good half-hour to fill in the gaps for each party.

"The trial resumes on Friday, Tom. D'you reckon you could be at Eversham then, so Mick can call you as a witness?"

Tom explained that he would need his Sergeant's permission, but it would probably be forthcoming. He would phone Mrs. Vickers with a message for Mick. In the meantime he'd hang on to Injun Joe on break and enter and assaulting a policeman charges.

The ride to Felix Creek wasn't going to be a comfortable one for the prisoner. Tom put him, still handcuffed, in the back of his vehicle, and attached the second pair of handcuffs to one of the steel bars fitted across the back of the cabin. Injun Joe was going to be stiff from more than his fall before he reached the comparative comfort of a Felix Creek cell.

Not long after the departure of the two vehicles the musterers returned with a small mob, mainly cows and calves, and Ernie helped them yard up. Then it was explanations all round again. Alec was the hero of the evening.

"Tomorrow," said Marion, "Serendipity is going to have more visitors than it has ever had at one time before. They won't get here before the middle of the afternoon, so we'll have to fix a place for them to camp. Should we tail the cattle out in the morning, Alec? And, Christy, me boyo, a day's school for you. You've missed enough so far, and you'll miss another two days this week, because I've got to go back to Eversham on Thursday."

Christy nodded seriously. "I'll do my Morning News bit first, Marion, and draw a picture. I'll tell the teacher all about what happened today, how Buzz and me, we went out all day mustering."

Ernie slapped his knee and burst out laughing.

Chapter 29
A man's got a right to protect his home and family

The jurymen made a holiday out of it. Those who were cattlemen indulged their natural interest in looking at a bit of new country, estimated the worth of the native grasses, eyed the grazing cattle speculatively, and inspected Mick's yards critically. (There is no cattleman born who cannot see a better way to build a set of yards when he is standing alongside someone else's.) Unconsciously they patronised the schoolteacher, clerk, publican and store-keeper, who, away from their own beats, were reduced to mere onlookers and listeners-in.

But on one point there was complete accord. They sat in groups on the top rail or peered through the lower rails to look at the brands on calves and older beasts alike. The TW was neat and standard, the M a little awry, and varyingly so. They asked to see the branding irons, and Alec brought them from the saddle-room, two separate irons, and demonstrated the process to the interested school-teacher on a little cleanskin calf. There were two others in the mob, and seeing he'd had to go to the trouble to make a fire, they might as well be done too. There was bawling and dust as Alec scruffed the calves, and a willing helper stretched out the hind leg while the schoolteacher applied the brands. The results were far from uniform. The evidence was conclusive.

Though Marion could willingly have entertained them, the circumstances decreed that the jurymen make their camp apart, and by mutual accord, they decided to go back along the road a few miles to the creek-bank near one of the permanent waterholes.

At Serendipity there was gleeful speculation about the trial result.

"They be proper cranky at Parrot Hill," commented Pansy.

They would certainly be apprehensive about the non-return of their man, and the almost certainty that the diary would be produced in Court to back up Mick's claim. The move the Yank had himself initiated in an effort to denigrate his neighbour had gathered a momentum beyond his control, which now threatened his own reputation.

""Serve him right!" said Marion somewhat pompously. "The stinker tried to get rid of us once before, and it didn't work. So then he has the nerve to have another go!"

"Don't count yer chickens yet, Ginger," warned Ernie. "He's got a mighty smart lawyer there, thinks on his feet, and remember, they got three days this time to think in!"

"Not that smart! And anyway, you said yourself, Ernie, there's eight Territory cattlemen and ringers on the jury, and that's got to count for something."

"But they got to convince the other four!"

"I reckon maybe the brands already done that, Ernie," said Alec pensively. "I was watchin' those fellas' faces this afternoon; they pretty sure now."

The trip back to Eversham was uneventful. Not that Marion had expected it would be otherwise. Even without her escort she did not think the Yank would be stupid enough to make any further attempt to get the diary. The best he could hope for now was that it had been burned in the fire, and a less-convincing new one begun after that event.

Mick had as yet had no message from Tom, so the first thing Marion did was to phone Felix Creek from the Post Office. The Sergeant answered. There had been a shooting accident at one of the little gold-mining shows near Mt. Blair, and Tom had left in a hurry to investigate; he wouldn't be able to attend the trial. Marion learnt that the prisoner's name was William Hale, and was asked if she wanted to lay a charge against him; he was being held for assaulting a policeman. Marion said she'd let him know. One thing at a time, she thought. The fact that he'd been caught was evidence, and that was all she needed for the present.

She reported back to Mick. He wasn't perturbed that Tom would not be there. He had a name and a piece of evidence that could easily be corroborated, that should be enough.

The Hall was once again transferred into a Court-house, and the protagonists in the drama re-assembled. Marion noticed that Elton-Smythe's over-bearing manner had subtly changed. Though his expression gave nothing away, Marion could sense a new tension. He almost seemed puzzled by the turn of events.

"Bet he wishes like hell he'd never started all this!" she thought. "Let his fancy lawyer get him out of it now!"

There was a hush when Mick took the stand. He repeated his claim that the calves in question must have been branded by someone else, and that someone else had a motive to blacken his good name in the eyes of the law. A ripple of sound ran through the Court when he picked up the diary from the table and read the marked extracts from it. The diary was handed to the school-teacher, who adjusted his glasses and read from it, and had to be jabbed in the ribs to pass it on to the next man when he obviously forgot himself and read on past the marked extract. It was some minutes before they had all done. The Quiet Fella waited patiently.

"There is only one point I would like to add," he said, when the diary had been handed to the Magistrate, who scanned it with interest. "You all heard the claim that this diary was only a figment of my imagination, and the implication that everything I said was just a fairy-tale. If my accusers did not believe there was an actual diary, why then was my wife's room searched at the hotel on Monday night, and why was Serendipity homestead broken into on Tuesday morning - the only day on which everyone knew there was unlikely to be anyone there, because you all heard me tell the Magistrate that I could send a telegram asking my head-stockman to muster."

Mick paused, and everyone waited for him to go on.

"Serendipity was broken into by a man who was in this hall on Monday. His name is William Hale, and he is now in jail at Felix Creek. The utility he was driving belongs to Parrot Hill!" Mick sat down amid uproar.

When the Magistrate had restored order the lawyer had the last say, and Marion realised that they must have worked out what might have happened to Injun Joe. The lawyer explained that the man in question was an American who had been in minor trouble with the police back in the States, who had begged Elton-Smythe for a job where he could get a new start. Because he was such a good worker Mr. Elton-Smythe had employed him, and up to the present time he had no complaints. When he did not return to the station by Tuesday evening Mr. Elton-Smythe was not unduly worried, because he believed the utility could have broken down, and the man was not a good mechanic. He knew there would be traffic on the road on Wednesday if such was the case. On Wednesday evening, when there was still no sign of the man, the head stockman was sent to search the road from Parrot Hill to the road junction in case some sort of accident may have occurred on that section, which would not have been travelled by the jurors. When this was found not to be so Mr. Elton-Smythe had, first thing on Thursday morning, sent a telegram to the Eversham police advising them of the theft of the utility. Obviously the man, believing there would be no-one home at Serendipity, had intended to rob the homestead of what he could find before making his getaway to the north.

"Good, but not good enough!" yelled somebody from the back of the hall. He was duly ejected, and the Jury after the usual caution from the Magistrate retired to the supper room.

It took them twenty minutes to reach the verdict and finish the smokes some of them had been tongueing for. The schoolteacher, mindful of his temporary important status, answered ceremoniously when asked how they found the accused.

"Not guilty, Your Honour!"

Marion, although she was almost certain that this would be the verdict, suddenly found the tears running down her cheeks. She was surprised at herself. That was out of character for her, the tough kid who never bawled - well, almost never! It must be the baby. But, thank goodness it was all over, and they could get on with their lives again.

But now the Magistrate was speaking.

"Obviously," he said, looking sternly towards the Yank, "there is more in this case than meets the eye; even grounds for further litigation, perhaps. In view of the fact that calves carrying the Serendipity brand, although legitimately owned by Parrot Hill, could be used for possible further dishonest claims if returned to Parrot Hill, I hereby order that the said calves be weaned and delivered to Serendipity as compensation in part to Mr. Hardy. Case dismissed; costs to the plaintiff!"

The Quiet Fella, a free man now, hugged Marion and shook hands with Ernie.

"I reckon Alan would have enjoyed being here today," he grinned.

"Well, it won't lose anything in the telling, when he gets home," rejoined Marion. "I won't forget any of it till my dying day!"

They were celebrities now. Outside the hall there were congratulations and offers of drinks to celebrate. Mick said he'd go back to the police station first to collect his gear, but before he could do so, Chet Wildean approached him.

"Look, Mick, I hope you don't think I had anything to do with any funny business on your place. I was just doing my job, I swear it. When I saw those calves I had to let the boss know, but, sure as hell, I didn't have anything to do with branding 'em with your brand!"

"Fair enough," said Mick. "I reckon if you're working on a place, you've got to do what the boss tells you, but I don't reckon he'd be fool enough to tell you to do that. No hard feelings."

Then the store-keeper tapped Marion on the elbow.

"Mrs. Hardy, I was reading what you said about losing your fridge, and I saw your place the other day. Sure need a fridge in the summer out there. Fella in town ordered one a few months back, and then, day before it arrived, his wife ran off with the bloke he had working for him. He packed up and left town, had more on his mind than fridges then. I was thinking maybe you could take it off me hands if I let you have it at cost."

"I don't think we could afford a new one," faltered Marion. "I only ever thought of a second-hand one."

"I got a fair bit of extra business this week with the court case on, and all. Maybe I could afford to drop the price a bit. Still in the crate, it is. Latest model on the market."

Mick, listening in, said they'd be down at the store to make some purchases before leaving, and they'd look at the fridge then.

"You're a good little mate, Honey," he told Marion, "and we really ought to have one with the baby coming."

All they both wanted was to get out of town quickly and get back to Serendipity. Mick had two drinks with Ernie, and steadfastly refused all the other offers. The publican said he'd never done it before, and he wasn't likely to do it again, but he refused to take the money for Marion's board, saying she wouldn't have been put to the expense but for the court case, and he felt bad about her having her room searched while under his roof. She thanked him and his wife, and she and Mick said a heartfelt thanks to Ernie, who said he'd better hit the track too as he'd neglected his place for long enough, and Lord knows what his blacks would be up to in his absence.

Then they drove to the police station, and Mrs. Vickers fluttered around them and insisted that next time they came to Eversham Mick would be welcome to a better room than the one he'd had this time. Last port of call was the store. Marion bought apples and oranges, an unknown luxury at Serendipity, and boiled lollies for the children, and then they looked at the new fridge. It had shelves in the door for bottles and jars; Marion had never seen one like that before. Mick pulled the storekeeper aside and talked to him, while Marion pretended to look at dress materials.

The crate was so big it took up all the available room in the back of the jeep. "Enough wood in that crate," said Mick with an impish grin, "to make a fair-sized kitchen table!"

They drove until the late afternoon shadows of the savanna-land trees stretched like tiger-stripes across the road in front of them, and then pulled off the road to camp for the night. Beyond the circle of camp-fire light the call of a curlew and the scutterings of little night-time animals were familiar sounds, and when they lay on their swag in the warm darkness and looked up at the panorama of the stars Marion experienced a great contentment that the child she carried would truly belong, like little Sammy, to this wild and beautiful land.

"Our baby's got to have a Dreaming too," she murmured drowsily to Mick. "I think I'll make it a star." Her eyes searched the heavens, and the constellations that Grandpa had shown her so long ago twinkled back at her.

"Orion's Belt!" she said suddenly. "That's the baby's Dreaming. And we'll call him Orion!"

"Could be a girl." Mick's voice was drowsy too.

"No matter. Orion will do for a boy or a girl. Maybe we could drop the O. Rion Hardy, that sounds real good, Micky me love!"

"Sounds okay to me. And I reckon Maggie and Grandpa will reckon it's okay too. They'll want to spell it R-Y-A-N though!"

Marion hadn't thought of the coincidence, but that seemed to make the choice all the more apt. She snuggled her head into the warmth of Mick's shoulder, and he placed his hand gently on the soft swell of her abdomen. Rion Hardy, who had been quiet and well-behaved for hours, responded with a ripple of movement.

"Hey," said Mick delightedly, "the baby reckons it's okay too! Rion Hardy, it is!"

When they crossed their boundary next day Marion felt a sudden wild surge of emotion. Mick glanced at her quizzically.

"You didn't really think we might have a slippery holt on the place, did you, Hon?"

"No, of course not!" she assured him.

"Never in doubt for a moment," he said enigmatically.

To Marion the week after the trial was as quiet as the preceding one had been fraught with excitement. Mick had lost no time in organising a schedule to make up for the time he had lost. With Alec's help he had installed the refrigerator in the bough-shed, and promised to build a kitchen complex like the one at Delroy once the cattlework was over. Now, he had taken Alec and Pansy and they had gone to muster the eastern section of the block to pick up and bring back the steers which would form part of next-year's turn-off, Serendipity's first worth-while sale. She still went cold as she thought of what might have been the situation if Mick had been found guilty of poddy-dodging.

The musterers would be away for a fortnight or so, but Marion, with quicksilver Sammy to keep an eye on, and Christy's lessons to be supervised, found her days as full as ever. Soon she would have to think about making arrangements to go to stay in Felix Creek, or Darwin, for the birth of the baby, due in early December, and she wanted to finish the year's schoolwork with Christy before she left. Christy had big ideas about going with the mustering team, but now he found himself working at lessons in the afternoons as well as the mornings.

When Saturday came around Marion kept him at it too, much to his disgust, but after lunch she relented and let him off to play with chubby Sammy. Then suddenly feeling the need to hear some adult voices again she decided to listen in to the galah session on the transceiver while she cut out and stitched the baby nighties from the pattern Muriel had sent her. She half-expected there might still be some talk about the trial, and she was not disappointed. But it was the reported aftermath which made her sit up and listen with sudden interest.

The disembodied voice floated across the verandah.

"I hear Parrot Hill's up for sale, and the owner's going back to America. That right? Over."

"8 Sugar Queen replying. Hadn't heard about it, Jill, but I wouldn't be surprised. Considering what happened, you know. Over."

A man's voice now.

"8 Tare X-Ray to 8 Mike Bravo. Hullo, Jill. Will you let Bill know I've got those horses in, and he can come over to see them anytime that suits him. Yeah, I think it's right about Parrot Hill. Anne just got back from Darwin yesterday, and she heard up there that it's coming up on the market. Over."

Marion grinned with glee. The Yank must really be scared that Mick might follow up a possible arson charge, and he was getting out while the going was good. Not that Mick would, of course. He had far more important things to do at home. One court case in a lifetime was one too many as far as he was concerned.

Sammy came into the bough shed and tugged at her skirt, and demanded "Biscuit?"

"Please!" she said automatically and cut an orange into quarters for him instead. Christy appeared and was given one too. Then they disappeared again, and she could hear the sounds of their voices and a rattle of stones in a tin from the shady side of the house. She should just have time to machine the little garments before it was time to think of kids' baths and the evening meal.

Marion was still half-listening to the chatting from the galah session when she sat down before her treadle sewing machine, and she forgot that she needed to start treadling very carefully because the belt had worn thin and one more snap would make it too short to join. She had sewn no more than three inches when the belt parted and flicked with a sharp sting against her leg.

"Oh blast!" she grumbled. Rion kicked her under the diaphragm. "Okay, okay, Rion. That's not real swearing, pet. Anyway, I can fix it myself." She could too. She was sure there were some suitable strips of leather somewhere in the saddle-room. She picked up the broken belt and her pocket knife and went to investigate.

There was nothing on the bench, and only some odd-shaped pieces in the steel bucket under the bench. Alec must have cleaned up the saddle room for something to do while they were away. She distinctly remembered seeing some thin strips of leather earlier in the year when Banner's bridle had needed repairs. Where could they be?

Marion never did know what made her reach up to move the sides of leather neatly rolled on the shelf above the bench. She had to stand on a box to do it, and it wasn't at all likely that the strips would be there. Perhaps she was thinking that if she couldn't find the strips she might have to cut a new belt from the side itself. She moved the side of redhide along the shelf, and tugged at the second roll. It seemed rather heavy. Then she remembered that she shouldn't be reaching for heavy things at this stage of her pregnancy. Maybe it was an old wives' tale, but she wouldn't take any chances. She gave the rolled hide an awkward shove, meaning to straighten it up, but instead she pushed it sideways and it fell with a thud on the bench below in a cloud of dust. Marion jumped backwards off the box, and sneezed.

She ought to put it back where it came from. She stretched out her arms and picked it up tentatively at either end. It *was* too heavy for a side of leather; there was something inside the roll. Her curiosity aroused, she picked up her pocket knife and cut the coarse string holding the roll together. Inside there was a long thin parcel wrapped in an old piece of tarp. It was the work of a moment to unroll it.

A branding iron was exposed, a shiny new branding iron, hardly used. At one extremity three neat letters stood side by side in perfect alignment - MTW.

Marion's eyes widened, and her jaw dropped open. She put out a hand and touched the letters, tracing them with her finger one by one. From afar, she heard Alan's voice say, "A man with guts, like Mick, 'e's not going to take this lying down, is he? A man's got a right to protect his home and family!"

A kaleidoscope of thoughts and pictures rushed through her mind. She saw the Yank's puzzled face, and heard her own earnest voice; she saw Mick's quietly confident demeanour in the court room. She began to giggle quietly. The supercilious lawyer's face swam into her ken - the first case he'd lost for years.

"Oh, Mick! My darling Quiet Fella! Mick, my love! I might have known!" She laughed aloud.

She picked up the brand and hugged it to her.

"A man with guts, like Mick, he didn't take it lying down. A man's got a right to protect his home and family - his bunch of strays!" she recited eloquently.

Then she began to laugh again, chuckles at first, then louder, then great whoops of belly laughter until the tears ran down her cheeks. Outside, right to the far horizon, the blue Territory sky vaulted over Serendipity, the Hardys' place; or well on the way to becoming so.

Marion, with an occasional half-smothered chuckle, manoeuvred the box to the bench, climbed up, and carefully replaced the rolled hide and its contents back on the shelf, all thoughts of the original purpose of her search quite forgotten.

She wouldn't let on to Mick, not right away, anyway. He'd got the strays back on course and they were nearly into the straight now; only depended on her to bring the last little stray safely into the world. As she walked down the verandah the last little stray kicked enthusiastically.

She unhooked the spout of the waterbag hanging from a bough-shed rafter and filled her pannikin as Christy's and Sammy's voices came fitfully from the shade where they played. She drank slowly, thought almost suspended, and then suddenly, her mind formed a picture, sharp-edged and clear. There was Mick, riding in the lead of a small mob of bawling steers, and two laden pack-horses on the wing with Pansy on her mount behind them. In the dust at the tail she registered Alec's silhouette. They were coming up out of the little creek near the big old carbeen tree not five miles down the track. It was a flash, a picture suspended in space for a brief fraction of a second.

"So that's how they do it, the blacks!" marvelled Marion, "and now I can do it too!"

"Christy," she called, a new urgency in her voice. "Christy, run over and bring me a nice big piece of salt beef from the meathouse. Mick and Pansy and Alec will be home tonight close-up suppertime. We'll have it all ready for them when they get here, eh?"

"The muster must have gone better than expected," she mused, as she selected potatoes from the wire framework on which they were spread at one end of the bough shed. "They're a couple of days ahead of schedule. I'd better stoke the boiler too. They'll want a clean-up before they eat."

The musterers yarded up just as the long shadow of the old gum tree fingered the bough shed wall. Saddles on the rail, horses turned out, spurs swivelled round over the instep and then Mick at the doorway, wide grin and big hat in one hand as he swept a courtly bow to his lady, with Pansy and Alec laughing behind him.

Later, lamplight on shining faces as they all sat together round the table, Mick sliced off hearty serves of beef on to enamel plates, already loaded with vegetables. Marion felt hugely content.

"Alan reckons we're just a bunch of strays," she thought, "but, all things considered, a lot of the regular mob would give their eye-teeth for what we've got!"

When all the plates were empty she whisked them away into the waiting bowl of hot water, dried them, and replaced them on the table.

"My surprise," she grinned. "The new fridge has got a freezer cabinet. I made ice-cream for dessert and jelly to go with it!"

"Oo-aah!" squeaked Pansy.

"Ice-cream!" echoed Christy, as if he couldn't believe it, and Sammy just stared, round-eyed. Mick and Alec grinned like kids.

The recipe from the booklet that came with the fridge had a note in brackets at the end which said 12 servings, but the chef had under-estimated the Serendipity strays - they ate the lot.